THE TRUTH OF LIES

THE ELEMENTAL KINGDOM SERIES BOOK 1

LILY ANNE ROSE

The Elemental Kingdom Series Book 1

the truth of lies

LILY ANNE ROSE

Copyright

The Truth of Lies is a work of fiction. Names, characters, places, and incidents are either products of the author's imagination or used fictitiously. Any resemblance to actual persons, living or dead, events or locales is entirely coincidental.

Copyright 2022 by Lily Anne Rose
ISBN (paperback): 978-1-7780249-0-0
ASIN (ebook): 978-1-7780249-1-7
ebook available only on Kindle Unlimited

Cover art by Ria at Graphic Escapist
Instagram: @graphicescapist
Editing by Lunar Rose Editing Services
Instagram: @Lunar.rose.services
Formatting by Peachy Keen Author Services
Instagram: @peachykeenas

For anyone who finds their place in the pages of a book.

PROLOGUE

I must be losing my mind. My hands begin to shake as my friend, Semira, buttons up my lace wedding dress. I don't want to tell her that I am going mad, so I simply chalk it up to wedding nerves.

I should be happy today.

Should.

Isn't that what everyone feels on their wedding day? Perhaps I would if it was under better circumstances. I was happy; I was more than happy. It was a dream to be married to him, but that was before.

Semira fluffs my long dark hair, letting it cascade in smooth curls down my back before placing a long lace veil on my head. I stare at myself in the mirror, my head spinning with incomplete thoughts. I try to think back to simple things to remind me why I am marrying this man, but nothing comes to mind. The harder I think about this arrangement, the more I'm unsure about it.

"Are you alright? There's no need to be nervous. You will be happy with him. I promise," Semira tries to reassure me, yet it doesn't fully penetrate. She has been my friend since we were both young, it was a forced friendship, but it ended up working out well. Her soft brown eyes have always reminded me of the beautiful deer in the forest by the chateau I lived in with my mother, leaving me to feel comfortable around her.

We aren't sure which kingdom she was born in, but I suppose the Earth Kingdom-unofficially- claimed her. Her parents had passed long before she could remember them and have lived with us ever since.

Semira stares at me, still waiting for my answer, her hand resting on her curvaceous hip.

"Oh, yes. I'm alright." My voice is shaky, but she gives me a small smile as she hugs me in a motherly way.

A bell rings in the distance, loud enough to vibrate our room. *Why can't I remember where we are? Am I in a church or close to one?*

Eleven tolls chime and echo through me as Semira says, "One hour until the ceremony." She walks towards the large wooden door behind me as she grabs the silver handle, "You relax. I'm going to make sure everyone is ready." With that, she leaves the room. Leaving me in silence.

Fear and anxiety creep into my bones until I can't breathe. My stomach churns, threatening to ruin my white dress. My first instinct is to run, my mother always told me to trust my instincts, but I can't even trust myself at this moment. The feeling is like waking from a vivid dream when you can't figure out where you are, or which is a dream, and which is reality.

I try to picture my mother's face, but I can't. *Why can't I picture her face? Where is she?* More and more questions pound through my head. The harder I think about my life, the less I know.

That's when my body takes control, and I run. I rip the veil out of my hair and leave the brightly lit room before the stranger even has the chance to come back.

1
The Fae

I watch the Fae men move silently through the trees, searching for their missing girl. I hope they never find her.

I'm standing at the borderline, waiting for the agreed meeting time. Growing more anxious and restless, I decide to head to the garden about a kilometer within the Earth Kingdom. I steadily walk through the lush forest, feeling calmer whenever I am around the flora and fauna.

I'm just hoping that everything will work out according to plan; I really don't want a reason to kill someone today- I'm just not up for it. I'm too strung out on impatience, my temper sitting on the tightrope with a hair trigger.

The gate to the garden creaks and groans when I push on the cast iron, decorated with swirling designs of flowers and vines, complemented by natural vines twining themselves through the bars.

I pace back and forth in the pavilion that rests in the center of the garden, looking out over the expansive flora of every imaginable type. I scan my surroundings again, growing more and more restless as time passes. I shove my hands into the pocket of my light, olive-green jacket. It's reasonably modern with large gold buttons down the front, simple yet warm in this evening chill.

Finally, *finally*, it's time to meet just like we planned. I stand tall and listen for any movement in the distance with my Fae hearing. When there is no sound out of place, I reach out to my senses to see if I can find out what is taking so long.

Nothing.

Shit! I curse loudly in my head; I should know something at this point.

I take a deep breath again and try my hardest to keep the panic down. One hour passes, then two. By this time, I am stomping through the garden and picking all the flowers, only to watch them die in my hand. I repeat this process over and over all night until there is nothing left alive in this garden. I've waited long enough; I can't take this much longer.

Summoning a leaf and pulling out a quill, I begin writing a message to my second in command on the leaf. I looked at it one more time before sending it away in the wind. It read the two most important words I've ever written in my life.

This message is my lifeline; it is my whole world. If it's lost, then so am I.

It read:

Find her

2

Amalie

The rushing sound of the frigid creek startles me awake, and I choke as my head slides off a piece of wood, submerging me entirely.

I gasp for breath, lifting myself with shaky arms. A small trickle of clear water drenches my white dress and long dark hair, weighing me down.

How did I get here?

Slowly, I stand on my trembling legs. My mind is as slow as tree sap oozing down the bark.

My heart beats faster in an almost painful rhythm as I wrack my brain for a memory, any memory. Starting with the easiest, I think of my name.

Amalie. I'm Amalie!

The relief is minuscule but strong enough to kickstart my brain into thinking a bit more rationally.

"One problem at a time. You're okay, Amalie. Just move," I whisper to myself while looking around the dense forest. There's a creek, which I am currently knee-deep in. There are trees, *great observation Amalie*, I think sarcastically. There is a large willow tree that looks like a good place to find some sort of cover. I move towards the edge of the creek bed, weighed down from my dress as I trudge through the water while the lace on my gown snags on every branch and rock. Gathering the water-logged fabric, I hike up my skirt to my thighs and head towards the weeping tree.

Stumbling over fallen logs and slippery, moss-covered rocks, I sit down under the willow. It provides me with enough of a canopy, so I can't see what is above or around me. It gives me a sense of foreboding comfort to be sheltered and unseen. Oddly, this willow tree feels like home, like a child being pulled into their mother's arms.

As if realizing I am, in fact, alive, I frantically search my body for any injuries now that I am out of the water. Starting from my head down, I touch my dark chestnut-colored hair. Feeling reanimated from my wet hair, I find the blood that coats my fingers is now creeping down my hand. There is a small cut on my forehead. *Thankfully not deep, but head wounds always bleed worse*, or so I'm told. I stop.

Who told me that? Do I have a family? Friends? Is anyone looking for me?

My thoughts threaten to ignite my panic all over again. Instead, I force myself to do something other than think.

I examine my body, noting only minor bruises and cuts. I move and twist my limbs in awkward and uncomfortable angles; the worst of my injuries stem from the gashes on my feet. I suppose walking, or running, through the forest barefoot would do that to a person.

The dress is sheer from lying in the cold creek, and my whole body is visible through the thin fabric. I pull my knees to my chest, trying to stop my shivering. "Think, Amalie. What do you know?" I mutter to myself.

My name is Amalie, and I'm lost. I know my feelings; I'm scared. I know my needs: food, warmth, and shelter. The rest I will have to figure out later.

I peek through the dense willow leaves as slight hints of sunlight shine through the forest canopy. Daylight. This is perfect! I have a time of day, perhaps not the hour, but at least I know it's daytime. Shucking off my thin, soggy gown, I stand bare in the forest, feeling the soft grass beneath my aching feet. I must have come from quite a distance or been here for far longer than I thought, judging by my state of disarray. I don't even want to look at my hair or my dirt-covered body. My extremities are green from grass stains. If I didn't know better, I would think I was turning into a moss-woodland creature. I'm sure I look like one too.

I hang my only article of clothing on a branch to dry in the gentle breeze, whispering through the trees before heading out to search for food. *Naked like the animals in the forest hunting for prey*, I think, as I carefully move through the forest, searching for berries, leaves, mushrooms, or anything that resembles food. There isn't a single sound. The eerie silence starts my heart racing again—the calm before the storm.

Spying some mushrooms growing on a water-logged branch, I begin to pick as many as I can carry. I don't know if these are safe to eat. Trial and error might be my best bet at this point. Who knows how many days I have been out here? The chilling breeze begins to pick up, signaling my need to return to my willow tree.

Taking my armful of mushrooms back to my "base camp" under the willow tree, I start trying to clean them as best I can by rubbing my hands over the tops of the mushrooms, then over the stems, removing any extra dirt I can find.

"Never eat the mushrooms with the purple stripes on the underside, darling. They will make you sicker than a dog with chocolate! Those are only for the woodland sprites to enjoy." The voice catches me off guard. My mother! A sudden thought of her wise words hit me like a bolt to my chest. My eyes ache, and I start to sob. I sob for the memory I lost and found, for the overwhelming fear strangling me and crushing my chest to the point of hyperventilating. I weep for my mother, who must be looking for me, who came back to me when I needed her wisdom.

Time passes as I wail my frustrations at the earth, at the trees at the cold creek that left me without dry clothing; to the sky for not showing me the way. I blame the land around me for everything I can think of just to get my anger, pain, and frustration out. I am not focusing on what truly matters. I am irrational, and I know it. I just can't think of anything else to do! I don't know where I am, how I got here, or how to get home. I don't even know where my home is! I search my memories vigorously until the throbbing in my head intensifies to almost blacking out.

I can hear the birds chirping and frogs croaking in the distance. Of course, my mind scolds itself. Great, even the animals are laughing at you. Pull yourself together, Amalie. You're stronger than this.

Taking deep breaths, I breathe in and out.

Breathe in.

One. Two. Three. Four.

Hold.

One. Two. Three. Four.

Breathe out.

I repeat the process until I can see again. Until the world comes into focus, and I feel like a human again and not an emotional storm cloud ready to rain and drown everything in my tears and fear.

I pick up the mushrooms and examine them with a new sense of comfort. I've done this before; I know I have. The memory of my mother's voice echoes in my head as I carefully turn the tiny fungus in my hands. No purple anywhere. The mushrooms are a fresh and plump cream white color. I devour them savagely with the rubbery and tasteless texture coating my tongue. Stomach growling like an unchained beast as the hunger pains slowly subside. I savor the taste of the earthy vegetable for as long as I possibly can, but the hunger is too much, and my armful of mushrooms quickly dwindles to nothing.

The trees whisper eerily as the breeze crawls through the forest, creating a haunting atmosphere. The ghosts of the earth are growing, deep and menacing. Fear strikes my chest as I stand to grab my garment from the creaking willow branch. I dress silently in my damp white gown, shimmying into it as it sticks to my skin.

"Stupid bitch! Where the hell did she take off to now?"

The voice stops me in my tracks. I'm paralyzed by fear, and the only thing moving is my shaking hands and the rasp of my breathing. That was not the wind. That was not the trees creaking or the leaves swaying. It was a man. I can see two large men moving roughly through the forest, and I bolt.

Instinct kicks in, and I run like a bird fleeing a thunderstorm. I feel the malice in those words; I know this is not a friend.

No.

This is pure hatred, pure danger. I know this voice is searching for me. I know this voice must be the reason I am where I am now.

My feet can't seem to run fast enough. I want to cry, I want to scream, I want to hide. I know none of this will help. The only thing I can do is move!

The fire in my chest is growing, catching flames to my organs with each intake of breath I take. Running between trees and jumping over the logs, I hike my thin dress up over my bruised thighs, feeling irritated with the train catching on each fabric of the earth. As I slow to a speed walk, I don't hear the voice anymore.

Did I imagine it? Am I going crazy now?

I've been wandering for hours, or at least it feels like hours. A stabbing ache in my torn and bloody feet threaten to drag me down to the forest floor. The setting sun breaks through the dense trees to unveil a gorgeous meadow full of lavender. The floral scent is so intoxicating that I could lay down and sleep without hesitation. Walking further into the wide-open field, I spread my hands out, grazing my fingers over the vibrant purple flowers as I move slower and slower through the field. In the distance, I can see a run-down cabin with smoke drifting from the chimney. Thank the stars!

Falling to my knees in relief, I quickly realize the mistake in my actions. I'm too drained to move, to even cry or shout for help. My throat is like sandpaper, and speaking is painful. I just kneel there, staring forward as my eyes cross and my vision blurs from exhaustion.

I wake with a frightened start when I hear my name being called and skirts rushing through the tall lavender stems. The swish, swish of a female's footsteps by my head forces my eyes open wide to stare into a soft young, silhouetted beauty.

"Oh! Amalie! Darling, we have been looking for you for almost three days! You look ghastly. Look at your face, look at your dress! Oh, your husband will not be pleased to see you like this." Her voice raises higher and higher as she continues yelling. Suddenly she murmurs to herself, "Oh dear, no. He will not be pleased, at all…"

"Hus-" I clear my dry throat and try more firmly, "Husband? I have a husband? I'm sorry, who are you?"

Helping me to my feet, she grabs my arm rather forcefully and places it around her shoulders to hold me up as we start walking. To where, I have no clue. I feel like for the hundredth time, I am searching my brain for an image of this woman or my husband! I feel like I should know if I have a husband or not. I have so many questions swirling through my head that I start to feel nauseous and dizzy.

"I-Darling, I'm Semira. I'm your friend. We grew up together, don't you remember?" Semira asks with a confused expression that mirrors my own.

"I'm sorry. I don't remember anything."

"Anything at all?" she clarifies for herself.

I softly shake my head no. Any more movements, and I may vomit. My feet drag as I heavily lean on my self-proclaimed friend. We have to stop a couple of times so I can take a small break, and each time Semira gives me a weary look like she's not quite sure what to think of my situation. Her growing concern for my condition is contagious. If I weren't so exhausted, I would probably have a panic attack, but my body can't work up the strength.

By the time we reach the cabin, Semira practically carries me through the doorway. The soft glow of lanterns shines through the window as she yells out to whoever is inside.

"Start the kettle! I will need some clean linens, a hot cup of broth, and to contact Asher. Now! Oh, and grab me one of my shifts!" The sound of her loud vibrating voice in my ear sets me over the edge, and my knees start to buckle as I begin to drift to the floor.

Semira, thankfully, keeps a tight grip on my slender waist and leads me towards a pallet. The pallet is small and looks like it was made for birthing cattle, not for a human to sleep upon. At this point, though, I couldn't care less. A bed is a bed; beggars can't be choosers, and I am not one to complain. I flop like a sack of grain onto the pallet. Straw and rough wool scratch my cheek and exposed arms as I fight the exhaustion pulling me into oblivion.

Moments later, an older, dirty, rough man walks into the room. He is carrying a steaming bowl and white sheets over his arm as he mumbles, "Uh… here. Broth. Linen, uh, shift." Then he loudly places the bowl and fabrics down with a thump before quickly shuffling away. I wonder how he didn't spill the broth as I take notice of a slight limp in his left leg. He stumble-stomps like it is an old injury, and I'm curious what happened to him. He has his shoulder-length hair tied back with a leather cord, and he wears drab, patched farmer's clothing. He's hugely unremarkable in every way. I feel terrible in thinking that he could be the type of man whom nobody would discern if they left the room.

Glancing over at Semira to assist in telling me who this man is, she simply says, "My husband, Alizar. He doesn't talk much, but he's nice enough. Highest bidder and all", she explains with a worried smile. I quirk my eyebrow as if to ask, *highest bidder?* But she just turns away towards the items he placed on the old table beside my pallet.

To keep my mind occupied, I try to get a good view of my surroundings. The cabin is small. There's no hiding that fact. It consists of probably two rooms and a den. The walls look roughly put together like a strong wind will come and take down this entire structure. There is a thin layer of dust and grime on every surface I can see, and the bedroom door no longer hangs on a hinge but is placed against the wall like it is on the fix-it list.

When Semira catches me glancing around the room, she gives me an uneasy stare.

"Amalie… What exactly do you remember?"

I don't answer right away as she brings the steaming bowl of broth to my lips, and I ungracefully slurp the liquid off the wooden spoon. It is foul. So, so foul that I could vomit right there. I turn my head abruptly, causing another wave of dizziness and nausea to seep through me.

"Really, Amalie, it's not that bad. I'm sure you haven't eaten in three days; it must be better than nothing. Eat. Please." I do as she requests while hating every minute of it. I admit that the pain of hunger does eventually subside enough for me to be able to lean back on the dirty pallet "Now, time to give you a fresh gown and bedding. I hope you don't mind. The pallet isn't quite what you are used to, but you should be back in your own bed in no time!"

Semira pulls her long, waist-length honey blonde braid over her left shoulder as she begins to help me stand up again to undress from my gown.

"Now, tell me what you remember, hm?"

"I know my name," I whisper self-consciously, shivering at the cold wind seeping through the gaps in the wall paneling. She stares at me like I've lost my mind. Maybe I have. Who doesn't remember their life, their own family, their own husband!

"Oh. That's a good start! What's the last thing you remember?"

"I-I don't know. I just woke up in a creek. I think I was running from something; my feet are all cut up."

"That's okay. It will come to you. We will get your feet fixed up and make sure you are comfortable." She pulls the clean shift over my still grimy body, letting it fall into place. I steady myself against the wall while she lays the fresh linens over the hay pallet. "Here, lay back down."

I grab her slender arm and slowly slide myself back onto the makeshift bed. The thick grey wool blanket is rough and scratchy against my bruised and sore skin. Sighing in contentment, my eyes fight to close again. My body warms, my stomach is full, and I am relatively comfortable. I may not know Semira, but she is kind, and I am so thankful she came across my body in that lavender field.

"I think we should wait until Asher gets here for more questions. He can help you find the missing pieces, I'm sure of it." She gives me a comforting smile that doesn't quite reach her eyes. I can tell she's concerned for me. She did say she was my friend. Therefore, she must know more about me.

"Asher is...my husband, right?"

"Yes."

"Okay. Um... Where are we?" I press the question because I need to know more. I don't want to wait until this man shows up to tell me about my life. I start with the easy question hoping she won't withhold too much information from me. I understand that she may not want to overwhelm me, but wouldn't she want to know what was going on in her life if she were in my shoes?

Semira hesitates for so long that I almost forget I asked a question. My eyes start to close again, and the room feels like it is beginning to sway as the breeze outside picks up.

"You're just within the border of the Air Kingdom, darling. When you're feeling better, we will travel inland to our home. Why don't you close your eyes and rest now, hm? I'm sure you've had a rough journey. I would love to hear all about it when you awake," Semira belts out quickly and stands, grabbing the now-empty bowl, then scurries through the open frame to the den.

"Where is she?"

"Sir, please. She is resting. She- Sir, she doesn't remember you..."

"What do you mean she doesn't remember?..."

I lost my battle of wills after that. My eyes are heavy and seem to be sewn shut. I can hear the voices, but I can't make out the words as my world slowly drifts to black, and then I dream.

3

Amalie

My soft sage green dress flows gracefully behind me as I walk along the moss-covered pathway. My garment is simple with tulip-shaped cap sleeves, a cutting neckline, and a keyhole back. My dark hair hangs long in loose curls, and I have an eloquent small flower tucked behind my ear. I feel stunning. The soft carpet of the earth beneath my bare feet calls me onward through the gardens.

I see vines of all sizes, statues of all figures, and flowers of all colors surrounding me. I have never seen anything more beautiful in my life. I hear the faint sound of a babbling brook as I move forward once again.

Gazing ahead, I see a man's silhouette against the shining sunlight. He's standing under a stone pavilion covered in ivy vines and a beautiful mix of flowers. He's tall with broad shoulders and a lean waist; I can't help but stop and stare.

The feeling of longing is so overwhelming that my hand moves to cover my gasp. The urge to run and wrap my arms around him drives my feet towards the pavilion.

This garden is my peace. This man is my salvation.

As I gather my skirt and climb the few stone steps up to the man, he reaches out and takes my hand. His hand is large in comparison to mine. He feels solid and sure in my grasp as he gently pulls me into his arms.

I'm safe. I'm warm. I'm loved. The words chant in my head over and over. I wish I knew who he was. I wish I could see his face, but it is cloaked in shadows.

His arms wrap around me in a blanket, and it feels like home.

"Come back to me."

His voice is like a caress down my spine, and my heart aches for us. For whatever this is.

"Amalie, come back to me, darling." The voice is stronger and more forceful. I stare up at the man, confused by the change in tone.

And then I wake.

Eyes wide, I startle and scurry backward, hitting my back off the rough paneling. I wince as my eyes dart back and forth between the faces staring at me.

"There you are, darling," the man says to me in a soothing voice. He doesn't look familiar, but I would assume he is around my age. Blonde hair cropped short over pointed ears and the shadow of facial hair are the first things I notice about him. The beard just doesn't suit him; there's something *wrong* about it. I stare into his eyes and see deep blue staring back at me. His eyes are the color of the ocean after a storm, churned up seas revealing all that was hiding underneath. I know him, I think as I stare longer.

No, Amalie. You know *of* him. There's a difference.

"Asher..." I whisper, remembering the name Semira told her husband to find. This man must be my husband.

"So, you do know me! Thank the stars for that. I thought we would have to start our relationship all over again when Semira here told me you bumped your head. How are you feeling?" He gives me a wide smile, showing all white teeth.

"Oh. I-uh, I don't." I look behind him to Semira for help explaining, but she only gives me an encouraging nod. "I'm sorry, I don't know who you are. I just know Semira was calling for someone named Asher. I assumed you were him."

The look of disappointment is undeniable. His demeanor instantly changes as my words continue to drive the knife into his chest.

"I don't know you. I don't remember marrying you," I bite out with more force than I intended.

The pregnant silence in the room grows to an unbearable awkwardness. The only sound is the howling voices of the wind outside the cabin. My head throbs from the effort of trying to remember, and my feet are starting to feel numb from the aching lacerations.

Asher coughs to clear his throat and answers, "Right, well. We will just take it one day at a time." He glances back at Semira quickly, exhaling a loud sigh. "Right," he repeats. "You're in the Kingdom of Air. You are my wife. Your name is Amalie. You're twenty-three years old. You are a human, and you are to be queen." He marks off each point of my life with his long fingers as he speaks. The moment he reaches fact number six, he hesitates and then continues, "Of course, once you are comfortable and we complete the coronation ceremony, you will be queen. And I, king."

He speaks boldly and proudly while I stare at him in utter confusion. I ran through his list of six facts I should know about my life and analyzed them all.

I am in the Kingdom of Air. Alright, that doesn't seem odd. I am his wife, where is my ring? Not important. Okay, I'm his wife; I will figure that one out later. He seems harmless, and he's attractive enough. My name is Amalie, duh. I am twenty-three, also, duh. I am human. I know there are humans and Fae; I just don't know how I know. As I don't have pointy ears like my dear husband here, I think it's safe to assume I am human. And I am to be queen, although that might need more explanation.

For some reason, my mind focuses on my ring. Or rather, lack of said ring.

"Where is my wedding ring?" I blurt out, catching him off guard.

Asher laughs, a strong and deep laugh that comes straight from his toes. "Darling, I never knew you to be so materialistic. If you want your ring, I have it kept safely at home." His smile widens again like my mention of the ring pleases him. "Now, most importantly, how are you feeling?"

"Okay," I shrug nonchalantly, but Asher raises one eyebrow in a knowing look. "Alright, my head aches, I feel like I was trampled by a horse, and I am utterly exhausted."

"Could you eat more?" Semira asks behind Asher as she shifts to reach for a bowl of broth.

"No! No, I'm okay for now. Thank you," I tack on the thank you to please her. I know she's trying, but that broth is the most foul-tasting liquid. I would rather eat the forest mushrooms again.

Semira smiles and grabs new cloth dressings to clean my lacerated and aching feet while I stare at Asher. My husband is observing Semira, as if he is making sure she is appropriately caring for me, which I find rather sweet. Maybe I did fall for this man.

"You have a beard..." I'm not sure why I said it. It's one of those thoughts that comes out your mouth before your brain can fully catch up, though I'm glad it said it.

Asher's smile grew again as he and Semira whipped their heads towards me. Shock and happiness are mirrored in both their faces.

"What?"

Asher shakes his head and chuckles softly before he lowers his voice and says, "You had a memory. I am always clean-shaven." He grabs my hand again and gives my fingers a soft squeeze. "I haven't had time to shave since you've been... gone."

"Oh," I mumble, staring at my thick blanket in embarrassment. That must be why he looked so different to me. That's what was off about him.

Semira and Asher return their attention to dressing my wounds. I feel it is unnecessary. I just need to sleep, but they are insistent on it. While they are busy murmuring between themselves, I close my eyes again, trying to reclaim the serenity of my dream.

What was it? A meadow? No, a garden. With a man, maybe Asher.

"Asher?"

"Hmm?" He slowly looks at me again.

"Were we ever in an overgrown garden with a pavilion? Like one of those botanical gardens that are full of vines and statues. Flowers of every color?" I ask, a smile on my face at the memory of the dream, but Asher's eyes darken.

"No," he says simply, turning back to Semira, deflating my euphoria almost as quickly.

I look away, embarrassed once again. I thought I had a memory, but it must have just been a vivid dream. I thought for sure the man I was standing with was Asher, but apparently not, at least not in this life.

I close my eyes again, sliding down on the rough pallet once Semira has finished with my dressings. My eyes close, and I give in to the exhaustion.

4

Amalie

Semira is reluctant to let me leave, but Asher thinks I would be more comfortable finally being home and in my own bed. I tend to agree with Asher. My headache is still making itself known, putting pressure behind my eyes and in my temples. My body is sore, but I think standing and moving around will do me some good.

Asher grabs me around my waist and hauls me to my feet. Once I am steadily standing on the floor, he moves his arms from around me and takes hold of my hand instead. Kissing my knuckles, he leads me outside to a small outhouse to take care of my needs.

The walk is short and slow but greatly appreciated. Taking in a large breath of the fresh earthy air, I look around to try to gain control over my surroundings. I don't recognize the area. We must have walked further from the lavender field than I realized. We are on a dirt road, wedged between a forest and a clearing with high snow-capped mountains in the distance. The road leads through the clearing and towards the mountains; I assume that is our direction to go home.

Asher waits outside while I relieve myself and takes my hand again to walk me back to the cabin.

"Asher?" I pull on his hand to stop walking, staring up into his storm blue eyes.

"Yes? Are you alright?"

"Of course! I just - can we just stay out here for a while, please. I need some air," I plead with Asher, hoping he will understand the stuffy and stifling feeling in the cabin. I just need time to breathe in the air, to feel the grass beneath my feet before we return to the Air Kingdom.

Asher sighs and turns his head towards the rising sun. He takes his time responding. When he does, the answer seems exasperated, "Amalie, we really should just get you back inside. There are creatures out here, and we need to send for the coach to take us home."

I simply nod and allow him to gently direct me back to the cabin. He turned to speak with a guard in the shadow of the trees surrounding us. I didn't notice the guard before now. I suppose Asher's guards are there only to see but not be seen; always watching in the shadows. That's something I need to remember. I catch the small conversation about calling for our coach before the door closes behind me.

Semira is inside tidying the pallet while we are outside, her husband nowhere to be seen. Giving me her usual smile, she gestures to a stool to sit on while waiting for the coach to arrive. She simply asks me how I feel using her facial expressions; eyebrows raised, nose scrunched, and deep brown eyes wide. My breath comes out silently in a quick laugh from her face alone.

"I'm fine, Semira, thank you," I tell her for what feels like the one-hundredth time since I arrived in this cabin yesterday. "Do you have something I can wear? I don't want to travel in my sleeping gown."

"Oh! Of course, I should have thought of that!" Semira runs

off, quickly returning with a black pair of pants and a loose shirt. The clothes seem to be in reasonably good condition, although too big for my frame.

I nod my thanks as I shimmy the pants underneath my gown and then lift the shift off over my head to put the shirt on. I tuck in the long ends and tie the collar tighter to not have my breasts exposed to the world.

Asher comes barreling through the door seconds after tying my shirt and calls out, "The coach is here. Let's go home, darling." Taking my hand, Asher leads me outside towards the coach that will take me to the capital of the Air Kingdom. Semira and Alizar follow behind us, and I glance back curiously.

"Asher thinks it would be beneficial if I come with you to get settled in. Maybe having a familiar face from your past will help with your memories," Semira says as she smiles at Alizar and me. "Alizar is only coming for my sake." She giggles to herself, taking his hand and entering the coach. I stare at the large carriage in front of us and then take a deep breath and prepare to meet my new life.

Hours pass. At least it feels like hours, but it could possibly only be a handful of minutes. Asher, Semira, and Alizar all stare in opposite directions, not allowing me to catch their eye or question anything I have learned about my own life so far. Looking around, I notice wealth, just an obnoxiously large amount of wealth that was needed to create this coach. The white-on-white interior casts a blinding shimmer on everything once the sun is entirely above the horizon. Everywhere I look, there is some sign of wealth. Plush white bench seats, hand-carved depictions of clouds and wind-blown skirts wrapping around slender female legs, and an image of a creature that does not match the atmosphere of the coach.

The creature is ghastly, to put it mildly. The sunken skeleton-like frame of the monster is unsettling and revolting. "What is that?" I question, perhaps a little too loudly in the silent coach, as all three of them startle and suddenly turn their eyes on me.

"That, Darling, is a ghoul. They live in the Kingdom of Air and are greatly feared by all," Asher announces with pride radiating off him. I just stare at him, willing him to continue explaining more about the ghouls rather than just name them. Asher continues, "The ghouls are creatures of Air. They start with the wind, carrying in fog and strengthening the gale as they approach. Once they have you in their sights, they trap you with fear before turning whole. They feed on the air in your lungs. They look like bone white reapers in part skeletal form, and their flesh hangs off the bones. They sleep in a field of husks, like corn stalks. The center of the stocks is the essence of the ghouls. Each kingdom has one fearful creature native to only that kingdom- ours is the ghouls. Luckily, the ghouls are obedient creatures and follow the rule of the monarchy. You have nothing to fear from them, darling. Others like Semira here may need to fear them more." He gives Semira a sly smile, hinting at an inside joke. I don't care to investigate it any further right now. I have more important things to ask him.

The ghouls were with me in the forest; I know they were. If Asher is telling me the truth about them, they were with me at that moment. For some reason, the willow was the only place I felt safe from them, as the wind never penetrated the walls of the willow tree. I could hear the voices of the ghouls and feel their eerie aura as they approached closer and closer. I shiver at the sudden realization of my close encounter. I wonder if they are why the wind was so unbearable in the cabin.

I still don't trust him, but perhaps he will unlock a memory for me so I don't continue feeling as confused or alone in this situation. I almost feel like a prisoner being carried off with her captor; I wouldn't know any different, and I am playing right into his hand. How do I know I can trust any of these people? I don't know them. They could be telling me lies to gain my trust, but to what end? If they were evil kidnappers, there would be some sort of sign as to their intentions or lies, but I haven't seen any. I don't feel like they're lying, just omitting some information that I need to know.

"Asher?" I attempt to gain his attention again while he is still willing to give me at least some answers, "How did we meet? Can you tell me the story of...us?"

Asher gazes out the window again, and for some time, I wonder if he is going to say anything, and to my surprise, he actually does.

"In the four kingdoms, we hold an annual gathering, if you will. We call it the Trine. As you probably still remember, our kingdoms are run on the four elements." I nod, allowing him to continue. "Right, well, every time a Half-Fae prince or princess comes of age, they undergo the ceremony of life-giving them a full Fae body, followed by five years of schooling to teach the Fae youngling how to control and understand their new bodies. Once they reach their full potential, they are ready to ascend the throne and take a bond. This ceremony, the Trine, is where we met. Stars, Amalie, you were radiant, and I knew you were my choice from just a single glance."

Confusion freezes my movements as he speaks. Yes, I remember how the kingdoms are made of the star's elements: Earth, Air, Fire, and Water. I know there are Fae, half-Fae, and humans. I have this knowledge integrated into my mind, but I don't fully remember it. It's like knowing how to breathe but not knowing how you know to do it. It just is. I stop Asher in his tracks before he continues again before I lose my train of thought.

"Royalty marries humans." It's not a question. I know they do; it only makes sense if there is a whole ordeal to turn a half-Fae into a full Fae. "Why?" I finally ask.

"Ah, well, there is the Treaty of Alignment. This allows humans and Fae to live in harmony in all four kingdoms. To keep the peace, each ruling monarch must marry a human as their child. The next heir would be half-Fae. The ceremony of life is given to reset the balance and begin again. That is how I chose you at the Trine. It was my ceremony to choose an eligible bond. I just completed my years of learning, and I was ready to ascend the throne." Asher leans forward, taking my hands in his larger ones, kissing my knuckles before continuing. "Amalie. Stars, Amalie. You were standing there in your beautiful starlight gown, and I knew I had to have you. You were mine the moment you turned to me and gave me your soft smile."

What do you say to that? What is the proper way to react to a random man saying he had to have you? It doesn't sound like an epic love story to me, but maybe there's more. So, I decided to press him for more, anything that might strike this sense of comfort or familiarity with my husband. "So, what happened next? How long did we know each other before we married?"

"Well, I chose you." He shrugs as if that's an explanation, "We married one month later."

Semira, who has been deliberately ignoring our conversation by looking out the window, finally turns her head to gauge my expression. I have no clue what my expression says to her, but I can tell her expression looks fearful. Her jaw tenses, and her eyebrows are furrowed. Are they afraid I won't like Asher's story? Because no, I don't *like* his story. I don't like that he just saw me and essentially said, "Yeah, that one. I want that one!" Like some cave-dwelling imp. This irks me more than I think it should. Maybe this is normal for our world, but it doesn't feel right. It doesn't feel right that I would be picked like fruit or chosen like an item at an auction. I am a person with a soul, a spirit, a life. I'm not an object to just be chosen. If this is a part of the human/Fae treaty for equality, it seriously needs to be rethought because this isn't equality. This is ownership.

I'm pretty sure Semira can see the thoughts going through my head as if she were a mind reader herself. She pursed her lips and gave Asher a look of disapproval that he nodded to. Asher squeezes my hands and lowers his voice, "Darling, I know this seems like a lot right now, but please give us time. We will work through it. It's not all that it appears to be. You were willing and ready to become my wife, my bond. I'm sure you will gain your memories soon. If not, we will build new memories. We will go at your pace."

And that's it. At those words, I feel comforted again; because clearly, a man would not just take me and then speak to me like this. He's so calm, confident, and sure. Asher sits back and stares out the window again. Clearly, this conversation is over in his eyes.

I glance around the coach's interior, staring at the faces that are distinctly not looking at me anymore. Everyone seems to be giving me space, allowing my thoughts to wander.

I lean back on the plush bench seat, closing my eyes to ease the growing headache and tension I feel brewing inside me. Asher is handsome enough with his close-cut soft blonde hair, his kind ocean blue eyes, and his tallness, although he's a bit thin-framed. Asher is the king, or soon-to-be-king of the Air Kingdom, and I'm not sure which but I make a mental note to ask about that later. He seems to care for me, or he wouldn't have traveled this far to bring me home. This does make me wonder, though, how did I end up so far away from the kingdom?

"Where are we?" I ask without opening my eyes or lifting my head. It's all too much right now.

"Oh, you were almost all the way to the Earth Kingdom! Good thing we found you when we did because-"

Semira's voice cuts off abruptly, causing me to open one eye and lift a brow, ready for her to continue. She doesn't. Semira casts her eyes downward while Asher casts a withering look in her direction. Throughout this entire journey back home, Semira's husband does not take his eyes off the window. He doesn't stir or shift from beside Asher; he doesn't even twitch. I'm starting to worry he isn't even alive until I see small breaths causing his chest to rise and fall. Alizar is utterly indifferent to our conversations and Asher's apparent hostility towards Semira for mentioning our location. He simply sits there in his slightly frayed outfit, staring out the window and rubbing his leg that must be aching from the trip. I watch as a gentle breeze blows through his brown hair, cutting loose a few strands from his leather tie.

"You traveled some distance while you were…gone. We were staying at our chateau when we discovered you were missing. We should be back to the capital by tomorrow afternoon," Asher smoothly interjects in Semira's place. Once again, ending that topic of conversation.

More hours pass, and I know this because I can now feel it in my ass. No matter how soft or plush this bench is, if you're sitting for this long, your ass will hurt. I open my eyes and glance at Semira sleeping peacefully against the wall of the coach, her husband still staring out the window, somehow in a trance from the endless path of trees.

Asher notices me shifting in my seat. He sits up straighter and whispers softly, "We're almost at Windhaven. We will spend the night there, get you some food and a proper bed to sleep in."

"Thank you, Asher."

His eyes crinkle as he smiles warmly at me, "It was really difficult not having you beside me. I'm glad you're coming home."

To that, I have no response. I only find myself observing him more closely. I can tell he was distressed by his growing beard, which he mentioned he always keeps shaven. His clothing is wrinkled from a couple of days' wear, which simply looks wrong on him. If he is the king or soon to be king, you would imagine his appearance would be immaculate. These past days have been hard on him as well, not just me, and I should be more considerate and grateful, I suppose.

The smooth rocking of the coach converts to rough jolting on cobblestone streets. I suppose Asher was right about being close to Windhaven. The trees disperse and morph into structures, homes, and taverns. The town seems almost deserted as we arrive at the inn for the night. The outside is worn down but not nearly as bad of shape as the cabin. I'm excited about a hot meal and a warm bed. Honestly, at this point, I wouldn't complain about anything as long as there is food and sleep.

The coach stops abruptly, and I barely have time to stop myself from flying forward into Asher's lap. Thank the stars, I am able to straighten myself before he notices my embarrassment. All four of us wait for the coachmen to open the door and assist us in our short descent onto the stone streets. Once he is out of the coach, Asher turns to grab my hand. I reach out to him and grasp his strong hand in mine. As cliche as it is, uneasy butterflies in my stomach flutter when our hands touch, and I can't help but stare up at him and think I could marry this man. I did marry this man.

Asher's frame is large enough to block my entire view of the inn, and once he shifts to the side, I can finally get a better glimpse. The inn is two stories tall, with small Juliette balconies on the second level. I can see the flickering of multiple lanterns on each table in the tavern below the inn as we walk through the insanely tall, creaking door. I glance up at Asher's blonde hair shining from the candlelight inside the inn. He is taller than me but still clears the door easily. He catches me watching him, his strong jaw and soft smile turn up at the corners. He is gorgeous.

The tavern is empty of humans and Fae. It looks like a dead zone, and I don't know how this establishment is still in business. One would think that being the only inn and tavern in this tiny village, it would at least have some people enjoying their evening.

"There's nobody here," I mention as if it wasn't obvious. Glancing around, there are at least ten picnic-style wooden tables on each side of the tavern and five round tables down the center aisle. Everything is made of dark, rich wood. The floors, walls, ceiling, tables, chairs, everything. It's so dark and masculine in this room that it gives off an oppressive atmosphere. I don't want to spend any more time here than I need to.

"Yeah, we sent some riders ahead to inform the inn of our arrival. They have our rooms and everything ready for us!" Semira answers excitedly.

Asher drops my hand and turns towards me, asking, "Did you want your meal in our room, or would you like to sit in the tavern?"

"Our room?"

"Yes… We are married, Amalie." Asher's chuckle causes my anxiety to soar and the butterflies in my stomach to intensify. I'm not ready for this; I'm not ready for any marital expectations. This is all too soon for me. I literally met my husband yesterday, or at least it feels like it. This man may be kind to me, but he's a stranger. Asher can obviously see my increasing distress because he quickly interjects, "Amalie, I don't expect anything tonight. You've been through a lot. We will just eat and sleep, that's all. I promise."

I nod a few times, reassuring myself, but I can't escape the fear of expectations for some reason. I need to pull myself out of my thoughts, but I know I will need to think about this issue later. What if I never get to that point with him?

"Thank you, Asher, but... um, can I have my own room? If one is available, of course," I ask in a quiet voice. I know he won't be happy about me wanting to be by myself after he just got me back. I'm still not sure how I ended up getting lost in the first place, but once again, that's another question for another time. I should really start writing a list of all the questions I have about my own life.

"Why don't you share a room with Semira? Alizar and I will have our own rooms, but I would feel more comfortable if you are not alone tonight, just in case you need anything."

Asher's request isn't unreasonable, so I oblige without further argument. "Thank you. I would like to eat in my room. I am pretty tired."

"Of course." Asher takes my hand again, gently kissing my knuckles, and gestures to one of his guards to prepare another room. I don't think that is in his job description, but I don't know the entire ins and outs of being a royal. I will have to interrogate some answers from Semira tonight, preferably while Asher isn't around.

5

Amabie

The loud banging on my door startles me awake. I shoot up in bed and panic as the blankets twist around my legs, making me feel as if invisible hands are holding me down. My heart stops and starts irrationally, I know I'm fine, but my body doesn't.

The wooden door screeches like a banshee as Semira walks into our room carrying two trays of steaming food. *Great, more stew*, I think to myself as she sets the trays on a small circle table by the hearth. The blazing fire casts a comforting glow through the room, and my heart begins to slow to a normal rhythm.

My eyes adjust slowly to the morning light dancing through the window into the old room. I glance around the space noting the small details to bring me back into myself. The warm fire in the hearth, the steaming bowl of food, and the crisp made bed beside my disheveled one. The room is dingy but clean. It looks a bit run down, but not nearly as bad as the cabin. The furniture is in good repair, and the bed is small but comfortable enough.

I untangle my legs from the bedsheets and stumble over to the table. I take a seat next to Semira, who has already eaten a couple of spoonfuls of her meal. She gives me a massive smile, and broth spills down her chin. I laugh at her embarrassment. She may not be the most classy or graceful person, but I have quickly grown to adore her in the short time I can remember. I know in my heart that Semira was-is- a friend.

As I eat, I study her. I don't think I will get any answers from her right now with her mouth stuffed full of beef and potatoes. Semira has a timeless face. She's the type of person who could easily be eighteen or thirty-five. Her smooth, tan-colored skin is free of blemishes or imperfections, making her even more radiant. Her husband is a lucky man to have captured her eye, if that's how their relationship started. She mentioned something about him being the highest bidder, which does not sit well with me. I know he's a human, so she did not participate in the Trine. But was she sold? Is she a prisoner as much as I feel like one?

Let's be honest, I know I'm being dramatic and that I'm not actually a prisoner. Somehow being taken to a kingdom I don't know of, with a man and his servants, who I also don't know, doesn't exactly scream comfort to me. I fight with my inner turmoil. It's a matter of knowing you're being ridiculous but not being able to stop the thoughts. I am literally complaining about having a family, about being a future Queen in a palace. I feel like a spoiled child, and my mood starts to sour. To keep my mind off my inner thoughts, I turn my attention back to Semira, who is too enraptured in her meal to realize my racing mind. However, she does notice that I haven't taken a single bite of my stew yet.

She takes her spoon out of her mouth and uses it to point to my bowl, asking over a mouthful, "You gonna eat that? I thought you were hungry."

I don't give her an answer, I just pick up my spoon and scoop up some chunks of beef and broth. The stew is hot and surprisingly delicious. I can taste the many different spices and flavors complementing each other in each bite. I'm sure this difference in food has something to do with Asher being present. I have the suspicion that if it were just Semira and I, we wouldn't be receiving such a good meal. The cook certainly pulled all the stops to please their future King. I suppose there are some perks.

We finish eating in silence. Semira piles the dishes and sets them outside our room for the housekeeper to take away. She turns back to me and gives me a hesitant grin, "All right. Spill it, Amalie. I can tell you are just dying to ask me questions. I've known you for a long time, remember?"

I thought she didn't notice my spiraling mind, but now I know Semira is much sharper than I give her credit for.

"Why did Asher not want you to talk about our location? Or the Earth kingdom?" I start with my most prominent question. I still don't like how Asher reacted to Semira when she began telling me about it, and I want to know how much she will say to me now that Asher isn't around.

Semira's eyes wandered, avoiding my gaze. Her avoidance is obvious. So, I decide to push. "Semira, please. Asher isn't here, and I won't say a word to him. I just need answers. Please." I add in again just to drive in the nail of guilt I know I hammered into her heart. It isn't fair, and I shouldn't pry if she isn't able or willing to tell me. They need to realize how frustrating it is to be around literal strangers and not know a thing about yourself, about your own life. I feel like a ghost walking around the world trying to find my purpose just to pass on to the afterlife. I am a phantom in my own life.

"Fine!" Semira hisses, "Amalie, you were born in the Earth Kingdom. Your mother was a dear friend of the current Queen." Semira keeps her eyes locked on the flickering fire warming our chambers.

"My mother was a friend of the Queen, is she-is she alive? And why would Asher be upset about me knowing where I grew up? Isn't that something everyone should know about themselves?" I can hear my voice raising a couple of octaves.

She just shrugs, still not glancing in my direction.

"Is that where I was headed to? Semira, what happened? Why was I in the woods for three days? Please tell me?"

"I don't know. I don't know where your mother is or if she's alive. I don't know why you decided to leave. I just… don't," Semira whispers her answer, and I don't know if it's my own frustration building, my unease, or if I somehow know Semira isn't telling me the whole truth.

If I learned anything from this, it's that I wasn't kidnapped. I left him. Stars! Why would I leave my husband? Angry tears threaten to escape my eyes. I quickly blink them away and move on as smoothly as possible before Semira realizes her mistake. If she realizes that she led me to believe I left Asher, she will never confide in me again.

I sigh, letting it go. I hope someone in the capital will know me and tell me the truth. I will find out whether they want me to or not. So instead, I move on to my other questions. "Is Asher a King?"

Semira seems more relaxed in my new line of questioning, perhaps thinking I didn't catch her slip-up. Her answer is quick and confident. This must be a topic that Asher will allow her to discuss. "Not yet. You two haven't had the coronation ceremony yet. Therefore, the crown title hasn't been transferred from his parents to you two. It's the law that there will not be a change in succession without a king and queen ready in waiting-one Fae and one human."

I can remember enough about the rules of the monarchy. The roles of the throne are the same in all four kingdoms. I remember the history enough to know that the Treaty must be upheld over the monarchy. There must be a bond formed, and there needs to be a potential King and Queen ready to take the throne together. One human and one Fae to continue the line of succession.

"Why did Asher say you would fear the ghouls over him?"

"Well, the ghouls are from the Air Kingdom, so they don't attack their own kind. Once you become Queen, you will also be in the safety of the ghouls."

"So, these ghouls are what, spirits?"

"In a sense," she replies. "They don't have physical bodies; they move on the wind and fog. You can hear their whispers and screams as the wind picks up. That's how you know they're coming."

I think back to my time in the forest when I thought I heard voices. *Was that actually a ghoul?*

I don't recall ever encountering a ghoul.

"So, what happens when the ghouls come?" I question, almost afraid to hear her response.

"When they attack, their bodies turn whole, like skeletons. They eat the air out of your lungs, suffocating you, strangling you from the inside out." I shudder from my close encounter with the beast.

"That was almost me," I say under my breath, causing Semira to give me an odd glance. She raises her eyebrow and tilts her head, waiting for me to continue. "I heard them in the forest, and I only felt safer when I hid under a willow tree."

"Ah, willows are the symbol of the earth Kingdom. Maybe it's your roots coming back to save you." She snickers at her own joke.

Giving her a courtesy grin, I let the moment pass. I don't want to think about what could have happened. I'm glad that I didn't get close enough to see their real faces. I can only imagine what a spirit, fog, wind, breath eater looks like with an actual body.

Semira and I move towards our separate beds. I curl under the soft fur blankets while Semira turns to the bag containing our bandages. We are still wearing our traveling clothes as we don't have anything else with us. The only things we brought with us were warm cloaks and supplies. Semira begins to redress my feet with clean bandages, and I stare at them. They're almost healed and don't hurt as they did, so small victories, I suppose.

My mind wanders to Asher again. I hope I didn't offend him by asking to be in a separate room from him. I'm so confused about what I feel instead of what I should be feeling. On the one hand, I'm grateful for everything he has done for me. He's been so kind to me, so protective, and he makes sure that I'm okay. On the other hand, I still don't remember him, besides knowing that he is always clean-shaven.

Maybe he didn't want to overwhelm me with too much information about where I come from. That could be why he didn't want Semira to mention the Earth Kingdom. Or maybe he didn't want me to have any memory of my home because I was trying to run back to it.

"Did I love him?"

"Hmm?"

"Asher, before all this. Did I love him?"

"Oh darling, that is for you to answer. That's an answer I truly don't know." Semira finishes wrapping my injuries and moves to her own bed, dowsing the lantern on the bedside table.

6

Amalie

I decide it's as good a time as any to find Asher and get going again. I'm still not entirely sure what to call my new home or old home that is only a couple of hours' carriage ride. Before I went to my room last night, Asher said that we should reach it by mid-afternoon. I trust his estimate as he was pretty accurate about our arrival to Windhaven.

When I open the door to leave, it creaks and groans obnoxiously loud, and I am happy never to hear that screeching noise again. Once it's silent, I begin moving down the stairs. The staircase is steep, wooden, and, you guessed it, creaky. It's narrow enough that I can put a hand on each side of the wall to steady myself as I descend. The wall at the end makes a sharp right turn. So sharp that I don't see Asher as I turn and almost fall over from running into his back.

"Oh, my stars! Asher, I'm so sorry, I didn't see you. Did I hurt you?" I ask him as I rub my sore nose. Of course, this is the perfect wake-up call. There is nothing better than getting a good smack to the nose from your husband's back to wake you up in the morning.

Asher turns, taking in my hurt expression with concern in

his eyes that quickly morphs into a peal of loud and booming laughter.

I glower at him.

"I'm sorry for laughing, Amalie. It's just-" He trails off and works into another fit of laughter. I raise my brow at him, also starting to fight a smile. His laugh is infectious. His storm blue eyes brighten like a sunrise over the sea. His whole aura changes when he laughs, the room warming at the sound. His sun bright, blond hair falls forward into his eyes as he leans into himself to hide his amusement. I can tell he doesn't laugh like this nearly enough, and I find myself wanting to make him laugh more. He clears his throat, trying to sober his expression. "I'm sorry. It was just your expression. I admit I was watching you come down the stairs. You had been so focused on not falling that you were looking down at your feet." His face softens with adoration. His laughter morphs into a small smile.

I remove my hand from my nose, no longer aching from the small impact, and I reach over to take his hand, smiling up at him. "You should laugh more, it suits you." I squeeze his hand and walk toward the tables set out for our breakfast.

Muffins, eggs, bacon, and coffee litter the table, and my mouth waters. If my mouth wasn't closed, I swear I'd be drooling like a dog teased with a steak.

I hear Asher's thumping boot steps following behind me. He starts filling a plate as I survey the table full of breakfast goodies. And when I say filling, I mean a mountain of food. He hands it to me. I raise my eyebrow at him and smirk. "I hope this isn't all for me. I'm not eating for two, you know."

"Not yet," he simply replies and loads his plate. My body runs cold as instant ice flows through my veins. I don't think Asher even notices my anxiety because he just continues filling his plate as if his comment is completely normal. Maybe it is, but to me, it's a shock. In my mind, I just met this man, and we're not even married. In my heart, I don't love him. I know this. My mind twists and turns like a whirlpool threatening to pull me under, bringing me back to the thought that I could perchance learn to love him. Maybe that's why I married him in the first place.

Asher takes his plate in one hand and guides me to a clear table with the other. There is no one else in the room, just like last night when we entered the inn. The early morning sun ignites the room in a warm glow, and the tavern is heated by the remnants of warmth from a wood stove that I overlooked last night. The only difference is that Semira and her husband aren't here, either. I stare at Asher, unsure if my appetite has gone away or if I am just too in my head to want to eat anything. Asher notices and nods towards me and gestures with his finger at the muffin on my plate. I pick it up and start pulling the muffin apart into tiny pieces, putting crumbs in my mouth one at a time.

"Are you alright? I thought you would be hungry."

"Asher... Why did we marry?" I blurt out. My mouth is moving faster than my mind can catch up. My head is still spinning within its own vortex to barely make me care.

He parts his lips to speak several times, only to close them again like he is trying to be cautious with his response. "Well... I mentioned that the Trine is where we met. In the Kingdom of Air, the monarch chooses whom they would like to be bonded to. You were there, as beautiful as I have ever seen you. There was something so enchanting about you that I could hardly take my eyes away from you the whole night. Once the Trine was almost over, I finally worked up the courage to ask you to dance." Asher smiles at the memory, never looking at me but rather down as if in embarrassment. "You made me laugh and smile for the first time in what felt like forever. When you smiled back at me, my heart felt like it would explode. I couldn't take it. I asked you to be mine that very night. Thank the stars you said yes because I don't know what I would have done if you had turned me down."

"Why did I say yes?"

"Well, I would like to think it's because you fell for me, too. However, I'm not a fool. I know what the offer means and what your future will hold. Many people would kill for the opportunity to be King or Queen of a kingdom." Asher shrugs as if it's a fact. He doesn't seem upset by the idea of someone agreeing to marriage simply due to his title. I don't believe I would be that shallow. Even now, I may not know everything regarding my past, but I do know that I wouldn't be the type to jump into something this life-changing so that I'd be queen.

I stare at Asher with an expression of self-loathing. I can feel it soiling my mood, slipping through the cracks of my armor and piercing my chest. Once it has penetrated, there is no reclaiming my lighthearted mood from earlier.

We've been on the road for hours now. My lousy mood still clings, and I'm sure everyone is aware. Asher, Semira, and Alizar all ignore me as we sit in silence, listening to the clomping of the horses' hooves along the gravel path to the palace. When I glance out the window, seeking to heighten my mood, I can't see anything except a fog so thick it almost looks like a white, grey curtain has been pulled over the coach windows.

"Asher?" I call out to get his attention, but I think my voice startles him because his head whips so fast towards me that I'm slightly concerned for his neck.

"What's wrong?" Always the protector. I wave off his concern with a smirk, leaning forward now that I have his full attention.

I pause for a moment, hoping for a dramatic effect. "My ass

hurts." Asher's eyes bulge in shock while Semira bursts out into laughter. Regaining his composure, he smiles from ear to ear--- just the look I was waiting for. Similar to earlier that morning, his smile warms me. My heart picks up in tempo, beating like a drum to his smiling song, hitting every note and octave in my heart.

There's something about Asher's smile that can put a dragon in a good mood. His straight, white teeth are on perfect display when he leans toward me and asks, "Do you want me to rub it better?"

Now I'm shocked! I didn't think that my comment would bring out the flirtatious side of him, but I don't find I hate it, either. My goal was to make him laugh or smile to improve my mood, not for him to throw it back at me. Semira is still chuckling beside me. She has a laugh that makes a wheezing sound rather than a typical laughing sound. It is so loud and odd sounding that even Alizar is grinning. I can tell he is trying to ignore us, but the sight of him trying not to laugh causes me to laugh until I have to wipe tears from my eyes.

"Don't worry, Amalie. We are almost there. You and your ass will thank me soon." Asher grins again and turns back to the window to stare at nothing while Semira and I laugh harder. We continue our silliness all the way to the capital and my new home in the Kingdom of Air.

7

Amalie

They weren't kidding when they said it was the Kingdom of Air.

I peer through the small window in the carriage as Asher points to a massive structure high up in the mountain.

The Air Kingdom Palace.

The palace looks like it is floating. It's enormous and resting on the edge of a cliff, peering through the clouds high above the city below. It takes me a moment to realize that's what I'm looking at. At first glance, I thought the palace rested on a cliff edge. Although the more I gaze at it, and the closer we arrive at the entrance of the capital, I see it is actually carved from the mountain itself. I wonder how we access the palace if it is so high up. It is like looking at a whole city in the clouds.

The carriage comes to a slow stop as the door is pulled open by a formally dressed guard. Asher exits first, followed by Alizar, then Semira. She grips Alizar's hand with a bright smile on her face. I take a deep breath and stand.

Asher's solid and supportive arm extends to assist me, and I place my hand in the bend of his arm. He smiles warmly and points out the palace as I turn in a circle to see my new home.

The palace is white on white. It is so well hidden that I'm sure you wouldn't even know it's there on foggy days. The large towers protrude from the mountain and wrap around the side. I don't see any greenery on or around it, and to me, it looks very intimidating. More like a formidable prison rather than a home. I glance towards Asher to see his expression only to find he's examining mine. His face is unreadable, and there isn't a single crease, wrinkle, smile, or frown. I realize he's waiting for my reaction before saying anything, so I humor him and ask stupidly, "You grew up here?"

That makes him smile and breaks up the cold expression on his face. Asher takes my hand, and we walk towards the mountain. As if I'm going to climb that, I think. We reach a metal gate, similar to a prison door which makes me think again that this isn't a home but my jail. A shiver runs frigidly down my spine at the dark thought.

"Welcome to Galeis, Amalie." Asher radiates pride for this place. I can tell how much it means to him to be back home. And even though this place terrifies me, I am excited to explore my new -or old home. I grin up at Asher, and he continues to guide me forward.

The fog in the streets cast the illusion of ghosts on the few people in the streets--disappearing and reappearing. Grey cobblestones and market stalls line the path through the town to the large gate door.

We walk through the gate and are welcomed by six fae guards. Asher is greeted sternly by a young and slender fae male. His hair is cropped short and light in color. He has two swords strapped to him-one on each hip. He doesn't look like a high-ranking soldier, judging by his stature. He doesn't have any pins or symbols on his military garb. The uniform is merely grey, closely tailored with pristine pleated lines on the jacket and matching pants.

Asher acknowledges the guard and gestures for him to

follow. "Hadden, this is Amalie. My wife. You will protect her, and you will guard her. Her life is in your hands. You are her shadow." Asher orders. He continues with a low virulence in his tone, "Her life is yours. If her life is no longer, so is yours. If she is harmed in any way.... You will receive the same punishment. Am I clear?"

Without hesitation, Hadden gives Asher a curt nod and growls, "Understood, Sir." Hadden briefly glances in my direction, and a shock of electricity runs through me. *This man is familiar. I know him!*

Of course, you know him, you idiot! He is Asher's general. But why would Asher introduce me to him if I know him already?

The feeling of *knowing* someone and actually recognizing someone are two completely different things. I know his face, like a tiny spider in my head weaving its shimmering silk web. The process is slow and delicate, but it dissolves before I can become ensnared in the web.

My nose begins to tingle with the sensation of tears welling, threatening to spill over. I am so frustrated and angry at myself for not being able to hold a good memory. As soon as an image forms, it dissipates and scatters in the wind.

"What do you think, Amalie?" Semira asks. Her eyes are so bright that I force myself to look around and see what she is excited about.

Galeis is like a perfectly placed dreamscape. I've never seen a city with such precision before. Every building and store are in a straight line, showcasing the same colors and decor. Without the signs on the front door, I don't know how anyone could possibly know where they're going. The iron, prison-like door we just entered through appears to be the only exit. The entire city is clean and either white or grey. It doesn't sit well with me that everywhere I look, is entirely devoid of color. The more I look around, the more suppressed I feel.

Semira is still waiting for my answer, and I stutter quickly to answer her, "Oh yeah. It's uh, great. It's very... clean and straight." Behind me, Alizar chuckles low on his breath. I don't think Asher catches our exchange. If he does, he doesn't say anything.

We keep walking through the streets while Asher quietly talks with Hadden.

"There will be a guard at every entrance and at her rooms at every hour."

"Yes, sir."

"I want daily reports every morn-"

I quickly tune them out when I hear discussions on the military and their safety protocols; I am too focused on my new home. Semira walks hand in hand with Alizar, and he seems to be very uncomfortable. I don't think he is uncomfortable with holding her hand, but I think it might be that he is so far away from his home kingdom.

I wonder what his story is; I want to know how those two met. Semira is so bubbly and bright, while Alizar is so broody and quiet. They just seem so odd together, but I suppose opposites do attract. Or he bought her, and she's forced to stay with him. If that is the case, she doesn't seem upset about it. Her statement about the highest bidder bothers me so much. I hope it was just a figure of speech.

Lost in my thoughts and evidently not paying attention, I feel a tug on my arm from Asher. I turn around with an apologetic smile on my face.

"This way, darling."

Asher leads me through many sets of doors. I didn't notice all these doors before, and they appear to go into the mountain like a tunnel. It takes a moment for my eyes to adjust to the moist and cold labyrinth. It's dimly lit with little balls of white light lining the walls down until I can't see anymore. The only sound in the hallway is the click-click of our shoes. Nobody breathes a word. Nobody in our group, at least.

I hear voices on a small draft creeping through the tunnel. Holding tighter to Asher's hand, I remember the whispers I heard in the wind when I was in the forest. Ghouls.

Asher leans down to whisper, "Don't worry about them. They won't bother us." Just as he says it, a thick fog creeps into the tunnel and hinders my vision.

"I can't see," I whisper, trying not to attract the ghouls' attention. Asher rubs my arm to try to calm my increasing panic. The fog moves around us in thick waves, causing my chest to tighten. I'm not sure how Semira is, I can't see her, and she's not saying anything. I doubt Asher would allow the ghouls to harm anyone here because he doesn't seem bothered by them. We keep walking, and he continues to stroke my arm to calm me.

After what feels like a lifetime, I can see the small globes of light shining on the walls ahead of me. The ache in my chest starts to ease after holding my breath for so long. Finally, finally, we are almost out of this stars awful tunnel. I don't think I can stand another moment being in a narrow, cold, barren tunnel with ghouls sweeping past you in a blind fog. It was almost unbearable.

Semira and Alizar are behind me, followed by Hadden and his men. I forgot Hadden was even there throughout the deafening silence and the whispers of the ghouls. I am quickly reminded that they're there once I hear their boots on the stone floor.

We enter a large foyer that is all white. White marble pillars, walls, floor, and grand staircase greet us. Not one person is waiting for our arrival, and I am secretly thankful for that. I don't think I would like the staff staring at me after two days of travel, three days in the woods, and only one change of clothes.

I know I stink and look like a pig that just rolled in shit, but there are not many options on the road.

Asher doesn't look that much better, to be honest. His beard is even longer than it was a couple of days ago. He seems more like a scraggly mountain man than a future king. As if realizing my thoughts, Asher laughs and says, "I will need to clean up before dinner. I will have Hadden take you to your rooms." He nods his head towards Hadden, who moves beside me. "Semira will stay in your adjoining room if that's alright. You will still have your privacy, but she will be right there if you need a friendly face."

"Thank you." And I genuinely mean it! Asher gestures to Semira to follow us, and my heart clenches at the thoughtfulness. I am grateful to have my own room. Asher, I'm sure, was assuming we would share a room, being married and all. Although after my suggestion in Windhaven, I am relieved he's changed his mind.

The walk to my room isn't very long, which is another blessing. I thought the inside of the palace would be a labyrinth because of how it looked from the outside. Thankfully our rooms are not far from the foyer.

The hallway is airy and exposed as we follow Hadden to the right of the hall. There is a wall on one side and a row of pillars on the other, exposing it to the elements. Moving toward the pillars, I take in the view and realize that we are on the side of the mountain. The chilled and eerie fog sweeps in through the passageway. While the plush clouds slightly obstruct my view of the landscape, they look soft enough to sleep on, moving slowly in the distance.

At the end of the hallway, there is a large white door. Beautiful swirling designs are barely visible as they appear to be painted in a slightly different shade of white.

"Your rooms, Ma'am." Hadden bows and opens my door. I enter my new chambers, and Semira follows closely behind me. Hadden closes the door and stands outside the door. I find myself feeling bad for him. I should have offered him to sit in the sitting area that we just walked through- but I doubt he would have accepted.

Semira walks through what looks like another foyer. It's in a giant circle with the exposed wall continuing inside. At the end of the hall, it splits into two smaller, white decorated doors. Semira opens the door on the left and walks inside, claiming it as her own. I think she expects me to follow her, but I don't.

"This is so pretty! I don't think I would mind living here. The only thing missing is some greenery or something," I mutter to Semira, not really expecting an answer.

"You certainly loved this room when you were here last." She replies curtly.

"Are you alright?" I only ask because she is usually bubbly or excitable. She has obviously seen these rooms before, but maybe she's upset that she's separated from Alizar? Guilt strikes me hard enough to look down and avoid her gaze. She's done so much for me these past few days, and now my selfishness takes her away from her husband.

"I'm just tired, it's been a long day, and it's not even time for bed yet."

"Semira, do you want to be with Alizar?" I question. I have learned by now all her little tells when she's not giving me the whole truth. She always turns slightly to the right when she's lying. It almost looks like she's putting her strongest side forward, bracing herself against any conflict.

"I just haven't spent much alone time with him, you know?" I glance up and find her cheeks flushed in embarrassment, and it all clicks. Oh. Oh!

"Oh, Semira! I'm so sorry! I will talk with Asher at dinner. Of course, Alizar can stay in your rooms with you, or you can go to his room if you wish?" I only hope she doesn't choose to go to a different room. Yes, our bed chambers are separate, but they are connected through a separate foyer. I feel a sense of comfort knowing that someone I'm relatively at ease with is close by.

Semira gives me a small smile and exits her room again, returning to the foyer. "Let's go look at your room! You're going to love it... again!" We both laugh at the weird exchange. How often do you hear someone saying they wish they could experience something for the first time again? I should be happy. If I loved this place the first time, I know I will soon love it again.

Except, I don't.

Semira opens my bed-chamber door with a flourish of her hands that makes me laugh harder. She looks like she's unveiling a new shiny sword rather than a door. When I pass through the frame, my laugh cuts off abruptly.

It's soulless. Feelings of emptiness creep through me like a shadowing depression squeezing the air out of me. How could I have liked this room? I move forward and glance around.

The right side is open to the mountainside, like the foyer and hallways. The room matches the palace in style and decor. White everywhere, to the point of blinding. I would be afraid to get my monthly cycle in this room!

The colorless room reminds me of the pale faces of the sick and dying. I don't know how I could ever find this comforting. Instead of telling the truth, I lie, just like Semira did moments ago. "It's gorgeous!" I enthusiastically hope she doesn't notice the panic and dread growing inside me.

Semira skips to the bed and flops down on it like a fainting goat that falls over when they're scared. The sheer curtains on the canopy bed gently blow in the soft breeze and begin to tangle around her feet. While Semira fights to disentangle herself, I laugh and move over to the loveseat and collapse. I start to worry that I might stain the cushions, but I honestly don't care right now.

I lay on the sofa and roll over to lean my head on my arm and look out over the open expanse. If I started sleepwalking and fell off the side, would I die? My thoughts are interrupted by Semira's voice.

"Amalie?" Her soft voice catches my attention, and I suddenly feel wary about what she will ask.

"Hmm…"

"Do you honestly not remember anything?"

"No, not really. I keep getting flashes of things that I think are memories. When I was in the forest, I remembered my mother's voice warning me about mushrooms." I chuckle quietly under my breath. "I thought Hadden looked familiar, but I know that isn't right because Asher just introduced us. I dreamed about a man holding me while we were in a garden pavilion. However, Asher mentioned we didn't do that, so there's another thing that isn't right. I don't know if I can trust my own mind at this point." I sigh in defeat. It's troubling to think back at all the times I remembered or almost remembered something. I would trade anything to have my memories back.

"Do you remember how you ended up in the forest?" she asks hesitantly.

"No, not yet, at least. That's one of my many questions. I'm almost afraid to find out. I can't think of a situation that ends with a happy answer."

After that, Semira is silent, and when I sit up and turn my head back toward her, I find her asleep. Her mouth is wide open, and she's snoring. I guess she indeed was tired.

I decide to take a bath and thank the stars that the palace maids are standing in wait in the foyer. I kindly ask for a warm bath, and they oblige without a word.

8

Amalie

A few hours later, I find myself in the dining hall to wait for Asher's parents, the King and Queen, to arrive. The dining hall is massive and intimidating. Grand high ceilings with one wall open to the mountainside and a table long enough to fit at least thirty guests.

Thankfully, the maids found me a beautiful gown. I wouldn't have been able to face the King and Queen in my drab attire from earlier. They put me in a dress that is, of course, white, with a breezy sheer overlay. The neckline plunges in a deep V, and the straps are off-the-shoulder. The dress is simple yet elegant- no beading or lace. I just hope I don't spill my dinner all over it. Semira's dress is similar but without the V-neckline. I guess they decided to give her some modesty while, in contrast, they thought to show off some of my assets.

Asher sits to my right and Semira to my left, her husband beside her. We're seated at the end of the table so the King and Queen can sit at the head. The table feels empty, with it only being set for six. What's the point of having such a massive room with nobody to use it?

I look behind me and glance at Hadden, standing straight as

a board against the far wall. Asher clears his throat, dragging my attention back to him. He's giving me a look I can't decipher, and then his eyes linger over my body, stopping at my chest. He doesn't even seem ashamed as my cheeks heat. He glances back up at my face and gives me a mischievous smirk. I raise one eyebrow in a dare. I've figured out that this is how we communicate. He gives me a flirty look, and I return it. I feel the most like myself when I'm tempting and teasing him.

Asher is now clean-shaven with his short hair slicked back, yet one piece falls slightly over his eyes. He looks good, *so good*. My husband is extremely attractive when he's all cleaned up and sitting proudly with an air of authority. I can tell he's definitely more comfortable in his own domain. He will make a great king. His whole energy shifted once we walked through the gates of Galeis; he's strong and overflowing with power. I think I want to kiss him, and that thought scares me so much. Asher hasn't pushed me at all. However, there's a spark between us that intrigues me. What if I don't live up to the expectations of the person I was before? I know I've changed, and who knows if I will find myself again or grow to become this new version of Amalie; a mix of my past self and current feelings.

My thoughts are interrupted by the announcement of the King and Queen's arrival. I follow Asher's lead and stand, bowing my head in respect. This is essentially the first time I am meeting them, and I don't dare look them in the eye. I am terrified. Without a word, they take their seats and gesture for everyone to sit. Immediately, they start a conversation with Asher.

"Asher, darling. I am assuming everything you set out for was accomplished?" she asks, peering at me. She means me, that he *accomplished* me. I don't have a good feeling about her. She is terrifying and cold, radiating dominance. The King, on the other hand, seems utterly indifferent to the situation, already starting on his bread before dinner is even served.

"Yes, mother. Please meet Amalie, my wife. Amalie, this is my mother, Everleigh. Queen of the Air Kingdom," Asher boasts with prideful bravado.

I look up and give Queen Everleigh a bright smile. "Pleased to meet you, Your Highness." I offer a slight bow of my head, hoping my action shows respect.

"Likewise," the queen replies with disdain. Great. I messed that up already. How can someone mess up a greeting? Stars know, but somehow, I did.

Asher looks towards his father and repeats the process. King Norin is at least a bit more hospitable in his greeting. I don't think he cares whether I'm here or not. He continues to eat his bread throughout the whole interaction.

An array of food and beverages are carried out to us by servants dressed in white and grey. Chicken, fish, beef, potatoes, garden vegetables, and wines of all kinds are strategically placed on the table in front of us, and our glasses are filled. I was secretly hoping they would top off my glass, but they didn't. I might need a bit more liquid courage to get through this dinner unscathed.

King Norin is a reasonably large man. By large, I mean he is more rounded than tall and broad, with buttons straining on his light grey paletot. His attire is complementary to the guards' sleek white uniforms. He wears white pleated trousers and black leather boots. A small royal crest sits at the breast of his coat, but it is hard to make out the details in the distance. It almost looks like the face of a ghoul encased in silver.

Queen Everleigh is a slender woman, however, with sharp and fierce features. She is the opposite of King Norin in every way, down to her clothing. The queen dawns a long and elegant black lace dress, the only black I've seen in the kingdom thus far. Her long sleeves rest artfully on her veiny hands. Everything about her screams malevolence. Her nose is turned up at a point, her eyebrows are razor-thin and arched, giving her a permanent scrutinizing expression. Even her fingernails are cut into sharp points like a dragon's claw, and it feels like she has the potential to rip someone's throat out if they cross her.

We begin our meal in silence. I look to Semira for guidance, but she is wolfing down food like she's starving. Her last meal was only this morning. Alizar is behind her in his usual ghost-like state. He hasn't said a word since the cabin, only a grunt here and there.

Asher and Everleigh begin having their own conversation about the kingdom, the guards, and other royal business. I keep my mouth shut and eat my food, even though it tastes bland in my mouth. I want to go back to my rooms but don't want to be rude, so I chew slowly and remain patient.

Finally, dinner ends after dragging on late into the evening. Asher grabs my hand, and we all bow to exit the dining room.

"Your mother doesn't like me much, does she?" We might as well clear the air before the night goes any further.

"Don't take it to heart. Honestly, she doesn't like anyone. She hardly tolerates my father, even though that's how most of the kingdoms work."

"What do you mean?" I ask him cautiously.

"We don't marry for love; we marry to keep the treaty and progress our kingdom forward for future generations. That doesn't mean that's the case for us, just for monarchs in the past." My face drops, and Asher clarifies, "My parents' marriage was one of convenience. My mother is Fae, my father is human, and they completed the bonding after I was born."

"So, your father is Fae now?" I didn't notice at dinner, but I had been trying very hard to keep my eyes off them. It never crossed my mind that they would go through the bonding if it weren't for love. Why would a human want to become a Fae and live forever with their spouse if they didn't even love them? My mind is boggled, and I know Asher can tell I'm trying to mull it all over.

"My father was a wealthy merchant and owned many cities, ships, and goods. Our Kingdom wasn't doing great financially, so my parents struck a bargain. My father essentially bought his immortality. He wanted to live forever, so he paid for it. My mother needed a spousal attachment in order to have a child. Mostly, I was raised by the staff." My heart aches for Asher, but he shrugs it off like it's not a big deal. I am saddened to think of the little boy neglected by his own parents. I can't wrap my mind around people who couldn't love each other enough to care for their children. Asher is the necessary product of a financial transaction, and I'm pissed. I didn't expect to get this defensive of Asher, but how heartless do you have to be? His mother could have at least tried to find someone to love her son the way he deserved to be loved.

"Were the servants good to you?"

"They were...around. It's weird to grow up essentially outranking most of the adults around you. With my parents never around, the servants pretty much adopted me. Once I reached adulthood, and they weren't needed anymore, my mother had them executed."

A shocked gasp escapes me. I didn't think his story could get more tragic, but it did. "Oh, Asher! I'm so sorry."

"It's fine. They weren't necessary anymore, I suppose." He shrugs, seemingly unaffected, but I can see the darkness inside his eyes, the sea blue in a hurricane.

I grab Asher's hand tightly, not sure if I'm trying to comfort myself or him, but either way, I need to ground myself. He squeezes my hand and leads me up a set of spiral stone steps. The passageway is incredibly narrow, causing him to put his arm behind his back so we don't lose contact. When we reach the top, I glance over his shoulder to see where he's brought me.

The view is unbelievably breathtaking. We are on a large terrace on the edge of the snow-capped mountains, but this view is different from the one in my room. It's nighttime, and the full moon and shimmering stars cast a tranquil reflection on the ocean far below us. The moon is so bright that I can see the boats floating in the harbor. There are more snow-capped mountains on my right, and the vast ocean to the left.

The chill in the night air causes me to shiver. A breeze blows through my long chestnut hair and causes my dress to shift around my legs. Asher smiles and moves behind me to put his arms around me. He rests his chin on the top of my head, and I heave a sigh of comfort and warmth.

"I never got the time to bring you here. This is a night of firsts for you, meeting my parents and now seeing my favorite place in the palace." He murmurs into my hair.

I turn in his arms to face him, putting my arms around his middle and staring up into his bright eyes. "Thank you." I place my cheek on his chest, and he kisses my hair again. After a couple of minutes, I remember the promise I made to Semira. "Can I ruin the moment for one second?"

"Of course, only for a second, though. I'm enjoying this," Asher says, chuckling softly.

"I promised Semira I would ask if Alizar could stay with her in her room. She misses her husband."

"I've already spoken with her and Hadden. The arrangements have been made. Hadden will stay in your foyer while Alizar is there. It's not that I think he would do anything, but that man doesn't ever say a word. I don't know what he's thinking half the time." I burst out laughing. My thoughts exactly. Alizar seems kind enough, but it's eerie when you can spend days with someone, and they hardly speak more than a few sentences total.

It feels good to laugh with Asher after what he told me about his parents. I don't want him to ever feel unloved like that, and a weird sense of protectiveness grips my heart. I think he grew up to be a reasonably normal person for someone who had the King and Queen for their parents. Perhaps a bit spoiled, but any child destined to become King or Queen would be. He is my husband, for better or for worse. We will grow together, learn together, and love together. I hug him tighter as we watch the stars twinkle in the night sky, whispering silent promises to each other. As a society, we have long sworn off gods and deities. We now pray to the stars, for it is the only constant in our lives. It is the only thing we can look up to and count on after a hard day.

Two hours pass, and we still haven't left the terrace. We end up sitting down on the hard stone floor, Asher behind me. His arms are still wrapped around me with his long legs on either side of my body. I lean back into his warmth and rest my head on his shoulder, my eyes slowly drifting closed.

"Come on, darling. We should get you to bed. It's late," Asher whispers in my ear, making me shudder. I reply with a slight nod, too tired to say anything. He quickly stands up and extends his hand to help me to my feet again.

With one last look, I peer at the stars and say goodbye to the sense of peace I feel. Asher leads me back down the staircase and through the numerous halls until we arrive at my chamber door, with Hadden standing guard outside.

Asher gives him a nod and turns to face me. "Sleep well, Amalie." He kisses my forehead and swiftly walks away. His soft affection forces me to catch my breath. He's being so respectful yet still showing me that he loves me in minor ways. For the one-hundredth time tonight, the butterflies flutter in my stomach.

When I'm ready, I turn to Hadden, who is standing there with the door wide open for me to enter my foyer.

9

Amalie

I wake with a jolt when Semira barrels through my door and jumps on my bed beside me.

"Good morning!" she bellows at the top of her lungs. Despite being exhausted, her good mood is infectious, and I laugh at her from my side of the bed.

"Morning," I mumble sleepily as I see Hadden place a bowl of strawberries on the table beside my bed. Semira and I chatter mindlessly while eating our fruit. "How did you two meet?" I ask, taking another bite of my strawberry. I want to get to know my friend again. Asking about her marriage may be a good start. She seems to open up then, giving me a smile before speaking.

"It's your fault, really. You're the one who introduced us." This shocks me. I introduced them? I stare at her in bewilderment, making her smile at me more. "It's so weird to talk to you about this because you were there, but you don't have any idea what happened." She shakes her head and continues, "We were at the Treaty Central Market when you brought me over to his stall. He's a blacksmith, and you commissioned him to make you a beautiful dagger for my birthday. I loved it so much. I asked where you got it, and it was Alizar. He bought my heart the moment I saw him work. He may not say much, but he has such a big heart."

"He asked you to marry him that day, right?" The thought came out of my mouth before I even had the chance to ponder it. It was a flash of a memory that I can think back on now.

Semira's eyes flash to me, as wide as the plates on which we are eating our strawberries. "Yes! Oh, my stars! Yes!" Her eyes start to fill with tears, and she leaps from my seat to give me a tight hug, and for some reason, I cry too. It's such a relief to finally have an accurate thought or memory. I was starting to think I would be lost in myself forever, but the more I think about that day, the more I remember.

"Do you think we could go back to that market? Stars, I miss it so much! Remember when we would each take the same number of coins and split up in search of the best gift for each other?" I say, laughing with more happy tears rolling down my face.

"Yes! I'm going to win next time. Oh, I would love to go back. You must bug Asher to allow us to go!"

"Allow?" I raise my eyebrow and snicker at her comment. "I'm not a servant. I'm his wife. I don't need to ask permission to go to a market."

"You asked him if Alizar could stay with me…" Her thought drifts off, but I answer the question she never asked.

"Yes, because he's my husband. I would want to be asked if a female—married or not— stayed close to where he slept. I respect him. But if he would have said no, I would have done it anyway." I giggle at the thought of it, even though Semira doesn't find any humor in it.

"Amalie, please don't push him. Asher can be…" she glances towards Hadden and lowers her voice, "he's the future king, that's all. He can be difficult."

"It's fine. I can handle him."

Semira doesn't have a retort to that, and I don't push her. Instead, I wonder where Alizar went off to or if he is still sleeping. We finish our breakfast and decide to get ready for the day as the maids enter the foyer with new dresses for Semira and me. We go to our separate rooms and vow to meet at the palace's main entrance.

About an hour later, I'm rushing through the palace hallways to keep up with Hadden's substantial strides. He still doesn't look in my direction, but his head turns back and forth, watching for potential threats. I honestly doubt there are any, but if I was kidnapped once before, maybe they will try it again. I make a mental note to talk to Asher about it even though I know he will not be in a good mood after.

In the foyer, I am surprised to see Asher instead of Semira. I glance carefully around the room, but it's just Asher, Hadden, and myself. As soon as I see Asher standing there in casual dark brown trousers and a white linen shirt rolled to the elbows, my stomach starts fluttering again, and my heart begins racing at the sight of him. I smile up at Asher as I move into his embrace. He pulls me close and tightens his arms around me, putting his face in my hair, that makes me swoon every time.

I pull back from him and stare up at his face, his ocean blue eyes shining in the morning like sweeping through the foyer, "Where are Semira and Alizar?" I ask him gently.

"I thought we would go for a walk this morning, just us," he answers simply, and I can't deny his offer. I'm as excited as I am nervous with him. I nod up at him while he glances towards Hadden to dismiss him for now. I take Asher's hand again, entwining my fingers with his, and allow him to lead me through a different passageway from the one we entered.

"How did we end up on a mountain if we walked through a tunnel? There weren't any stairs." I ask him curiously, remembering how we entered the palace in the first place.

Asher doesn't even look at me but continues walking, eyes focused forward. "The wind you felt in the tunnel wasn't only the ghouls passing through, that's more of a distraction. The wind acts as a type of portal. You might have felt nauseous or anxious, that's the portal working." I don't have anything to say to that, so I keep my eyes focused on where we are going.

He takes me to the water's edge where we were last night from up in the mountain palace. Asher helps me steady myself as I step off the dock into a medium-sized sailboat. Shortly after, he follows me, pointing at the crew to depart from the pier. I sit quietly and take in my new surroundings. We wade through the water, surrounded by snow-capped mountains, and a glacier in the distance peers over at us like a white island.

Asher comes over and sits beside me on the wooden bench. There is a chill in the air, I realize, as he drapes a warm blanket over my shoulders, covering up my thin, light blue dress. I smile my thanks but keep my eyes up towards the mountainside.

"Asher, what happened that day?" I don't need to clarify which day I'm talking about; he already knows.

He puts his arm around me, and I lean into him, hoping to ease my nerves, but it only builds the longer he withholds his answer.

"Asher?" I ask again, looking over at him now. He's troubled, I knew he wouldn't like my asking, but I need to know. I feel like it would be a big key to my locked memories.

"It was our wedding day." That makes me stop breathing from the shock of his words—our wedding day. "We said our vows and committed to one another. We were preparing for the bonding ceremony, and then you were gone. Nobody saw you leave, and nobody saw if you were taken. Amalie… it gutted me." Asher's voice breaks at the end, and that guts me. He holds me tighter as if telling me will make me disappear like a ghost in the fog. I interlace my fingers with his to lend him a bit more comfort when he continues, "We looked for you for three days.

Finally, a rider came up to me and told me Semira found you passed out in a field, and I thought I would die all over again. I thought you were dead, Amalie. When I saw you laying on that pallet, you were so pale and cold. You didn't wake for hours. Then when you finally did, you had no clue who I was. It was the worst torture I've ever endured."

Asher and I don't speak for a while after his confession. We just sit in the silence of our combined sadness, confusion, and frustration. We would have been crowned by now. We would have been happily together by now. I understand the fact that I had taken ten steps back must really bother Asher, and I know that isn't fair to him, but I'm just not ready for anything more. I think if I had to marry him right now, I would say no. Of course, I am attracted to him, I have the nerves and the butterflies to prove it, but I've known him for only a week. It's all so new and raw for me, and it must be painfully raw for him, too, though differently. He lost me, then gained me only to lose me again. I couldn't imagine that pain.

"We will get back there. Together," I promise him in a whisper.

He kisses my hair and murmurs, "I know."

We arrive at a small and secluded cave towards the end of the bay. The boat sways viciously for a couple of seconds while the crew ties it to the rocks by the cliff's edge. Asher holds me steady while I'm starting to feel nauseous from all the swaying movements. I am more than happy to leave this boat. Grabbing Asher's hand for support, I finally step out of the boat and onto land. I now stand on dark grey flat rocks just before the cave mouth, waiting for Asher to join me.

The mouth of the cave is like walking into a whole other

world. While it's bright, airy, and snowy up the mountains, it is lush green and warm in this cave. The darkness is illuminated by thousands, if not millions, of tiny glow worms hanging from the insanely tall ceilings. They cling to every surface like barnacles on a ship. The further we move into the cave, the wider and lusher the flora becomes.

Hot tears well in my eyes and slide down my cheeks at the aching comfort of it all. While it felt so cold and remote at the palace, here, it feels like home.

Asher notices my tears and slides his thumb over my cheeks, wiping away the tears spilling over them. He gives me a look I can't figure out. His strong jaw tightens, his bold brows lower, and his nostrils flare. If I didn't know better, I would think him angry. But the expression is gone as soon as I realize it was there in the first place. He takes my hand again and leads me to a moss-covered sitting area where an iron bench has been installed. Evidently, this isn't some remote cave, then.

"What is the place?" I ask, genuinely curious. It feels so comforting and familiar that I know I've been here before in my other life.

"It's the passageway to the Earth Kingdom," he says hesitantly, not wanting to give me that answer right away. Does he think I'm going to run home? I don't even know where home is, let alone how to find it. It could be anywhere in the Earth Kingdom. I just nod and give him a nonchalant shrug.

"Do you know my parents? I remembered my mother's voice when I was in that forest. She was warning me not to eat those purple striped mushrooms." I laugh at the memory, excited to know more about her and maybe even my father. Asher frowns more at the question causing my heart to plummet into my stomach.

"I never knew her. She's not with the living anymore. You told me she was long gone before we even met. I'm sorry, Amalie." And he does seem genuinely sorry, which causes my sinking heart to drop even lower. If she is long gone, wouldn't my body know it instinctively? But no, it's all coming back to shock me as if it happened weeks ago instead of years ago. I don't know what to say or ask or do. I feel so awkward showing my emotions to Asher like this. *Is he looking for a strong wife? Should I still be upset over someone long gone?*

I fold my hands in my lap and sit softly on the iron bench, unsure of my feelings and how much to show to him. He follows behind me a moment later, and we stare out into the glowing cave, watching the worms twinkle and move like the midnight stars. Silent tears cascade over my face, and I don't dare look at him. I can't stand having his pity any longer. I want to move forward.

"I'm constantly overwhelmed by your strength, you know."

His words grab my attention again. Here I am silently crying and moping about the loss of my long-gone mother, and then I start to cry about how the cave looked and made me feel. I sob about pretty much everything that has happened along this mysterious journey to find the old Amalie. I don't feel strong. And I tell him so. I tell him how weak I feel when I cry about long-lost memories.

Asher puts an arm around me and squeezes my shoulder, "You're strong because you're still fighting. You haven't given up. You're still moving forward with your life, with us. You're trying to remember, and you're trying to find us again. I don't think I would be able to do the same thing if our roles were reversed."

I look up at Asher, gauging his expression only to find sincerity. He truly believes what he just said. I sit a little straighter and rub my hand over my face, catching the last bit of wetness only to rub it on my soft blue dress. Now I see why I'm wearing this color, I match the luminescence of the glow worms surrounding us. Asher truly thinks of the small details. He's always a step ahead of everyone else; he would make a great King.

I turn in his arms to face him more fully, and our eyes lock together, unblinking. Asher's eyes roam my face, moving downward to my lips. Am I ready for that? Is it such a big deal to kiss your husband? And there is my answer. He's my husband, not some random stranger like I have been making him out to be. He has supported me, comforted me, and cared for me. The least I could do was attempt to show him affection in return.

My stomach twists and turns with nerves. It's like my first kiss all over again, and it's surprising to find myself this nervous. It takes such a long time for me to decide what I'm going to do that Asher chooses for me. He gives a soft sigh and turns his head back towards the glow worms, but I'm not one to give in so easily.

I lean up closer to him, grabbing his face in my hands so he has to turn his head to look at me. I watch his eyes widen in shock before I close mine and lower my mouth to brush his.

Asher is so still that I feel like I'm kissing a corpse. His shock is undeniable, so I press myself harder toward him, to show him that this is my choice. Finally, after what feels like a lifetime, Asher relents. Humming low in his throat, he kisses me back with a powerful possession urging to the point of pain. The heat is burning through my body, and I can't tell if I want to push him away or move closer to him.

Asher breaks the kiss with a sigh, "Amalie. Amalie, Amalie." his voice trails off in a whisper as he chants my name repeatedly, running his fingers through my hair. I rest my head on his chest while he tightens his arm around me. We made more progress than we thought possible for the first sort of re-date.

"What do you think of having our bonding ceremony in a few weeks? I can finally give you the ring you so desperately want." Asher laughs at my glare.

"First of all, I didn't mean it like that! And second of

all...okay." Asher's smile widens more and more as I talk. I think he initially expected me to protest, but I don't see a point since we are already married.

"Okay? As in, yes?" he clarifies, but he already knows what I mean, so I give him a kind smile in return. Asher gives me a quick kiss, elated like it's our wedding day again.

My mind drifts back to my earlier revelations about the day I went missing. I left him. Semira said she didn't know why I left. Nobody took me, she knew that much. If she knew that, so did Asher, most likely.

I suppose I have only a couple of weeks to figure out exactly what I was running from.

10

Amabie

I think I just saw Alizar smile! It's akin to seeing a dragon walk right down the street without them anything over! It's possible, but you certainly don't see that every day. Alizar sits on the plush sofa with Semira sitting in his lap, reading a book. It's so cute, the way he watches her read. He takes in every expression that crosses her face and tries to mimic it with his own. Semira is very visual when she's reading, every sentence that describes facial features, she attempts to replicate them with her own. I find it so funny to see her face change in so many ways while staring at the pages, and now I just find it adorable that Alizar does the same thing.

We are in the library, enjoying the gentle breeze sweeping through the large windows, which allow for so much light to come through, making the white marble floors shimmer. Each wall is covered in shelves and shelves of books, while the center of the room houses a circle of sofas with a large coffee table in the middle. The room must be in one of the towers because there aren't any corners. Everything is in a giant circle.

"Alizar, have you been to the Treaty market lately? Semira

and I were saying this morning that we would like to go back there." I try to get Alizar to engage in a conversation, but no such luck.

"Not recently."

How does Semira have a full-on marriage with this guy? I got two words from him, and he didn't even look up from Semira's book to acknowledge me. I'm not one to give up, though, so I press harder.

"So, did you want to come with us? I'm thinking we will go tomorrow morning. I can't wait to see what they have this time. Do you still work as a blacksmith? I really could use a new dagger." I think Alizar is going to murder me if I don't stop talking because he slowly looks up at me and glares. Oh boy.

"No, I don't want to come. No, I'm not making you a dagger."

Semira looks up from her book now at Alizar's tone towards me. She gives him a be nice look, but I don't think he gets the memo. He clearly has no interest in interacting with me. I wonder what changed if I was the one to introduce them? Why does he hate me now? Do I ask? Do I drop it?... Nope, I ask. I don't care if he hates me or not, but I'm not going to keep tiptoeing around him.

"Alizar, did I do something wrong?"

Semira stiffens as Alizar abruptly moves her off his lap and stands. I watch him move towards the door, his limp more prominent after sitting in the same position for a while. Glancing back at Semira, she's now glaring at me.

"What?"

"Just leave it alone, Amalie."

"Really? Is it a personal thing or simply just his personality because I can't tell the difference? I can accept it if he doesn't like me, but I'd at least like to know why," I shoot back at her. I can tell I'm being unfair, but I honestly don't care.

She closes her book with a loud sigh and moves over to the sofa I'm lounging on. I move my feet off the seat to give her room to sit down. She drops her head to my shoulder and whispers, "I'm sorry. It's not you, I can promise you that. It's just this situation. He isn't happy being here."

"Oh, does that mean that you're leaving?" I am so torn by the thought of Semira not being here with me that my throat clams up, and I can't speak anymore.

Semira sighs loudly. "We are discussing it. I promised you before all this that I would stay with you until the wedding but then. You know, everything happened. Alizar just wants to go home. He and Asher don't get along, they have a history."

"What do you mean?"

"Asher was a spoiled child," she says, with a wave of her hand like it's obvious. "Alizar made a sword for him that Asher didn't feel was up to par, apparently. Alizar's limp was caused by the guards traveling with Asher."

I put my hand over my mouth, shocked. I don't even know what to say. No wonder Alizar isn't a fan of mine. I'm essentially dragging him from his home to live with someone who hurt him. "Why didn't Alizar stay away?"

"He says he is worried about me. He thinks Asher is still the same person he was years ago, but I don't think so. He's been very different since he met you. He laughs, he cares, and he thinks about your needs before his. I promised you I would help you, and Alizar promised to protect me."

"What do you mean?"

Semira hesitates before answering, "Asher grew up desperately wanting to be loved. He did everything he could to please his parents. They're not the best, either, by the way. I think Asher wants the best of everything just to get their approval. When he met you, maybe he thought he found the best." She shrugs, giving me a sorrowful look.

I give her a small smile that doesn't reach my eyes. My feelings are mixed about Asher. On the one hand, he was horrible to Alizar, yet on the other, perhaps it is true that he genuinely did want to please his parents.

Last night after dinner, we made plans to visit the market. Asher didn't put up a fight like Semira thought he would. He actually agreed pretty readily. His only condition was to bring Hadden with us, which is entirely fair and understandable. Hadden just nodded at the order as usual.

Waking up this morning, I slept much better than the night before, despite my excitement for today's adventure. I slide out of the large bed and find a simple blush pink dress. It has long sleeves, a sweetheart neckline that hugs my breasts, and a flowy A-line skirt. Feeling giddy, I loosely braided my hair to one side and did a little spin before turning around and seeing Asher smiling at me from my bedroom door.

"Don't stop on my account, I'm rather enjoying the view." I run to Asher and throw my arms around his neck. He catches me and stumbles backward a step or two. "What's that for?"

"I'm just so excited for today. The Treaty Central Market is the only thing I truly remember from before all this. I'm just happy to be in a place that I know… Does that make sense?"

Asher smiles and holds me tighter, putting his face in my neck. I hear him whisper in my ear, "Perfectly."

"Are you sure you can't come with us?" I ask him again because I really do want him to join us. I would love to see Asher interact with other people. I want to know what he would buy at the market, who he would talk to.

Asher hums in my ear, "I might be able to catch up with you

a bit later, if that's okay? I'll come get you from the market, and we can walk home together." My grin widens at the thought. I'm in such a good mood that I don't think anything can ruin this day.

11

Wren

I need to get to her.
　I need to talk to her again.
　I need her to explain.
　I'm stalking the Fae man through the forest, not daring to cross that border. Watching him move back and forth, patrolling and protecting his kingdom from enemies like me. I'm the worst thing out there right now.

　I genuinely feel bad for this poor bastard. He should be fine as long as he gives me what I want. He doesn't wear any badges that I can see to signify his rank. This poor lowly guard is so far down on the list of essentials I'm sure they won't miss him if he suddenly goes missing. It might be a couple of days before they even notice, right?

　I step out from behind the trees, intercepting his path and crossing into his line of sight. He's dressed in the standard pristine white military uniform that all Air guards wear. I just want to throw a big ball of mud at him. He would probably have a fit for dirtying his outfit. I laugh loud enough to get the attention, "Oops! Sorry there, I didn't mean to startle you." I grin at him.

　"State your purpose." The man stands tall and robust, raising his voice to boast some sort of authority. Unfortunately, it falls on deaf ears.

"So... funny story, I'm looking for someone, and I think you might be the perfect person to help me out with this little issue." I lean against a tree crossing my arms nonchalantly while remaining on my own land, simply waiting for the man to mess up and cross the border. Once he does, it's free game for me. "Her name is Amalie. I'm sure you've heard of her. You know, cute little thing about this high." I raise my hand to my collarbone to elaborate on her stature. "Long brunette hair, curves so smooth it's sinful." I continue listing her attributes to the man, waiting for a reaction. "Is this ringing a bell, or should I keep going because stars could I keep going!" I give him a suggestive wink.

"You will not speak of our new Queen that way!" The man bellows, losing his confident stance. He doesn't notice he's moving forward in his rush of anger, and I don't give him any indication that he's about two steps away from the border. But he stops. Of course, he does. I guess I will have to try a bit harder now.

"Have you seen her thighs, though? Silky smooth and kissably soft. I could run my hand up and down her-"

"THAT IS ENOUGH!"

Gotcha.

The Fae man takes that step over the line, and before he can even think, I raise my hand, and a massive poplar tree flies up from the ground impaling the man through his stomach with a massive branch. My tree quickly lifts him off the ground, legs swinging as he starts to scream. He's hanging with a branch through his stomach like a grotesque execution. I just knew one of the egotistical Fae of the Air Kingdom would lose his cool soon enough; never speak ill of their royals, for they simply can't help but defend them.

"Great, while you're just hanging there. Let's chat," I repeat, hoping this man doesn't die before I can get some answers out of him. Being the Prince of the Earth Kingdom has its perks. We, higher Fae, can heal just as quickly as we can grow a flower. Like in a garden, we can create life or take it away. I decide to let him heal just a bit so he doesn't pass out on me. It would be easier if he would stop screaming, in any case. "Tell me where I can find her, and I will nicely set you free. I swear it."

The guard gurgles a reply, but it's hard to hear him through the blood running out of his mouth. The ground is now puddled red below him and the white of the tree, well, let's just say it's not white anymore. I heal him some more and try speaking again, "One more time, man, you know my word is a bond. I can't go back on a promise." The Earth Kingdom prides itself on honesty and integrity. Breaking a promise is just as bad as breaking a spine.

"To-tomorrow... She's going... Treaty market." He coughs a few times, causing more blood to fountain out of his mouth. I sag with relief. Finally, I get somewhere.

I slowly decay the tree back down to the ground, nicely like I promised, and take a step back from the male's broken body. He's breathing hard, gasping for his next breath, sounding more like a wheeze than a proper breath. "Heal...me," he gasps out slowly.

The man's chest is slowing more and more as I watch him with a stern gaze, not allowing my actions to penetrate my mind. I stand there for so long that finally, everything stops. His eyes are open, clouding and gazing in my direction even though there are no signs of life remaining in his body.

Before turning to walk away, I give him my parting words. "Sorry, that wasn't a part of our deal."

12

Amalie

My eyes devour our surroundings as Semira and I walk through the crowded marketplace. Stalls of every delicacy from the four kingdoms, handmade craftsmanship of every element, toys for children, and so much more. I feel euphoric while watching the vendors sell their life's work to eager buyers.

Semira and I venture through the market with a little coin from Asher jingling in Hadden's pocket. Unfortunately, as beautiful as my dress is, it's not exactly the best item of clothing to wear if you're carrying coins. Semira stops at a fire stall selling smoked meats from Alizar's kingdom. She purchases some for her husband and turns with the bag of meat in her hand towards Hadden. He sighs but takes the satchel from her, tying it to his belt loop. Semira and I giggle at his expression and keep walking, glancing at more stalls.

Scanning around the vendors, I spot a familiar man, and my heart stops for a moment as my dream of the pavilion comes crashing back in full force, making me feel unsteady on my feet. My heart jumps and races as soon as I realize there is some truth to my dream. I'm feeling stunned and intoxicated all at the same time. Simply seeing not just a familiar face but *his* face gives me hope that maybe not everything is lost.

Maybe there is hope that I won't be trapped in my mental prison forever.

"Amalie!" Semira grabs my arm to steady me, "My word! Are you alright? You look like you've seen a ghost." She glances around to catch my line of sight, trying to see what could have set me off. There she spots him too.

So, he wasn't just a dream.

I start walking towards him as he stares straight through me, scowling. For some reason, his frightening scowl doesn't hit home. There's great pain behind those emerald green eyes, he looks like a lost man wandering through life, and I know in my heart that I am the cause of this man's pain. I can't say how I know, I can just feel him. His dark hair is tousled and messy, likely from running his fingers through the shorter length too many times. I eye him, top to bottom, trying to conjure a song in my mind to match the drumbeat in my heart. He wears a similar green tunic that he wore in the dream. This time it is darker, almost black. Buttoned with golden leaves up the front, embroidered with matching leaves around the hem. His trousers are black and tucked into tall leather boots with no significant designs. I can't distinguish between his rank from his appearance alone. He holds himself as a royal but dresses in humble attire. His eyes, however.

Those eyes.

He could stare at me with those forest-green eyes, and I could lose myself for hours.

"Don't." Semira grabs my arm again to stop me from taking a step forward towards the man. "Asher won't be happy about this. It's not safe, Amalie," she warns in a low tone, not wanting the stranger to hear.

The man stands straight now, no longer leaning against a vendor's stall, and starts his advance towards us. My heart restarts in my chest as I watch his tall, muscular body move through the crowd of people, never taking his eyes off mine. Hadden doesn't seem upset about this situation, so he can't be that bad. Right? I don't let myself think too long about the situation. Clearly, Semira doesn't want to be here anymore, so I offer an out.

"It's fine, Semira. You can go browse the market, please."

"No. I am not leaving you with... him," she adds with spite in her tone, narrowing her eyes at the man.

"Semira, it's fine. Hadden is with me."

"Asher won't like this," she repeats, which only increases my curiosity. What does this man know? How do I know him? Why do I feel so safe when I stare into those eyes, especially when Semira believes he is the exact opposite?

"If I am to be the Queen, as you and Asher say, please don't make me pull rank. I don't want to force an order, but I will if I need to. Please, Semira, it's important. I know it." I can feel it in my gut, my inner voice screaming at me to move towards him. It's like my lungs are burning to take in air. I try to keep my voice as even and as confident as possible. However, I am unwilling to back down, not even to please Asher.

Semira hesitates until the man is almost right in front of us, but she finally relents, "Fine, but when Asher has my head for this, it will be on your conscience that it will be haunting your dreams." Semira storms off before I have the chance to reply to her dramatic statement. I'm just talking to a possible friend. I need answers, that's all.

The tall man stops a couple of feet from me, and I can tell he is Fae. Not only by his pointed ears but by his demeanor. He demands authority, respect, and grace in every movement. It causes my stomach to tighten in anticipation of his words. I don't know where to start, so I remain silent, waiting for him to say something, anything.

"I'm surprised you're here. Didn't think your *husband* would let you off the palace grounds," he sneers with blatant hatred towards Asher and even maybe hatred for me, too.

"Why do you hate him so much? I can tell by how you are speaking now that you do." The question slips out of my mouth dumbly. That wasn't the first thing I wanted to say, but it's out before I can stop it.

I know it's not the right thing to say because his eyes tighten in a glare, and he snarls, "Are you kidding me right now? Please tell me you're joking, Amalie. I swear to the stars. Do not test me. You're the one that left me for him."

His words rip a hole through my chest and pierce my heart, shattering me into a thousand pieces. I don't know how to react. I don't know what I did because I don't remember what I did! The odd thing is that Hadden still doesn't react. Even when this man is yelling at me, he still doesn't move.

You're the one that left me for him. Oh stars, no. I knew there was some sort of connection. I could feel it tightening in my chest as he spoke. I feel so strongly for this man in front of me, so strongly in such a way I did not feel for Asher. Why would I leave him? Instead of asking him that question or explaining that I have no clue what he's talking about, my mouth vomits another idiotic question.

"Were we ever in a garden? With a pavilion?" I stare straight into those green eyes, and I can almost see the truth staring back at me. It wasn't a dream. It was a memory.

The man takes a large breath, staring at the leaves hanging over our heads, and breathes out slowly in an audible rasp as if it physically hurts him. Maybe it does.

"You promised you would come back to me..." Those eight words break my heart all over again. Tears threaten to spill over as I reach for his hand. The need to touch him, to end the agony for him, is overwhelming, but he takes a step back, not allowing me to reach for him. My hand drops, and my eyes go blurry with tears.

"I'm sorry..." Even though I genuinely have no idea what I am apologizing for. "I'm so confused. I don't know who you are. I barely know who I am. I know there was something between us because I can *feel* it, but..." I shrug since I don't know what else to say to him.

His eyes widen with shock and quickly turn to fury. His snarling reply causes me to flinch. "What did he do to you?"

I open my mouth to speak when I feel large, muscular arms encase my waist, and suddenly, Asher is standing beside me protectively. "Wren, I didn't think you had it in you to show your face here again. Why don't you run home now, hm?" Asher taunts, causing my blood to boil. I look up at him in disbelief. I've never heard him be anything but kind to everyone, but that's not entirely true, is it? I think as my eyes find their way back to Wren.

"What the hell did you do to her?" Wren growls through his teeth, and I can feel the danger and darkness spilling from him.

"You better watch your tongue, Prince Wren. Amalie is my wife. You will watch yourself with her in your presence. Or better yet, not be near her at all." Asher smirks, standing taller and more confident in front of Wren. He used the word Prince like it was an insult. He's trying to make Wren feel inferior, and I am not having any of it.

"Asher! I chose to talk to him. You have no right to step in as you did. You need to leave-" I never got to finish my sentence before Asher spun me around to block my view of Wren.

"Hadden! Take her home, now. We will have a discussion later." Hadden nods and gently grabs my shoulder, urging me to follow him, but I refuse.

Instead, Wren decides to antagonize Asher again. "You better watch yourself, Asher. By the color of your face, people might start thinking you're the king of the Fire Kingdom." I hear Wren chuckling to himself behind me, enjoying his snide remark.

Asher's face grows hotter by the second, getting more impatient.

"Amalie, return to the carriage. Now. I will be along in a moment." He grabs my other arm and pulls me towards an approaching Semira. Hadden looks between Wren and Asher like he's unsure of what to do now. I don't understand what's going on. My head is spinning. New and old memories are mingling and mixing. I can't tell what is up and what is down, right or wrong.

"Don't you dare touch her like that again. I don't care if there is a treaty, I will destroy you," Wren promises with violence in every syllable.

"I will touch her in any and all ways I want to, for she's my wife," Asher seethes back, suggesting more than a hand on my arm. He's goading Wren, urging him to try something. I can't let that happen, not here, not today.

Semira reaches my side, and I relent, allowing her and Hadden to guide me down the path towards my home. I just hope my submission will help ease the tension.

I hear Wren call behind me, "Willow misses you!" And that does it.

I stop in my tracks, unable to move forward anymore. Willow, my leaf, my gift, my life. The memory assaults my head so suddenly that white-hot tears pour from my eyes. *Willow!*

Wren gave me a tiny, leaf-shaped baby dragon. She used to fit in the palm of my hand. She would fold into her vibrant green wings, resembling a little leaf. I named her Willow. Wren would always laugh at me for naming dangerous and fearsome beasts after the flora in the Earth Kingdom.

I spin back to Wren, staring at his anguished expression, and my tears turn into sobs at the assaulting memories. My Willow...

"Is she-" My voice breaks. I clear my throat and continue, "Is she okay?"

Wren's expression is torn between fury and sadness. His eyebrows slope and close as if in pain, and he repeats, "She misses you."

"That is ENOUGH!" Asher bellows in rage. He grabs my shoulders and pushes me towards Semira once again. "You!" He points back at Wren. "You have no right putting your nose in our business. You will leave her alone, or you will have more troubles than a lost love," he promises with malice in every word, but Wren doesn't seem so easily deterred.

"You're all secrets and lies, Asher. The day will come when she realizes what you're doing to her. I do feel bad for you, you know. Amalie is formidable when she puts her mind to something. I'm afraid there might not be much left of your kingdom when she's done with you." Wren seems confident in his taunt towards Asher. I don't think I agree with him. A human can't do much against a whole kingdom.

I give Wren one last glance, still unsure of what the hell just happened! I know Wren has the answers but am I safe with him? I feel safe with him, but Asher and Semira don't feel as confident. I give Wren a final glance, pleading with my eyes for something I'm not sure of. Wren gives a quick nod to Hadden, who discreetly nods back. I turn away, continuing down the path to our carriage with Semira, Hadden, and Asher trailing behind, still red-faced with anger. I can feel his ominous malice, and I don't dare look back at him. I suppose this is the first and only trip to the market that I will be permitted for the rest of my new life.

I'm angry. Angry at myself, not because of the connection I feel with a man who isn't my husband. But I'm even angrier that I don't know *why* I feel this connection.

I'm furious at Asher. His actions were appalling. No matter the reason for their quarrel, he is a Prince and needs to hold himself to a higher standard.

"I'm sorry," I say quietly, not entirely apologizing for my

actions. I'm honestly not sorry at all, but I am hoping that my apology will prove to be a start to gaining Asher's trust again because, in the end, I am going home with him. I need to know the reason behind the animosity and if apologizing first is the way to do it, then I will swallow my pride and do it.

The only thing I'm sure of, is that Wren has answers, and I need to find a way to get them from him.

13

Amalie

I'm waiting for Asher to explode; the anticipation and suspense are driving me insane. The four of us are packed into the carriage and are on our way back to the palace. Nobody dares to speak, nobody except me because, for some reason, I have recently developed no filter. It's like as my memories come back, I learn more about who I and what was hiding beneath the surface.

"Asher?"

"Don't"

"Don't, what?" I counter. I'm not ready to give this up. I only apologized in an attempt to smooth everything over, although I didn't do anything wrong. I was simply talking to a person--fae--from another kingdom. Last I checked, you're allowed to do that, especially at the Treaty market since it's neutral grounds.

"Don't speak." He mutters under his breath.

Excuse me?

"You have no right to do what you just did. I am not your property. I am your wife, your equal. In my kingdom, that means something!" I begin to shout at him. I want a reaction. I want him to tell me what the hell is going on. I want him to argue with me.

"You're not in your kingdom anymore. You're in mine." He takes a breath, trying to calm his rising anger again. "Amalie, please. Just don't fight about this. Wren is no good. He's a washed-up prince who thought he could con you into loving him, that's all. He's still bitter that you chose me instead."

Hadden clears his throat and shifts beside me while Semira pretends none of us exist and stares out the window. Asher is somehow still holding his anger at bay. Maybe the further we get from Wren and the market, the calmer Asher will be.

I decide to wait until we are back at the palace to speak with Asher privately, my guilt increasing as I glance between Hadden and Semira.

After what feels like hours but in actuality is only about ten minutes later, we arrive. I don't wait for Asher to assist me from the carriage. I am the first one out, and I keep walking towards the tunnel to bring me to the palace. I can hear the other three behind me, guards surrounding the entrance, and the possibility of ghouls passing through… All of which doesn't deter me from speed-walking.

I walk through the open tunnel straight to the foyer and decide to go to the observation terrace. I think it's the best place for me to sit and think about everything that happened today. I'm upset the market day was ruined, I'm fighting with myself for being so stubborn, and I'm heartbroken for Wren and Willow. I'm so lost in my thoughts that I don't hear Asher approach behind me. He carries a bottle of red wine and a blanket, which he hands to me before sitting down on a bench. I didn't notice the bench here the other day, but I'm too emotionally distraught to care. I feel like I'm being buried in an avalanche, fighting for my way back to the surface.

"I'm sorry." Asher is the first to truly apologize. He looks so upset and defeated that I almost give in and immediately accept his apology.

"It's not right for you to speak to me like that. It's not right for you to touch me like that," I scold him sternly.

"I know. I'm trying. I'm not used to having you. My whole life, I've gotten everything I've wanted with no bumps in the road, but not you. You are the one thing that is worth fighting for, and I am terrified of losing you, especially to him."

I move towards the bench, slowly sitting down and wrapping the blanket around my shoulders. I sigh, allowing Asher to take a long swig from the bottle. He didn't bring any fancy glasses, which is so unlike him. He is the guy who follows the role of being a King; he's been preparing for it his whole life.

"You sure you want to be drinking for this conversation?" I try to joke, but it falls flat. This somber feeling is blanketing the whole terrace. I think we are both drained from today's emotions that it's not easy to feel anything else. "Can you tell me about him?"

Asher sighs, taking another swig of wine. I watch him as his jaw tightens and his nostrils flare. I can't tell if it's anger at my question or his hostility towards Wren. Asher extends the bottle out for me, but I just shake my head. I want to remember every word he says. "You both grew up in the Earth Kingdom. You told me that your mom was good friends with the Queen, and you lived in their chateau, so I guess you and Wren were friends. He is a year younger than I am, so he wasn't happy when I had the Trine before him. You and I, we chose each other, but he didn't like that. He thought you were meant to be his. He didn't want to give you a choice!" Asher's voice starts to rise again as he tells my story. His white shirt is partially unbuttoned and askew. He looks like he couldn't care less if he was a prince or a peasant. His blonde hair is unkempt and flopping to the side, unlike his usual slicked-back formal style.

Wren intended to marry me because of our connection

through our mothers. Asher believes it was an arrangement made a long time ago. I'm not too fond of the idea of being owned by anyone or having my choice and future taken away. His story makes sense to me. I most likely did say yes to Asher just to spite Wren, no wonder why he's pissed. This is my doing, I made an enemy out of the Earth Kingdom, and now less than one year before Wren is to ascend the throne, he is without a Queen by his side. If he doesn't find a Queen, he can't become King. It's the law of the treaty.

As my mind runs through the possible scenarios, I lean on Asher's shoulder, caving into his warmth. "I'm sorry, I didn't realize what was at stake. I didn't realize asking Wren questions would cause this."

"You wouldn't have known. I don't blame you. I'm angered more by his inability to give up. He needs to move on and let us be happy." Asher strokes the top of my head in a soothing motion that dissolves any hesitations I have about him.

"Things will be better once I get all my memories back. Please just stick with me until then," I plead. I wouldn't want Asher to give up on me because I pose too much of a problem for him. Selfishly, I don't want to end up alone in the end. I don't know what bridges I may have burned or what connections may have remained after all this, but right now, the only constant in my life is Asher. Sure, Semira is here with me as well, but she also holds a grip on my former life, even though she does have Alizar. I can't hold her back from her future because I can't remember my past.

"You never need to ask." Asher soothes me until I fall asleep on the bench with him beside me.

"Wow, thank you...I love it." I try to keep the sarcasm out of my voice, but Wren sees right through me. He's laughing at me now, and I scowl at him, fighting the twitch in my lip that's threatening to smile at his gorgeous laugh. His bright green eyes are shining brighter today, and my heart melts at the sight of him. "It's a leaf. You know there are about a billion or more in the world. In fact, you can create them with just a thought! I don't know what to do with a leaf."

Wren grabs my hand and turns it so my palm faces upwards. He gives me a sly smile while gently placing the leaf in my hand, and I'm surprised to feel the warmth. I examine the leaf with an eyebrow raised; it is a perfect forest green salal leaf. It starts large at one end and tapers to a sharp point on the other end. The little leaf fits perfectly in my palm, and I notice a tiny lizard foot sticking out from underneath it. My eyes widen more, and I have to remind myself to blink and breathe. Staring up at Wren's smile, I smile wider back at him, mirroring his pleasure. I cup my other hand together now that I realize this creature is a living thing, not just a leaf. I'm so worried I'm going to drop the little guy.

Wren grabs the leaf and gently pulls on it to separate its...wings. The leaf is its wings folded together, beautifully ticked together like a bird after landing. "Wren!! Be careful!" I scold him, now officially in mama bear mode. That's it, this thing is my baby!

"It's fine! Dragons are durable." He laughs loudly, and I glare at him all over again. He's going to wake my baby! Wren notices my expression and sobers up quickly.

"You got me a dragon?"

"She was abandoned by her mother. I found her on the forest floor, nearly crunched the thing." He mimics the gruesome act by stomping his foot.

I stare at the little creature again, a little girl. I can't believe Wren brought home a baby dragon! Where the hell am I going to put it when it's fully grown? Honestly, I don't care. I will build a structure for her if I have to. It only took one glance at the tiny foot to seal my heart with hers. The vibrant leaf-green dragon spreads out in my hands, *revealing a thumb-sized head, four gorgeous little feet, and an insanely long tail, roughly the same length as her body. Her tail stretches out and slides off my hand, alerting me that the baby is fully awake now. Her forest green eyes match that of Wren's, and her scales are shaped like elm and birch leaves, tucked tightly against one another.*

"Oh, my stars." My heart melts, and I sit down right in the middle of the greenhouse floor. Wren follows my movement and lowers himself beside me.

"Do you like her?" he asks nervously. Has he not been seeing me melt at the sight of her?

"Wren... I love her. Thank you."

He smiles wider, putting his hand on my wrist to slowly guide my cupped hands down to my skirt. I let the baby dragon splay out on my lap, but she bounces up just as quickly, staring at us. Surprisingly, she doesn't flee from us. She simply turns a couple of times as a dog does before laying down and flopping onto her side, and tucking her wings in again. And she's back to being a leaf. I laugh at how adorable she is.

"What are you naming her? Another plant, I'm assuming?" Yeah, I have a habit of naming every creature I come across. So far, I have Lily; a forest cat that visits my garden, Sage; a little pixie that steals cheese from the kitchen, and Oak; a little river troll who wanders around the creek behind the chateau.

"Willow," I whisper, my little willow. Willow trees are the mother tree of the Earth Kingdom.

"Willow," Wren repeats, testing the name on his tongue. "I think it's perfect."

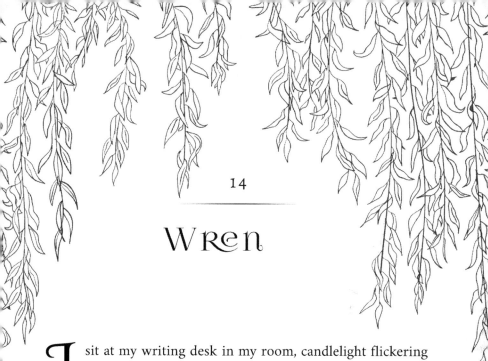

14

Wren

I sit at my writing desk in my room, candlelight flickering and casting a dingy glow throughout the room. I stare at the letter I've written to her. I read it over and over before grabbing the paper, crumpling it up, and then throwing it across the room. I don't even know where to begin.

Amalie wasn't herself. I knew something wasn't right, I just didn't know what it was. I don't regret the actions I've taken to see her again. I would do it all over if I had another five minutes with her. I would take her anger, her pain, and her confusion just to kiss it all away.

My fists clench at the thought of her with him, but if that were indeed her decision, I would let her go. Amalie is strong, she can take care of herself, but she shouldn't have to. That's the issue I'm struggling with. If I try to swoop in and save her, will it all be for nothing, or am I missing a key factor here? Is she being held prisoner by him? She certainly didn't seem safe; I didn't like his hands on her, and she didn't even fight him. The Amalie I know would have kicked him in the balls for that, stars know she's done it to me a time or two.

I lean my forearms on the solid wood desk, staring at the little doodles she carved into the top with my dagger. The same dagger that I misplaced days ago, another memory of her gone.

I pick up my quill and try to write her again,

Dear Amalie,

Please help me understand your decision because for the life of me I can't. I think of your words from over a month ago, again and again, of you telling me you're going to marry and bond with him. It doesn't seem real.
How did we go from planning our lives together to you being gone?
I am alive but not living. I'm breathing but not thriving.
I'm empty and confused.
Please. Just help me understand your decisions. Please tell me it's because you love him. Please tell me you're happy. Just please, please tell me you're okay.
I will be all right as long as I just know.
Amalie, I love you. Stars, I love you. But you're not mine. Not anymore.
I need to know if this is the end.

-Wren

"Damn it!" I shout, tossing this letter aside too. What am I thinking? She chose him. She left me for him! A week before her wedding, she came to me saying she wanted out and didn't want to marry him. We spent the whole afternoon planning how to get her out. She was going to run away and meet me in the pavilion. I am not able to cross their borders without a proper declaration. Kingdoms can only visit rival kingdoms through an invite or for political reasons. Any other manner could be seen as an act of war, so she would need to come to me. That's why we picked the garden, she knew where it was by heart. It's close enough within the Earth Kingdom that her human legs can run to.

I waited all night for her, but she never came. My right hand, Finley, helped me search for her as much as we could. Since I was young, Finley has been my best friend, and I trust him the most out of anyone, sometimes even more than Amalie. Where she is unpredictable, he is a constant. I asked him to search within the Air Kingdom because he is human, and there are no laws prohibiting humans from crossing between borders.

And then it hits me. The plan starts forming as soon as I realize Finley is my secret weapon. He is the fox in the hen house, and I'm about to set him loose.

I run to my chamber door and throw it open with so much force that it cracks against the wall with a loud bang. Finley smirks and raises his eyebrow at me. He's always standing guard outside my room, even though I tell him to leave me alone.

"Fin, come in and shut the door. I have a plan brewing."

"Great," he drags the word out like it's a considerable effort. "Can you make it a bit more fun than the last couple? I know you're going through some shit lately, but stars, man. The tree impaling and leaving them to hang is getting rather old."

Okay, yeah, I might have had to torture a couple of people to get some answers—big deal. "Don't be dramatic, Fin." I wave his impending remark off with my hand. "Anyways, this plan is for you to be a spy for me." At that, Finley raises his eyebrows in shock, his expression full of excitement and intrigue.

"I'm listening..."

"Well, I saw her today, and I'm pretty sure her new guard is next on the list..." I leave the sentence hanging in the air, but he doesn't catch where I'm headed with this. Finley cocks a thick eyebrow, unsure of what I am insinuating. He is a massive warrior of a man, but sometimes I swear his energy is spent moving those bulging muscles rather than working his brain, so I continue, "You will replace her guard, Fin."

Finally, light connects in his eyes, and I can see now that he understands. Fin has long black hair partially dreaded with silver leaves twisted through the locks and his beard. He's tall enough to intimidate the strongest man with dark eyes to match. Sometimes, when he is preparing for battle, he will line those eyes with coal, making them darker. I can see four swords strapped to him, two crossing his back and one on each hip. To put it simply, he is quite terrifying. I would not like to be on the other end of his sword, which would just stroke Asher's ego. He will take one look at Finley and know he needs to have the biggest man to protect his girl.

Once you get to know him, he is the most protective and fun-loving person you've ever met. I would trust him with my life, but more importantly, hers.

"I'll set everything up for you, get your papers in order and all that. First off, though, you need to take those leaves out. Even though we know Asher isn't that bright, they're a dead giveaway. Any blind man could see that you're from the Earth Kingdom with those in your locks." I move back over to my writing desk, drafting a letter to some nameless people who would be more than happy to forge some documents for me.

Behind me, Finley is removing the leaves from his hair, and I catch his eyes wandering around the room and falling on the mountain of crumpled letters I've tried to write to Amalie. "Anything you want me to tell her, Wren?" Finley knows a fair amount about our relationship, or former relationship.

"No. She pretended she didn't know me, so just play along if she does the same to you. All I want to know is if she's okay. Just watch her. Make sure he's not threatening her or holding her against her will. If anything happens, you get her out of there, no questions asked. I don't care if she fights you. I trust you, Fin. You're the only one at this point I do trust."

"Only me and that dragon, right?" Finley laughs at his joke; he knows that Willow is shady at the best of times. I think the only one she actually likes is Amalie. She had me make a whole "Dragon Garden" for the young creature. It's more of a vast forest with a large pergola to keep it warm and comfortable on rainy days. I've never seen a wolf-sized creature skip around like a puppy, but she does it every time Amalie is around.

I snort at Finley and continue writing my letter. "Just remember, let her live her life if that's what she wants. It's her choice, but if he does anything, she comes back here. Whether she wants to or not." It's easier to ask forgiveness than permission, right?

I hand Finley the letter and give him instructions on whom to deliver it to. He nods, takes the letter, and walks right out the door; no goodbye, no see you later. That's how Fin and I work. Most of our exchanges are silent. I just hope I didn't make a huge mistake.

I sigh and head over to my bed, grabbing this ridiculous book about 'Dragon Behavior' that Amalie picked up at one of the local shops in town. I flop onto the bed, flipping through the pages. She thought it would be important to learn the dos and don'ts of owning a dragon, even though I'm confident that no one has ever actually owned one. They're not exactly the most obedient creatures.

I flip through the book, looking at the flowers she dried between the pages as bookmarks.

I still remember her serious and stern look when she told me, *You can create and kill flowers all you want. I think it's only fair that I can too.* When I looked at her in confusion, she continued, *Don't underestimate me, Wren. I'm just as strong as you are. I may not have magic as you do, but I can do the same thing, just in a different way.*

I close my eyes, ready for this day to be over. I start to drift off when I hear the stars awful roar of a very hungry Willow. *Shit, I forgot to feed her*, I think as I get up again and head out to feed the cranky two-month-old dragon. Amalie better thank me for this later.

15

Amalie

I wake up from the dream with tears in my eyes. They are falling down my cheeks as I slowly open my eyes for the day.

I remember.

I remember the day Wren brought Willow home to me; she was so little. I wonder how big she is now. It's probably been close to a month since I last saw her. This hits me hard because I understand running from Wren, but why would I leave Willow with him?

I slide from my bed, not bothering to change into my outfit for the day before leaving my room. I need to apologize to Semira about yesterday, but as soon as I step through the door, I stop in my tracks. In front of me is a mountain of a man. He must be at least six-foot-five; he's enormous!

"Umm… hello," I say dumbly. I've gotten so used to seeing Hadden every morning, but now I feel exposed. I cross my arms over my breasts as if that will help. "Who are you?" I ask, even though he's obviously a guard of the Air Kingdom. He's wearing the exact same uniform that Hadden wears.

The man winks at me, actually winks! Oh dear, this one is

trouble, I can tell by his jovial aura. "Names Finley, new recruit. Asher put me on rotation, so I'll be here about half the time." He smiles kindly, which makes me wearier of him. He looks familiar, but I don't think about it for too long. Many people look familiar to me, I just have no idea who they are.

"Where's Hadden?" I ask Finley.

"Word on the street is he got canned." He gestures with his finger and crosses his neck in a slicing motion, making my eyes widen in horror.

"Are you implying something, sir?" I stand taller, on the defense. I don't like what he's suggesting. Asher would never make that decision. I know they needed to talk about the situation yesterday, but I thought it would be a verbal warning and he would be by my side again.

"Are you insinuating that I'm implying something?" he fires back at me, and I'm exasperated just speaking with him. With a huff, I walk to Semiras' room without even knocking when I enter—completely forgetting that Alizar also shares her room with her. They're both cuddled in their bed, startled by my entrance.

"Stars! I'm so sorry! I completely forgot. I'll wait in the foyer." I start to retreat backwards out the door, but Semira stops me.

"It's fine. Come sit, Amalie," she says as she gets out of bed. I move toward the small seating area to the left of the room, flopping down in the chair, exhausted already. "What's wrong?"

I shrug because I don't even know where to start or what to say, or not say. Do I ask her about Willow? Wren? Or don't ask anything at all? I'm so confused I can't even decide what I'm confused about!

"Asher and I spoke last night, and we seem to be fine now."

"Okay... why are you upset about that? You don't seem too pleased," she asks cautiously. I glance over my shoulder towards the door, where Finley is in the foyer.

I lower my voice, "Hadden is gone. Finley," I nod my head to the foyer again, "the new guard is making it seem like Hadden is dead, not just gone."

"Oh."

"Oh?"

Semira hesitates so long that Alizar gets up from the bed, his shoulder-length hair loose. He's wearing cream-colored loose-fitted pants and no shirt. I must admit he does look good now that he's cleaned himself up, really good, actually. He walks over to the small sofa with his slight limp and carefully sits down beside Semira. She watches him move with such tenderness in her eyes that it makes my heart ache.

"Amalie, I'm going to say this, and I know you won't like it. Trust that I have my reasons. This doesn't leave the room." I simply nod my head in agreement at Alizar's words. I've never heard him speak so much; that was two sentences! I keep my mouth shut, not wanting to scare off his openness. "Don't underestimate Asher. He may be acting nice to you now, but there's a motive behind it. There's always a motive behind it."

Semira looks between Alizar and the doorway and startles, sitting up straight and then looking back at Alizar with wide eyes. She's afraid, I realize. Is Asher here? I slowly turn around and peer at the doorway, following Semira's wide eyes. Finley is leaning against the doorframe, arms crossed with a broad smile on his face. To put it simply, he looks terrifying. My blood runs cold at the sight of him. I can feel the fear seeping through me. Finley is going to tell Asher. If Alizar is right about Asher, I don't know how to stop him from saying anything. I stand up quickly and run to the door, pushing Finley out into the foyer.

"You, we need to talk. Now." I lead him next door to my room and slam the door behind us. I put my hand on his broad chest and shove him further into the room.

"Oh, I'm liking where this *talk* is going. Should we go talk on the bed, or we can talk on the couch." He wiggles his eyebrows suggestively. And I realize he doesn't seem upset at all about our conversation that he was just eavesdropping in on.

"Not that kind of talk, you pig!" I take my hand off his chest and take a step back from him. "I mean, about what you overheard, please, Finley. Please don't mention anything to Asher. Alizar didn't-" Finley halts my rambling with one hand held up in my face. I crane my neck to look him in the face, hoping he will understand.

"I'm not going to say anything. Calm down. You're going to hurt yourself, pop a blood vessel or something."

I stand there confused as to why wouldn't he run straight to Asher? Isn't that a part of his job? I'm almost afraid to ask, but my stupid mouth doesn't have a filter. So it comes out anyways, "Why?"

"Because he's right."

Now I'm dumbfounded. Asher's guard is seriously saying this? It must be a trick or something, "How do I know you're not playing me? You're probably going to run to Asher, and then Alizar and Semira are going to get hurt in the end. If what you say about Hadden is true…" I let the words trail off. If Finley is correct about Hadden, Alizar won't stand a chance against Asher.

Finley moves to the couch and sits down on it, rather unprofessionally. He seems to be enjoying himself. He's leaning back on the white sofa, looking out the mountainside, seemingly in thought. I decide to walk over and join him on the couch. I know I need him on my side. I need him to trust me as much as I need to trust him. We are now a part of a team with secrets.

He reaches slowly into his jacket to grab what seems like a crumpled piece of paper and pulls it out. He holds it in his hands for a moment as he contemplates his decision and then hands it to me.

"Read it later. I'm going to get in shit for stealing it, but some things need to be said. Don't show anyone, burn it after. It's more than your life on that paper." And with that, he stands and walks out of the room. In the short time I've known Finley, I've learned he isn't a bad guy though I can't decide where his cards lay. I guess I just have to wait until they all fall to find out.

I pretend the day started like any other day and try to ignore the piece of paper that I've tucked into the bodice of my dress. I'm restless and jumpy, and this dress feels rough and itchy against my irritated body. I play ignorant when I see Semira and Alizar again, knowing I can't discuss anything with them so out in the open like this.

I decide to take a walk around the palace. There's no garden, no color, or people anywhere. It seems cold and deserted. The only thing this place offers is a nice view and a steady breeze.

I hear footsteps behind me, and I know it's Asher before even turning around. Finley is surprisingly silent as he follows me about ten paces back, then I hear Asher call out, "Amalie!" I spin around and give him a warm smile, waiting for him to catch up with me. "Hi, are you alright? I haven't seen you at all today, and it's almost time for dinner."

I honestly overlooked the time of day. I just decided to walk the palace and utterly lost track of time. I tell him so, and he nods, seeming to accept my excuse. "Did you want to accompany me to the dining hall? My parents are out, so you won't be interrogated by them tonight." He laughs even though the joke doesn't land quite right, but I do give him a courtesy grin for his effort.

Asher links his fingers through mine and leads me through the hallways to the dining hall. When we walk through the large double doors, I see candlelight casting everywhere, creating a soft and romantic glow. I look up at Asher curiously.

"I may have asked to have privacy tonight." He turns and waves Finley off. He seems like he doesn't want to leave, hesitating for a moment before moving out of the dining room and standing beside the door. "You are dismissed for the night. I will take Amalie to her rooms." Asher's voice is full of authority, which scares me, although I'm not entirely sure why. It's not like I haven't heard it before, but I also haven't heard it with this warning in my head.

We move to the one end of the table where plates and wine are waiting for us. Asher, being chivalrous, pulls my chair out for me and tucks me gently into the table. I glance around the dining room. Besides the candles, there's nothing different or unique about it. I catch Asher's eyes watching me, and I give him a soft smile. "Thank you for tonight."

"You're welcome. How have you been settling in? Have you remembered anything yet?" Immediately my red flags go up. A voice in my head screams No! And finally, my brain and my mouth communicate when I repeat the thought to him, shrugging as if it's not a big deal. I observe him closely for his reaction, but he doesn't give any.

"Ah, well, I'm sure it will come to you. If not, we will make our own memories." That sounds...nice. Even if these people have their reservations about Asher, he has been kind to me, and he admits his faults which is more than I can say for many. I decide to push all those thoughts aside. He is trying to be a better person, and I have no right to judge when I don't even know who I really am.

"So, where have you been all day today?" I decide to ask him to move this conversation along.His answer is interrupted by the servants bringing meals out of the connecting kitchen. Pasta with a fantastic smelling tomato sauce lands in front of me, and my mouth waters, forgetting my question. "Mmmm," I moan from the smell alone.

I glance at Asher, who gives me a flirty look. "I'd love to hear that again," he suggests, but his comment makes my body tingle from head to toes. Butterflies return, and I can't tell if it's excitement or nerves. Probably a bit of both. We take a couple of bites in silence. *Well, this is awkward now,* I think as I chew my food.

I dare to bring up the question that's been bugging me since we left the market yesterday, "Will I ever be allowed back at the market?" I ask it like a question, but the real question is, *Will you throw a fit when I return to the market? Because I am not taking orders from a man, king or not.* He may be my husband, but he isn't my captor.

"I think after we have our bonding ceremony and coronation, then you will officially be Queen. Nobody will bother you then." All right, that isn't a no. It's a compromise, and I can live with that. It's only about two more weeks until our ceremony.

We finish dinner with easy conversations. Asher calls out to one of his guards, and I stare at him in confusion. The sound of footsteps approaching draws my attention to the large entrance as a young woman walks through the large double doors holding a paper and pen. Asher looks up as she's almost at the table, and he gives me a huge, bright white smile.

"Surprise," he cheers quietly while the woman simply stands slightly to his right, like a ghost haunting his presence. I examine her while Asher speaks with her. She's wearing a white off-the-shoulder shirt with little capes on her arms starting at her shoulder. Her skirt has a long slit on each side, and it's in a deep, rich grey color. Her auburn hair is long and cascading down her back in soft curls while her eyes shine emerald, like the forest floor after a rainstorm. To put it simply, she is stunning. I find my jealousy emerging from deep within me.

The emotion shocks me into action, and I give Asher a *'Who's she?'* kind of look, which he thankfully picks up on immediately. "This is Kirah. She's the palace event coordinator. She works on all the events we host here."

"And what event is she working on now?" I ask, not too

kindly, which I should feel bad about, but she's giving him sultry eyes. It's making me wonder if they have a history with one another. Asher is walking on a tight line right now, even though I know it's irrational because I'm not even willing to be very intimate with him right now. However, it does rub me the wrong way to see a woman making eyes at my husband, regardless of our current situation.

Asher stands up and moves around to my side of the table, pulling the white wooden chair out beside me and sitting down. He takes my left hand in his and smiles wider. "We never got to celebrate our marriage, so I thought we should hold a ball for our union and your safe return. Kirah, here, she will make your every wish come true. I've told her the mandatory things we need like food, music, décor, but you get to pick the specifics."

My anxiety increases at the thought of the task and all the eyes on us. Asher sees it in my expression and laughs. "It will be fine. I'm sure you and Kirah will make it beautiful. Anything you want, let her know. She will make it happen," he assures me kindly. I nod because I'm not sure what else to do. I sit up straighter in my seat and turn my full attention to Kirah, who is now standing behind Asher. She doesn't appear too happy about me taking the lead on this. She sighs dramatically and turns to look at me, readying her pen as she does.

"Well, uh, I would like greenery. Flowers and plants and twinkling lights everywhere, like an enchanted garden." Asher looks in my direction with a slight frown but nods his agreement while Kirah scoffs at my suggestion.

"Wouldn't you like something... less cluttered and more airy? Why don't we have stars and sheer panels cascading the walls?" Kirah suggests instead.

Asher interjects immediately, cutting off Kirah's suggestions. "That doesn't sound anything like what Amalie requested. Should I find someone more agreeable?" He gives her a pointed look, and I straighten a bit more, giving her a sly smile as if to say *ha, I win*. I know it's childish, but sometimes you just have to surrender to the urge.

"Yes, Sir. Amalie has a beautiful vision for the evening," Kirah tries her best to backtrack. She writes my suggestions down on her parchment and looks at me, waiting for me to continue.

"Um, I think we should have lots of sweets. They're my favorite and maybe a table of various foods so people can have their choice of foods."

"You don't want an elegant sit-down dinner? I think my parents would be happy with something a bit more formal." His suggestion saddens me a bit. Having a solely formal event would please many, but in my opinion, if we are celebrating something, it shouldn't be so traditional.

"Oh, okay," I speak low and give Asher a small understanding smile while Kirah writes down his suggestion with a sneer on her face.

Asher stares into my eyes, and after a moment, he holds his hand out to Kirah. "Cross that out. I don't care what will please my parents. This isn't about them, it's about us. Amalie will have her choice." It is in that small motion where he thinks of me first, that makes my heart melt and the butterflies return. I give him a quick kiss on the cheek.

"We should have benches and comfortable sitting areas out on the terrace, surrounded by flowers and the stars above." I swoon at the image.

We continue brainstorming ideas for our upcoming celebration ball. I think this might be the first time that I remember I would enjoy a social gathering since usually the more people around, the more uncomfortable I become.

As Asher and I walk to my rooms hand in hand, I begin to feel calm with him. He still gives me butterflies, but I now embrace them rather than feeling like I want to run from them. When we reach my door, I decide to give Asher a full kiss before entering my room. I press my entire body against his until I can hear his low moan in the back of his throat.

"I'd love to hear that again," I repeat his suggestive words from earlier, "Maybe later." I give him a wink and slip into my room, closing the door tightly behind me.

As I move to my closet to change into my night shift, I remember the paper that Finley gave me earlier today. I pull it out of my bodice and set it on my night table while continuing to change for the night. I take my hair out of its long braid and brush the tangles out, making it falls in soft waves down my back as I pick up the paper again and move to the sofa. Sitting down, I curl my legs underneath myself and unfold the crumpled paper. I read the first line, and tears immediately well up in my eyes.

Dear Amalie,

Oh Stars! Please no, I just decided to forget him. I decided to move forward with Asher and make this work! However, I can't contain my traitorous tears spilling over as my eyes continue reading down the page.

Please help me understand your decision because for the life of me I can't. I think of your words from over a month ago, again and again. You had told me you were going to marry and bond with him, it didn't seem real.
How did we go from planning our lives together to you being gone?
I am alive but not living. I'm breathing but not thriving.
I'm empty and confused.
Please. Just help me understand your decisions. Please tell me it's because you love him. Please tell me you're happy.
Just please, please tell me you're okay.
I will be alright as long as I just know.

Amalie, I love you. Stars I love you. But you're not mine. Not anymore.
I need to know if this is the end.

-Wren

Stars I love you. But you're not mine. Not anymore. Those words echo through my head throughout the night. The tears don't stop, and I can feel my heart breaking for a man I don't even know.

16

Amalie

I fake a headache the following day, refusing to leave my room. I stay in bed nursing a broken heart on behalf of Wren. His letter tore me apart like a parasite that slowly eats your body from the inside while excruciatingly devouring me. I feel raw and overwhelmed.

The servants enter my room to bring me water and fruits, but I don't even look at them. I do, however, look up to Finley, who is staring at me from the doorway. His expression is full of contemplative concern. He looks at me like I am a mystery he is trying to solve, and I can't stand it. Once the servants bow and leave my room, I sit up in bed and motion for Finley to approach. He does so, closing the door quietly behind him. He must know something is going on, and it's not just a headache.

"Do you remember him now?" Finley asks me while sitting in the white wooden chair across the room, opposite my bed. He leans forward, placing his forearms on his thighs, and watches me.

"Where did you get it? How do I know it's actually from him?" I'm still in shock and denial, I think.

"I found it."

"Really? It was just lying around?" I counter, not believing his story.

"In a way, yeah. I found it in Wren's room. He would probably impale me for taking it and giving it to you. That's kind of his thing lately." I'm oddly not bothered by the impaling portion of what Finley just said, however, the part that does stand out to me is that he found the letter in Wren's room.

"And you were in his room because…" I leave the sentence open, waiting for him to fill in the blanks for me.

"Because," he continues, "he asked me there." I huff out a deep breath. This man is so irritating; It's like pulling teeth just to get a simple answer from him.

"Okay, here's the thing. I'm getting sick of these half-answers and fake truths in my life. Could you give it to me straight or not at all? I'm so over this shit!" My voice raises by the end of my small rant. But Finley just smiles at me. Standing up, he grabs the white wooden chair he was sitting on and positions it right in front of my bed, so he's closer to me. He sits down on the chair and stares at me like the happiest person in the world; this only confuses me more.

"There she is. I missed the little fire in your bones." I stare at him like he's lost his mind, and he just laughs harder. "Well, Wren told me not to say anything, but I'm not always the best at listening to orders. He asked me to come here. He knew after the market Asher may be in the market for a new guard."

"Oh, so this mysterious man who writes letters but doesn't send them sends me a babysitter instead? Does he want information on Asher? Is that what he's doing?"

"So accusatory! Calm down, kitten, your claws are starting to show." I give him a more extensive glare. My goodness, this man is irritating! I sit still with my mouth closed, once again waiting for him to continue, "He loves you, even though he won't admit it to anyone. I found the letter crumpled on the floor. He had been too distracted talking about how I am to make sure you were happy to even notice I grabbed it. He sent me here to ensure you were safe, and I think he just wants to understand your decision."

I stare at him dumbfounded. This doesn't sound like the same man I've been informed about by Asher or even cautioned against by Semira. How do I know whom to trust? My head says to trust Asher because he's my husband, but my stupid heart is warring with my head. My heart says to trust Wren.

"If I write a letter, would you be able to give it to Wren?" The only way I can get answers is by going straight to the source.

"I might be able to arrange something." Finley's smile grows brighter, and I do have to admit, it's gorgeous and infectious.

I slide out of my bed and walk over to my writing desk. I grab a piece of paper and a quill and begin to write. I already know what I will say to him, the words flowing easily through me onto the page. Once I'm done, I carefully fold the paper, not bothering with a wax seal. I stand up again, taking the letter with me and handing it to Finley.

"It might take a few days for him to get it, but I promise he will get it," Finley assures me.

"Thank you. Now go do your job, guard. I need to get back to faking a headache." Finley laughs loudly but stands to leave the room.

Before he exits the door, he stops and turns around, staring at me with a serious look. "It's good to have you back, kitten. Even if you're not quite whole right now, you will be." And with that, he walks out of my room, softly closing the door behind him.

I crawl back into bed, thinking about the conversation with Finley. For some odd reason, I'm starting to feel okay with this decision to reach out to Wren. It feels right to trust Finley. This is the type of confidence I haven't had for a while now.

Semira comes running into my room a couple of hours later, waking me from a deep sleep. I didn't realize I was that tired, but I suppose staying up all night will do that to a person.

Semira jumps on my bed beside me as she did before and yells, "Wake up! You weren't at breakfast. What's wrong with you?"

"It's fine, Semira," I say as I roll over to face her; I look at the door to see Alizar smiling warmly at Semira. "I just had a small headache, that's all."

"Are you okay now?" she asks, glancing at the uneaten fruit the servants left on my night table beside my bed.

"I'm fine, Semira. I just didn't sleep well."

She seems to accept my answer because she moves on quickly, looking between Alizar and me. "Asher was looking for you. He asked if I could check on you. I guess he didn't want to come to your room. What happened last night? He seemed nervous."

I shrug, posting an illusion of not caring. "He set up a candlelight dinner, we talked, flirted, I kissed him, and we separated. Nothing serious." By Semira's expression, I'm guessing it is serious. "What?"

"Nothing! I just didn't think you felt that way about him. At least with your condition, I thought it would be a bit longer before you enjoyed his company."

"He's my husband," I stupidly remind her, like she's forgotten. "It's been a couple of weeks since we've been married. I think I should at least try, right?" I look to Semira for confirmation. I hate feeling so indecisive.

"Just don't rush into anything you're not ready for," Semira warns. She speaks to me as if I'm a daughter and not her friend. We are the same age, but she exudes wisdom while I lose my wits more with each passing day. I give her a slight nod.

"Alright, let's get you in the bath then dressed to see Asher. Sorry, girl, but you're starting to get a little ripe."

I laugh at her as we both slide off the large bed. She gives Alizar a 'shoo' look, and he leaves the doorway, closing the door behind him.

A few minutes later, the servants come in and fill the tub with hot water. Alizar must have told them our intentions when he left. Semira grabs the scented oils, soaps, and any lotions she can find before turning back into my room. I watch her move and sit down on my sofa, staring at the mountainside in front of her. "I'll be here when you're done," she calls from the couch.

I turn my back on her and shut the bathroom door. Shucking my night clothes off, I lift them to my nose and inhale. My stars, she's right! I've been too distracted with my wayward mind fighting with itself that I haven't really been taking care of my body. I drop the garment to the floor, hoping the servants will just burn it.

I ease into the scalding water, hissing as my body descends. I think about Wren and how he will react to my letter. Will he be pleased? Will he be upset? Why do I even care? It has been made clear that I left him for Asher, but it's also been implied that I left Asher on our wedding day. I still don't know what truly happened that day, so I run through the different scenarios in my head, ticking off other options with my fingers.

One possibility is that I was kidnapped. That would easily explain my sudden absence; thus, it would be no fault of mine. But if I was, that means I'm still in danger because they never found who did it. Also, who were they targeting? Me or Asher?

The second possibility is that I was running from Asher. Right now, I don't see this as a likely option. He obviously cares for me, and I get butterflies every time I see him, so there is an attraction there. But I've been warned about Asher's temper, so maybe things got out of hand, and I ran?

The last option is I was running to Wren. He said I left him for Asher. What if I changed my mind and decided to go back to Wren. If that's the case, then how pathetic am I? Man-obsessed, and I can't make up my mind, so I jump back and forth between them? It doesn't sound like me, yet I don't really know who I am anymore. Maybe it was the old me.

I'm sitting in the water for so long that it starts to turn cold, and I can hear Semira speaking on the other side, "Stars, girl! Are you almost done in there, or did you die while I was sitting out here waiting for you?"

I laugh at her dramatic comments and stand up to get out of the bath. Grabbing a plush white towel set on the floor beside the tub, I wrap it around myself before exiting and putting Semira out of her misery. Semira is pacing back and forth like a caged animal. "I'm alive! I feel human again." We both giggle at my joke and stars does it ever feel good to joke around with her.

"Come on, let's get you dressed."

Half an hour later, we are walking through the open hallways to the library, where Semira and Alizar spend most of their time. I'm surprised to see Asher sitting in one of the chairs in the middle circle, reading a book all by himself. I look toward Semira and ask, "Where did Alizar go?"

"He prefers not to be alone with Asher if he can help it," she whispers in my ear. I nod, understanding a little about his hesitations and finding I have a new respect for Alizar now that he's opened up to me more. I clear my throat a little louder to alert Asher of our arrival in the library.

He stands so quickly that the book he is reading slaps the ground with a loud thud. "Amalie! We missed you this morning. I hope all is well."

"It is, thank you. I just had a slight headache. But I'm much better now." I smile up at him kindly.

Asher gives me a look like he's not entirely sure he believes my lie, but I try to change the subject quickly, "So what were you reading?" I ask, bringing the focus back to him.

"Honestly, I wasn't. I was just lost in my own thoughts. Would you sit with me?" I take a quick glance at the cover as he lays it down on the table beside him.

The Kingdom and the Throne: The Rise of the Elements.

It appears to be a history book judging from the title. I wonder if Asher is trying to get some insight into his new role or attempting to impress his parents. Or perhaps I'm looking at this all wrong. What if Asher simply wants to impress his subjects, to become a good ruler.

I sit down with Asher on the sofa beside the chair he was previously in. Semira has slipped out of the room, most likely to search for Alizar. I didn't even notice she left until I sat down. I look around the space while I wait for Asher to put the book back on the shelf. I love this library. Here and the observation terrace is the only two places I truly love about this palace. It's almost like they don't belong here. They give off this sense of calm, like a blanket covering your shoulders on a chilly day; it's comforting and serene.

Asher sits down on the chair adjacent to mine, taking both of my hands in his. He leans forward and looks me in the eyes before speaking, "Are you alright with this? With us?"

"I-uh-why do you ask?" I'm not sure how to react to his question. Does he know about Wren's letter? My anxiety increases, and my palms start sweating in his hands, but I don't think he notices, at least. I'm trying to ponder a couple of steps ahead. I want to assure him that I don't have any doubts until I get more answers, but he's asking me direct questions, so he clearly has reservations as well, it seems.

"I thought maybe you were having second thoughts about last night when I didn't see you earlier today." Second thoughts? About a kiss? He's thinking way too hard about this, not that I'm one to talk, but it was just a kiss. Last I checked, a husband and wife can kiss without it being weird. But we're not a typical husband and wife.

"Asher, it's fine, honestly. I just had a headache." It's fine as long as he never finds out about the letter, or the hesitations from Alizar...or that Finley isn't really his guard. Oh, what trouble I've gotten myself into this time.

Asher abruptly changes the subject, finally accepting my excuse, "So I've spoken with Kirah. We have decided to have the ball tomorrow night. I have sent out all the invitations on our behalf, and Kirah put a rush on all the decor and plans. It will be perfect." He seems excited, and I can't seem to hold back my excitement, so I end up mirroring his expression.

"Do you think I could take Finley to the shops in Galeis? I would like to pick out a dress. I want it to be a surprise for you." Asher smiles back at me with a seductive smile that makes my heart beat faster.

"Any specific color I should look for to match?" he asks me, still smiling.

"I'll let you know." I kiss him on his cheek quickly and run off before he can catch me. I'm a giddy girl on a mission. Once Finley returns from his day off, we will head out first thing in the morning.

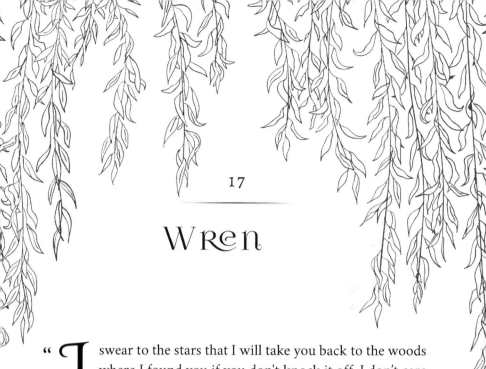

17

Wren

"I swear to the stars that I will take you back to the woods where I found you if you don't knock it off. I don't care if Amalie rips my balls off, I'll do it, and it will be worth it!" I threaten the green beast. Willow huffs out a huge breath right in my face, and I almost gag. It smells like corpses and rotten meat. Sure, the only thing Willow actually enjoys is meat, but with her growing size, fresh meat is in short supply for dragons. Willow can eat her greens, Amalie read it in her Dragon Care Manual, which is by the same ridiculous author who wrote Dragon Behavior, but she doesn't want to eat her greens. Thanks to Amalie, she has been spoiled with the best food she could find and a perfect feeding schedule that I'm botching.

Willow knows something is wrong. She's been hanging closer to the Manor than usual ever since Amalie's mother died suddenly. She fell ill a week or two before Amalie decided to leave us. I thought maybe she was lashing out from the loss, but she was gone before I could help her.

The beast uses the flat top of her snout to thump me in the chest for more food. I forgot where I was for a moment, daydreaming, I suppose. Willow is now tall enough that her head is right at my chest. Her wings are about fifteen feet from tip to tip, but she usually keeps them tucked away to resemble massive leaves covering her side and back. She doesn't have regular reptilian scales, her scales resemble salal leaves, and each individual scale looks like a leaf. For a creature so large, she still has no issue camouflaging herself in the forest.

"Fine! You nasty beast, I'll see what I can scrounge from the kitchens." I walk out of the adjacent forest towards the ivy-covered Manor, only to hear Willow stomping through the brush. I'd tell her to stay back or go to her gardens, but the thing never listens to me, only Amalie.

I approach the half door leading to the kitchens on the east side of the manor, sticking my head through the open top half and leaning my arms on the bottom. "Hey, uh Cahira, do you happen to have any leftover meat? Willow is being a brat again." I call through into the kitchen. I hear pots and pans banging around inside before Cahira comes running around the corner.

"Oh yes, I have just the thing for her. Poor creature." Cahira coos at Willow standing behind me, giving her best innocent look. Cahira is a tiny thing with fiery red hair and a face full of sun-grown freckles. Even though she is the tiniest of our staff, she is fearless with Willow.

I scoff at her comment about the poor creature. "She's a spoiled overgrown dog," I mutter back to Cahira, and I can hear her laughing as she walks off to find more meat. Looking inside the kitchen, I always find it a bit dingy with stone floors, a stone hearth, and hundreds of fresh herbs hanging from the ceiling to dry. The only thing it needs is more sunlight. I've always said it's too dark on the bottom level of the Manor.

"Oh, Wren. You don't mean that. If you did, you would have left her in the forest. I see right through you." Cahira's voice grows louder as she approaches with an enormous raw steak in her hands. She passes it to me through the split door and smiles at Willow. I roll my eyes, thank Cahira, and walk towards Willow's garden. I throw the steak far ahead of us, like a ball, and Willow chases it like a dog. I can't help but smile at the odd sight of her.

"Sir! Wren, Sir!"

I turn around in the small field to see who's calling my name so frantically.

"Sir!" Hadley stops in front of me, holding a piece of paper. I stare at Hadley. Even winded as he is, he still doesn't have a hair out of place. A young guard whom my parents insist I have in my employment. It was a compromise because I didn't necessarily need any guards. I live in the Manor house while they rule in the Chateau. Hadley came with me to the Manor for "my protection," but he's such a thin, gangly man; it's me who does the protecting if needed.

"What's this?" I ask, taking the paper from his outstretched hand, giving him a curious look before opening it.

"I was given it from Finley! He was at the Treaty Market on his rotation day. He says she's well, and she wasn't pretending, whatever that means." Hadley drew his eyebrows together, mirroring my confusion from two seconds earlier, but I am now staring at the folded paper in my hands as they begin to shake.

"Hadley, please take Willow to her garden," I mumble quietly before walking back to the manor as if in a trance. I feel drunk and unsteady. My mind goes blank, and I don't know how I ascend two large staircases to find my room, but I do. Slamming the door loudly, I unfold the letter where I stand, expecting to see Finley's chicken scratch, but it's an elegant cursive instead.

Dear Wren,

I wish I could give you the answers you seek, but I can't. I don't know them either. I can tell you what I know and remember, but

first, I want to know it's actually you. My trust is a thin line these days.
If you answer mine, I will answer any of your questions that I can remember.
Am I safe with the new recruit? And yes, he told me your plan.
I would like to see you again, but I am not sure it's possible any time soon.
I have dreams about you, you know. I remember the day you brought her home. I hope you are feeding her properly. I'm serious.
I want to end this letter with a question. Were we ever in a pavilion?

-Amalie
I've never gotten a letter from a river troll...

I slide down the door, hands shaking so hard I don't know how I might have read that letter. I can't even be angry about Finley telling her I sent him. I would do it over again one hundred times just to get this letter again.

I read it over and over. Feeling confused about her forgetting me, laughing at her scolding me about Willow, I can even feel tears threatening when she says she dreams about me. However, the last line below her name strikes the chord and plays the perfect tune; she is asking a question only I would know.

The letter I write back to her, I will sign it Oak, the name of the river troll we encountered that one day. She asked for its name, and when it couldn't provide one, she named it Oak.

18

Amalie

"Message delivered, kitten," Finley says the next morning as I emerge from my bedroom. I stare at him in confusion for a minute. It's too early to figure out his riddles until I finally understand it isn't a riddle. He's just telling me that Wren received my letter.

I sigh with relief, feeling like a weight has been lifted off my shoulders. It was almost like a lump in my chest that wouldn't disappear until I heard those words. Now I'm nervous all over again for a new reason. I'm not scared about Wren or his reaction, or even if he will understand what I am trying to convey in my letter. I'm nervous that someone will find out about the letter, specifically Asher.

I don't want to know what Asher would do. I still have difficulty believing he would be vicious to anyone, stern perhaps, but I don't see him hurting anyone. Honestly, I just don't want to end up being on my husband's bad side.

"Thank you, Finley," I say sincerely, genuinely meaning it. I know it couldn't have been an easy task, but he didn't seem to mind or hesitate in the slightest. "We are going to the city today. I need to find a dress for this celebration ball."

Finley raises an eyebrow. "Ball? I hope I don't have to be a guard that day. I don't get paid enough for that." I laugh at his exasperation. Leave it to this massive warrior of a man to hate balls. I couldn't imagine him in the ocean of people dancing and holding conversations with anyone. The image of him doing so strikes me as hysterical, making me laugh harder. I grin up at Finley to see him trying not to laugh as well. "What are you laughing at?"

"I'm just picturing you in a fancy outfit waltzing around with your big bulky boots and weapons strapped to you, it's such an odd image."

Finley smiles wider. "Sure, it would be fun if you want to see me trample everyone I try to dance with, but if there were some girls who would like to volunteer for a different kind of dance, then I am all for that!" Both of us chuckle at his joke as we leave the foyer of my rooms and head out to the coach waiting at the base of the mountain.

About half an hour later, Finley and I are walking through the city of Galeis. He seems unimpressed while I am ecstatic. There are little shops all over the place in clean and organized streets. Modern-looking shops with glass windows display chocolates, clothing, furniture, and toys. You name it, they have it. Street after street of various shops continues for an immeasurable distance.

Finley sticks out like a sore thumb in this setting of pristine streets and pedestrians. Yes, he wears a typically regulated uniform in its crisp, clean appearance, but the rest of him just doesn't quite fit. His sheer size is insanely tall, with a barrel chest that has partially tressed hair. His skin tone doesn't even match those around us. Where everyone in the Air Kingdom has been ghostly pale that I've noticed, Finley has a dark tan coloring. I love his uniqueness. Though I suppose in the Earth Kingdom, he might not be as unique. I remember Wren with his dark hair and vibrant green eyes, he has an olive complexion, so

I'm assuming a higher degree of diversity exists in that kingdom.

I spot a shop with some of the most beautiful gowns I've ever seen displayed in the window. It may be the only place in this whole city, in the entire kingdom, with a splash of color. In the shop window, there are about five dresses in different colors: purple, green, blue, yellow, and pink. They also have varying cuts and styles; long train, knee-length, off-the-shoulder ball gown, and mermaid cuts. I love every single one of them.

Pulling Finley's arm, I guide him into the shop. He allows me but lets out a loud groan of displeasure, yet I can't tell how genuine it really is.

The shop owner is jumping in front of me before I even get Finley through the door, "Hello, Miss! What are you looking for? I have almost every style and color you could imagine!" Her enthusiastic demeanor is infectious, and I grin widely at her.

"Honestly, I'm not sure. I am attending a celebration ball at the palace tomorrow, and I need a worthy gown. It is to celebrate my marriage to Prince Asher."

The kind woman's eyes widened in shock. "Oh, dear! You must be Amalie! Oh, it is so nice to meet you! Anything you want, I will put it on the kingdom's bill. Don't you worry, we will get you started right away." She eyes Finley with a look of intrigue, but he stands stone cold by the door, making sure nobody comes in or out. I suppose this shop is officially closed until I am ready to leave because it doesn't look like Finley is planning on moving from the doorway anytime soon. He gives me a nod, and I turn towards the woman to start my search.

She sashays as she moves about, swinging her curvy hips in a seductive gesture, and I honestly think it's all for Finley. The way she scanned him up and down, and then how he returned that look, I'm sure they will have a little rendezvous later. I look her up and down as she leads me towards the back of her shop.

She has long, sleek straight sapphire blue hair. She's a fae, I can tell by her pointed ears and skin tone, which is a bit darker, leading me to believe she isn't from the Air Kingdom. Is it rude to ask where they came from? Is it the fae equivalent to asking a woman's age?

She has soft blue eyes that remind me of a lapis lazuli stone, its blue with tiny flecks of brown woven into her iris. She has a smooth face that radiates kindness, and after my examination, I decide I like her.

"What's your name?" I ask curiously, loud enough for Finley to hear.

She looks back at me and smiles. "Seren, my lady." The manner in which Seren says my lady sounds like she's not quite sure what to call me. I'm almost positive she isn't from Galeis or any part of this kingdom. Everyone here seems to be trained in proper etiquette, so it almost becomes second nature. Where everyone is stoic, formal, and devoid of color. Seren is peppy, unrestrained, and full of color, which is reflected throughout her shop. It's the only shop I've seen while walking the streets of Galeis that actually has any colors besides white, grey, or black in its windows.

"Seren, please call me Amalie. I'm not from the Air Kingdom, so formalities make me uncomfortable. If that's all right with you," I say primarily for her benefit. I can tell how awkward her demeanor is around me, and I want her to feel more comfortable.

"I was born in the Water Kingdom. We don't dwell on titles or formalities, either. Everyone in my kingdom is seen as an equal," Seren explains to me, and I'm somewhat shocked by their customs. Their way of life sounds amazing. I can see why Seren is so open and friendly. A bit more of her makes sense now.

"Do you not have Kings and Queens?" I ask, genuinely curious.

"Oh, we do! But they don't live in a huge palace or roll around in large carriages. They listen to the people and put themselves on the same level." She realizes her implications and immediately seems panicked. Looking from me to Finley, she sputters with wide eyes, "I'm sorry! I didn't mean anything by it. I know you're a part of the monarchy now, and I didn't mean that you were prudish like them." Then her eyes grow even wider, putting her hand over her mouth in shock and distress. "Oh stars! I don't mean that Prince Asher is prudish, either. Stars! I only meant that it's a different custom and that -"

I cut her off by raising my hand before she has a stroke right there on the floor. I can't help it. I start laughing at her so hard my eyes water. "Stars, Seren! It's alright! I don't take offense at all. Don't worry about Finley. He cares less about the monarch than anyone here, I would bet." I notice my slip-up on Finley's true role, though I don't necessarily care. The look of relief on her face is unmistakable. I notice she has tiny freckles blanketing her nose that stand out more when she blushes brighter.

"Thank you, Amalie." She gives me a small smile as I reign in my laughter. I look at Finley, who has a big grin on his face. Seren continues, "I tend to ramble when I'm nervous. It's a bad habit then I end up getting myself in more trouble. My grandmother would always give me a smack when I wouldn't stop talking." She chuckles to herself at the memory, and my heart swells for her. I am dubbing her my friend, and I don't care if she wants to be or not.

"Why did you leave the Water Kingdom, if you don't mind my asking?"

Seren's smile drops, and her gaze falls to the floor. "I-uh, that's a story for another time, miss."

I note her embarrassment and try to apologize for my boldness. "I'm sorry, I didn't mean to pry. I'm just interested in learning about the other kingdoms."

"It's alright, I will tell you all about the water!" Her pleasant mood returns like the ocean tides after a storm. "We have water giants instead of ghouls. Our giants are huge! Well, they are giants, so that's to be expected, but they aren't mean. They form the bridges between the islands. When people need to travel between the seven islands, the giants lay in the water, and you wouldn't even know they are living creatures! They are made of hard river stones and the vibrant coloring of moss. I wish you could see them. I promise they are simply amazing."

I give her a wide smile as I move to a blush pink velvet chaise, urging her to continue.

Seren sits down on the other side of the chaise and turns to face me. She crosses her legs as she reminisces about her past life, and we sit together like lifelong friends. That's when I come to terms that maybe Seren and I could perhaps be great friends. Both of us have a past that we've left behind, and both of us are trying to move forward the best we can.

"The Water Kingdom is made up of seven islands, as I mentioned. Each island helps provide for everyone in some way. It may appear to be divided, but really, we work together and make a peaceful home. *They* work together. Not *we*, I suppose." She gives me a sad smile again.

"What did your island provide?" I ask, distracting her again.

"Well, my island worked with seaweed harvesting. Did you know that you can make so many things from seaweed! That's how I became a dressmaker. Seaweed was harvested, and we crafted a type of fabric with it."

I'm impressed with the ingenious idea of turning seaweed into fabrics and Seren making beautiful clothing from it. The more I learn from her, the more excited I am to have met her.

I glance up to see Finley leaning against the door, eyes closed like he is taking a standing nap, and I giggle.

"Let's look for dresses, shall we?"

It only takes about an hour to find the perfect dress. It's an A-line emerald green color with a lacey vine overlay on the bodice that cascades down the hip and onto the skirt of the dress. The top is set in a deep heart-shaped neckline with a dual one-shoulder strap set in emerald lace vines that match the bodice. One side of the strap rests at the top of my shoulder right by my clavicle and splits at the shoulder joint to wrap around the base of my shoulder, giving it an off-the-shoulder look.

It is simply gorgeous, and I *feel* gorgeous. I find I have a bit more spring in my step when I twirl around the shop. Seren is grinning from ear to ear and jumping up and down to show her excitement. I look at Finley, who about five minutes ago looked like he was ready for a nap, and even he has pulled himself together to grant me a crooked grin.

"If there wasn't history between you and Wren, I think I would fall in love with you right now," Finley says with a dead-serious tone. Seren turns to look at him with wide eyes, and I can't tell if she's shocked by his statement or upset about it. I suppose it can be confusing for her, but I ignore it, not letting her think too deeply about his comments.

"I think Asher is going to love it! It matches our theme perfectly!" I squeal excitedly.

"I think Wren is going to love it…" Finley mutters under his breath. I sigh and roll my eyes, ignoring him again. Turning to Seren, I ask, "Sooo… What are you wearing?"

She looks down at herself. "Well, right now, I'm wearing a pink blush top with a navy-blue skirt…" She stares at me in bewilderment, and I chuckle at her again.

"I mean to the ball. There is no way you can pick out a dress like this and not come to the celebration."

"I-You-What?" she stutters out, trying to form a cohesive

thought. She clears her throat and tries again. "I'm not royalty or important enough to attend." Her voice is almost a whisper, like my invitation should be a secret.

"You're important to me, and that's more than enough. I understand we don't necessarily know each other well. However, I would love to get to know you more. You're a lot of fun to be around, and I would love to have you there," I insist, hoping she will accept. When she finally does, I jump for joy again. Both of us are squealing while Finley mirrors a crooked smile as he stares at Seren.

I decide to stay with Seren for a couple of hours more, her whole aura is so infectious, and I'm genuinely sad when it comes time to leave finally.

Walking down the streets again towards our carriage that we left with the horsemen in the center of the city, I peer up at Finley. "You liked her, too." It's not a question, he knows it's not, and he knows I mean more than what I'm saying.

Finley looks down at me and gives me a dreamy look when he thinks back to Seren. "Yeah, I liked her."

19

Amalie

I am so excited about the ball tonight that I barely slept the night before. I notified Asher about Seren attending the ceremony as my guest and, thankfully, he was more than agreeable about it. He informed the guard she is allowed to pass and be escorted to my rooms once she makes her arrival. This is where we all are now; Semira, Seren and myself. We are all sitting in the foyer with our servants, who are curling, braiding, straightening, brushing, and primping our hair before moving on to a few cosmetics to enhance our features.

Semira has decided to have her hair straight for the evening, her long sleek blonde hair hanging down to the middle of her back.

Seren has asked for a braided updo, which naturally elongates her neck, along with a perfect choice of a choker-style necklace. I haven't seen her dress yet, but I'm sure it's stunning.

I made the decision to keep my chestnut hair down, curling it and putting a leaf-shaped pin on one side to hold it out of my face while keeping the other side free and flowing. My hair is so long now that it rests just above the small of my back. I stare at my reflection in the mirror, and I'm almost astonished at the mere image of myself. I haven't gazed into a mirror in what feels like a lifetime. Probably since my wedding, which I don't remember.

Bright coal-lined amber eyes stare back at me, a small nose dotted with faint freckles and lush pink rose-colored lips, a stark contrast with my dark chestnut curled hair; I don't quite feel like myself. I feel beautiful and confident but also uncertain, like I'm staring at a beautiful stranger.

Semira approaches behind me, carrying my green dress in her hands.

"Ready?"

I nod at her, feeling anxious for the night to come. I don't want all the attention on me, although I am very excited to dance and laugh with friends. However, I am most excited to see Asher all dressed up.

Finley escorts us to the main ballroom. I can't tell if he is happy or disappointed about not working the event tonight. Unfortunately, guards are not allowed to be royal guests; therefore, he can only attend up until the entrance. His eyes keep catching Seren, a slight grin on his face.

She looks exquisite with her sapphire hair and bright blue eyes; she's wearing a long red dress that hugs her every curve and accentuates the sway of her hips. Of course, Finley insisted we walk ahead of him for safety reasons, but he refused to elaborate further. I think he just wanted to watch Seren sway her hips because he didn't guard anything except her ass. I roll my eyes at the thought, as a small smile forms on my lips.

I glance back at him a few times, but he is so focused on that one aspect of her that a tornado could have blown through, and he wouldn't have even noticed.

I take a deep breath before turning the corner and walking into the main foyer. Asher stands there with his back to me, talking to an older man with greying hair in a lavish navy-blue long overcoat and black slacks. I quietly approach him, not wanting to interrupt, but I also don't want to stand there awkwardly waiting. I take the final step and gently place my hand in the bend of his arm. He turns to me with surprise in his eyes, which grows even wider when he takes a better look at me.

"Excuse me." He politely bows to the man, putting his hand on mine and leading me to a private corner of the room. "I, uh, wow. You are simply breathtaking, just like the day we met. I couldn't take my eyes off of you then, and I don't think I will be able to tonight, either."

I give him a large smile, taking in his figure for the first time tonight. His long overcoat coat with slacks and green shirt underneath match my dress. The overall outfit isn't spectacular, it's the man in the outfit that makes it special. I've never seen him in anything except white or grey. "You look pretty good yourself." I wrap my arms around his neck and give him a chaste kiss on the cheek.

"My wife, my queen," he murmurs into my neck, and I have to force myself to stay in this moment with him. I try to empathize with his side of our situation. Of course, he must be missing his wife as he once knew her, but I'm not the same person he once knew. I'm not sure if I ever will be. My heart beats faster when he's this close; he is the lighthouse that guides me to shore.

I place my hand on his chest, giving him a slight push to break the moment. "We have guests. Should we begin the celebration?"

The dreamy, lustful look in his ocean blue eyes slowly begins to slip away. "I'm really starting to regret having this celebration. I don't think I would like others' eyes on you."

My face flushes crimson. I can feel the heat running up my face and a tingle in my ears from nervousness.

He takes in my flush and smirks a cocky grin, nodding in my

direction. Asher grips my hand again, leading me through the large double doors that enter the main ballroom.

As much as I don't like Kirah, damn, she does do a good job. Everything is perfectly decorated to resemble an enchanted garden. Flowers, vines, trees, cast iron benches, and twinkling lights line every available space. In the center is a beautiful large wooden pergola over the dance space. Glancing to my right, I see a long table full of finger food and desserts, my mouth waters at the sight. Hypnotizing melodies intertwine throughout the room, and my body sways involuntarily.

"What do you think?" Asher asks me at my side, not even looking around the room as his eyes wander over my face. He's watching my expression intensely.

My eyes start to water and spill over with tears. I lift my hand to his smooth cheek, staring at his face while trying to obtain my voice again.

"I... I love it. It's everything. It feels like home." The tears come a bit faster. Asher gives me sad eyes, wiping my tears away with his thumb. "Thank you, Asher." I genuinely mean it because I know deep down that this is home. I may not remember being born in the Earth Kingdom, but it's still a part of me that I can feel in my soul. Whenever I see a leaf, a plant, or a flower, I feel a fluttering inside me. For Asher to create the perfect scenery of his rival kingdom right inside his own palace speaks volumes. I know it won't please everyone, but he made the decision to forgo others for my sake. The thought warms me to him.

Once I pull my emotions back and my tears finally dry, he takes my arm and hooks it around his elbow again. "Let's go dance." I giggle my agreement and excitement as he leads me to the dancefloor under the pergola. I can almost imagine a small dragon sleeping in the corner of the pergola, cuddled in so tightly to herself that she resembles a leaf.

As he spins me on the dancefloor, my mind starts to wander, and I realize I don't even know where Semira and Seren are. Did Semira find Alizar? Is Alizar even attending? I'm so lost in my thoughts that I am startled when Queen Everleigh interrupts our dance, "We need to talk, now. Both of you." Her voice is hard and stern, full of authority as she stomps towards a room I never noticed before. I glance at Asher with worried eyes. I can feel my nerves tighten, anticipating the wrath of the Queen.

Asher nods and follows her through the crowd to a small door far off to the side of the pergola. Inside is a dark wood and leather office that gives a very modern and masculine feel. It is the opposite of the entire white and grey palace it's housed in, and I wonder whom it belongs to. Queen Everleigh signals for us to sit down in the chairs by the large window while she stands over us like a mother scolding her children.

"How dare you." Her voice is so low it's frightening, like the calm before the storm or the eye of a hurricane. I am waiting for the winds to pick up and the storm to take hold of us.

"What are you talking about, mother?" Asher asks in a calm demeanor, one to rival Everleigh. I'm wondering why I'm here in the middle of this, but I don't dare say a word for fear of drawing attention to myself.

"You will address me as your Queen for this conversation. This is a matter of the courts, not of the family." She stares down at Asher until he nods. "The theme of tonight is revolting. I understand she is from the dirt of the forest, but did you need to bring that dirt to our kingdom? I was under the impression she would be washed before you brought her into our lives. Now she has soiled you, too."

The shock of her words hit me so hard that I don't even know where to begin to defend myself. I understand that the kingdoms are rivals, I anticipated that she wouldn't be pleased, but I didn't think the hatred ran this deep. My hands begin to shake at her aggression.

Is she insinuating my mind needed to be washed? Is that why I lost my memories?

Asher stands up so fast it startles me. I forgot how graceful and quick the Fae could be; they always seem so human until they lose control.

"I understand perfectly well who you are, but you will respect your future Queen. You may be the Queen now, but you're on your way out." I stare wide-eyed back and forth between Queen Everleigh and her son. I've never seen Asher get this heated. I don't even think he was even this mad when he saw Wren. "This is a celebration of us, Amalie and me. What better way than to have her culture displayed in the middle of mine?"

Everleigh's face is turning redder and redder with each word Asher says. I suppose realizing she can't do much except abruptly end the ball would cause more of a scene and speculation that she wouldn't want.

"I certainly hope you are smarter than this when you become King." She glances down at me from the bridge of her nose. "And you will do well to remember, you're only here to give him an heir. You are nothing more than a birthing cow."

Tears are in my eyes and threaten to spill over, but I stand up, grow a backbone, and say, "Really, is that advice coming from experience? I certainly know a cow when I see one." And I walk out of the gloomy office before she gets a chance to recover and comment back.

I need a minute alone to gather myself. My hands are shaking uncontrollably, and I feel like I am going to have an anxiety attack at any moment. I keep my legs moving through the crowds of people and out to the terrace connected to the ballroom. I sit down on the iron bench furthest away from the ballroom. I'm surrounded by plants, creeping vines, twinkling lights, and the stars shining above. Asher lowers himself to the bench beside me, taking a deep breath and letting it go. He puts his arm around my shoulders so I can turn and put my face into his chest. Finally, the tears start to fall for the second time within as many hours but for two very different reasons.

20

Amalie

"I'm sorry I called your mother a cow." I sniffle into his chest, leaving a disgusting wet mark on the front of his shirt. Asher laughs loudly at that as I look up at him in surprise. I thought he would be more upset with either his mother or me.

"I'm not. She deserved it. The look on her face was priceless." He gives me a sad look, taking my chin between his thumb and forefinger. "I'm sorry," he says it so effortlessly, but it means everything. The two words are giving me strength. He stood up to his parents for me. He defied the rules of his kingdom to allow me a night of happiness, and I know I could love him for that alone. The thought stops my reflection in their tracks.

I'm falling for Asher.

I may not be in love with him yet, but I do love him in my own uncanny way. He's become important to me.

While we wait for my tears to dry, we both lean back and stare at the stars. "What are you thinking about? Wishing on the stars above?" Asher smiles knowingly.

"I wish on the stars for an air sprite to jump down from the clouds and perform a ballet act in nothing but its birthday suit."

Asher laughs softly beside me. "Why are you wishing for that?"

"I figured if I wish for funny and unreasonable things, all my real wishes won't seem so impossible."

"What do you truly wish for?" His expression turns grave. I can feel his gaze on me as I keep my eyes focused on the sky. As I turn towards him, I see that he's genuinely curious about my response.

"I wish I had all my memories to start with." Asher just gives me an understanding smile before turning back to the stars.

"I wish for a massive and terrifying ghoul to go to the salon for a makeover. Complete with cosmetics and an elegant gown, just like yours." I couldn't hold back my laughter at the thought of this grotesque half skeletal creature getting pampered to look pretty for a ball.

Asher and I continue our silly game, trying to one-up each other after every round. I started wishing for a dragon on ice skates while he wished for a water giant in scandalous swimwear. By the end of our little game, I learn that even though I'm more creative, Asher's serious tone makes everything that much funnier.

"Are you ready to go back inside?"

I nod, taking a deep breath and standing. Asher waits for me to stand with his hand extended. I reach for it, and together we head back into the ballroom.

I spy Seren by the food table, stuffing her face with pastries. I sneak up behind her, giggling.

"Busted." She jumps and drops her pastry on the floor, scowling at me before kicking it under the table. She glances at the prince over my shoulder, eyes widening and cheeks flushing, and she bows.

"Sir! Stars, I am so sorry! I will pick it up." She begins to get to her knees to crawl under the table, but I lift her back up under her arm.

"Seren, it's fine. No formalities tonight."

Asher gives her an amused chuckle and kisses my cheek affectionately. "I have to go speak with someone, I will be right back."

I watch as Asher leaves, a bright smile still on his face, weaving his body through the crowd of people huddling in groups and twirling under the pergola. I turn back to Seren, and she is giving me one of the biggest knowing smiles I've ever seen.

"What?"

"Oh nothing… You and Prince Asher seem cozy tonight." Seren just couldn't help herself. She started off trying to be smooth but couldn't wait to point it out. I've never really confided in her about our odd relationship, so she only knows the minor details of our story. Still, even she can see that tonight is a good night for us.

"I hear a certain guard of mine is off duty tonight…" I counter smugly while the light in her eyes brightens.

"If I go missing for the night, don't come looking for me." She wiggles her eyebrows in excitement, but then her face suddenly goes serious and stern. "Unless I don't show up tomorrow morning. Then please come looking for me, he is a bit terrifying, and I might end up dead. And I told you not to come for me so nobody would know I'm dead. My body would never be found, and you would have to spend the rest of your life wondering what happened to me while Finley lives his life in peace being a murderer, and nobody would even know." Seren takes a deep breath and continues, "So… you know. Just wait a bit before you come looking for me." She nods, proud of herself, and gives me a happy smile.

I just shake my head and laugh even harder. "Seren, you're fine. A little bird told me that Finley is quite smitten with you. He's a good guy, and I trust him. He has that familiar feeling about him." Seren places her hand on my arm and squeezes it before running off to search for Finley.

I glance around, staring at the guests dancing and enjoying the company of their loved ones. I see couples in shadows and corners in passionate embraces, kissing behind the greenery.

I don't see Asher approaching until he steps right in front of me, startling me out of my reverence for these lovers.

"I brought you some wine. We can probably get in a couple more dances before calling it a night." I take the glass of wine from him, giving it a sniff before taking a sip. It's a sweet wine that soothes my fluttering stomach and warms me from head to toe.

"People of the Air, I would like to thank you all for attending the celebration of the union between Prince Asher of the Air Kingdom and Amalie of the Earth Kingdom. Please raise your glass as a symbol of good fortune and a prosperous future." His voice carries on the wind, creating a perfect announcement.

Wouldn't that be a boring air trait, I think, before turning to Asher with a curious look.

"I assumed you did not want each of us to make a public speech, which is usually done at these ceremonies. I asked Carron to make a short and sweet announcement instead." I snake my arm around Asher's neck and give him a full kiss on the lips that he deepens with a moan in the back of his throat.

"Thank you."

He smiles at me and leads me back to the dancefloor, placing our glasses on a nearby table as we move.

We dance and dance until the crowd starts to thin, and the night grows late. The whole time Asher is twirling and waltzing me around the floor under the twinkling lights on the pergola, laughing and making silly faces at one another.

My mind wanders again; I want to *feel* like I have a husband, not just believe it because I am told so. Asher has been so kind and patient with me. Perhaps if we act as a husband and wife should, maybe it will start feeling true.

"Asher, I think I'm ready to leave now," I say in a low voice, still not entirely sure about my decision, my brain arguing with itself.

One part of me thinks that I owe him for his kindness and patience. The other part of me is telling me to take it slow and not rush anything. I have so many emotions tonight that I don't allow my mind to overrule the latter part of myself. I am ready to play with the hurricane tonight.

Asher takes my hand and leads me through the long hallways to my rooms, strolling and taking our time. We don't speak, but we can't help but stare at each other every couple of steps we take. His thumb rubs soothing circles on the back of my hand, and unbeknownst to him, he is solidifying my decision further. I can feel his love, power, and compassion radiating from him.

We enter the foyer of my room. There aren't any guards with us tonight, and I don't hear Semira or Alizar in the next room. Approaching my bedroom door, Asher gives me a long, languid kiss, moving his hand up to caress my cheek while I move closer to him and press my body even closer against his.

Asher breaks off with a gasp and takes a step back, leaving us both breathing hard. "I, uh, I should go." I can tell he's fighting with himself. Battling with what he wants to do and what he should do. Asher is still trying to give me the time and space I need, but I don't need it anymore. I am ready to move forward with *us*.

"What if you didn't leave?" I give him a nervous look, taking a step toward him.

Asher takes a deep breath and stares up at the tall foyer ceiling. When he finally looks back at me, I see his walls starting to crumble as I take his hand.

"No expectations," he says softly as I lead him into my room.

"No expectations," I repeat.

21

WREN

It's been three days since I received her letter. Three days I've been visiting the Treaty Market. Three days I've been waiting for hours while the regulars and vendors stare at me. I make the excuse that I am buying fresh meat for Willow, but there are only so many days in a row before people start thinking I actually like the thing. Which I don't, by the way.

I have officially banned Hadley from the market because people might start recognizing him. He's pretty pissed about it, but he will get over it. I keep bringing him daggers, treats and even tried a living bird once, but he can't be bribed. I don't know if he's mad that I went to the market without him or if it's because he isn't allowed to go there anymore. Either way, I tried. Now the kid needs to get over it.

By the time the sun sets on day four, I am ready to walk straight into the Air Kingdom and kick some Asher ass. I would, too, if he wasn't such an Ash-hole and invited me into the kingdom, but he's too afraid Amalie will come to her senses.

My grim demeanor is killing all the flora as I walk along the path back to the Earth Kingdom, the flowers and leaves shrivel and die after my every step.

"Wren!"

I turn around at the sound of my voice, seeing Finley running down the path towards me. He looks like he just rolled out of the sack after a fun night, his long hair is standing up all over the place, and his military uniform is half untucked. We are standing eye to eye in the forest just outside the border of my kingdom. I give him a pissed-off look. "Oohh, how nice of you to finally show up."

"It's been a busy couple of days."

Finley seems like he's holding something back; he never hides anything from me. The hair on the back of my neck rises as fear and anxiety grips me. "What happened?" I say in the calmest voice I can muster. If I come on too strong, Finley might not want to tell me even more. My blood is boiling the longer he stands there, and I am two seconds away from making a Fin-kabob.

"Wren, man… She's happy." Finley looks down like her being happy is a bad thing. I suppose selfishly it is. Deep down, I wanted her to be miserable so she would come back home.

Maybe she really did choose Asher in the end.

Maybe she really did change her mind about meeting him. Did she run back and marry him? Did she even run in the first place? There are still so many unanswered questions that make my head spin.

"Right, well. Good for her." My false bravado isn't fooling anyone here, not even me. I feel torn apart inside, but I guess I got one answer at least. She chose him. "I don't have a letter for her. Just tell her one thing."

Finley looks at me with sad eyes. "Yeah, anything."

"Oak."

I find myself sitting in Willow's garden; she's sleeping soundly beside me, her large head is crushing my leg. She's curled so perfectly around me that I can lean back on her while she leans on me. Right now, Willow is my last tie to Amalie, and I don't think I'm ready to let her go.

I stare up at the stars debating on what to do. I pull the letter I was going to give Finley out of my jacket pocket, taking each side in my fingers and ripping the paper repeatedly. It doesn't matter what I wrote anymore; the only thing I need to focus on is moving forward. But how do I move forward when there's nothing worth going forward for. I don't want to be King; I never have. If Amalie had wanted me to be King, I would, but I never thought she was the type to want that. It seems I was wrong about that too. Willow misses her terribly. I could let her go, but a dragon won't be welcome in the Air Kingdom. They prefer their nasty precious ghouls.

I hear soft footsteps enter the garden, the iron gate groaning as it's being pushed closed. I roll my head to the side to see a short little Cahira bouncing in with a large piece of beef in her hands.

"Oh! Wren, I didn't think you would be out here with the beast." She gives me a small smile. I can tell she sees my somber expression. She's trying to make me feel better, but I'm a stubborn bastard. I raise one eyebrow at her and look back towards the night sky. "Hey, what's going on, Wren? This isn't like you." She sits beside me, curling herself around Willow, who is starting to stir now that she can smell the meat.

Willow comes to life a second later, dropping me on my back. I don't bother to move; it's a better angle to watch the stars from, I guess.

"She's not coming back. She's happy."

"Amalie?" I give her a look that says duh, but Cahira just chuckles at me. "Oh, you're so dense sometimes, Wren. She may be happy at the moment, but those moments pass."

Cahira thinks she's this great philosopher, but in reality, she's just saying things that are obvious. Clearly, a moment will pass, that's why it's called a moment.

"Wren... She was safe here. She had a purpose. She had love. If what you say is true and she doesn't have any idea she had all this, she will spend the rest of her life looking for it. She won't be content, not for long anyway. The Amalie, I know, likes to have a choice. Give her time to make it." I don't allow the seed of hope to grow in my chest. I destroy it like the rest of the earth around me. The only thing I will leave untouched is Willow's garden. She's innocent, even if she is a little brat of a beast.

Sitting up, I look over at said beast, but she's enjoying her beef snack that Cahira brought her.

"It's time to move on and move forward. I owe her that much; I promised her that much." Cahira nods in understanding. "Come on, let's head back to the Chateau. You'll be really tired tomorrow when you make me a cake if you stay up too late." I give her a cocky grin that I know always gets on her nerves.

"Oh, and why, pray tell, would I bake you a cake?" She stands up, folding her arms and cocking her eyebrow.

"Because I'm heartbroken! The best remedy is cake. Everyone knows that!" I smirk, one corner of my mouth lifting in a smile. Cahira smacks my arm, and I burst out laughing at her.

"Fine. I'll make a cake tomorrow only because I got you to laugh. It's a reward for me. You have to share, though!" I laugh harder at her as she joins in on my amusement.

Great, well, the best thing about today is I get to look forward to stuffing my face in the morning.

22

Amalie

Asher and I lounge on my sofa facing the terrace while staring at the shining stars. I am curled up on one end with Asher's head lying on my lap. There's a calming and natural feeling between us tonight. Relaxing as a husband and wife should. I run my fingers through his blonde hair, breaking down his pristine image and revealing the true Asher underneath.

It's my turn to ask a question. Without looking at him, I ask, "What's your favorite memory from when you were a child?"

"Hmm..."

I look down at him, and our eyes meet, "This shouldn't be a hard question." I try to joke with him, but it falls flat as he sits up to lean against the back of the couch. His eyes drift to the twinkling lights of the city as they meet the stars on the horizon.

"When I was six, I accidentally poisoned myself."

"Wait- what?" The statement shocks me, that is his favorite memory? "How is that a happy memory?"

"You asked for my favorite memory, not my happiest one. Nonetheless, it was my favorite because it was the one and only time my parents came together. They genuinely never left my side until the palace physician cleared me." The energy in the room turns cold. I inch closer to him and grip his hand tightly, trying to give him strength and support through our physical touch.

"How did you accidentally poison yourself?" I ask.

"There were these weird little mushrooms with purple stripes on them. I saw the staff cooking with mushrooms and decided to eat them."

I think back to the forest and remember the warning not to eat those mushrooms. I'm sad for this man. He never had someone teach him something as simple as avoiding mushrooms. His favorite memory is when he was sick, simply because his parents were with him. My heart pangs with sympathy.

It's Asher's turn to ask a question, and his whole mood brightens again as he does, and we are back to our comfortable leisure. "If you could do anything, what would it be?"

"Oh, this is easy. I would travel to all the kingdoms. I want to see how every culture lives their lives. I want to meet everyone and see how they live and what they deem worthy. The only way to learn is to educate yourself through someone else's eyes." My voice trails off as I think about my desire, realizing that perhaps that won't happen if I am meant to stay in the Air Kingdom. And I am not sure where my feelings lie on that matter.

Before he can reply, I ask my question, not looking at him. "What do you want most in your life?" I'm expecting him to be sweet or funny. I expect him to say something like, *I only want you. Or the crown.* Instead, I get an answer that I don't know how to reply to.

"Acceptance. The thing I would want most is to be accepted and know that I am good enough."

"I have something for you, if you will accept it." Asher and I lay together, my head resting on his chest. We stayed up most of the night talking, laughing, and getting to know each other.

Asher didn't push for more, and I didn't offer.

His words make my head rise, and I peer up at him with a soft grin. He opens his hand, revealing a beautiful white gold and opal ring. I stare at it in shock. Even in the darkness of night, it still sparkles like the stone is forged in magic. The circular opal in the center is white and iridescent, with three small diamond brackets on each side of the beautiful stone. The ring is simply elegant and airy. It is perfect coming from the future King of the Air Kingdom.

"Asher, it's beautiful," I finally say when my brain and mouth decide to work together.

"I was hoping we could have a private bonding, then have the formal ceremony together. If you choose to accept this ring, we will be bound as husband and wife. You will have a small source of my magic, so you will always be safe. If you're in distress, I will feel it and come to your aid. It's not a normal ring. It's a symbol of us, of our bond. Will you accept it? Will you accept us?" Asher holds the ring out to me, allowing me to decide our fate. My eyes start to water as I think about how he's giving me a choice. It feels like the easiest and most important decision I've ever had to make.

"Yes, of course!"

As he slides the ring on my marriage finger, I feel a push and pull within my heart, a small game of tug-of-war in my chest. Not only can I see the adoration on his face, but I *feel* it inside me. I look down at my finger, glistening with my ring, and it looks like it's meant to be there as if it's the missing piece to this puzzle. I lean back down, resting my head on his chest again and staring at my ring. My eyes start to close when I hear Asher's whisper in my ear.

"I love you, Amalie." He kisses my hair, running his fingers up and down my spine in soft rhythmic movements. I fall asleep soon after, listening to the beautiful heartbeat of my husband.

I wake up groggy and confused. It takes me a moment to gain my memory and focus on the room around me. Asher isn't beside me, and it is cold where he once was, so he must have left a while ago. I glance at the sun shining through my bedroom terrace. The late morning breeze caresses my cheek, causing the hair on my arms to rise. I can't help but smile as I turn my face into my soft pillow, giving it a tight squeeze.

Semira must be magic because she came waltzing into my room moments later with fresh fruit.

"You're a star sent, Semira. Thank you," I tell her sleepily.

I slide out of bed and scurry like a scared rabbit to the partial wardrobe fold in the far corner next to the bathroom.

I hear Semira call from my bed, "So, you seem to be settling in…" I hear the note of hesitation in her voice. She seems reluctant to speak, which puts me on edge. Remaining silent, I will her to continue. "Are you happy?"

"I-I am." Suddenly, I realize that it isn't a lie. Asher has been everything that I have needed. He stood up for me against his mother, he's given me time and space, and he even allowed me to decorate the ball to make me feel at home. I just never gathered how quickly Asher had become my home. "I didn't expect to love him. It's weird not remembering someone but feeling this close to them. I'm happy here." I slide on my shift quickly and peer out at Semira from around the folding divider. She's staring down at her hands nervously. I walk over and sit on the bed with her, turning my body to give her my undivided attention. "Semira, what's wrong?"

"I have to go home, Amalie. Alizar isn't happy here, and I promised I would only stay while you still needed me." She shrugs sadly. "You don't need me anymore."

"I will always need you." Semira looks at me with the saddest expression I've ever seen from her. Her eyes are starting to fill, threatening to spill over. "Do you think Alizar could ever be happy here?"

She sighs, looking as defeated as I feel. All my good feeling bliss has been thrown right off this mountain. "Amalie, they have a past. You already know that Asher and Alizar don't see eye to eye. I don't think they ever will. Listen, I'm glad you're happy. I really am. But it's time for Alizar and me to be happy too."

I think this over for a couple of seconds; Semira does deserve to be happy, Alizar too-but I hate the idea of her not being here. She was the first person to bring me comfort and friendship. She was my rock through all this. She helped me and guided me through everything. As much as it hurts, letting her be happy in her own kingdom is the right thing to do. So, I let her go.

"When will you be leaving?" My voice is small. I can't fake enthusiasm for her, not after I was so upset earlier.

"Tomorrow morning, I already spoke with Alizar. He's more than ready to go home."

I nod again, taking her hands in mine. "Just because you're leaving doesn't mean you will be gone forever. I will come to see you off in the morning. This isn't a goodbye, it's a … I'll see you later!" I give her a smile, swearing to stick to my promise. Who knows, visiting Alizar and Semira someday could be an adventure.

23

Amalie

Finley is leading me back to my room after my private dinner with Asher. He said he would join me tomorrow morning because he has some sort of ceremony preparations. He's been so focused on the bonding ceremony lately, while selfishly, I'm just happy to finally have Asher's ring on my finger. I don't think of myself as materialistic, but the ring symbolizes everything I've been told to be true. As difficult as it has been to believe my situation, the physical reminder of the ring on my finger solidifies my future, my chosen future.

I told Asher about Semira and Alizar leaving in the morning, and he seemed pretty upset as well. Maybe the bad blood is only one-sided between Alizar and Asher. Asher has welcomed Alizar into his home. He invited him to live here while I was recovering, so I just don't fully understand the hatred there.

"So," I stare up at Finley with a big bright smile. "How did last night go?" Finley gives me a confused look. I don't know if he is playing dumb or truly confused. "Uh, Seren…." I coax.

"Ah, right. Yes." He gives me a smug grin so wide it looks like it's got to hurt.

"That's it? Really? Finley, you need to give me more than that!"

"Oh no, Kitten. I don't kiss and tell." I squeal at his admission, so happy for my friends.

I walk through the hall picturing their wedding day. Tiny little Seren in a gorgeous gown with massive warrior Finley, his hair pulled back, waiting for her at the altar. I describe the scene to Finley, but he rolls his eyes and laughs.

Is that a blush I see?

When I enter my room to change into my night shift, I notice a letter sitting on my bed. I walk over to it, sitting down on the side of the bed. My feet dangle over the side as I open the letter and read.

Amalie,

I'm sorry to be the one who will write a letter and run. However, I couldn't tell you this and then face you in the morning. I know it's the coward's way out, and I am so sorry.
Amalie, please understand I did it to help you, and I had no idea it would go this wrong. It's my fault you lost your memories. It's my fault you're in this situation. I only wanted to help you.
I understand if you don't keep my secret, but I hope you do.
I'm a Caster. I can't stay here. I'd be dead if anyone in the four Kingdoms ever found out.
I know you don't remember, but Casters are not welcome. We are seen as nothing more than a menace. I am a fae without specific elemental magic. I don't have fae features because I am not claimed by a kingdom.
I tried to cast a memory spell on you, so it would be easier for you to forget Wren, but something went wrong, and you lost everything.
I'm so sorry!
It's not possible to remove a memory spell. You can only gain back

the memories from the Caster's death or by making your own new ones. I hope you can understand. I thought it would be easier for you to live with Asher if you didn't have anything tying you to your past.

I also know how Asher could be, or how he used to be before he met you. I was scared!

I was scared for you and for myself. I know what he is capable of, and you ensured me you truly wanted to be with him. I just wanted you to be happy.

I remember the day you met him. Stars Amalie, you were so smitten. After your mother's passing, I didn't want you to have any more pain or loss.

I hope you can forgive me for my mistake. I would love to see you again someday.

I love you, Amalie. You're my best friend even if I am no longer yours.

-Semira

I sit on my bed for stars knows how long. I don't know what to think. I don't know what to feel.

My hands shake, and my stomach churns with indecision. My mind feels like a fog that can't find its escape. On the one hand, I understand why Semira did it. If I had her ability, I think I would have done it as well. On the other hand, I am so mad at her that I can scream. Everything that I've lost is because of her. I am not even sure I had a say in it or not. I don't know if I asked her to take my memories of Wren.

I have so many questions that I need to speak with her face to face before she leaves. My emotions settle on anger as my teeth clench, and I hop off my bed with the letter in my hand, walking to the door to speak with Finley.

"Kitten, what's wrong?" Finley can barely get the words out before I shove the letter in his face.

"I need to find Semira, now. Before she leaves." I run to her room, already knowing she isn't there, but I need to see for myself. I swing open her door to find an empty room. There's not one item in the room that belongs to her or Alizar. I turn back to Finley, who folds the letter and extends his hand to return it to me. I take the note and tuck it into the bodice of my light lilac-colored dress.

"Let's go. Hopefully, we can catch her before she leaves the palace," Finley encourages, ushering me through the foyer door into the halls.

We rush towards the main foyer, assuming they would be taking the tunnels out to Galeis city square, when suddenly Finley grabs my arm and pulls me into a dark corner beneath a set of stairs. Peering around the corner, I can see Asher and Semira in conversation at the mouth of the tunnel. Asher stands tall and broad-shouldered, almost like he is trying to appear larger, while Semira has her hand gripped in a fist so tight it's shaking. Her cheeks are flushed red, and I can tell their conversation isn't friendly.

"Asher, I've already told you. I need to leave now. Alizar is waiting for me."

"Here's the issue. I didn't say you could leave. Amalie still needs you here," Asher counters, sounding upset, but I can't read his facial features since he has his back to me.

"She's fine, I talked to her. Now, if you will excuse me." She attempts to turn around, but Asher grabs her arm with a bruising force. My blood boils, and I move to step out from behind the corner staircase, but Finley pulls me back so I'm standing flush against him. I watch in silent fury Asher's actions towards her.

"I know what you are, little caster. Only I know what you did. If you don't want anyone to find out, I suggest you reconsider." Asher leans closer to Semira, whispering so low I can barely hear his threat.

"Amalie will know soon enough! She's the only person I was worried about finding out the truth. She is the reason I'm here at all. I would have run if it wasn't for your threat against Alizar-"

SMACK

Asher's back hand connecting with Semira's face echoes through the main hall, bouncing off the stone walls like a morbid symphony.

"I'd also watch your mouth, Caster. I'm not afraid to threaten your husband's life again," Asher spits his words like it leaves a foul taste in his mouth. "I wouldn't mind breaking his other leg."

Finley holds me tighter, placing his large hand over my mouth so I don't shout out. "Shh. You don't want his attention right now," Finley whispers very low in my ear.

"Screw. You." Semira spits blood onto Asher's pristine white coat. "Alizar is so far from here by now, you can't threaten me with shit!"

Everything happens so fast, it takes a moment for my brain to catch up to what I am observing, what I am *feeling*. Asher lifts his hand in the calmest gesture I've ever seen from him. Initially, it appears like he's going to caress her cheek, but instead, she starts gasping. The air is stripped from the room instantly, and she holds her hand to her chest, folding over and trying to catch her breath. I can feel the wind increasing, but none of it is bellowing near Semira. No, the air, it seems like it's being taken from her. The breath from her lungs is being ripped out of her while she struggles to inhale. I can feel a pull within me, startling the breath out of my own body. My shock and horror cloud my judgment as I begin to cry out for her, yet nothing comes out.

Whatever Asher is doing to Semira, I can feel it too. Perhaps not with the same severity, maybe because I am several feet away, but it doesn't make it any less painful. The excruciating pain and shock are evident on her face as she falls to her knees, placing both hands on the floor. She tries to scream or cry, but nothing comes out. She can't make a single noise without any air. I start thrashing harder against Finley, tears pooling in my eyes and running over. Finley's fingers are wet and slick with my tears, but he doesn't dare release me. I feel as if I am going to vomit, my head swims and I am dizzy with the pushing and pulling within me. It feels like my essence is being ripped from me, my soul ripping from my body.

Can't Finley feel what's happening? Doesn't he know what Asher is doing?

His grip on me never loosens. He is the only thing tethering me to my body. I feel as if I am adrift in the seas, and Finley is the only beacon of light in the far distance.

I watch Asher lower his hand and take a step back, revealing a wide-eyed Semira lying flat on the ground. Her skin is as colorless as a ghoul. Then it hits me; Asher doesn't only control the ghouls, he can also harness their powers as well.

"Good riddance," Asher murmurs before walking off in the opposite direction, most likely to find someone to clean up his mess.

I freeze, ice running through my veins as my brain registers that Semira is dead.

Asher killed Semira.

My body goes cold. My mind focuses on the oddest thing, my fingers. They're numb. I can't feel my hands, I can't move my fingers. The pinpricks of a sleeping limb are so painful that I can't think of anything else except that same sensation in my fingers.

Finley takes the opportunity to lift me into his arms, and I stop fighting. I just give up. My brain isn't working, my body isn't working, and the numbness in my hands is spreading up my arms, encasing me in an icy tomb.

Maybe I'm dying too. It certainly feels like it.

My fault. It's all my fault.

The chant repeats over and over.

"It's not your fault, Kitten. You didn't do this."

I don't realize I am speaking out loud until Finley replies. His voice sounds so far away, not right next to me as he carries me.

Finley moves gracefully like a wraith in the night, unseen and unheard, as he holds me through my foyer and walks into my bedroom. He places me on my plush sofa even though I don't feel it beneath me. I'm having trouble breathing, and I start to hyperventilate, thinking Asher is doing this to me too.

My eyes dart back and forth, trying to focus on something, *anything*.

"Kitten, listen to me. You need to breathe. I know it's hard, but you need to. I will get you out of here, I promise." Finley kneels in front of me, trying to catch my eyes.

"I'm going to vomit." It's the first words I truly manage to say, and the sound of my voice sounds odd even to my own ears, like they're stuffed with cotton.

This isn't real. This can't be real.

"It's alright, you're in shock. Listen to me." I take a deep breath and open my eyes to stare straight into his dark ones. "Good girl, great job, Kitten. Keep breathing." I take a couple more breaths, starting to regain feeling in my limbs. I can now tell I am silently crying, the tears won't stop, but I'm not screaming, at least. "I will get you out of here. I just need a day or two to work out the plan. Please, try to act like everything is normal. Pretend you didn't see anything. I know it's hard, Kitten, but you need to."

"I-I can't," I hiccup, trying to breathe through my oncoming sobs. "Finley, I don't have anything left. Semira is dead, Alizar is gone to only the stars knows where, and Asher is..." I leave my sentence unfinished because I have no idea what Asher is anymore.

Finley gives me a small smile. "Oak."

"What?"

Then it hits me. The answer to the question I asked Wren in my letter. Wren, oh my stars! "I- Wren. Wren came up with the name Oak when I wanted to name the river troll. I asked Wren to come up with a name. He chose Oak."

"That's a memory, you know," Finley says to me in a soft and gentle tone. "It might be overwhelming for a while as they start to flood back to you."

I just nod stupidly.

"Please try to get some sleep, Kitten. I will fix this the best I can. I-" He takes a deep breath looking up towards my bedroom ceiling. "I'm sorry about Semira. She didn't deserve that."

And with that, he walks out of my room. Leaving me to cry alone.

The issue with being alone is allowing your thoughts to overpower you. The last thought before the shock is too much and my body pulls me under is, *What if she did deserve it?*

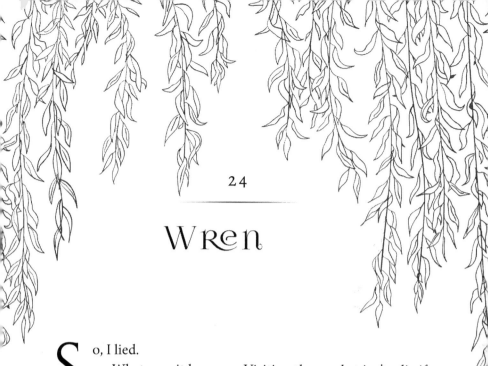

24

Wren

So, I lied.

Whatever, it happens. Visiting the market isn't a lie if you're going for a different reason, right?

Cahira needed some spicy herb from the Fire Kingdom, and because I am a gentleman, I volunteered my services. Thank the stars for me because her food would be bland otherwise.

I tell myself the lie repeatedly when really, I just need another update from Finley. It's like some addiction I've developed. I know she's happy and all that, but I just want to *see* her happy. I want to see her smile, then I'll stop.

Liar, my voice echoes over and over.

I walk down the forest path, hands in the pocket of my brown trousers, staring at the trees swaying in the wind above me.

I barely make it a foot when I hear Hadley calling me, "Wren!! Wait!"

"Ugh, go away," I mumble under my breath before stopping and turning around to face him. "No, Hadley, I don't need your guarding services today. Just go... do something." I wave him away with my hand, but he reaches for my arm as I begin to spin around.

"Wren! Listen to me!"

Okay, this is new. Hadley never raises his voice to me. I mean, I wouldn't mind if he did, but it's just so out of character for him that it alarms me for a moment. Eyes wide, I jerk my head back to look at him. He's a couple of inches shorter than me, but I don't need to duck to stare straight into his eyes.

"Okay, you have my undivided attention."

"It's Finley, he-" Hadley pauses to take a breath. He's winded from running to find me. I cross my arms, nodding forward. I'm trying my hardest not to be impatient, but this kid is testing me today. "Finley," he continues, "he came home to the chateau. He was looking for you."

"Well, what the hell Hadley! Couldn't you have started with that? Did he say why he came back?" I ask while I walk past Hadley, back to the chateau.

"No, Sir." I gave Hadley a pointed look. "Wren, sorry. He just showed up and asked for you."

I take off running. I have a pit in my stomach. Finley wouldn't leave her without a proper reason. I know that in my soul. I run so fast, that it takes me no time to reach the chateau. Spying Cahira with Willow, I call out, "Cahira, where is he?!"

She just points towards the half-open door of the kitchen. I don't stop running until I whip open the door, smashing it into the wall. Finley leans around the stone island in the middle, ducking his head around the hanging herbs.

"Why are you here?" I bellow. I am so worked up right now, I'm having trouble focusing. It takes me a moment to realize Fin is still wearing his guard uniform. "Oh, man! If someone saw you coming here in that," I gesture with my hand, like he doesn't know what that is, "you would be so dead. Asher would kill you."

"Yeah, well, Asher's already started," Fin says, taking a sip of water he pulled out from behind the island. "He killed Semira, man. Right in front of us."

"In front of who?" I know the answer, but I don't want to believe it.

"Wren, he has the power of the ghouls. He doesn't just control them, he literally has their power." Finley walks towards me, ignoring my stupid question. He places a hand on my shoulder. "Semira was a Caster. She made Amalie forget you, now that Semira is gone..." Finley lets me fill in the blanks. Now that Semira is gone, Amalie will regain her memories. Oh Stars! She must be thinking she's going crazy. She must be so confused. Not to mention how she would feel now that Semira is dead.

"I need your help getting her out," Finley interrupts my thoughts.

I wrack my brain thinking of what to do and how to get her here safely. At this point, if Asher is willing to murder someone close to Amalie so out in the open, who knows what he would be willing to do to keep her.

"How did you get here?" I ask, moving around the island to grab a bag and fill it with as much food as I possibly can. Nuts, berries, and dried meats are all shoved in the bag haphazardly; I don't have time or care to make sure everything is packed properly.

"I went through the cave portal. I don't think anyone saw me take the boat."

"Okay, okay." I nod to him, trying to form a plan, but my head is still spinning. I give the appearance of calm and collected, but inside, it feels like my stomach is full of bees. "Go back through the Market path. It may take longer, but you don't want to raise suspicion. Are you still good with the Ash-hole?" Finley grins at my joke, taking the bag from my hand and slinging it over his shoulder.

"Oh yeah, wrapped right around my little finger." He lifts his pinky, giving me the most prominent and brightest smile I've seen in a while.

"Careful there, your face will get stuck that way." Finley's little finger morphs into a giant middle bird, making me laugh. Leave it to Fin to make the best of every situation. "Alright, before you go, I need to write a letter."

Finley sobers up, giving me a slight nod. "You'll find me with the beastie. Stars know you don't give her enough love." I roll my eyes but watch him walk away without a retort.

Turning, I move around the kitchen to the opposite end, down the narrow hallway into the main room. The room is warm and homey, with simple and inelegant furniture neatly placed around the room to invite conversation. Sofas and chairs facing one another, bookshelves line the wall around the hearth, and wood paneling on every vertical surface. I love that even though it is a prominent place, it still feels like a family home. It makes me feel like a human, not a royal fae.

I move to the sofa, sitting down with a huff. I grab the quill and paper on the table beside me and begin to write.

Amalie,

I have to keep it short. I will be waiting for you, I promise. I can't cross the border without causing a war, but you know where to meet me.
I know about Semira, and I'm sorry. You're probably losing your mind and heart all at once. There is nothing I can say to make the hurt go away, although I know you're strong enough to power through it. Please keep fighting, even when it's hard. It might not seem like it now, but this will get easier.
Until I see you again, Stay strong.

-Oak

Don't form the bond.

I take the letter, folding it up enough to fit in a small pocket. I march through the main room, back through the kitchen, and out the half door to Willow's garden, where I find Fin giving the thing a belly scratch. Willow rolls on her back, her vibrant green wings splayed flat on the ground.

"She's not a dog, you know. She's a dragon."

"Hey, don't be nasty. She's cute." It's hilarious to see Finley making soft cooing noises at a dragon, mainly because he is such a huge man.

"Here." I pass over the letter to him. He takes the paper and pockets it swiftly. "As I said, take the market route. If you're able, try to convince Asher to take Amalie through the markets. If not, you better get her through that cave. She will know where to meet me. If you don't show up in one week, I will come looking for you. I don't care if I have to cross that border to do so. If I don't see or hear from you in one week, I swear on the stars there won't be an Ash-hole anymore."

Finley nods his understanding. "Thanks, man. Uh... another thing." Oh great.

"Oh, don't tell me, you shacked up with some girl, and now you want to run away with her and Amalie in tow?" I'd been only joking; I definitely didn't think I would have hit the nail on the head.

"Uh, yea. Her name is Seren, stars Wren. I can't leave her there either! If Asher killed Semira that easily, imagine what he would do to someone he just met. She's important to me, and she's important to Amalie." Finley almost sounds like he's pleading for my understanding, but there's nothing to understand. If I were in his position, I wouldn't even ask, I would do and beg forgiveness later.

"Fin," I place my hand on his shoulder and stare at him with the most severe look I can muster. "I will see you in one week or less. With *both* girls."

Finley gives a visible sigh, his shoulders sagging as he grabs me in a tight embrace. Finley and I are pretty close, but we rarely hug one another. Things must be worse than I thought. He must be more frightened than he led me to believe.

I pull back, waving him off. Taking a deep breath, I give him a slight shove. "Go."

As I watch Finley walk down the path, I turn and yell to Hadley, only to find him already standing behind me. "Stars, Hadley! Make some noise when you're creeping, will ya? No wonder we made you the spy."

Hadley just smiles up at me, like a praised child. "How can I help, sir?" I cock my eyebrow at him for calling me sir; we've talked about it over and over.

"I want you to personally deliver a message to my parents, tell them about your experiences with the Air Kingdom. Tell them about Amalie and tell them that nothing changes." Hadley gives me a perplexed look, but I just nod to him. "Repeat what I just said."

"I am to deliver a message to your parents. I am to tell them about my time in the Air Kingdom, about Amalie, and that nothing changes." His smile is so vast it makes him appear much younger than he is.

I nod and wave for him to go. Without a second glance, he takes off running to the capital of the Earth Kingdom.

25

Amalie

I wake late evening to a pounding headache at my temples and long dried tears crusted in my eyes. I lift my hand to clean my eyes before opening them when I hear a voice, "Finally, you're awake. I thought I would have to call the palace physician."

My eyes fly open to the sight of Asher sitting on a chair in front of me. He has dark circles under his eyes, almost like he hasn't slept in days. His features seem sharper, more angular, and gaunter, but I must be observing him from a new perspective now. People don't change that quickly, right?

He's changed into a darker grey garb than he usually wears. Tight, tailored chesterfield overcoat that defines his figure underneath. I can't stop staring at him. He's never worn anything other than white or light grey. The charcoal color brings forth the storm in his eyes and malice in his aura.

I glance around the room to notice he's pulled the chair from across the room. *How long has he been here?*

Asher reaches to brush my hair out of my face, but I flinch involuntarily at the chill of his fingers on my skin. His eyebrows rise in question at my movements.

"I'm sorry, I'm just not feeling well," I mumble as I sit up further, trying to calm the inferno in my heart while feeling like a bee trapped in a jar.

Asher gives me a small smile. "Perhaps I should have called the physician then." He studies me with those storm blue eyes. They used to bring butterflies to my stomach, now, they just bring nausea. His face is still an image of concern which bewilders me more. He knows what he did, but there is not an ounce of guilt within those eyes.

"I don't need a physician, just some rest, I believe." I stand slowly off the couch, trying my best to smile at Asher. When I smile at him, his eyes light up, and my traitorous heart flutters like a bird trapped in a cage. I turn away from him, pursing my lips, so I don't cry.

"Here, let me help you to bed." Asher grabs my arm gently, so softly that if I hadn't witnessed what he'd done, I wouldn't believe it happened as I fight the urge to shake off his hold. "Are you sure you're alright?"

"Yes. Don't worry, I'm just a bit tired," I assure him, hoping he will leave me alone.

Now that my memories are coming back, I feel like I am going mad. I can't tell what is true and what isn't.

I lie in my bed and listen to the door softly close as Asher leaves the room, allowing me to sleep. When I close my eyes, I see images of Wren and Finley. Flashes of pictures and words from a past life. I see a small figure with golden brunette hair and a curvy frame. My mother, I realize as tears soak into my pillow—the same female who helped me through the woods, her words of wisdom ringing through my head.

Voices surround me; giving me information, telling me jokes, crying, singing. All the sounds that I've heard before over the course of my life.

My mind turns to Asher. The memories of my husband, I now realize, were never built out of love. They were built out of fear. I don't remember everything. There are still blank spaces in my mind that need to be filled, but it's a start.

I sit up and slide out of bed, then take Semira's letter out of my bodice, almost forgetting it was in there. A small drawer in my writing desk is the only place in my room with a lock and key, given I don't exactly know where the key is, but it will only be there for a few days until I can leave this place. I slip the letter into the drawer where it lies stacked with Wren's letter.

Moving to my wardrobe, I change into a simple shift and wrap a long house robe around myself as I make my way to the library that I saw a few days ago. I figure if I need to find some solid answers in my world, this would be the place to find them.

The library is empty as I crack open the large wooden door and sneak inside like a shadow. I keep the torches extinguished to not draw any attention. I don't think I could handle Asher right now. As angry as I am at Semira for what she's done, she didn't deserve her fate, and I need to know why he decided to kill her.

I search the shelves for anything that may jump out to me. I run a shaking finger along the spines, feeling books and tomes bound in leather, felt, and wood until I come across a book called *The Bond: The Joining of Two Lives*.

Taking the heavy red leather book down from the dusty old shelf, I drop it down to the floor and flip open the pages.

"The bond is a sacred union between Humans and Fae. Joining the two worlds to continue the Treaty of Alignment is essential to keep the balance within society. Modern human traditions have been happily accepted into Fae culture, creating a unified world.

The merging of rival magic is strictly forbidden, causing insanity within the host. Half-fae who have inherited magic-even dormant-may not bond to a full-blooded fae, for the result will be the same.

There has never been a successful bond between rival elements.

Bonding with a human is the only acceptable option for a full fae, as it continues the legacy of the Trine and is the safest route for the Monarchy.

Magics alliances are as follows:
Air and Fire
Earth and Water

Air and Fire are complementary elements. With the aid of Air, Fire will be able to grow, and Air would have no warmth without Fire.

Earth and Water are complementary elements as Water aids the growth of the Earth, and Water would have no path without Earth.

Allied Elemental Kingdoms share goods, services, and cross-border travels.

A Fae or Human may change their Elemental Kingdoms only by denouncing the throne, exile, or bonding."

The chapter about the Treaty of Alignment continues into a blur, and I read until I can't understand the words. That's when a loud bang startles me out of my reading trance. The library door flies open, threatening to crack off its hinges.

Asher strolls in with a look of malice, eyes dark and scorching. It almost appears as if a dark shadow is looming behind him as he approaches me, snuffing the air out of the room. In his hand is a piece of paper, and I know it must be one of the letters that I have kept hidden in the drawer. Asher must have been going through my room to find it. I curse myself for not taking care of it sooner, too eager for answers.

Judging by the elegant, feminine scrawl, it's Semira's letter.

"How long did you plan to lie to me?" His words are thick with anger and another deep emotion I can't place. His voice seems to crack with the effort of remaining calm. "Are all your memories back?"

I stand, not wanting to face Asher while sitting on the library floor.

"N-no. I don't have any of my memories back. Semira just left it, so I'm stuck in the dark unless she undoes this spell." I try to maintain as much irritation in my tone as possible while thinking about her betrayal but more of Asher's. I don't want him to realize that I know she was murdered. If he finds out, I'm afraid I will be in the same situation.

"Don't *lie* to me!" Asher yells, his body becoming unhinged. He storms closer, causing me to back up involuntarily. "You lie so prettily, my dear." His voice softens as he firmly grips my chin, tilting my head up to look him in the eyes. "But still, we both know a lie when we hear one."

I jerk my head to the side, breaking his grip on my face. I have no hope of hiding my returning memories. He may not suspect that I have witnessed his deeds, but he knows my memories are coming back, perhaps not all at once as I expected but like a steady stream on a lazy creek.

I just stand still and stare at him with fury in my eyes, not giving in an inch. I can see him growing tense with frustration, his anger building higher than my own. I stand so still, it's as if I am made of stone. I don't dare move or breathe too loudly as his hand balls into a tight fist, body shaking with anger.

"I felt your distress earlier. Was it because Semira left? I only searched for her letter after she told me about it. I thought I could break the news of her departure to you myself. It seems I could not save you from her inducing heartache upon you." His demeanor changes once again as if he believes his own words. His eyebrows pull together, and the sides of his mouth sag in sorrow as if he is actually sad that she is gone. Still not admitting to his deceptions. His head cocks to the side again. "Are you afraid, my dear?"

I am.

As much as one can hide emotions from their expressions,

nobody can hide them in their heart. Fear is a faceless friend, one I've come to know well.

"Please, darling, don't fear for her. I can sense your anger, and I believe you should feel angry." He moves closer, arms extended to embrace me.

I peek around him, searching for Finley, or anyone really. Anyone or *anything* that I can use to draw Asher's attention away from myself.

"Semira was a despicable friend, to begin with. I apologize I read your letter, but I truly believe if someone cared for you as she said she does, she would not have taken something so vital from you." His whole demeanor is giving me whiplash. He builds his words like a blacksmith with a forge, creating pretty and elegant double-edged swords. My mind races, trying to find a way out of this room without him. "I truly hope we never see her again for all she has done to you."

That's when I lose control.

All my careful planning and plotting have gone out the window with the swipe of his sharp words of irritation against Semira. I can't hold them back anymore. I slap him so hard across the face that my hand violently stings. My fury rises even more when I notice *another* flicker of change in his eyes, and he smiles like a cat that finally caught his mouse.

"You bastard. She didn't leave, you killed her!" I stand up taller as I scream in his face, no longer afraid of him or his actions.

He smiles brighter at my red-faced anger. "Oh, Darling. Of course, I did. I'd kill you too if I didn't need you alive."

"Yeah, and why is that? Am I just some sort of pretty show wife to you now?" I scoff at him, turning to walk away, but he grabs my arm in a bruising grip refusing to allow me past.

"No, no. You will no longer be seen, and I will continue my life and find a new wife after the tragic disappearance of my *darling Amalie*." He pouts a lip mockingly as I narrow my eyes into a heated glare.

"What are you talking about?" I ask, genuinely confused and curious. Asher is now speaking in riddles; all his secrets and lies are coming to the surface.

Asher laughs a loud bellowing laugh. He's officially gone mad now. "Amalie, darling. You don't know, do you? I only need your powers through the bond, I don't need *you* for anything more. You wouldn't be fit for a queen anyways, too emotional."

His grip on my arm tightens as he nods to a guard waiting for his signal at the doorway to the library. The guard slowly approaches us as Asher says to him, "Take Amalie to the cages, make sure she is fed at regular intervals. She must remain alive."

"You're making a mistake, you know. I don't have any powers. I'm human!" I try to reason with him because clearly, he's sick, unwell in the head."

Asher laughs louder like it's me who is the wrong one. "I suppose you're right in a sense. You don't have powers...anymore. The bond forced your Earthen magic out and into me. Now you're just a little half-fae with nothing to show for it."

Half fae? Earth magic? I give him a bewildered look. I don't understand any of this. "What are you talking about? I'm human! Have you lost your mind? Is that how you murdered her, with my *supposed* magic?" I spit the words at him viciously.

Asher smiles even wider, noticing I know the truth now. "Yes! Finally, you're catching on. Earth kingdom can grow life as easily as they can take it away. Now I have that power. I just harness it in the same way a ghoul would. Isn't it amazing!" He stares down at his hands like they hold the whole world.

When I accepted his ring, the push and pull must have been the magic of the bond, the trading of our elements. My mind is so furiously frantic that I don't even realize I've acted until I see the blood trickle down Asher's cheek. Oh stars! I hit him *again-*

my ring must have caught him this time, but he barely flinched or moved.

I take it off my wedding finger and throw it at him.

"Here, take your ring back! Now we aren't married or bonded anymore!" I shout and begin to turn away again, hoping to feel the pressure of our bond breaking yet I can feel it didn't.

His guard steps into my path, and Asher grabs me tighter than before. It feels like he's crushing my bones. His face turns ghostly white and his nostrils flare, almost displaying a pained expression. My eyes fill with tears, glaring at this man. The same one I accepted, the one I chose to have my future with. Only to learn it was all a lie.

"Well, you're half right, again. You *are* clever." His tone condescending. "We were technically never married. I just needed your consent to the bond, and you accepted. Ring or not, we are *bonded*, darling."

I feel an odd sense of relief to know we never officially married. Maybe I left before the wedding? But on the other hand, my heart sinks at my mistake. If it is true and I had magic in the first place, now he has full access. "So, what do I get from this bonding?" I ask him, not caring at this point.

"Usually, I would say you have my protection and love, but really… you get nothing. Besides a meal enough times a day to keep you alive." Asher shrugs, nodding to his guard to remove me from my room.

I kick and squirm and scream like a feral cat, but the guard pulls my hands behind my back, taking both of them in his large one.

"Subdue her in any way necessary," I hear Asher mutter behind me as the guard raises a fist, catching me in the temple with a savage force. My vision goes black, and I slump to the ground, still conscious but slowly slipping away. He kicks me in the ribs for good measure, and I feel a rib or two crack under the aggression of his violence while Asher yells in the distance.

Voices and the sound of a struggle fade as if they are in a tunnel, moving further and further away until I don't hear anything.

I lost the fight.

"Amalie, no. You can't go in there. There's nothing you can do for her." Wren holds me tighter as I cry, trying to fight my way through the open door. I can see her from where I am, but I can't stop her from dying.

My mother became ill suddenly last night after our evening tea. It started with a mild fever and vomiting, but now her organs are shutting down. Or so the castle physician says. I know the truth, though. She's dying because of me. It's all my fault and my stupid decisions. My foolish heart led me to this. I was warned, and I decided to call Asher's bluff.

I suppose I lost.

"Wren, it's my fault. It's my fault." I repeat it over and over, but I can't tell him anymore. The second letter arrived this morning.

Amalie,

My condolences to your mother. It would be a shame if Wren caught the same sickness, wouldn't it?
Come to the Air Kingdom to avoid any further illnesses spreading through the Earth Kingdom.
You're a smart girl, don't allow the dirt of Earth to tarnish you as well.

-Asher

I know it wasn't an illness. He has spies in this castle, he has spies everywhere. There is nowhere to run or hide. I can't risk Wren. I can't lose him too.

That night, my mother passed. I spent the whole night crying in Wren's arms, he never complained once, but in the morning, I left before he had the chance to wake. I slipped out in the middle of the night like a coward. Only telling one friend of my intentions to marry Asher.

26

Amabie

My memories come trickling in like a strange form of torture, a flower here, a candle there, or one word on repeat in my head. It's like watching things pass by a window too quickly to catch any details, you know what you saw, but you're not sure if your mind was playing tricks on you. I don't know how long it will take to regain them all or if I ever will.

I remember why I left Wren, and it's like mourning the loss of my mother and him all over again. I'm starting to form a long list of heartache, and the only conclusion I can come to is that it's all my fault. I made these decisions, I was naive to my own identity, and I let Semira die.

I try to roll over to gauge my surroundings, only to find myself in a cell and my ribs screaming in pain with my every movement. I can feel a lump on the side of my head, increasing the headache that I woke up with earlier today. *What day is it anyway?*

I try to take in my surroundings, but it's so dark that all I see are bars and stones. I am lying on the dirt floor. My robe is hanging off my body without much regard for decency, but there is a small crack of light illuminating grungy trousers and a black undershirt to the side of the cell. Not much to keep me warm, but it's better than being exposed. It's cold, so cold I can also see my breath in the chill air. I'm trying my hardest not to shiver; I tense my body to keep it as still as possible. Every little shake and movement of my body causes agony to rip through my middle as I lean over and grab the garments.

I take the bottom of my robe and tear it along the hem. Gathering enough to wrap it around my torso, I feel the burning pulse of my broken ribs grinding as I circle the fabric tighter around myself.

Anger overwhelms me—white-hot anger for Asher, anger at Semira but most importantly, anger at myself. I hate myself for what I've become, for the situation I put myself in.

That's the problem with emotions; they demand attention. You always have the choice of facing it or suppressing it, letting it fester like an infected wound. One option will give you strength, while the other will tear you down and make you a liar. Like an infection, all lies spread and consume the body until nothing is left.

I wouldn't allow myself to be suppressed anymore.

The cold of the iron bars bites at my palms, and I test the door for any weakness, of course, not finding any. I survey the lock, the spaces between the bars, and the ominous hallway in front of me, all to no avail. The walls are a hard stone that meets a dirt floor. To be honest, this cell doesn't seem to be used often, which I find surprising. I suppose that would be a good thing if it weren't for me being stuck in here. The ground is full of loose gravel and sand and that's when an idea strikes me.

Much like Oak, my sweet river troll in the Earth Kingdom, I could dig under the cell bars, just enough to squeeze through. I drop to my knees and cup the dirt in my hands, digging like a mole burrowing into the ground.

I remember Wren would yell at Oak for ruining the

riverbeds as he made tunnels full of water throughout the chateau grounds. He would burrow under the bridges and walls, creating his own path. I can imagine his cute green curved hand shoveling the dirt, and the slight grin of peace reflected on his face.

I dig and scrape the ground until my fingers bleed. Nails ripping from my fingers, blood soaking the soil, but the cold and adrenaline have numbed my hands. I don't feel the pain in my ribs, head, or hands. I only feel anger and determination.

That is until the echoing footsteps sound down the hallway, giving me enough time to cover the hole with my dirty, torn robe.

I wasn't given a blanket or a pallet to lay on. So, I lean against the wall, trying my best to look injured and pathetic. I close my eyes and wait.

I don't know how long passes until I hear someone opening the heavy iron gates, their screech and groan echoing through the cell.

I force myself to sit up, groaning in pain from the seizing ache and panting from exhaustion at the movement. My blood is still pumping fast, so I don't have to fake my movements anymore.

"Food," a guard grumbles to me. I can hardly see him, but I can see the outline of a tall, frightening man. He looks so menacing on the other side of the bars that I am almost thankful I'm locked in here.

I hear a latch click open, and a small hole at the bottom of the cell door opens. He slides the tray with food on it and locks the hatch again. I don't move towards the food; I don't have the appetite for food right now. I know it isn't smart, I know I shouldn't skip meals, but I don't really care.

I take as deep a breath as I dare, inhaling deeply in small intervals. I scoot myself back against the wall as I release a ragged breath, keeping my mouth shut so I don't scream from the pain. *Yup, definitely a broken rib and most likely a concussion.* With my eyes closed, I try my hardest not to fall asleep as I wait for the guard to leave. A traitorous thought passes through my mind, but I shove it aside, not allowing my old habits of submission to win. *At least if I'm sleeping, I don't have to deal with this or the pain.*

More footsteps carry through the cell, and I'm getting annoyed with these guards. An irrational annoyance, but they keep interrupting by stomping around which causes my head to bang with each footstep.

The ache in my head and the exhaustion overtake me, making me lose track of time.

I open my eyes to see Finley holding a torch. He turns and places the torch in the wall sconce, giving the room a soft yellow glow.

"Finley…" I croak out, my throat so dry and my body so tired I'm not able to lift my head as I call his name.

Finley doesn't look or talk to me for so long that I'm starting to believe I'm imagining him.

"Fin," I manage to speak louder, catching his eye in the torchlight.

"Shut up!" Finley bellows, startling me and causing a small whimper of pain to run through my body at the jolt.

This can't be Finley. I trusted him. My confused and traitorous mind turns on me again. You *don't have the best judgment in friends lately, do you?* it sneers at me.

That thought halts my hope, *is Finley allied with Asher and not Wren as he led me to believe? Would Finley actually betray Wren and report all my secrets and movements to Asher?* I never got a letter back from Wren. What if Finley never delivered my letter but gave it to Asher instead.

Oh Stars! I need to take a breath and calm down. I remember Finley. I know who he is, but the memories swirling in my mind aren't exactly straightforward. It feels like I am reading a book out of order, as if someone has torn the chapters out and is giving me one page at a time.

My eyes start to cross with fatigue, resting my head back against the wall. I close my eyes again, hoping to fall back asleep.

Time moves differently with little to no light. It's hard to tell the time of day or how much time has passed. It could be hours, it could be minutes. The only indication that time is different is that Finley has left me, and a new guard has replaced him. I never saw if he tried to communicate with me somehow. He seemed so different, so cold. I know it must be an act. I've never even seen Finley get angry before. His anger is expressed through teasing and jokes, taunting and sarcasm.

A low bone-shaking moan vibrates through my ears like an earthquake, rattling my whole body as a thick fog pools around the guard's feet. The air in the room feels stale and dead.

And then I see it.

A ghoul.

The shoulders of the guards tense, hunching forward involuntarily as the fog grows thicker and thicker, snuffing out the lit torches. The metal of the wall scones rattles and clangs against the thick stone walls. Bile rises in my throat as I glimpse the decaying, skeletal figure.

It slides along the floor like it's floating on the fog. *That's because it is*, I think. Becoming frustrated with myself for my stupidity. I should be thinking about how to get out of here and keep out of the ghoul's clutches. Instead, I can't focus. I'm too entranced with the grotesque figure approaching.

"Don't move, Charlie," a guard urges.

I notice the shake in Charlie's shoulders and hands. His back is turned to me, but I can faintly see the paling of his features when he turns his head to stare wide-eyed at the approaching ghoul. The wind increases, dropping the temperature in the dungeon while the thick fog begins to rise higher. It circles the guard's knees. I stand on shaky legs, feeling dizzy as my head throbs. A small flame ignites in my chest. A feeling of a kindred spirit towards the ghoul. This is completely insane because it's a ghoul!

But for some strange reason, I don't feel scared as the ghoul drifts closer. I've always been able to connect with animals or creatures. Wren would get annoyed that I would bring home or name the dangerous beasts, but to me, they were living things. They deserved the respect and love that any human or fae would.

That is how I feel about this ghoul. Perhaps it is because of the bond between Asher and me. I know he has gained the abilities of the ghoul, thanks to my fae side. *I wish I had known about that earlier.*

Maybe, I did. Maybe that's why I can connect with the creatures of earth and now death.

"H-Hello," I stutter. I edge towards the cell bars, not taking my eyes off the ghoul. It falters, almost hesitating, before turning its lifeless eyes towards me. Deep holes blacken its eyes, white ivory skull clanging against a rusty chain around its neck.

I didn't notice the chain before, but it seems to be enchanted. Every time it hits the stone floors, a soft white glow emanates from it.

Clink, clink

I raise my voice over the sound of the chains, "Are you trapped here?"

"Shut up!" the other guard yells at me, taking his eyes off Charlie for a split second. His round baby face turns a deep red, anger creasing his eyes. "Charlie, pull yourself together. They're ordered not to do anything to us."

"Why is it here?" I ask, glancing back and forth between the ghoul and the guard. I wrap my fingers around the cell bars, peering through them as much as possible.

"They're here to punish prisoners when they misbehave." He gives me a cruel sneer, his teeth showing in his grin.

"They're trapped here." It's not a question, and nobody answers me, but my heart aches every time I see the dead eyes of the ghoul. I lift my hand and snake it through the bar, reaching out for the beast. Charlie snaps out of his fear-induced trace and grabs my wrist. He squeezes it in a bruising force, enough for me to cry in pain as he shoves my hand back through the bars.

The ghoul moves so fast that I lose it in the fog. I can feel the power radiating through it, charged like lightning during a storm. Both guards begin shivering from either the cold or fear, but as I pry my eyes from the ghoul, I see a darkening puddle spread across Charlie's uniform pants.

He wet himself! I lift a hand to my mouth and stifle a laugh. "I can help you, if you allow me," I say in a calm voice, giving the creature my full attention.

The ghoul gives a soft moan that carries on the wind. I realize it is wrapped in a cloak of fog. I always thought that the clothing the ghoul wore was actual fabric. It reaches for the chain wrapped around its neck, but a bright burst of flame sparks from the rusted links. The ghoul gives a soft moan, creating an ache in my heart.

I feel the sadness radiating through it. The feeling shocks me. Coming to the Air Kingdom, I was always terrified of the stories. Moving through the tunnels to the portal, hearing the ghouls moan and the fog increase set my body trembling in fear. Now, my feelings have changed even if It's a bad idea. Even though I am trapped myself. If I can save this creature, then I will.

"Can I take the chain off you?" I coax the ghoul closer. I am holding my breath and waiting for its approval.

The ghoul moves closer to me, silent except for the *clink, clink* of the bones and chains. I slowly move both my hands through the cell bars again. I glance at the two guards, still frozen in fear, and reach for the chain. My eyes return to the ghoul, and I give it a soft smile before my finger grazes the chain.

No spark, no flame. The chain is cold and solid, but there is no lock. The chains remind me of fire shackles, an enchanted metal that only burns the one encased in the metal—invented in the land of ideas and creation, the Fire Kingdom. Of course, it would be the shackles. The Fire and Air are allies. One born from hatred, and the other with enough fury to encourage it. The metal won't hurt me because it isn't meant for me. It's intended to trap and control this ghoul. *Maybe they wouldn't be so foul if they were treated properly.*

I take the end of the chain, careful not to touch the skeletal figure in front of me. I drag the rusty metal off the neck of the ghoul. The instant the chain is free, the ghoul dissolves into a stream of thick fog. It flows like a flooded river through the bars of the cell. The fog lifts my hair in a cold caress, and I can almost feel the appreciation through the soft whisper. It drifts back through the cell, and the ghoul turns into a solid skeletal decaying figure once again.

I blink, stunned at the sight. The ghoul rips the breath out of the nameless guard, leaving Charlie frozen with a silent scream. He's shaking in fear, his mouth is hanging open, but only a small whimper escapes as his fellow guard falls lifelessly to the ground.

The ghoul turns to Charlie tauntingly. It circles the guard, running a sharp boned finger over his chest.

I can't help myself when I blurt out, "What did you do to it?" It's apparent that this creature has an intense hatred for the guard. The air seems thin, like standing on the top of a mountain. The fog grows thicker, making it difficult to see what the ghoul is doing to Charlie until I hear his scream. "I think it wants you to answer my question," I say with a grin.

It may be wrong of me to be enjoying this man's torment, but if he did do something to the ghoul, he deserves everything he gets.

"I-I didn't," Charlie's shaking voice whispers into the fog. The ghoul uses his sharp boned finger like a knife, dragging it over the guard's chest until blood wells to the surface.

"I don't think that's entirely true, Charlie," I taunt, really enjoying this. "You see. The ghoul killed your friend easily, with no toying. Now, why would it keep you alive for this long?" I ask rhetorically. I give a slight pause before leaning against the cell bars. I lay my head against the cold metal as my headache throbs in my temples. "It looks like revenge to me."

"The- the chain!" he stammers. "I put the chain on it. I whipped it," he sobs harder, "I beat it when I was angry. I'm sorry! So sorry."

My face pales at his admission. How could someone do that to this poor creature, deadly or not? One does not chain an animal and use it as a punching bag. My anger heats inside me, and I want to wrap the chain around Charlie's neck myself.

I never get the chance to.

The ghoul lunges for Charlie's neck, piercing him with the sharp bone of his fingers. I watch as he coughs, spitting blood *through* the ghoul as it turns to fog again. It takes off through the dimly lit hallway, leaving me alone with two dead bodies.

A couple of hours must have passed because two new guards are standing outside the bars of my cell, but what really surprises me is Asher's form staring back at me. The bodies are gone. I must have slept harder than I thought.

"I'm happy I didn't have to wait long; I would have had to reconsider your gift." I stare at him, refusing to indulge in his childish taunting. "Aren't you curious, darling? I think you're truly going to enjoy this one." His smile is so big that I can see the white of his teeth through the darkness of the dungeon cell. The faint glow of the reignited torches in the sconce cast a flickering silhouette of his body.

I roll my head to the side, opening one eye as I hear loud boot steps descending the stone staircase and the clank of chains behind Asher.

"Ah! Here it is now! I thought you might enjoy some company." He is still smiling like a thief who pulled off their ultimate heist, and it's not far from the truth.

My mind goes to the ghoul. *Did he know it was me who helped the ghoul?* The chain I took off its neck is gone from view; I buried it in the useless hole I dug. I realized before I fell asleep that under the soft dirt and gravel were bricks.

I watch as Finley reaches the bottom of the staircase, pulling a chain harshly to bring his new prisoner forward. I gasp, then wince in pain at the sight of a very pissed-off Seren. I have never seen her so angry in the short time we've known each other. I try my hardest to sit up straighter, to stand or speak, but my body doesn't cooperate with my mind. I stare in shock, silent warm tears run down my chilled face, making me shiver harder from the contrast in temperatures.

Asher nods towards one of the guards on his right side, still grinning at me like I am a caged animal on display. The guard grunts and moves around Asher to open my cell door. Finley yanks the chains again, causing Seren to stumble forward. She mutters a curse but regains her footing.

Finley refuses to look at me as they pass through the cell doors, and Seren stays silent, shooting dagger eyes at Asher and his guards. They walk to the far wall I'm leaning against, across from the door they just entered. Finley takes Seren's chains and locks them to the chainring beside my head. He gives her a final look I can't decipher, though she nods with determination in her eyes before he turns away and leaves the cell without a word or glance towards me.

I am so pissed off at him, Asher, and myself that I can feel my face heating at its emotion, more tears escaping my eyes without my consent.

"Oh, my love, don't cry. Your friend is safe. As long as you behave, that is. She will remain chained but fed at the same time you are. Not a bad deal, hmm?" Asher taunts me, and the best thing I can do is slowly raise my hand and give him the middle finger.

Take that Asher, and screw off while you're at it. But the words don't come to my mouth. Asher just laughs before he gestures for Finley and another guard to leave with him. In the dungeon now, there are only three of us; me, Seren, and one guard.

Seren looks down at me and practically leaps on me, her chains just long enough to wrap around my middle and squeeze as she slides down the wall to sit.

I scream in agony. As much as I love having her embrace, it doesn't feel great with broken ribs. Seren's eyes go wide in shock, and she quickly pulls back. If it weren't for the residual pain from her embrace, I would have thought I imagined it.

"Stars! Amalie! What did they do? Are you okay?" Seren asks with a hint of fear in her voice, her eyes start to water, but I raise a hand before the tears spill. I don't want to be the cause of her sobs too. I just shake my head at her, but she continues talking, faster and faster as she does when she's nervous.

"I didn't know what was going on! I thought everything was okay, but Finley came to my shop and told me I needed to come to the palace with him. He seemed so serious that, of course, I couldn't refuse. And honestly, I don't think I would have refused because, *hello*, Finley! But as soon as we got out of the sight of the locals, he slapped these cuffs on me! They're not the most comfortable things to have to wear either. But then he said some things that I, um," she looks towards the guard who's purposely ignoring us, cleaning his nails with his dagger, and rubbing the dirt on his white uniform pants, "I forgot what he said." She lowers her voice as she finishes, nodding towards the guard.

I clear my throat, speaking for the first time in what feels like days. My voice comes out raspy but firm, "I'm fine. Sorry I got you into this."

"Shh, you didn't get me into anything I don't want to be in. Even the chains, although I would prefer chains in much more enjoyable circumstances." She gives me the biggest grin, and I can't help but smile, giving her a small chuckle.

As awful as it sounds, I'm glad she's here. I think I would lose myself entirely if I dealt with everything alone. Now I have more drive to get the hell out of here.

27

Amalie

"Amalie, Amalie!" I hear a voice down a long tunnel, but I find it harder and harder to open my eyes. I crack one eye open to find I'm still in this windowless, cold cell. Seren is slightly shaking me awake, causing a dull ache to run from my ribs to my toes. "You've been slipping in and out of consciousness for the past couple of hours. You've already missed one mealtime." She gestures to the half-eaten tray of food that was slid under the door. It rests about a foot away from where I'm hunched on the back wall.

I groan and sit up straighter, keeping both eyes open. "I'm not hungry. Thanks, though," I murmur to her, fighting the fatigue. I'm not sure my words are clear enough because she gives me the strangest look, like I'm speaking a foreign language. "How are we getting out of here? Any ideas?"

Seren grabs my face with both of her hands, the cold metal chains rest against my chin and chest. I flinch from the chill feel of them. She doesn't seem to notice since she's too focused on inspecting me with the bit of light we have available.

Her eyes go wide when I jerk away from her hand as it grazes my left temple. I know she felt the goose egg-sized welt on my head. "Stars! Amalie! Turn your head towards the light, let me see." She grabs my face more fiercely as I try to pull away more. I don't want her worrying about me. I don't want to be a hindrance to her or anyone. It's one of those situations where nothing can be done, so it's better not to acknowledge it.

"I'm fine." I sigh, relenting to her fierce determination.

Seren gasps when the left side of my face hits the light, "Oh Stars! Your face is all bruised! Girl, you probably have a concussion, if not a cracked skull! How did this happen? Last I saw, you and Asher were all over each other." I never allowed Seren to see the extent of my injuries when she was deposited on my right side. She's talking so fast I have to hold up a hand to halt her.

"I'm fine! It's okay. There's nothing we can do about it. Please stop stressing." I give her a small smile, but Seren doesn't mirror my own expression. She repeats her question, jogging my memory about the whole situation I got us into. "Asher lied to me; the only reason he wanted me was to take my powers. I didn't know I even had any." My voice drifts off, trying my hardest to hold back my tears. Seren rubs the back of my hands, urging me to continue. "He killed Semira. She... she was a caster. And now we're here."

She knows I'm keeping information out, but she doesn't force me to tell more. Seren grabs the tray of food, sliding it forward within my reach. "Eat." Her voice is as forceful as I've ever heard her. She's so stern that she sounds like a mother scolding her child.

Sighing, I take a piece of stale bread, breaking off a small portion before putting it in my mouth. I force myself to eat as much as possible, satisfying Seren. While I chew, I wonder why she isn't more scared or trying to escape. Seren doesn't strike me as the person who would just accept her fate. "Why did they chain you?"

"Water fae, remember?" She holds up her chained wrists, and

I see the slight glow of the enchantment. Seren sits back, sighing loudly into the echoing dark. She takes a quick glance at the guard. "We aren't stuck here," she whispers in my ear. I lean my head back against the wall, closing my eyes again. She slowly shakes her head back and forth, portraying a message I don't quite understand. "Just close your eyes, rest for a bit." And I do just that.

I fall asleep pondering her words when the noise of grunts and fists hitting flesh startles me awake. My first thought is Seren, my eyes shooting open to ensure she is still beside me, but the torchlight is snuffed out, and the cell is so dark I can't see anything.

"Seren?" I whisper into the dark, holding my breath for an answer. Once I hear her soft reply, I let out a breath of relief.

"I'm here. It's okay." I open my mouth to ask what's going on, but my blood runs cold when she continues, "It's Finley. He's here to get us out."

"No!" I yell into the dark. "You can't trust him, he's with Asher. Seren, I thought he was with us too! He brought you here, remember?" I pull myself up the wall, lifting my arm and searching for her.

"Oh, I'm offended if you truly think that, Kitten. Or perhaps I should give a bow for my delightful performance." Finley's voice is so deep and low that it seems to amplify off the stone walls.

My hand finds Seren's, and I link my fingers with hers, feeling her cold chains against my wrist. "It's alright. Fin gave me the plan before putting me in here. I couldn't say anything because of the guards."

I see a faint, massive silhouette of Finley approaching Seren.

Keys rattle in his grip as he unlocks her chains, freeing her from the wall.

"Can we go and talk later? We're in a bit of a time crunch here." Finley asks, rushing us out of the cell.

I keep my mouth shut, running through my options. I could fight Finley, most likely injuring myself further, and then I would still be stuck in the cell. Or I could comply and go with Finley. I could accept the offer to escape. Whether it is a lie or not, I'm out of the cell and will have a chance to escape later.

I decide to follow Seren and Finley; they're my best bet at getting out of here.

"Careful, Fin. She's hurt," Seren says as she puts her arm around my shoulders, keeping me steady as I move away from the wall towards the cell doors. I suddenly feel so claustrophobic that I just want to leave before these doors close again.

"I'm fine," I grumble.

"Shit," I hear Finley say in the dark, but I don't bother looking in his direction. The chaos has caused my brain to focus on one task at a time. "Let's get out of here, and then I can take a look."

Seren and I follow Finley through the silent and eerie hallways. The drafts are sweeping through us, tousling my sweat-soaked hair, causing me to shiver. I fear encountering guards more than ghouls in the tunnels.

I know in my soul that Finley wouldn't side with Asher, but I believed the most in Asher, and I ended up bonded and in a cell.

Finley leads the way while Seren keeps her arm around me. She's gently pushing me to move faster and faster. The harder I breathe from the exertion, the more my ribs ache, but I push through, desperate to feel the fresh air again. Desperate for freedom and life instead of a dark and lifeless cell.

Finally, we reach a crossroads in the dark tunnels, and we don't venture up the stairs like I initially thought we would. Confusion and fear hit me so hard that I think I hear footsteps behind me. I whirl around so fast that I almost knock Seren over, but I don't see anyone following behind us.

The path in front of us spreads into a Y-shape, though after a short breath, Finley nods his head towards the right, and we move again, descending more stairs into more darkness.

I can't hold back my anxiety anymore, and I whisper through my teeth, staying as silent as possible.

"Do you know how to get out of here?"

"Nah, I just thought I would wing it and hope for the best." Finley gives me a sarcastic smile, and I can't help but grin back at him. Okay, I admit it was a stupid question. "Don't worry, Kitten, we have to detour a bit, but I will get us home."

Home.

No word has ever sounded so sweet to my ears. My heart aches, and I am so eager to get home that I pick up my pace, ignoring all of my aches and pains.

"Okay, now I'm starting to think you're walking us into, Fin. How is it possible that we haven't run into a single person through this whole escape plan?" Seren asks after a few more confusing turns through the underground tunnels.

Finley slows his pace, evidently feeling more at ease and less urgent. "Well, I heard that there is a certain mushroom with purple stripes that will make people sick. Unfortunately, the cook accidentally mixed some into their dinner. Crushed up real fine too... I don't think the cook even knew the difference."

I burst out laughing, imagining the whole guard quarters fighting over their chamber pots and the closest outhouses.

"My mother used to tell me to avoid those. It's one of the only things I remembered when I was running from this place." The hellscape I unknowingly went back to will haunt me for a while.

"I ate one on a dare from Wren." Finley pauses to laugh at the memory. "Man, was I ever sick from both *ends* for days."

Seren just shakes her head at him, grinning widely. She grabs my hand and guides me up a narrow slope towards the end of the tunnel. I know it's the end because the only light shining through is the beautiful shimmering stars high above us. There are no town lights, no torches, and no noise of movement or life. The cool breeze feels fresh against my dirty skin, and I take a breath as deep as I dare, cleansing my lungs of the filth.

"How long was I in that dungeon?" I ask Finley and Seren, genuinely curious. I lost track of the hours or days.

Finley gives me an odd look before answering, "I- I don't know for sure. It took me a day to get here. I had to walk back through the Treaty Market so I wouldn't raise suspicion. Then another day to plan once I found out where you were. So about three days?" Finley gives me a sad look. "I am so sorry I wasn't there for you. I promised I would protect you, I promised to be your friend and be there, but I wasn't."

Finley's apology demolishes the wall I had slowly started to build against him. I grab his sleeve, tugging gently to halt his steps.

I wrap my arms around his waist, giving him a slight squeeze as I say, "It's okay. I'm sorry I didn't trust you. Thank you for getting me out of there." I groan and hiss in pain when Finley hugs me back, resting his chin on my head and squeezing me tightly.

"Ah, shit!" He drops his arms and steps back so quickly, shaking his head in apology. "Let's find a place to get you looked at."

"I'm fine. Honest."

"She's lying," Seren says, rolling her eyes as she steps up, grinning softly and taking my hand again. She leads me to follow Finley down a stone path. Finley hikes a fabric bag over his shoulder. It had been so dark I never realized he was carrying it until now.

We walk along the path, keeping off to the side, close to a tree-lined forest. In the distance is a cornfield, or what looks like one. The corn stocks are thicker and all white, like bleached husks. Finley slows his steps, holding his arm out to halt Seren and me.

"Don't make a sound. Don't touch the husks."

"What is it?" Seren breathes into the darkness, the only light given to us is from the stars and moon above.

"Ghouls. Well, not quite. The Kingdom of Air uses these husks as their death ceremony. They wrap the bodies in the white corn husks, and once they start to decompose, they will reanimate as a ghoul. Given life again to serve the kingdom." I put my hand over my mouth to stifle my shock and disgust.

"So, there are dead bodies in there?"

"Yes, as I said, don't touch them and don't make a sound. If we wake a ghoul in transformation, our lives will be gone in the breath of a moment," Finley warns us sternly, not taking his eyes off our frightened faces.

I've never heard of something so disturbing as a kingdom essentially harvesting their dead to create an army of soulless monsters.

"When I was in the cells, a trapped ghoul reached out for help. I removed the chains from around its neck. Was that you that cleaned up the bodies?"

"Uh, is that a new trick of yours?" Finley hesitates, raising a hand to rub the back of his neck. "Anyway, I didn't want Asher finding them. Even though I'm positive he already knows. They've been taken care of." He takes a moment to breathe before quickly changing the subject, "Well, is everyone ready?" Finley hitches the bag higher up his shoulder and begins walking towards the field of corpses without looking back.

28

Amalie

I don't know what I'm more shocked at, the fact that there is no dead body smell, or the way ghouls are born–created? I honestly have no idea.

The tension in Finley's shoulders is unmistakable, even though he is trying not to show his anxiousness. Seren has moved behind me to form a single file line as we enter the field. We move slowly and silently between the rows and rows of stocks like a giant labyrinth threatening to swallow us. I don't know how long we've been walking through, but apparently, not as long as it feels. When I look back, I can still see the entrance we just came through.

When I turn back around, I stumble and almost fall into a completely covered stock. I don't see any ghouls or corpses around, but that doesn't mean there aren't any here. I can *feel* eyes on me, watching my every move. The silence is deafening, and I'm afraid to even breathe too loudly. Finley slides sideways so as not to brush the stocks with his broad shoulders, while Seren is so petite she can skip right through with no problem.

I stop in my tracks, causing Seren to bump into my back, nearly throwing me off balance. She glares at me but thankfully doesn't say anything as I look directly beside us, staring face to face with a decaying corpse.

The man looks like he was in his late forties, but maybe he looks older than he is because his face is so white and grey, eyes sunken in and missing. I glance down further to see he is half laying out of the corn husk. The man looks like he is trying to escape the bondage of the stocks that he's trapped in. He is leaning so far out of the stock that his hand grazes the ground, stiff and unmoving with rigor mortis.

I want to scream or vomit, my body hasn't decided which yet, but my mind is pushing me to keep moving. To not look at the macabre figure beside us.

I can hear Seren's frightened quick gasps behind me, and I shift my hand back to reach for hers, giving her comfort. I wish there were more to do, but there truly isn't. The only thing to do now is to keep moving forward. And I think that is becoming a symbol of my life.

Coveted secrets have constantly surrounded me. Grotesque monsters masquerading as something else, just waiting for you to mess up so they can take what they want. It is a beautiful white cornfield from the outside, but on the inside, it's these creepy monsters. Last week was the gorgeous palace and Asher's warm embrace, only to turn into a nightmare of heartbreak and deception. The only thing guaranteed in both situations is the reaction to move forward and get through it. Weirdly, this horror gives me the strength to guide Seren through.

The man isn't the only one we've seen who is either trying to escape or isn't held correctly in the husks. We pass three more half-decayed transformation stocks, the smell increasing the closer we get to them. It's almost like they are soaking in their essence and stench; yet only the ones falling out have the gag-inducing, rotting stench of the dead.

My eyes fill with silent tears as we pass a child. I stare at the little girl, trying to piece together her story. I would place her age at about six years old, even though half her face is only a skull and the other is an oozing gruesome slice of flesh. Her skin has slithered off her bones, allowing the flesh to slide to the side as she leans out of the stock. Her arms are bound behind her back with a thick rope that is beginning to give way as her muscles deteriorate. I wonder if she died bound or was she bound after her death. Did she die of injury or natural causes?

I find the answer to my question as I lean closer, noticing a slice of gaping tissue along her tiny neck. Through the crevice in her spine, I can see that this child was murdered.

I can't help but wonder if her murder was for the sole purpose of building an army. If I had been asked a couple of days ago, I wouldn't have believed it. However, now I know better.

I hear Seren's quiet sobs behind me, and I pull her forward past the young girl, so she won't have to look into the face of the slaughtered child anymore.

Ice runs down my veins when I hear a tearing sound coming from behind us. Almost like cloth ripping or a farmer shucking corn, and that's when I realize what the sound truly is. I spin around, pushing Seren around me towards Finley. I see the body of the little girl flop onto the ground making a sickly wet sound. I look back at Seren and Finley, gesturing for them to keep going. I hold my breath, hoping for none of the bodies to reanimate themselves.

The child's body lays on the floor of the field, unmoving. I let out a breath and keep walking, turning my back on the girl. Finley moves faster, dragging Seren along as he does. Just as we reach the end of the field, a low thick fog encircles around my feet like a snake in the grass.

I don't bother keeping my voice down, it's too late for that.

"Run," I yell to Finley, who doesn't hesitate for a moment. He grabs my wrist in one hand while still holding Seren's hand, and we run before the ghouls sense us as they begin to wake. Peering back, I see the murdered child crawling through the thick fog, barely visible. Her head hangs at an abnormal angle as the only thing holding it together is her spine and thin tissue.

"Mama…" the ghostly voice travels on the wind.

"Oh my stars!" Seren cries. "She's someone's daughter! A baby girl." Her cries become unbearable as Finley releases my hand and swings Seren up in his arms. She clutches his shirt, body shaking with sobs as we leave the little girl behind.

We run until we find a stone path at the water's edge. It is so dark out that I only recognize the water from the reflection of the stars and moon above. Up ahead, I recall the harbor as we approach the docks.

"Are we taking the cave?" Finley gives me a *how did you know* look while I continue to explain, "Asher took me to the cave entrance to watch the glow worms." He's silent after my words, as he guides us towards a small rowboat and tosses the sack into it.

Finley reaches for Seren's hand to help her steady herself in the boat. She lifts her dirt-covered skirt and lowers herself onto the bench seat before he turns to me.

I'm breathing so hard I want to scream from the pain in my ribs. Finley turns to help me into the boat but stops when he notices my arm around myself, bracing my middle to stop the pain of exertion. Taking in my face and then gazing down at my torso, he sighs loudly and reaches for my hand as well. Seren stretches out hers, and I am braced on both sides to steady myself on the rocking rowboat before Finley jumps in without a care. He grabs the oars, rowing us towards the cave.

Towards home.

The mouth of the cave is illuminated by the glow worms within. They shimmer and shine like the night stars. As much as I now hate this place, I know I'm going to miss this part of the Air Kingdom.

"It's about a half day's walk through the cave to the Earth Kingdom portal." Finley's low vibrating voice startles me out of my reflection. I sigh, wishing for a horse or something to carry us through.

As we enter the cave, I abruptly stop, afraid to go further. I can't explain the feeling, but something tells me not to go. Finley and Seren keep walking ahead of me, not noticing that I have stopped.

"No," I whisper into the air, hoping it travels to their ears. Seren stops and turns with a confused look on her face. I refuse to go further into the cave. Slowly walking backwards, I try not to slip on the hard rocks at the entrance. My fingers tingle and my chest feels as if it's going to explode. Something isn't right, I know it. My anxiety is growing the longer we stay here. "Something's wrong."

As soon as the words leave my mouth, Finley moves with such speed that I would think he's fae. He rushes towards us, grabbing our hands and leading us back to the rowboat.

"What's going on?" Seren asks, still confused by this sudden change of plans. We enter the rowboat, and Finley starts to row as fast as he possibly can.

I look back at the mouth of the cave to see white, mist-like shadows escaping from the entrance. Ghouls, more ghouls! We were about twenty steps away from the ghouls. I realize I felt their essence, their malice.

I open my mouth to speak, but Finley cuts off my words, my mouth left hanging open. "Don't. I know what you're thinking. You can't talk twenty or more ghouls off the ledge like you did with that one."

I was ready to argue with him. I wanted to say that the ghouls are simply misunderstood.

As if to contradict my assumption, Seren starts gasping in the seat beside me. She is holding her throat like she's strangling herself. Seren looks like a fish out of water, eyes wide and mouth open, gulping as much air as she can.

"Finley!" I scream at him to move faster, taking Seren's face in my hands to try to reassure her. "It's okay. Try to calm yourself a bit. Once we are out of their range, you will be fine. Just a couple more meters."

Finley moves frantically, every muscle bulging and sweat collecting on his brow. I can see the ghouls now taking form, skeletal and grotesque. Seren slumps to the side, putting her head in my lap as she breathes more easily now. She gives Finley a small smile, "Thanks."

He simply nods, still not looking assured of her safety. He doesn't slow or ease his efforts to get as far away from here as possible. Now that the ghouls have spotted us, it will be worse. Asher will now know we left if he doesn't already. The ghouls will be able to point out our location to him.

I'm not willing to go back there. Ghouls or not, I refuse to give up after we made it this far. I look back again, but I don't see any fog or skeletal creatures, making me breathe a sigh of relief.

"What now?" Seren gasps, finally sitting up.

Finley secures the oars so we can start drifting with the current. He slides forward on the bench to put both his hands on Seren's face and kiss her fiercely like a starving man deprived of nourishment. I turn my head away to give them some privacy, my cheeks flushing at the intimate moment between them. I've never seen Finley so fear stricken.

"Are you alright?" Finley breathes, touching his forehead with Seren's. When she gives a slight nod, he continues, "Stars,

Seren! If I had lost you, I would tear down the entire Air Kingdom to get to that bastard."

She grips his forearm tightly, a lone tear sliding down her cheek. Finley wipes her sadness away with the pad of his thumb. "I'm okay, Fin." She gives him a small smile before turning to me again, "How did you know?"

I clear my throat, not wanting to explain and relive my mistakes. "I just felt it. I felt that something was wrong." I look at Finley, giving him an apologetic look. "Fin, we're bonded. I didn't know what that meant, and I accepted his ring thinking it was simply a marriage ring. I didn't know." I peer up at him, waiting for the anger, but it never comes.

He just nods and smiles at me. "Well, I'm more scared of Wren than that twit. He will find a way out of this. If he doesn't kill me first, that is." Finley laughs at his own little joke, but it leaves me feeling cold all over again.

Wren, the one person who has loved and believed me, and I betrayed him. I lost him to my own stupidity. I couldn't go back to him like he's a second option. I haven't gotten all my memories back, only bits and pieces, but from what I remember, I screwed Wren over and left him. My shame hits me hard, my face heating from the embarrassment that I'm sure Finley and Seren can see plainly on my expression. They avert their eyes, allowing me to wallow in my self-hatred while our little boat floats further and further into the frigid sea.

Hours later, the air changes from frigid to breathtakingly frozen. Seren and I are huddled together, shivering so hard my ribs are screaming, and my whole body is aching. The sheets of ice are banging into our small boat, causing an awful cracking noise that I'm not sure if it's the boat or the ice. Snow is falling in silent drifts, coating everyone in a small layer of white. Finley looks like a statue in front of us. He hasn't moved an inch in the past hour, and I'm wondering if he's sleeping with his eyes open. The snow is stuck in his locked hair and broad shoulders. I glance to my left, squinting through the snow and mist of our mingling breaths to see white, snow-covered land.

"Fin? Where are we?" I whisper so I don't startle the sleeping statue in front of me. His eyes shift in my direction, looking so defeated as he takes in my face.

"We're in the Nightlands. If we time it right, we will have one day to spare before Wren loses his shit."

"The Nightlands are unclaimed territory, right? So does that mean that Asher can still come here?" I ask cautiously.

"He can, but he won't. Running to the Nightlands is the same as admitting he lost his wife. He's all about image and reputation. If word gets out that you're gone, his parents will be on him quicker than poison ivy on a wet dog." I giggle at his analogy, hoping for the truth behind his words. "Just a little further, and then we can make a camp once we go inland. Tomorrow will be a long day of walking, and we will be just short of the border by tomorrow night."

I do the math in my head; roughly three days in the cell, one day escaping and sitting in this boat, two days traveling, and then we are at the border. "About six days altogether. Did he give you a timeline?" I glance at Finley, not wanting to say Wren's name.

Finley nods, "One week." I nod back and look out towards the horizon, ending the conversation. I feel dead on my feet, well, I guess not my feet. But it sounds better than being dead on my ass.

We have been through so much today I am surprised Seren is as wide awake as she is. She doesn't look tired or defeated like Finley and me, but I suppose that is just how Seren is.

Finley grabs the oars again, steering us towards the snowy

shoreline before the ice becomes too thick and we're stranded. We reach a small ice-covered beach area to dock the boat, then Finley jumps out into the freezing water with no hesitation or complaint. He moves to the bow, pulling the front end of the boat onto the shore and reaching his hand out to steady me as I stumble out of it and land safely onshore.

Finley turns back to Seren with a big grin on his face. She stands on the bench and leaps into the air, into Finley's arms. Seren laughs as he catches her and gives her a stern look. Patting his cheek, she smiles and walks away to look at the snowscape ahead of us. Finley and I share an amused look at her sudden elation, and I think she is just so happy to be out of that boat. I turn back to see Finley grabbing his bag from the boat, hiking it over his shoulder, and nodding towards Seren.

I follow silently behind, trying to keep my shivering to a minimum and failing. The walking and cold aren't helping much with my aching ribs, and my headache is slowly returning. I don't say anything to anyone because I don't want to be a bother. I don't want to seem like the weak one, even though I clearly am.

We walk until the sky grows dark and the stars start to shine through. There are barely any trees around us. It looks like a barren arctic tundra, and I have no idea how Finley knows where to go.

"We will rest just up here." I raise my head to see where our camp will be, nestled between two large boulders, blocking the wind and chill. Reaching the boulders, Finley pulls the fabric bag off his back and begins to pull out some blankets and bread. "Here, wrap yourself up and stay here. I'll go look for something to burn."

Both Seren and I nod at him, quickly reaching for the soft blankets. I wrap the blanket around my shoulders, inhaling the intoxicating scent. It smells woodsy and warm, like home and comfort. I sit on the ground, curling the blanket around the rest of my body to shield myself from the bitter cold.

I fall asleep leaning against the boulder, barely bothering to check if Seren is doing the same before my eyes close and the memories trickle in.

29

Amalie

I knock another arrow into the bow and pull the string tight, never taking my eyes off my target. I see him running through the forest, blending in with the flora around him like a chameleon. I line up the bow, take my aim and breathe out the release of the arrow.

The satisfying scream of my target as the arrow pierces his flesh causes me to grin. Even the future King of the Earth Kingdom cannot outrun my bow.

"Stars, Amalie! That hurt like a bitch," Wren says, pulling the arrow out of his shoulder as he walks towards me.

"Oh, you're fine, don't be such a baby. Maybe you should hide better next time, hm?" I shoot back at him, giggling at my triumph. Wren's expression is torn between amused and irritated. He's always been my biggest supporter, but I don't think he's entirely too happy about being my practice target this time.

"Excuse me, I was hiding better this time. You must have some keen sense in the forest or something. I used magic and everything..." Wren pouts, rubbing his shoulder, which is already starting to heal. Damn Fae.

"Ooohhh, so you're saying you cheated. Now you deserve to get *another arrow in the shoulder."* I pick up the arrow from the quiver on my back and tap him on his shoulder with the feathers on the grip. *"Even if you heal five minutes after."*

Wren laughs loudly as he hooks his fingers behind his head and begins to walk back down the wooden path to the chateau. The trail is lined with little wooden bridges as the forest floor starts to flood from the marshlands in the spring. My steps cause the boards to creek and rock while Wren walks so lightly and gracefully that there isn't a sound from him.

"What's it like being a fae?" I ask out of genuine curiosity. I've never thought about the difference between our species in my fifteen years of life, but it's been on my mind lately. Now that he will be going through his full fae ceremony in two years, I want to know how he will change. Will he still be my best friend? Will his heart grow cold like the rest of them?

"You know I'm only half-fae, right? I can let you know when I'm eighteen."

I roll my eyes at him. He's always so literal, or he does it to drive me nuts.

"Never mind." I shake my head, defeated.

"I'm just teasing, Am." Wren stops walking, taking in my expression. He lowers his hands and crosses his arms, finding a tree to lean against. *"I guess... I don't know. I haven't thought about it much. I don't know any different. It just feels like me. From what I've heard from humans, my hearing is better and I'm faster."*

"And you can heal," I add in, gesturing to the healed skin at his shoulder. The only reminder is a small red stain on his white shirt.

"And I can heal faster. Humans heal too. You know, I think humans are stronger than the fae. They need to fight harder. They feel everything and suffer longer. It sounds awfully difficult to be a human."

"Gee, thanks, Wren." I roll my eyes at him again. But he laughs low in his throat.

"I didn't mean it like that. I didn't mean that humans suck or

anything. I just mean that they're better than fae. Fae have their lives so easy. Everything they do is more accessible, while humans have to exert more energy, use more knowledge, and fight harder. They're incredible. For a creature that could so easily be defeated, they don't give up. Humans are the strongest creatures I know. "

I stare at him, trying to figure out if he truly means his words or if he is just trying to humor me. In the end, I don't really care. "Well, I'm looking forward to being a weak fae when I'm older."

Wren raises an eyebrow, "You want to be fae? And how are you going to do that?"

"I'm going to marry you, of course! Who else did you think you were going to marry?" I challenge him, waiting for him to shut me down, but he doesn't.

"Are you proposing to me, Miss Amalie? You do know that the Earth Kingdom requires love to marry, we aren't all about convenience and alliances." I cross my arms and stand taller in front of him. He's still taller than me, but at least I can show him I'm serious.

"I could love you, you know. You're my best friend, and our mothers are best friends. What a better arrangement!" I grin widely at him as his eyebrow raises even further. I don't know which part of my statement shocks him, but I decide to push him a bit further. I quickly lean forward and plant a soft kiss on his lips before turning and running down the wooden path back to our home. It takes a couple of seconds for Wren to recover from my assault, but once he does, I can hear his footsteps behind me, no longer bothering with stealth.

I laugh loudly into the afternoon air, still feeling the tingle of him on my lips.

I wake suddenly, my body jolting forward in an upright position. The sudden movement jars my ribs, causing me to whimper at the pain.

I can still feel the memory burning in my mind. My eyes start to well with tears, threatening to spill over. I raise my head to see Finley staring at me with soft eyes. Beside me, Seren sleeps soundly while curled in the warm blanket.

"Aren't you cold?" I whisper to Finley. He is sitting by a dimly lit fire, but he still has snow collecting on his shoulders and settling in his hair. Fin shakes his head and turns back to stare into the fire. After a couple of moments of silence, I start to read the somber mood he's in. "What's wrong, Fin?

He sighs heavily, still not looking at me. He leans over and reaches for the fabric bag he brought with him. "We should rewrap your side." He pulls out a bandage kit full of different supplies of tonics, antiseptics, and bandages. "Here, let me wrap your ribs. It will help the pain to have it done properly. I assume that is your handiwork?" He nods towards the tattered strands of my robe I tied around myself. "At least until we can get you to a healer."

I let the blanket fall off my shoulders. I'm still wearing the filthy trousers and black undershirt from a couple of days ago, but Finley doesn't seem to mind. He takes one end of the long-ripped material and unwraps it as I sigh a breath of ease and pain. It feels good to be cared for, even though I don't deserve it.

Finley pulls up my shirt below my breasts to assess the damage. I can hear his sharp inhale of shock as I quickly look down at myself—blue, purple, black, green, and yellow bruising. Every color you can think of has been painted across my abdomen like a gruesome piece of art. He takes a breath, not bothering to poke or prod, he's seen enough. The new bandages wrap around my bare skin in a tight but relatively secure way.

When he's done, he lowers my shirt and drapes my blanket around my shoulders again.

He shakes his head again like he's angry with himself, but I can't understand why for the life of me. He already apologized for not being there, which wasn't his fault.

"What's wrong?"

"I never got a clear look at your head and face until now," he admits.

"Finley, please don't do that."

"Do what?" he says as he moves back to the spot he was sitting at by the fire.

"None of this is your fault, it's mine. I was the idiot who trusted the wrong people. I'm the one who left Wren. Stars, Finley, I even agreed to the bond!" Tears build in my eyes again, this time spilling over at the memory.

Finley places one of his large hands on my small one. "Kitten, I'm sure you had a reason. You always do. I think that's why Wren was so confused. Everything you do is so selfless, but nobody could figure out your reason for this."

"I had a memory, well, more than one, but my mother's death wasn't an illness. Asher has spies in the castle. She was poisoned, Finley. He sent me a letter threatening Wren's demise next." The tears come more now, turning into silent sobs. "I couldn't lose Wren, even if he hated me. The Earth Kingdom needs him."

Finley's eyes catch mine. "I-Stars, I'm sorry, Kitten. Here." He ties off the remainder of the wrapping bandage, throwing the rest into his sack. "I have something for you." He sifts through the bag and pulls out a small, folded piece of parchment paper.

I reach out for it, hesitant to open the letter I know is from Wren. Taking a deep breath, I unfold the paper and read it.

Amalie,

I have to keep it short. I will be waiting for you, I promise. I can't cross the border without starting a war, but you know where to meet me.
I know about Semira, and I'm sorry. You're probably losing your mind and heart all at once. There is nothing I can say to make the

hurt go away. I know you're strong enough to power through it. Please keep fighting, even when it's hard. It might not seem like it now, but this will get easier.
Until I see you again, Stay strong.

-Oak
Don't form the bond.

My shoulders shake from the river of tears flowing down my face. *Don't form the bond*. The one thing Wren has ever asked of me, and I couldn't even do that right.

Finley wraps his large arms around me and lets me sob into his chest. My mind spins with memories and sorrow. Finley never pushes me away or complains. He just holds me until the tears stop and my breathing evens out.

"He signed the letter with Oak," I murmur into Finley's chest.

"What?"

"My last letter to him, I wanted to verify it was actually him. I said I never got a letter from a river troll." I smile at Wren's humor, still present even when our world has gone to shit.

Finley sighs loudly, then laughs. "Ah, that's why he said it. Do you mean that awful, moss-covered thing you found by the creek?"

I smack his shoulder lightly, "Oak isn't ghastly! He's delightful once you get to know him."

"Right, and I'm a teddy bear once you get to know me." Finley scoffs at the idea.

"Uh, Fin. You *are* a teddy bear. I know you try this whole macho thing, but you're truly a softie." I laugh at his appalled expression; his face turns so red, and I can't tell if it's anger or embarrassment.

"I am not!"

"Yes, you are," I hear Seren's quiet, sleepy voice answer behind us, and I laugh even harder at Finley's expression.

"That's it! I'm leaving you both here," Finley promises in vain, holding one hand to his chest as if he's offended by Seren's confirmation.

"Yeah, right, your soft heart wouldn't let you," Seren counters, her voice gaining strength as she moves towards the fire.

Finley huffs, "I-well- you… I'm going for a walk to kill someone. If you hear screaming, it's just people dying as I torture them… to death." Fin stomps off into the darkness, leaving Seren and me laughing so hard I have to clutch my sides to stop the ache.

It takes quite a while for our laughter to die down, but I feel like my soul has been cleansed when it finally does. I think back to the letter Wren sent with Finley, and it gives me strength knowing how much Wren believes in me even though I betrayed him. I pick up the letter again and hold it out for Seren to read.

"He asked me not to bond with Asher," I say as she takes the letter from me and unfolds it.

She remains silent as she reads, then finally, she replies, "Do you think there's a way out of it?"

I shrug. "If there is, Wren would know or know how to get the answers."

Seren nods but doesn't say anything further. She simply stares at my letter until she folds the paper and hands it back to me. I take it and slide it into the pocket of my trousers.

"Ah, are you finished slaying people?" Seren giggles as Finley walks through the snow, glaring at her.

"As a matter of fact, I slaughtered many." He sits down with a thump and grins up at Seren, who mirrors his expression.

Finley looks over to me, still with a grin on his face. "Wren said you would know where to meet?"

I'm hoping I'm right in my assumptions. "I think his letter was referring to the pavilion," I tell Finley. "It was where we were supposed to meet when I was running from the wedding."

"Wait, why would you run from the wedding if you decided to marry Asher?" Seren interrupts. I must admit it's a good question.

"I wrote a letter to him, telling him about my doubts and how sorry I was for my decision. On the day of my wedding, everything started to fade away, and the only thing I remembered was to run to the pavilion."

"Well, the pavilion is easier to get to. We should be there by this afternoon. A lot sooner than I thought. It's about a kilometer over the border between the Air and Earth Kingdoms." Finley lifts his hand towards the slowly rising sun, signaling early morning. "Just through there is the Earth Kingdom, then we have to backtrack a bit, about ten kilometers to reach the pavilion."

Seren reaches for some bread that Finley packed, and passes it around to us around the fire.

"I'm ready to go home," I say, pulling the blanket closer around my face and taking a bite of my bread.

"So am I, Kitten. So am I."

We walk for hours, and I lose track of how many, but the sun has risen over the horizon. When we first started traveling, it was high above, and now it's on the other side of the sky. My feet are aching, and I have sweat gathering on my brows. I am dry as a desert, but I don't complain, and I refuse to give up.

Something about Wren's letter gave me strength. His understanding and words of encouragement motivate me to see the man behind the words.

"Look!" Seren points forward to a grassy area. It looks like a straight dividing line of the different territories. Sparkling white snow on one side, bright green grass on the other. I can't help myself when I smile at Seren, and then we run. I let all the worries and emotions from the past wash away as I move through the snow towards the grass.

Before I reach the border, I see Finley smiling at me from about thirty feet away. I wait for him to catch up; I wouldn't want to enter the Earth Kingdom without him. I wouldn't be here if he didn't choose to help me, even when I didn't know I needed it.

I reach out my hand for his, grasping him tightly while he takes Seren's hand with his other. The three of us take a breath and cross into the Earth Kingdom.

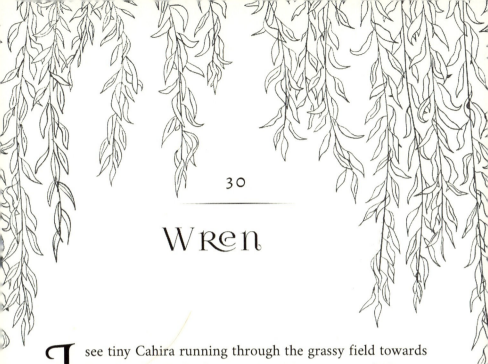

30

Wren

I see tiny Cahira running through the grassy field towards the chateau. She looks scared and frantic, arms flailing as she yells something to whoever will listen. Last I knew, she was with the beast. The thought stops me in my tracks.

Shit, what if Willow is hurt? I ran down the front steps of the chateau towards Cahira. As I get closer, I can hear her calling my name louder and louder. And now my run isn't just a human speed anymore.

Something is wrong.

My heart is racing as I reach her, grabbing her by the shoulders to steady her. "Cahira, what's wrong? Is it Willow?"

She smiles wildly while nodding her head and trying to catch her breath from her sprint. Her freckled face is in such a vast mix of emotions that I have no idea if I'm supposed to be happy or concerned.

"Willow ran off!" she says, still smiling.

I pause, waiting for her to elaborate or change her expression. I can't see how this is a happy moment. Sure, I don't wholly love the beast, but I wouldn't want it to leave.

"Can you pretend that I'm a child because I'm not following?" I finally say once I realize I'm not getting any more information from her.

Cahira laughs, tears springing to her eyes, and now I'm genuinely concerned that this girl has heatstroke or something. I'm about three seconds away from calling Hadley to take her inside for a glass of water, but the next words out of her mouth chill my blood and stop my heart.

"She's here."

I can't breathe. I don't move or blink.

"Wren, she's here! Willow felt her, I know it." I just stare at Cahira. Maybe I'm the one getting heatstroke. Can Fae get heatstroke? She grabs my forearms and moves them off her shoulders. She moves her arms around my torso, hugging me tightly. "Our Queen is home, Wren!"

That snaps me back into reality. *Is she our queen? Does she want to be our queen?* There's a lot to talk about, I suppose. *Does she remember all the promises we made to each other?* I've never even told her I loved her until she was gone. I didn't comprehend that I did love her. Is she even able to be our queen if she's married to Asher?

"I-I need to go find that beast," I mumble out, stepping out of Cahira's embrace. I turn around and walk into the forest area closest to me without peeking back. Finley is early, so I didn't have time to prepare.

Prepare what? Dumbass, she's your friend. I take a breath, calming myself a bit before I actually try to find this beast. I close my eyes and lean against a tree, grounding myself with the earth.

I reach out with my senses to try to find Willow. I listen to the trees, feeling the movement and vibrations through the ground. I see the leaves move through the wind, and I see the blades of grass flatten under large claws. My eyes snap open, knowing where Willow has gone off to.

I take off on a casual walk, not wanting to rush the reunion of Willow and Amalie. She loves that creature more than anything. It should be the thing to welcome her home.

It only takes me about an hour to walk the distance until I hear them. I can hear Amalie's soft cries and the gentle grunts from Willow. I risk a glance through the trees to the clearing at the border. I see Finley first, standing off to the side with a petite, vibrant girl at his side. I can see her bright smile from this distance, she's staring up at Finley like he is the most important person in the world. Perhaps, he is in her world. However, *my* whole world is kneeling just fifty feet away from me on the grassy floor, cuddling a green and overgrown dog.

My nose tingles as my eyes start to water at the sight of her. I can see her bruises from here, but she's alive. She's laughing and smiling. She is still the most beautiful thing I've ever seen.

Taking a deep breath, I compose myself and fortify my walls again. With an air of nonchalance, I strut out of the forest and call out, "What? No love for me? That damn thing gets everything." Amalie's hands freeze, and her head jerks up in my direction. It takes a second for her eyes to lock with mine, but when they do, all the air is pushed out of me all over again. I glance over to Finley, giving him a nod of thanks before looking at his girl. "Glad you decided to whip this one into shape. He needs all the help he can get." When she laughs, I walk over to her, extending my hand. "I'm Wren."

"Seren," her reply is simple but good enough for me.

I give her a wide grin. "Nice to meet you, Seren." I glance up at Finley and wink before turning away to finally see my girl.

The tears are streaming down Amalie's face, but she still hasn't moved from her spot on the ground in front of Willow.

"Wren." Her voice is so low and shaking that it takes everything in me not to grab her and hold her close.

"I hope those are good tears. I don't think I would be able to take your tears if you didn't want to be here." That gains me a snort of laughter from her as she stands up to meet me.

It's only been a short time, but for some reason, I'm checking her all over for any changes. I expected her to be taller, to be slimmer, to be anything but herself. She's just as short and curvy as sin as I remember. Her beautiful long hair is tied back in a messy braid, and her clothes look like men's clothing. I scowl at the thought. She's wearing a dirty white button-up shirt and dark trousers. Her face is bruised, yet her freckles that have always reminded me of the stars look as if the clouds are covering them at night. My blood is boiling, but I try not to think too much about it now. The most important thing is that she's alive and with me again. Lastly, I glance into her eyes. *Stars,* her eyes. The exact shade of amber as before, with tiny flecks of light penetrating through them, small enough that you have to gaze for hours to notice them, but they still grip my heart, bending me to her every wish.

As she steps directly in front of me, she is only as tall as my collarbone. She is the perfect height to rest my chin on the top of her head, and that's precisely what I do.

I grab her so quickly I hear her small gasp of surprise as I put my arms around her, resting my chin on her head and closing my eyes. Nothing has felt like home until this moment. My heart is beating so fast, that I'm almost sure she can feel it through my shirt. I'm uncontrolled. My powers stir the trees, releasing leaves as they float around us from the nearby forest. The grass sways and small violet flowers bloom around us. I place one hand on the back of her head, not wanting to let go again.

Amalie clutches my shirt tighter as her silent tears turn into sobs. I rub her back, and my heart breaks for her. I can't imagine what she's going through, how she's not even safe in her own mind, never knowing what's real and what's not.

"Are you alright?" I whisper into her ear, I know she isn't, but I need to hear her lie. I need to hear her voice again.

"I'm sorry. I'm so sorry, Wren." She sobs harder and harder after every word she says. The physical ache in my chest tightens at every tear, every sniffle I hear.

"Shh, don't worry about it now. We will talk later. Look at me, Am." She does as I ask, glancing up at me with those bright, beautiful amber eyes. I run my thumb over her cheek, wiping away her tears and examining her face.

My fingers brush the bruise on her left side, causing her to wince. My mood darkens when I see the bump on the side of her head too. This wasn't an accident like I was naively hoping.

"We will get you a healer as soon as we get back. I'll send for one now." I hold out my hand, willing a leaf to land in it. A small maple leaf floats down from the closest tree, and I catch it out of the air. Grabbing a quill from my jacket pocket, I write a note to the healer requesting her assistance, more like demanding her assistance. But if anyone asks, I requested very nicely.

I throw the leaf into the air for it to travel on the breeze to the closest town. I try my hardest to keep my voice low and calm, but my anger is building, and I'm about ready to murder a certain Ash-hole. "What happened?"

Amalie just shakes her head. "We will talk later." She mirrors my words, reflecting them back at me. I give her a long look before nodding and whistling to the beast still lying at her feet. Willow jumps up so quickly, long tail wagging with joy. The dragon is now so tall that she stands right at eye-level with Amalie as she runs her fingers over the soft leaf-shaped scales of Willow's back.

"I'm starving, so I hope you were getting some food prepared for us. It's been a long journey. My friend, I can't survive on bread alone," Finley bellows his orders. I just raise an eyebrow at him, causing him to laugh at my expression.

"I'll see what Cahira can whip up when we get back to the chateau."

I move to the side, giving Amalie a bit of space. I'm not sure what to do in this situation. I know I just want to pick her up and carry her home. She must be so tired and sore, but she's also strong. Stronger than she will ever know and just as stubborn. She would hate me treating her like she's weak, so I just let her be. Walking silently the rest of the way to our home, together.

31

Amalie

Wren doesn't look at me the whole way back to the chateau. Not a single glance, and I'm left wondering if I did something wrong besides the obvious.

He seemed happy to see me, but once he took in my face, he pulled back, not speaking or looking at me again.

Willow hasn't left my side since I crossed the border into the Earth Kingdom. Seeing her running towards me, still too young to fly, wiped away all my bodily complaints. As we approach the chateau, I wonder if Wren will let Willow sleep inside, but it may not be the most comfortable for her now. It is incredible to see how quickly she has grown in the past two months that I almost miss the wee little leaf that used to fit in my hand. The memory of her grows more solid, clearer, the more I am around her. I remember playing with her, feeding her, smoothing her scales until she falls asleep.

I inhale the fresh forest air, allowing the scents of my home to fill my lungs. It feels like I haven't taken a breath since I left. Just because I was in the Kingdom of Air doesn't mean I was able to breathe. Air could be just as suffocating and heavy as quickly as it could be light and refreshing.

Seren lets out a long whistle beside me as we approach the chateau. "Well, does the size of this place reflect the size of the meal tonight because I'm starving!" Seren looks up at Finley, genuinely curious. He laughs and gives her a light kiss on the top of her head.

"Don't worry your pretty little head. I will find you something to eat." Finley pulls Seren through the kitchen doors at the side of the chateau, leaving Wren, Willow, and myself to stare awkwardly at the ground.

"Um, do you mind If I take a bath? I've been in these clothes for a few days," I ask Wren quietly, unsure what I should do next.

Wren gestures to Willow to stay outside, she doesn't seem pleased, but she flops down on the ground to wait for our return.

"You don't need to ask for anything. This is your home too, Am." He opens the chateau's front door, and I am amazed by its beauty. Wren gives me an odd look before asking, "Do you not remember living here?"

I shake my head. "I have bits and pieces of memory. We were at the castle when my mother was murdered. But they are slowly coming back."

"Your mother was sick, Amalie," he says in a soothing tone as if he is trying not to upset me, but I know the truth.

"We have things to talk about," I say simply, trying not to dwell on the subject for too long. I want to keep it easy between us for as long as we possibly can. Wren just nods and guides me up the main stairs, placing a hand on my lower back as we walk.

The chateau looks like a greenhouse. Plants and creeping ivy are everywhere you look, and the roof is full of skylight after skylight. The colors are warm and inviting neutrals, allowing the greenery to shine. Every table has a bouquet of flowers, and every railing is wrapped with vines.

I stop at the top of the stairs, looking around the main foyer. "It feels like home. The Air Kingdom felt so cold and eerie, but this...it's so warm and inviting. It's comforting, almost like the blanket Finley packed." I smile at the memory of how that simple warm blanket gave me as much comfort as this whole chateau.

"I-uh. I packed the bag. Finley came here for help to get you out. I put the bag together, and I thought you would like your favorite throws." Wren shrugs as if it's no big deal, but he couldn't be more wrong.

"Wren." I wait until he looks at me to continue, "Thank you for everything you've done. Thanks for not giving up on me."

Wren doesn't answer, he just carefully wraps his arms around me, giving me a soft hug. "Go get yourself washed up. I will call Cahira to help you."

"It's okay, I'm fine." I try to protest, but he puts his hand up to stop me.

"Am, you stink. You will need help, trust me." I laugh at his teasing and slap him in the arm. He chuckles at me before turning around and descending the stairs quickly.

"Wren! Which room is mine?" I ask him, still laughing.

He smiles back from the bottom of the staircase. "Oh, shit. Yeah, that's going to take a minute to get used to. Go down this hall, and it's the second door on your left. It's the garden view so you can see Willow. Your orders, not mine!" He holds up his hands like he's innocent in all of it. Whoever had that idea was brilliant.

I turn around and walk down the hallway he directed me to. When I reach the second door on the left, I take a breath before grabbing the handle. Letting out the breath I was holding, I grip the doorknob and twist, the door swinging open silently.

The room, my room, is beautiful. Fresh flowers line the

small table in the center of the room. As I walk in further, I see double doors leading to a large balcony overlooking Willow's garden. Mandevilla vines of every color crawl up the side of my balcony and wrap around the banister. To my left, there is a large open door leading to the bathroom, and to my right is a large canopy bed set against the far wall with more vines and flowers wrapping around the poles of the canopy. The floral mix and woodsy scent of fresh-cut pine bring me back to the garden from my first memory.

My first memory of Wren.

A knock on the open door behind me jolts me out of my reverence. I turn around to see a petite young woman with beautiful auburn hair and freckles all over her face. Something in the back of my mind sparks, and recognition suddenly ignites.

"Wren filled me in, so it's okay if you don't remember me. I understand! I'm Ca-."

"Cahira, you work here at the chateau, well actually, you were my lady's maid, but then I was gone, as you know," I cut her off, reciting the information that came to me. I want to hug her. I want to apologize, but I stand there, unmoving.

The silence is awkward, and her nervousness reminds me of Seren. *They would be great friends.* Perhaps that's why I grew so close with Seren so quickly; she felt so familiar when we first met.

Cahira nods. "Right, well, I will draw your bath," she says before walking to the bathroom and turning on a tap. I hear the groan of pipes and the splash of water before I grasp that the Earth Kingdom has running water systems. I remember my mother telling me about the Water Kingdom alliance allowing the Earth Kingdom to share their benefits and vice versa.

As the bathtub fills, Cahira exits the room with a bathing robe in her hands.

I unbutton and shuck off my dirty undershirt, revealing my bandaged ribs.

"Mind if I unwrap your bandages there?"

I glance at Cahira, feeling no sense of unease or awkwardness as we did mere moments ago. The acts are familiar, clicking into place like a puzzle. I nod to her as she moves closer. I lift my arms slightly, holding them away from my side so she can take hold of the wrap.

Cahira gives a loud gasp, and I look around frantically, thinking maybe I left the door open, or the water overflowed, but when I look at her, I notice she's looking at my torso. My body is so bruised and discolored that it seems like I'm wearing another shirt. Cahira glances up at me, eyes wide as saucers.

"What happened to you?" She whispers to me like it's a secret.

"Um, I was a punching bag for Asher's guard. Well, more like a kicking bag before I was put in a cell. I-I haven't truly seen myself since then. I know I probably have a rib broken, but it will heal. I'm fine." I try to explain as quickly as possible to drop the subject. It only reminds me that I should have done more. I should have fought them more.

"Does Wren know?" She looks behind her like she's expecting him to be summoned by his name alone.

"Not really. He saw my face obviously, but he doesn't know the extent."

"Good. Your ribs are slightly bruised, that's all. You fell. Any more information, and he might cause a war." I give Cahira a look of disbelief. Yeah, he won't be pleased, but he wouldn't do anything more than scowl. "Is that how you ended up with that bump on your noggin too?" I nod my reply and assurance to not say a word to Wren. She seems to understand because she leads me towards the bathroom, completely undressed now.

Cahira follows me, helping me lower myself into the bath before turning off the tap. The tub is large enough for two, made of a solid piece of hollowed wood from a massive tree. The scent of the lavender buds she sprinkled into the water is heavenly, and I sigh in relief. I feel her hands running through my hair, untangling my braid, and using a small jug to rinse my hair before adding an exquisite citrus-scented shampoo.

"Sorry for the rat's nest," I say, apologizing for the mess of my hair. I can't remember a time it's been this tangled. I wouldn't blame her if she just cut it at the scalp.

"Oh honey, don't worry about it. I've had worse with your hair. One time you decided to roll in the mud and then let it dry before coming home! Oh, was your mother ever angry at you, but you never took that grin off your face through her whole lecture about being a proper lady." Cahira laughs at the memory.

"I must have been pretty young to have done that!" I muse, trying to recall the memory.

"Actually, it was only last year! Wren dared you to jump in, he didn't believe you would, but you sure showed him how fearless you are." Fearless, right. Fearful of a mud pile. I roll my eyes at the thought. I crack a smile at Cahira, still giggling to herself as she thinks of my antics.

I don't feel like the same girl that Cahira and Wren knew. I don't really know who I am anymore.

I lay back, allowing Cahira to scrub my hair and body from head to toe. I am almost falling asleep in the warm bath when I hear a knock on my bedroom door.

"That must be the physician now. I'll be right back." Cahira drops the cloth into the tub and moves to exit the bathing room.

I take the cloth and squeeze out the water before rubbing it over my face and behind my ears. Once I've finished, I grab the side of the tub and haul myself up into a standing position. My body screams in protest, and I groan in pain.

"Stars, girl! Stubborn as ever, I see." Cahira pokes her head into the bathroom just in time to see me step out of the black, gritty water. She hands me the bathing robe before placing her hand on my lower back to guide me into my room. "Here, sit on the bed. This is Leeha. She will help you heal faster and relieve some of the pain."

I straighten myself out on the bed, turning my head to look at Leeha as she begins to speak, "Hi, Amalie. I use magic herbs to heal from within. I'd like to give you a tonic if that's okay. It will make you sleep, but you will feel much better once you wake."

I look at Leeha, a white-haired older fae. In human years she would be about sixty in fae years, she is probably about one hundred twenty years old. Then glance back at Cahira, who nods encouragingly.

I sit up slightly as the older woman brings me green liquid in a crystal-clear glass. Before I think too much about it, I take the glass to my lips and drink the mouthful in one swallow. The effects are quick but not immediate. I remain conscious as she asks me questions regarding my injuries. I glance at Cahira again to confirm how much honesty I should be giving. Complete transparency is the way to go with healers, apparently.

Before I finish speaking of my trials and woes, my head hits the pillow, and everything goes dark.

32

Amalie

I wake to soft light and a gentle breeze on my cheek, like a lover's caress. I turn my face towards the comfort. Opening one eye, I see Wren sitting in a chair beside my bed. His eyes are closed, but I have a feeling he's still awake. However, I don't dare make noise and rouse him.

He's sitting with one leg crossed over the other at the knee, and one hand on his cheek while his elbow rests on the arm of the chair. His dark hair is tousled like he's been running his fingers through it for hours. A shadow of blue lines his eyes, showing how tired he really is. I sit as still as possible, just watching the man in front of me. I think about how Wren could fall asleep in any position and how I was always so jealous of him. The memory of me finding him in random rooms, napping without a care in the world, makes me chuckle without warning.

Wren's eyes fly open, staring at me with narrowed eyes. "What are you giggling at over there?" The relief in his eyes is immediate, as if he's been waiting on edge for hours. His shoulders relax as he takes a deep breath and lets it out.

"I didn't mean to wake you. I was simply remembering how

you could sleep anywhere. Do you recall that time when I found you in the library, sleeping with a book covering your face and your legs hanging over the side of the sofa? I didn't want to wake you, so I sat on the floor until you woke up." I smile widely at him.

"You remember that?" Wren asks, unsure and weary of hope.

I nod at him in affirmation. "I'm remembering things, but I can't tell if it's a thought or a memory."

Wren leans forward and takes one of my hands in his large one. I use my left hand to push myself up on the bed to rest against the headboard. Only then do I take in my ribs with a dull ache now, no piercing pain when I breathe or move.

"Wow, that Leeha is a miracle worker, huh?" He gives me a slight dip of his chin, eyes still sad. "What's wrong, Wren?" I almost don't want to ask the question. I know there's a lot wrong, but Wren was always the light in the darkness. No matter what was going on, he always brought humor and confidence to every situation. Now, seeing him look so defeated makes my heart contract in empathy.

Without answering, Wren sits straight in the chair and pulls the letters out of his jacket pocket. I forgot I hid them in my pockets—both letters from Wren. "Cahira found these when she was cleaning up. Where did you get this one?"

"Finley." I don't have to look at the letter he's holding up. I already know he's talking about the letter Finley found. "He said he found it, but I think he was hoping it would spark a memory of you." Wren stares at me for a moment. His eyes are unreadable and stern. He looks like a man engaging in an internal struggle, and I don't know how to help him. "Please don't be mad at him. I'm sure he was only trying to help."

"I'm not mad at him. Stars, I couldn't be mad after all he's done for me- for you." Wren licks his dry lips and clears his throat before asking in a low voice, "How are you feeling?"

"Much better, thanks!" I put some enthusiasm behind my

voice, hoping it will lift his somber mood. To drive in the nail further, I jump out of my bed and stretch dramatically. That gains me a small grin, but there's still a hint of sadness behind his eyes. I want to know the cause so that I can fix it, but there are still some missing pieces of the puzzle in my head, and I can't decipher how to help without them.

"How about you get dressed, and we can take a walk." Wren doesn't allow me to answer. He walks out of my bedroom, leaving me confused and uncertain.

I stand beside my bed, staring at the door he just left through. Taking a breath, I move over to the armoire by the bathroom and open the doors to glance at my own clothing. It's a weird feeling to see your own items but not recognize all of them.

I find a pair of dark brown pants and a long green tunic, and I slide the bathing robe I fell asleep in off my shoulders, letting it pool onto the floor in front of my wardrobe. I find some undergarments in the drawers of the armoire and quickly put on a brassiere and undershorts. One of the small things that I missed when I was away from home were my personal belongings.

Next, I take the pants and shimmy them up and over my hips, fastening the clasp before sliding the long tunic over my head. The sleeves end at my elbows, and the front has a deep V tied together with a thin leather lace. I walk into the bathroom to stare at my reflection in the sizable floor-length mirror.

My amber eyes are the first thing I notice, not the bruise or lack of bruise on my head. I run my fingers through my dark hair, feeling for the bump at my temple. I don't feel anything but my smooth skin and silky hair. I haven't felt this clean and put together in quite some time - a few days at least - and I smile at myself in the reflection.

My nose is small with rosy lips, the bottom one is slightly larger than the top, and I have tiny freckles covering my nose and cheeks. I can remember days spent running through the forest and fields with Wren and some other local children who are now grown and married by now. The time spent in the sun danced along my face, leaving dozens of the freckled kisses I see today.

I'm nervous about going for a walk with Wren because I know this is more than just a pleasant stroll through the chateau grounds. Wren will want to know what happened. I just don't want to tell him I did the one thing he asked me not to do. I'm embarrassed and ashamed. My mind is constantly at war, two opposing thoughts battling to be the successor. On the one hand, I wouldn't change anything because Wren is alive, and my kingdom is safe. On the other hand, I feel foolish for allowing my best friend to erase any memory of my home.

I allowed Asher into my heart, and for a short time, I believed his lies and thought there could be a future. I sigh at my reflection and turn away with a shake of my head.

Tying my long dark chestnut hair back with a leather cord, I untie it again, my anxiety making me fidget.

Once I can't stall any longer, I look for a pair of flats or boots to put on. A pair of tall, knee-high black leather riding boots are at the door resting against the wall. I decide to grab them before Wren comes looking for me.

I exit my room, making my way to the main foyer, but I don't see Wren. I decide to search the chateau grounds and bump into Seren, literally.

"Ow! Stars, girl, where are you going in such a hurry? Don't tell me you're running away. If you are, I won't let you. I like this place too much for you to leave. Did you know you can pretty much do whatever you want here? Last night, I played with your little dragon there. At first, I was scared, but then she rolled over like a puppy!" Seren's excitement makes me chuckle. She's wearing a simple green dress with white embroidered flowers around the collar. Her sapphire hair is tied elegantly up in loose braids. I don't think she breathes when she gets talking.

I should mention to Finley to remind her to breathe, or he will find her on the floor every time she opens her mouth. I smile at the thought, shaking my head at Seren.

"Have you seen Wren?"

She huffs in annoyance, probably because I ignored everything she said, but she lifts her hand and points at nothing in particular. I stare at her in confusion, cocking an eyebrow as I wait for her to elaborate.

"He went that way," she says simply before turning away. Seren is in an odd mood today, but I will have to sit down with her later. While I am determined to clear my sins and get these secrets off my chest, I have to find Wren.

I take off in the direction Seren points to.

"Your ass looks great, by the way!" I turn to see Seren cupping her mouth to make her voice louder. I laugh loudly and continue walking toward Wren.

I find him standing on the edge of a cliff, looking at the ocean. Behind the chateau, there is a small dirt path through the forest. I follow it to the end, feeling that sense of familiarity to find myself here.

Wren is wearing a forest green cloak billowing in the wind off the ocean. His hair is tousled back off his forehead as I approach him. I put my hand on his arm, but he still doesn't look at me.

"If you fall, nobody will ever find you," I half-joke, trying to start a conversation, but I'm also nervous about how close he is to the edge.

"Perhaps that's a good thing," Wren says low under his breath. His deep voice makes it difficult to hear him.

"It's not. I'd miss you. I would have to jump after you." That makes him turn towards me, and I give him a shy smile, but he just stares sadly into my eyes.

"I'm sorry for what he did to you. I wish I could have stopped it." Before he even gets the words out, I'm shaking my head.

"Don't. There's nothing you could have done."

We stand together in silence, the wind blowing his cloak around me, wrapping me up in his warmth. I slide my hand down his arm and twine my fingers with his. He grips my hand tightly like a lifeline before lifting it to his mouth and kissing my fingers gently.

Wren lets go of my hand, slowly sliding himself to the grass and straightening his legs out in front of him as he leans back on his arms. I follow his movements, sitting down beside him.

"I don't know where to start," I admit, curling my legs tight against my body and placing my chin on my knee.

"What do you remember?"

I stare at the ocean, remembering the blue of Asher's eyes and how I believed they were calming. But instead of the calm before the storm, he was the storm. I just didn't realize I was in the eye of the hurricane.

"I woke up laying in a creek. I only knew my name. Stars, Wren, it was terrifying!" Wren stiffens but doesn't say a word. He allows me to tell my story at my own pace. "I just wandered around until somehow Semira found me, she-she was so kind, and she felt familiar. Even if I didn't remember her, I felt comfortable with her. I was told I had a husband, and that's when Asher showed up. He allowed me to heal. He listened and was everything I thought I needed. I convinced myself I could love him someday." I stop talking, trying to gather my thoughts and feelings.

"What happened, Am?"

I sigh and continue, "He wooed me, Wren. I fell right into his trap like an idiot. I accepted everything he said. Every word, every touch, and every promise. I just believed it." A white-hot tear rolls down my cheek, turning ice-cold from the ocean breeze. I wipe it away quickly. I can't tell if I'm crying because I'm frustrated or sad. "I never married him."

Wren's head snaps in my direction so quickly. "What?"

I shrug, "I don't remember all of the details of that day, though I do know why I decided to marry him. Asher confirmed it himself that we did not actually wed. I was just led to believe we did. I suppose Semira's spell was a blessing in disguise for him. I don't know if it was fully her idea or if it had a bit of his influence as well."

Giving my head a slight shake, I continue, "Anyways, Asher killed Semira. He didn't know Finley and I were there. Finley made sure I got back to my room safely. He took care of me, Wren. And when he had to act as if he was allied with Asher, I believed him. I felt so bad for not trusting him!" Another tear slips from my eye. This time, it lands on my knee before I can catch it. "But he already got what he wanted, so I was disposable. He didn't hesitate to throw me in the dungeons to rot," I say with disgust.

"What do you mean?" Wren asks me, fighting to keep the calmness in his voice.

"I accepted his ring, Wren." My voice is so quiet that he wouldn't have heard me if he weren't fae. But I know he has. His whole body tenses again. It's one blow after another for him. "I didn't get your letter in time. I didn't know what the ring truly meant; I didn't know I was half-fae. Did I always know I had this power dormant inside me?"

It takes a moment for Wren to answer my question, he seems to be deciding how to respond. Wren sits up straighter, crossing his legs under himself, and sighs, "No, you didn't know. I didn't either until after you left. I tried to find as many answers as possible. You didn't want to go, and I couldn't fathom why you would; I spoke with my mother. Do you remember her?" he asks, and I nod. "I thought if anyone had any ideas, it might be her. She knew your mother, and the way your decision changed so quickly after her death scared me." Now it's Wren's turn to pause as I hold myself as still as possible. I don't want to deter him from telling me the truth, just like he was holding himself together while I told him my truth.

"Your father was fae. My mother said he was sent to death. I didn't end up finding any answers beyond that. I am not sure what he did, but it must have been severe enough to warrant his execution."

I flinch at his words as I imagine a father I never knew being executed before my birth. *Or after my birth, did he ever get to see me?*

Wren continues, "I suspected that Asher's intentions weren't honorable, but I would have let you go if you truly chose him. Not that you were truly mine to let go of." The last part of Wren's confession wavers. His voice starts to break, so I put a hand on his arm again, permitting him to end his confessions.

"There's no way any of us could have known. I'm shocked, but it really doesn't change anything. I'm sure I will have a panic attack about it later, but for now, I'm just in shock."

"When the panic sets in, let me know. You never did well with stress." Wren smiles softly at me as a memory flickers through my mind.

"It wasn't my fault. The guard was teasing me, so he deserved the kick to the balls."

Wren laughs loudly at that. "He bothered you so much that you couldn't deal with it and ended up attacking him. Rightfully so, I was torn between doing it myself or letting you figure it out."

"I should have taken an arrow to his kneecaps."

Wren laughs again, and the sound is so lyrical that it brightens my heart as his smile reflects on my face.

When our laughter slowly dies, and the only sound is the water hitting rocks below us, I ask, "So, any ideas on how I can break this bond?"

"No, but I will. I promise you that. We will figure it out." Wren leans over, wrapping his arms around my shoulders in a comforting embrace.

We sit like this for what feels like hours, just enjoying each other's company. I close my eyes and take in the scent and feel of him. Wren smells like fresh rain and male musk. The same scent you get after a rainstorm, and the sun comes out to warm your face. My head rests on his shoulder, listening to his steady breathing. It's one of those moments you wish could last forever, but you know it can't. It's the peace I've longed for, for so long, and I'm not willing to let it go.

33

WREN

I'm fuming. Stars know I'm trying to keep it together, but I'm about five seconds away from beating the shit out of that Ash-hole. The only reason I'm still sitting here is literally right beside me, wrapped in my arms. She is my anchor in this sea of fury, the only thing tying me to my spot.

I try my hardest to appear calm and collected with everything, but I'm not. If anyone says they are, they're either an idiot or an asshole.

I'm not mad at her. I could never be mad at her. She made a mistake and trusted the wrong person, big deal. I'm mad at myself for letting her go, for thinking she would be happy there. Our kingdoms don't get along. Why would he treat a girl from the Earth Kingdom any better than any humans who have crossed their border?

"Why did you leave?" I know I shouldn't ask; I know I'm on edge, but I need to understand. I need to know if she left because of me. I'm no better than him.

I'm a killer too.

She takes a deep breath, sitting up and pulling away from my arms. I let my hand drop from her shoulder. Laying back on the grass, I close my eyes, not wanting to look at her face when she tells me.

"I couldn't lose you." Her voice is a soft melody, like the saddest song. I tighten my jaw, forcing myself not to speak, for I don't trust myself. I'm fighting with my inner monologue here.

What does she mean? She doesn't want to lose me, so she *left me?*

I take it back. I can be mad at her.

"Asher had my mom poisoned." My eyes fly open, not quite believing her words. "He threatened to kill you as well." She shrugs like the decision was easy. "I couldn't lose you. Even if you hated me forever, at least you would be alive. You would be okay." Her eyes start to glisten, and here I am, staring at her like a buffoon.

All of this was because of me, just not in the way I initially thought. If she made the sacrifice to "save me" then I need to do the same for her.

I sit up so quickly and grab her, pulling her tight against me. I run my fingers through her hair because I just need her to stop crying.

"I don't hate you. Stars, Amalie. I-I don't even know what to say. I wish you would have told me, but I understand why you didn't. If roles were reversed, I would have done anything to save you." I hug her tighter as she looks up, staring into my eyes. Her gorgeous amber eyes are welling up with tears, and I kiss her forehead fiercely.

I don't give a shit. I'd sacrifice anything to keep her with me.

I whistle loud enough for Willow to hear, hopefully calling the beast to Amalie will bring her comfort. I wait a minute before I hear the loud thumping of the dragon running through the path.

With a deafening roar, Willow sees Amalie and runs faster to her, sliding to lay down beside us. Amalie is smiling so wide with tears still in her eyes as she grabs the beast's head and kisses her snout. Willow lays her head in Amalie's lap before closing her eyes in comfort.

"Thank you," Amalie whispers to me, still looking at Willow as she strokes her green head.

"For what?"

"For everything. For listening and understanding. For Willow. For the past. Just...everything." She looks at me again, her small nose scrunching up in amusement. "So, about that letter, did you mean every word?"

"No, I got bored and was trying my hand at poetry."

"Well, you're shit at poetry." She laughs when I scowl at her. "Love letters, on the other hand, those I enjoy." Her smile is infectious, but I fight the urge to grin at her.

"Hmm..." I lay back on the grass, closing my eyes again. "Sucks you're not getting any from me. It's your loss, really. I've been told they're delightful."

I laugh out loud when she smacks me in the arm, cracking open my right eye. I watch her for a moment before closing it again, listening to her soft laughter and the grumbling of a sleeping dragon.

It's close to sunset when we decide to walk back to the chateau, with Willow leading the way through the forest. Amalie has my hand in one of hers and the end of the dragon's long, leaf-tipped tail in her other. When we break through the forest, Willow leads Amalie to her pergola in the garden. I take my hand out of hers, telling her I'll meet up with her later before she leaves to feed and put Willow back in her own bed.

I watch as she moves away from me, my eyes staring at her perfect round ass as she sashays through the garden gates.

Finley suddenly appears to my left. "Can't take your eyes off her, huh?"

"She looks pretty good walking, it's rather hard to look away," I admit to him, no shame in my voice, only adoration.

"She sure does." Finley lets out a slow whistle and then bellows his laughter at my expression. My fae male instincts kick in, and I growl under my breath, trying my hardest not to impale Finley right here.

"Watch it, Fin." Finley pokes me in the chest just to drive in his teasing remark.

"Touchy, touchy. I got a girl of my own. You don't need to worry about my ability to steal her away. I'm not interested." I raise an eyebrow at Finley. He is an inch or two taller than my six-foot-two frame, but I know I never had any competition with him. He's just trying to get my blood boiling.

I nod my head towards the chateau, taking one last glimpse at Amalie as she rounds a rosebush to the shelter for Willow.

A male servant is there replacing a broken torch on the side of the stone wall. I move around the ladder he is standing on while Finley walks right under it. I give him a vicious smack in the back of the head for his stupidity.

"Oh, come on, don't tell me you're still superstitious!" Finley laughs and moves to walk around the ladder.

I wave up at the servant before replying, "I wouldn't say superstitious. Just a little-stitious."

Finley laughs even harder at me, but I'm utterly serious. "Do you truly believe that you will keep the peace by avoiding certain things or by doing a specific action?"

I stare at Finley. "If this is the best that things get, I don't want to risk anything to lose it. If that means avoiding bad luck, I'll do it."

"Oh, shit, man." Finley's mood sobers at my words. I can see the thoughts churning in his mind as he ponders my thoughts.

"If one action as small as walking under a ladder made you lose Seren and you had the choice, you would regret that choice every day." I didn't realize a little quirk that I've developed in the past month suddenly meant so much to me, but my words ring true.

"Okay, I'm out." Finley walks away without a further reply. He's never done well with heavy topics or conversations. Ever since I met Fin about ten years ago, he's never had a proper heart-to-heart. In his eyes, that makes him the bigger man, I suppose.

I find Seren in the library, curled up on the plush sofa with a romance novel on her lap. She jumps up when she spies me, losing her book on the floor as she does.

"Oh, I'm so sorry. Uh- Prince Wren. I was just reading, I wasn't snooping around the library earlier. I just wanted to look for something to read." I put up a hand, shaking my head at her so she will relax a bit.

"First, it's just Wren. Second, if you wanted to snoop, might I suggest the treasury. My parents like to keep some valuables there. And third, I was wondering if we could chat for a second." I sit opposite her on the decorative wooden chair with carved ivy leaves on the arms.

"Of course!" She plops down on the sofa, sitting straight and proper, still not relaxed around me.

I lean back and try to gain a posture of comfort and relaxation, hoping she will mimic me and feel a bit more comfortable, but she doesn't.

"I know you and Amalie are close, correct?" I know the answer already, but she nods fiercely. "I was wondering if you could do me a favor?"

She's nodding before I even finish my sentence. "Yes, anything!"

"Can you please just look after her? If she knew, she would kill me. I know she is strong and can look after herself, but would you, please, for my own peace of mind?" I give her my sincerest look. I don't think she fully understands my question. I don't want to ask her to be a spy or tell me all of Amalie's secrets, but I just need to know she's okay.

"Can I be honest?" Seren asks me, and I nod in affirmation. "That's a stupid request. If she's my friend, why wouldn't I look after her? Just like I hope she would look after me, it's what friends do!"

I smile at her honesty. "That's exactly what I needed to hear." I stand up, ready to leave Seren to her book, but she stops me with a hand on my wrist.

"I haven't known her as long as you have, but I've known this Amalie longer than you have. She won't like you tiptoeing around her. Be honest with her. She's had enough secrets and lies in her life."

I consider her words, understanding that she is a much better friend than that caster was. I think Seren would make Amalie go through the pain of memory and sacrifice rather than allow her to suffer confusion and manipulation. Sometimes, the best thing to do is the most challenging path to follow. Sometimes your good intentions lead to more hurt and destruction. Sometimes suffering is the kinder solution.

"Hey, what are you two plotting in here?" Amalie's soft voice floats in from the large double doors of the library. I turn to smile at her.

"Oh, I'm just whipping this one into shape." I give Seren a small grin, and she giggles before settling in with her book again.

Amalie rolls her eyes at me but takes a step back as I walk through the doors towards her.

"Hungry?" I ask, not giving her a chance to answer before I pull her towards the kitchen to grab some dinner.

34

Amalie

It took me a few days to be entirely comfortable at the chateau again. It also took a while for Wren and me to get over the awkwardness when we would see one another. Now, we talk, joke, and play with Willow like we used to, and it almost feels like no time has passed at all. I've hardly seen Finley and Seren since we've arrived, and I'm content to believe they are enjoying one another.

I'm sitting on my balcony, watching Wren and Willow play in the garden below. Wren is creating small trees and flowers for Willow to fly over. She's beating her wings so hard, but the poor girl isn't getting off the ground. I can hear Wren's words of encouragement to her, telling her how to flap her wings to gain air.

I give her small cheers when she gains a moment of gliding before falling back to the ground. After each accomplishment, Wren and I shout in excitement like proud parents.

That is when my day turns dark, like a giant cloud creeping across the sky to cast out the sun.

A servant walks in with a letter in his hand. I thank him kindly, sitting down on the bench and spreading my lilac skirt around me. The letter is from Asher, and I should have already expected it. However, when I unfold the parchment and stare at his elegant cursive, my blood runs cold, and I want to vomit.

Amalie,

My Darling, I miss your company. It was unfair of you to leave your husband, for sneaking off with my guard is a serious offense. I wouldn't want to put a bounty out for you. Why don't you come home like a good wife?
We can marry and be a family like we were always meant to be. I am sorry for my actions. I'm trying to change, but I need something to change for. I was wrong for what I did to Semira, I know that now. I'm also sorry for the actions of my guards, they should not have been so rough with you.
I promise you will be happy if you come back.
I know I already have your bond, but I want your adoration again. I miss us.
I don't want to have to force your hand again, but I will if necessary.

Your Husband,
Asher

My hands shake so violently that I almost drop the letter off the balcony. My body is frozen, and the world's noise is beginning to fade as I stare at the blurring words on the cream-colored parchment. I didn't hear Wren calling my name until a small rose suddenly blooms from a vine on the railing in my peripheral. My head snaps up at the movement in front of me.

"Hey! What's wrong?" Wren's tone changes from excitement for Willow to concern for me. I lean on the railing with the letter in my hand, extending it for Wren to take. A vine rises from the ground, wrapping itself around the letter and disintegrating in a slow descent to Wren's height again.

Wren takes the letter and examines it.

Willow is now lying flat on the ground in exhaustion, with her wings splayed flat to her sides.

I don't want to cause Wren any more problems, but we had promised each other that we would be honest. I don't want to hide anything from him.

I can see his expression darkening as he continues reading the words on the page.

"He really is an idiot if he thinks you will be going back to him," Wren says with such confidence. "Do you want to send a letter back, or do you want me to send a personal letter?"

I'm shaking my head quickly before he has the chance to get the whole idea in his head. The last thing we need is for Wren to lose it on Asher. Yes, Wren is stronger than anyone I know, but my opinion is biased. With Asher now having access to my magic, I am unsure what my magic can do.

It will end in a war.

I shake my head at Wren again before turning away to meet him in the garden below. I enter my bedroom again, sliding on a pair of black flats, and I exit my room, walking down the hallway and taking the stairs two at a time. I bump into Wren at the bottom of the steps to the front door, and I put my arms around him, taking his comfort as much as I'm giving him mine.

"Please don't go to him. It's not my lack of faith in you, it's my fear of him," I confide in him, holding him closer.

"When are you going to get mad and fight back? The Amalie I knew would have already tried taking him down. And if she failed, she would have a plan to do it again."

I ponder his words because, as usual, he's right. I should be fighting harder, but at what cost. Fear keeps people safe; fear is the natural instinct for safety. Where do you draw the line between cowardice and bravery?

"I am mad, but how can I fight to regain something I never knew I had. I don't feel any different." I counter Wren's argument.

"What about your friends, your kingdom? You wanted to be my queen, but you're unwilling to fight for it?" I stare at Wren, pulling back from his embrace. I know he doesn't mean to have cruelty behind his words, but they hit me all the same like an arrow to the chest. The truth always hits the hardest. "Do you remember when you found Althea, the nymph?"

I think back, trying to recall the memory.

The sun shone through the canopy trees, glistening off the leaves, bringing the forest alive every time the breeze stirred them.

I was practicing my archery while Wren was strengthening his magic, creating beautiful targets out of flowers for me to aim at. Another breeze blew through the trees, bringing the strong scent of pine; the scent of my home. I inhale deeply and close my eyes, calming my mind before knocking another arrow into my longbow.

I open my eyes with an arrow at the ready; I raise my bow and pull back the string to caress my cheek like a lover's kiss. I point the arrow slightly above the bloomed flower target, hoping my trajectory is accurate. With a breath, I release the arrow and watch as it soars through the air.

And misses the target.

A startling female scream sounds through the forest, chilling me to my bones. Stars! Did I hit someone? I rush towards the sound, Wren yelling at my back to stay where I am. But if someone was hurt and it was my fault, I wouldn't be able to just stand in place and watch. I wouldn't be able to have Wren take care of my mistake.

Ignoring him, I keep running, searching for the injured female.

"Am! That wasn't human!" Wren cries out beside me now that he has caught up.

"It was a girl!"

The scream of pain comes again, accompanied by a male's gravelly voice. They are too far for my human ears to make out the words, but I can see Wren's jaw clench beside me, nostrils flaring in anger. I slow my advances, trying not to trip on the forest floor, and ask him, "What is it?"

He cocks his head, listening. "Shit."

I hear the man more clearly as he approaches, weaving through the trees a short distance away. I can see his loose-fitting clothes, most likely a farmer or carpenter from the village nearby. His bald head shines with sweat as he drags a creature through the woods.

No, not a creature. A girl.

A green girl, but a girl, nonetheless.

Her long, tattered sheer dress drags and shreds more as she is pulled through the forest over sticks, rocks, and logs. I can only imagine the cuts and bruises she will endure at the hands of this man. Her olive-green legs are kicking and thrashing, trying to get purchase on the ground as he holds her by her mossy hair.

My body burns with fury. Instant inferno ignites, and I stomp through the forest, readying my bow as I do.

"Drop her, or you will get an arrow in your heart."

Wren is behind me, allowing me to take the lead. Perhaps allowing isn't the correct word because he wouldn't have a choice at this point. My aura is oozing malevolence, and this man doesn't realize the trouble he stumbled upon today by encountering me.

His beady eyes and bulbous nose somehow make him look more furious than one would think. Generally, the features would almost seem comical, but he is mad. Evident by the fire-red flush to his features.

"Mind your place, girl." His voice is thunderous, loud enough to echo through the woods.

I clench my bow tighter and raise it to position. "I am not afraid to add a couple of holes through your chest. Now, drop her. I won't repeat myself."

The villager's small eyes go wide, resembling an owl hunting in the night though he does as I say. I expel a soft breath of relief for the girl as she skirts away from him, crawling on hands and knees to hide behind the closest tree.

He steps toward me as I ask, "What business do you have with her? That is no way to treat a lady."

The man scoffs at my term. "Lady, right. That is no lady. This forest nymph has been ruining my fields for the past month."

"She is still a lady regardless of race, and you will treat her as such," Wren's voice carries on the breeze from behind me.

"My-my prince! I'm sorry, you must understand. This creature," he points at the nymph curled tightly to a tree several feet away, "she has been growing trees in my field!"

I take a step towards the female as I speak to the farmer, "There are always two sides to every story. I'd like to hear from her." He glances between Wren and me, looking for guidance from his prince, but Wren only nods in my direction.

I approach the nymph slowly as if she is a wounded animal. And perhaps, in a way, she is.

I lower my bow and place the arrow back in my quiver as I crouch in front of her.

"My name is Amalie. Do you mind telling me why this man was treating you so?" I try to keep my tone even and soft, my language simple, just in case she does not speak the same tongue.

I notice the beautiful green glow in her eyes as she looks into mine, almost like the aurora borealis; magical greens, blues, and purples dancing in her irises. Her skin is a soft shade of olive-green with tiny brown freckles that cover her face, ear to ear. She wears a silk organza gown, most likely made of real worm silk. Her hair is darker green, giving the illusion of moss and vines cascading down her back.

"He cut down my home." Her voice is whisper-soft like the brush of leaves in the wind.

"Lying creature!" the foul man yells. I snap my head up, standing so fast I grab my bow, knocking an arrow in the notch and releasing. The arrow hits a tree beside his head with exceptional accuracy. Even impressing myself.

"Speak out of turn again, and the next arrow will not miss. Do not test me, Sir." I gaze down, and the girl has curled into a smaller ball than before. Creasing my eyebrows in sympathy, I lay my bow down again and crouch in front of her. "I apologize. Please continue. Nobody will hurt you."

"H-he cut down my home. I was living in a large oak tree. He cut down my home and many others to increase his land plot. I swear, miss, I only wanted to restore our homes." Her words break with a sob, and my heart aches for her.

"Ah, so you decided that you would take more land than you have been given from the kindness of the crown? Or am I mistaken?" Wren asks the man.

"I- Your majesty, you must understand. I need the land to feed my family, my villagers!" he stammers.

"Is the plot that was given to you not been enough? You should be well aware of the protocols. If you wish for a land increase, you will need to meet with the crown. To avoid this exact situation."

"Yes, sir. I understand. It was my mistake." He hangs his head in shame, but this isn't enough for me. I am still furious on behalf of this poor girl.

"You do realize you have decided to destroy her home to make yours better. You are purposely harming others for your gain. This is her *forest, not yours!*" My voice raises to a yell. I wish I could send an arrow into this man for his actions.

To his credit, the man does show enough expression to look ashamed. His head bows and his fingers twine together in nervousness.

"This will not be a repeat occurrence. The crown will be informed, and you will have a meeting with them to petition for your land increase. You will await a letter informing you of the date to arrive at the castle. You will not be permitted to take an ax or any other tool to another tree or flora without written permission. Are we clear?" Wren stands tall, his whole body emitting authority. His back is straight and features firm, green eyes as dark as moss.

"Understood." The farmer nods, bowing before running off into the darkest part of the forest.

"Would you come back to the castle with us? I would like to get your injuries attended to," I ask the Nymph.

She gives me a small smile, showing her razor-sharp teeth. "Thank you, your highness."

"I am no royal, not yet anyway. Can I ask your name?"

"Althea, miss."

"Beautiful name, Althea."

I glance back at Wren, and the smile on his face is the largest I've ever seen. It reminds me of a proud brother, standing broad-chested, boasting about his successes.

I remember the Nymph. The Earth Kingdom is my home. It's where my magic has been claimed. It's where my mother birthed me, where I found Wren, and where I must be to protest its inhabitants.

This is my time to fight for it, to fight for myself. Sure, there has been no official declaration of war, but there will be. As soon as I send my letter back to Asher, I will be shocked if there isn't any backlash for it.

"You're right."

I straighten my back, putting as much confidence in my posture as possible. My insides still feel like they are churning, but if I pretend that I'm brave, maybe it will come true.

"Alright, that settles it. Ready to go to the capital?" Wren asks me with a big grin on his face. "I think it's time we figure out how to break this bond. We can't allow him to have the upper hand, even if you knew it or not. That power is still yours."

"Do you think your parents will hate me for what I did?" My voice is filled with shame, and I can barely look him in the eyes. He may have forgiven me, but his parents won't.

"They can screw off if they do."

I bellow out a loud laugh at the sudden shock of his words, unable to hold it in. I look up at Wren, who seems deadly serious, making me laugh even harder. He cocks an eyebrow at me, giving me a confused look.

"Stars, Wren! You can't be serious. They have every right to be upset, even I understand that."

"And I have every right to tell them off if they are. The situation isn't as black and white. The treaty shouldn't even hold because it was formed on deception. I want to go to my parents and protest the bond between you and him." Now it's my turn to give him a confused look. I take a step back again, sitting down on the front stairs of the chateau, the cold of the stones chilling me more than his words.

"What do you mean protest it? You just say, 'hey, I don't like it!' and it's done?" With a sigh, he moves to sit down on the stairs beside me. He gives me enough room that our bodies aren't touching, and I miss his warmth, but I don't want to press anything yet.

"Well, not exactly. We need to request an audience with the council. First, we need to have proof of his deception. The treaty was built to empower humans, not strengthen fae."

His words spark a sense of false hope. The only evidence we have is the letter from him. It doesn't reveal what he did, it only implies I ran off with one of his guards on some weird affair.

"What if we don't have evidence?" I'm afraid to ask, but I know it will be sitting at the back of my mind if I don't.

"Don't you worry your pretty head. I had this plan in motion before I even realized I needed it. He isn't the only one with spies in the kingdoms." I give him a look, but he just shakes his head and stands up again, holding his hand out for me.

I take his hand, allowing him to pull me to my feet and lead me towards a small shed at the side of the chateau. I guess shed is an awful name for this beautiful but small structure. It looks like a small log cabin, with full flower beds lining the sides, leaving only the front door for access. Wren pulls open the door and steps inside. I decide to stand outside the shed and wait, it's not that large, and it might be too cramped for two people to move around.

Wren emerges with a beautiful longbow and leather quiver in his hands. I immediately recognize them as mine. The beautiful creeping vine hand carved into the bow matches the dyed leather engravings on the quiver. The memory of this gift hits me so hard that I stumble and have to catch my breath.

"Happy pre-anniversary! Ready for your gift?" Wren shouts at the top of his lungs. His nineteen-year-old frame isn't as full and robust as he is now at twenty-four.

"Pre-anniversary? Really, Wren. There's no such thing!" I cross my arms and roll my eyes at him.

"Our mothers agreed to our plan, in any case! In six years, you will be my wife and partner. I thought we should start our anniversary celebration early." He almost looks embarrassed, like he's unsure if this is what I truly want now that it's a possibility.

"I didn't get you anything..." I hang my head and pout, my bottom lip prominently exposed for the world to see. Wren steps forward and pokes my bottom lip. I laugh and squirm away from him.

Without a word, he begins walking along the castle corridors to the weapons room. He takes the door handle and sighs before entering the room. I glance around, taking in every weapon of shape, size, color, and lethal ability. My stomach tightens in anxiety. "Did you get me the gift of death? If you didn't want to be my husband, you could have just said no."

Wren chuckles at my fear-filled statement. "Quite the opposite, Am. I want you to be able to defend yourself, so you will live longer. If you're going to be Queen, you will always have a target on your head." He gives me a serious and stern look. Wren is never serious; everything is always amusing to him. He walks to one end of the room, across the fighting mats, and reaches for a long and beautifully decorated green box before bringing it back to where I stand. My apprehension is noticeable enough for him to roll his eyes before setting it on the ground.

"Open it" His eyes are so bright with excitement I can't deny him another moment. I reach for the long green box. It is about as tall as I am and almost as wide.

My eyes go wide and unblinking as I slide the lid off the box to reveal a beautiful longbow. Elegant hand-carved vines sweep from tip to tip, and the matching quiver lays beside it.

I gape at Wren, looking for an explanation, but he just grins back at me like the happiest person in the world.

"I think my wife should know how to fight back. You've always been good with a bow; I just thought you should have one of your own." I can tell Wren is getting nervous because I just keep staring at it in the box, not touching it.

"You got me a bow for a pre-anniversary gift?" I look up at him now, watching as he runs a hand through his hair.

"If you don't like it, I can get you something different."

I shake my head frantically, "No, no. I love it. It's just so beautiful and perfect. I-I don't have anything for you."

Wren shrugs, I know he doesn't care, but I do. I see the kindness and happiness in his eyes now. I jump up from my crouching position in front of the box. Without thinking, I round the gift and throw my arms around Wren's neck. Whispering small thank-you's in his neck before I pull back and kiss him.

We share our first kiss when it is meant to be saved for the altar, as customs declare. Although, I just threw those out the window. Wren grabs my hips, and I think he's going to push me away, but he doesn't. He pulls me closer and places a hand on my cheek to cradle my head.

I push my body up against his as he moves his other hand from my hips and up my back to entwine it with my hair.

I pull back slightly to breathe while staring into his eyes as he gives me a cocky smile. "I think we're even now." He gives me a quick peck on the lips for good measure.

"That's not why I did it. I don't want you to think I kissed you because I owed you." I peer up at his mouth again, then his eyes as I start to back away. Maybe he will think that now that we are committed to one another, he can give me gifts, and I need to reward him. Thoughts quickly demolish my bliss, and I can tell he knows mine have turned bleaker by the slight frown forming on his face.

Wren pulls me close again, putting one palm against my cheek, "And that's not why I did it. I can see the wheels turning in your head. I want you as my Queen, Am. I couldn't imagine having anyone else by my side."

"I don't love you." The words slip out of my mouth before I can reign them back in. "I don't want to be with anyone else, though."

"I don't love you either. But I could." He shrugs. There is a big difference between love and lust, friendship and relationship. Wren and I are dancing along those lines, unsure of which side we will fall on.

"My bow."

I realize my voice sounds like I am a thousand miles away, but I can't help it. I step back and stumble, the memory of our first kiss wreaking havoc in my head. I want to laugh and cry at the same time.

Wren drops the bow and moves so fast to catch me before I trip over my own skirt.

"Am? Amalie, what's wrong?" His frantic voice grows louder as I struggle to speak. For some reason, this memory was ripped from my mind with such force, unlike before. As my memories come back, most are thoughts or dreams that I'm not sure are real or not. This memory had power behind it, pulled from me by a triggering object.

I shake my head at him, trying to calm him and myself at the same time. Taking a breath, I finally put him out of his misery.

"It was a memory."

"A memory of what?" he replies with the calmest voice, urging me to keep talking.

"Of us. The day you gave me the bow. The day I kissed you for the first time. Do you remember?" His mouth turns up on one side at my stupid question. Of course, he remembers, he wasn't the one who was spelled to forget. "I'm sorry." I shake my head, fighting with myself.

When Wren doesn't answer, I look up at him. He looks equally tormented.

"I don't know how to feel. I need to know what you want. I can't bear to hurt you again. I need to know if you're okay with this, if you still want me as your queen. If not, we are still friends. I'll understand, Wren."

And there it is. Wren can either say he wants to stick to our plans, or he can say he wants me to leave. Wren has all the control and all the power.

It takes a minute for him to answer. "Friends," he repeats, staring at me with that sad and troubled expression, his fingers running through his dark hair and tousled hair.

"Things have changed." My heart stops beating. "You're not the only one who has lied. I haven't been honest with you about everything." I can feel my breath coming out in shallow pants. I know I told him that I would accept his decision, but I can't. I can't deal with it if he decides not to have me anymore. I left one lie to be thrown out by another. "That day," he continues, "when you kissed me, I lied to you then. I said I didn't love you, either, but I did. *I do.*"

I hiccup a sob, a very inelegant ugly sob at his confessions. My walls begin to crumble, and my body feels like it is ready to collapse.

I take a deep breath. "I don't remember loving you then. I don't remember all of our moments or the exact moment when I knew I wanted to be your queen. But now, without any idea of how or when, I feel you in my heart. It aches every time I see you."

Wren's hesitant to believe me. He still thinks I left him for Asher because of a different reason.

"How can you be sure?" he asks, his voice breaking on the last word.

"I-I don't think anyone can be sure. But if this is love, it makes sense to me. Love shouldn't be butterflies and anxiety. Love should be peace and warmth. When you meet the person you are meant to be with, you should feel a sense of rightness. Like everything clicks into place. With Asher," I shrug, "I was nervous and full of anxiety. Nothing felt calm or certain. It felt like fear, especially in the end. I'm not going to lie to you and say it was horrible the whole time I was with him, but something just felt *off.*" I swallow a breath, trying to calm my nerves. "All I know for sure is that you are my safe haven. Everything about you brings peace to my body, to my mind. You are everything life and love *should* be." The tears are running freely down my face now.

Without hesitation, Wren pulls me into his arms, kissing me like a starving man.

I don't know if my tears are from my confession or because I can't help thinking of Asher while Wren is kissing me.

35

Amalie

I grab my longbow from the ground where Wren dropped it earlier. It took a moment for us to regain our composure. I wish I knew what was going through his head right now. I still worry about so many things, but being here with Wren, in my own home with my memories coming back, I feel like I can finally move forward.

"Can I practice?" I ask him, waving the bow at him. He smiles, leading me into the forest to practice. We reach a small clearing with targets set up all around, and by targets, I mean vines with miniature red roses just like we used to do. Wren would make the vines dance, grow, and move all around us so I could practice my aim on a moving target. Once I became a better shot, we stopped using Wren as target practice. One too many hits to his body, and even he wouldn't be able to heal himself.

I grab my loose hair and braid it towards one side so it falls in a long chestnut twine over my shoulder and down my chest. Stringing the quiver over my head to rest on my back, I lift my bow and take a firm stance, tightening my core as I look forward and gauge the distance of my targets.

Wren stands behind me. "Still remember how to fire an arrow?" His tone is genuine and not condescending, more curious.

I nod, hoping I'm not wrong. I inhale, grab an arrow, and knock it into place. Once it's set and my eye is on my target, I tighten my core again and raise the feather of the arrow to my cheek as I let go on an exhale.

The arrow hits a tree with a thunk, severing part of the vine. I didn't hit the small red flower, but I did hit the vine, and that to me, is something to be proud of. I smile, straightening my back again as I reach for another arrow to fire. I hear Wren's low whistle behind me, but I ignore his praise.

Lining up the arrow with a vine again, I pull and release. Again and again and again until I finally hit my target.

In excitement, I jump up and down, almost hitting Wren with my bow. If Wren weren't a fae, he would have been hit across the face.

"Stars! Sorry!" I move my hands to cover my mouth in shock, almost hitting him again.

"Am, are you trying to kill me already?" he asks as my bow swings again as I raise my hands. Wren laughs at me, grabbing my bow from me and placing it behind his back. "Maybe we need to practice bow safety again. I'm just glad I didn't get you one with a blade on the tips."

I stare at his childlike demeanor. I haven't seen his eyes this bright in a while. My shock turns to laughter as I leap towards him. I put my arms around his neck, it's quickly becoming my favorite place to be.

Wren catches my newest assault, moments after recovering from my bow attack, and holds me tight against him. He breathes in my hair, placing his face in the crook of my neck.

"You did great. You may have lost your memory, but you haven't lost your touch." I roll my eyes at him.

"That was so corny." I tip my head back and laugh, feeling so carefree. And for the first time in a while, I feel strong and capable.

Our moment is interrupted by the obnoxious sound of my stomach rumbling. It seems I lost track of time, and it's almost after dinner as the evening light is showing through the forest trees. Wren grabs my hand, leading me back to the chateau. We walk through the doors, hand in hand for the first time for the chateau staff to see.

Wren places my bow by the front door while I untie my quiver and remove it from my back. Setting it down beside my bow, I give it a final glance and then follow Wren through a hallway on the main level. Turning to the left, we enter the kitchen and turn to a small private dining room again.

I sit down, waiting for Wren to do the same, but he holds up one finger and leaves the room, walking back into the kitchen. I skim around this intimate dining space. It almost looks like a sunroom or a greenhouse. Three of the four walls are floor-to-ceiling windows with beautiful greenery everywhere. Candlelight illuminates the room in a soft glow, wall sconces shining amongst the leaves.

I hear the door creaking behind me, and my head swivels to see Wren carrying multiple trays of food, balancing them on his forearms. Wren places the food down on the table and arranges our meals. "Where are the servants tonight?"

"I decided to give them the night off. I don't need them to serve if it's just us." I take the plate of food that Wren hands me. On the plate is a little bit of everything: cheeses, bread, and assorted meats. I look up at Wren with a questioning look. "I didn't have time to cook a full meal."

"It's perfect," I tell him as I take a fork and begin eating.

Wren sits opposite me but doesn't immediately grab his fork. I stare at him questioningly before he licks his bottom lip and grabs his fork, skewering the cheese.

"If you're still up for it, I'd like to go to the capital the day after tomorrow." I nod my answer. I'm willing to follow his lead on this because I have learned that my judgment isn't the best as of late.

Our dinner is awkward since there's not much to say or do. We've already confessed, played, and went down memory lane. Now it's time to just live.

"I'm excited to see the castle again. Remember when we would play in the fountain out front, and your mother would come out of the castle every time just to scold us?"

"She was so pissed, but we never stopped." Wren and I laugh together at the memory.

"Think she would still scold us if we decided to jump in again, now that we're older?" Wren laughs even harder at that. His voice is so lyrical and infectious that I can't help but laugh.

After dinner, Wren leads me to my room. I had helped him clean up our dishes, taking them back to the kitchens to wash and put them away. I even grabbed a handful of bubbles and slapped them carefully on his nose. My fingers are still wrinkled from the water.

We finally reach my bedroom door. I open it and walk in, expecting Wren to follow, but he doesn't. He stands on the threshold like the vampire myths the humans believe. I smirk at him when I notice. "Are you waiting for an invitation?" He still seems undecided. "Wren," I take his hand, pulling him into my room, "I'm not ready for anything more, but I'd like you to stay. If you want to."

His features decide on an emotion and snap into place, regaining his carefree attitude. He kicks off his shoes and throws himself onto my bed, putting his hands behind his head.

I laugh at him before going to my privacy screen to change into my evening shift.

The thin white nightdress lands just above my knees, exposing my legs, and the thin straps of the top plunge down into a soft sweetheart neckline. I glance at myself in the mirror, feeling a bit nervous. Before changing my mind about my outfit, I step out from behind the screen, unraveling my braid as I walk toward the bed.

Wren's eyes go wide at the sight of me, and my cheeks burn hot. When I step closer, I notice he has made himself comfortable as well by removing his shirt, though his pants are thankfully still firmly in place. When I slide onto the bed, I roll onto my side to face him, putting my right hand underneath my pillow. We stare at each other in comfortable silence before my hand moves to run my fingers up and down his forearm.

His hand flexes in response, but he doesn't pull away. I can feel his eyes on me while I study his muscular arm flexing beside me.

"Am, if this is real...if we're doing this, I won't be able to let you go again. I need to know if you're with me. I need to know if our plans are real." Wren's self-doubt causes my heart to ache. I did this to him. I've never known him to be this way. He was always so self-assured that nothing got under his skin until now.

"I'm with you." I feel him nodding beside me. I move closer, resting my head on the crook of his arm as he moves to wrap it around me. This is how I fall asleep, wrapped up in Wren and ready to start our lives again.

I startle awake with the feeling of Wren bolting from the bed. I hear his feet hitting the floor as he runs to the balcony. I roll over to see a flickering glow of fire in the garden below, and my first thought is of Willow. Still too young to fly over the garden gates.

"Stars! Wren!" I scream, jumping off the bed and running beside him, putting my hand on his arm to steady myself. "Where is she? Wren, where is she?" My voice gets louder and louder as my eyes frantically search for her.

Wren gives me a quick look before leaping over the balcony and landing softly in the blazing garden of fire. It takes me a moment to decide what to do, but I turn on my heel and run for the front foyer as soon as my mind catches up. Barefoot, I grab my bow and quiver out of instinct and run through the front door, down the stone steps to Willow's garden.

36

Amalie

I can feel the heat of the flames as I round the corner of the chateau. Wren is nowhere to be seen, and I start yelling for him. When I reach the gates of Willow's garden, I notice that someone put a chain on the gate doors and a large key lock to keep them closed.

My blood runs cold as I begin to comprehend that this is intentional. Someone purposefully set fire to Willow's garden and locked her inside. I uselessly pull on the chains holding the gates closed when a set of large arms encase my waist and drag me away. I start thrashing, kicking, and screaming to escape.

"Ow! Stars, Kitten! It's just me." Finley's deep voice reverberates in my ear, calming my efforts.

He lifts me and carries me away from the locked gates, the embers of fire brightening behind us. I am set down beside Seren, who is hugging herself like she's trying to hold it together. I've never seen her so quiet before as silent tears run down her face. It makes me grab her and hold her tightly to me.

"Willow!" I scream, tears threatening to spill from my eyes.

"She's fine. She's a dragon," Finley tries to reason, but his logic is wrong.

"Finley, she's an *Earth* dragon! She doesn't breathe fire. Fire can still hurt her, just like every other creature in the forest." A gasping sob catches in my throat, making it difficult to get the words out.

Finley takes off running again, leaving us to watch in terror.

"Seren, use your water magic!" I yell in fear, but she doesn't move, doesn't even react to my words. "Seren!"

"My baby," Seren mutters to herself, still hugging her knees.

"Your water! Seren, please!"

Her lineage is from the Water Kingdom, she must still have her powers, but she freezes when we need her most.

I can't sit here and watch my home burn. I can't watch my Willow burn. My eyes search the grounds for anything to help. If I attempt to get in there, I would only be a distraction. Behind me, I hear more footsteps approaching. I see Cahira running up to me from the light of the flames, still in her bedclothes. Her bright red hair matches the inferno as they reach the gate.

"No, no, no," Cahira chants over and over. I try to keep my panic at bay, but I need to move. I need to help in some way. I reach for Cahira, pulling her close to Seren.

"Shit. Stay together. I'll be right back!" I take off running, searching for anything to help. I don't bother looking back when Cahira begins to yell after me.

My bare feet hit the soft grass as I move silently through the night, the only light coming from the flames at my back. I pull my bow out, searching for the one who started the fire. Maybe if I can find them, we can get some answers. I have to believe Wren will be okay, and that he will get Willow out.

I stand, scanning the forest for any movement. I think I spot a shadow moving through the trees, the shadow only a shade darker than the night. Moving behind a tree, I ready my bow and wait. After a breath or two, I see the same movement through the darkness. Pulling the string of my bow back, I aim and fire. The satisfying scream of pain rings through the forest, alerting me that I've hit my target.

Running towards the figure, I knock another arrow into my bow. Keeping it loaded is my best option for safety right now. Once closer, I notice that it's a man—the chateau servant who brought me the letter from Asher. My internal alarm bell begins to ring on high alert.

"My-my lady. Please." The servant lays on the ground with an arrow through their left knee, right at the joint. Sure, I was aiming for his chest, however, the knee works too. He won't be going anywhere.

"Amalie!" I turn to see Wren running towards me, with Finley following closely. "What did you do?" Wren says while Finley laughs, "Damn, Kitten! You got claws."

Both men are covered in soot. Wren has dark smudges all over his face and bare torso. At the same time, Finley looks just slightly disheveled. I find myself searching Wren for any burns or injuries as I move closer to him, putting my hands on his chest.

I expected Wren's reaction, I knew he wouldn't be happy, but once I explained everything, he would understand. "He was creeping through the trees, and he's the same man who brought Asher's letter. It can't be a coincidence." I look up into his eyes. He has a sad and haunted look that I just want to kiss away. "Are you hurt? Where's Willow?"

He shakes his head. "I'm fine," Wren says simply, walking up to the moaning man on the ground. "Finley, take Amalie to see Willow." I'm so excited she's alive that I don't protest, and his words don't kick in until I try to catch his eyes again.

"Wren?" I'm afraid of asking, *is it Willow? Someone else?* I look at Finley, but he doesn't want to look me in the eyes either. I step forward and take Wren's hand, still ignoring the groaning man on the ground. "Is it Willow?"

He looks at me finally, biting his lip in nervousness as he nods. "She will be alright, although she does need your comfort. I'll take care of him."

Tears sting my eyes, even though I refuse to cry right now. I need to hold it together for Wren and Willow. I nod, kissing him gently on the cheek before turning to Finley and running back to the chateau, Finley in tow.

Finley is faster and quickly catches up, leading me to the kitchens. When I reach the half door, I swing it open with a fury. Finley stands off to the side, allowing me to enter first.

On the cold stone floor lies my beautiful Willow. She raises her head when she sees me and gives me a small groan, breaking my heart. I run to her, kneeling on the hard floor, and taking in her broken form. Willow's right wing is burnt through her wing's soft and thin membrane end, revealing a singed and tattered edging. I gasp at the image in front of me, not believing it's real. Her left wing has minor burns, and I keep searching her body for more wounds.

Minor burn marks sparkle on her green skin, likely from falling embers landing on her. But for the most part, she looks okay.

She is still tiny, roughly the size of a giant wolf, but the end of her tail is curled up tightly around her side, hiding the leaf-shaped tip from my view. I peer up and around the room, spying Seren and Cahira mixing some herbs. Seren looks pale and in a state of shock, but Cahira is giving her gentle orders. I only hope they have contacted Leeha to come help.

I stroke the long muzzle of the dragon soothingly, whispering soft words of affection to her. Her soft grunts and snorts are the only thing ensuring me that she is still alive. She is so motionless that I watch and wait for any movement to show she's still breathing.

"Here, see if you can get her to eat some of these herbs. It will ease her pain." I take the bundle of herbs from Cahira and speak softly to Willow.

"Raise your head, honey. Please," I coax the dragon to lift her head so I can pry her mouth open to place the crumbling, dried leaves in her mouth. Her large teeth graze my hand as I reach into her mouth to place the herbs. I followed it with a funnel of water that Cahira handed me.

Sliding the funnel into the side of her muscle, I tilt the glass of water slowly into the funnel. Forcing Willow to swallow, I take her head and tilt it up further to rest on my shoulder so the water can run down her throat. When I see her throat contract from the water, I remove the funnel and use both hands to pry her mouth open.

"That's a good girl," I coo, giving her a kind caress under her chin. I lay her head back down gently on my lap, letting her fall into a peaceful sleep. I sigh, closing my eyes and laying my head down on top of hers.

I must have fallen asleep on the floor with her because the next time I open my eyes, warm sunlight is shining through the top half of the kitchen door, and Wren is sitting cross-legged on the stone island in the center of the room. His eyes meet mine, and he uncurls his leg before jumping off the counter. I watch as Wren moves towards me, slowly sitting down by my side. He sighs, unsure of what to say, so I decide to begin.

"Is he still alive?" My voice is monotone and without a care. I only wish he were alive so I could kill him myself. I don't think Wren would allow that on my conscience, though. Wren nods solemnly, so I keep pushing him for answers. "Did he say anything?"

With a sigh, Wren states the truth. "He admitted to working with the Air Kingdom. They made plans to set fire to the garden and numerous houses on the path to the capital." His voice is so low that I have to strain to hear him. Willow doesn't stir at the sound of our voices, and I'm glad for that. It's not her fault, she was caught in an inferno because of a vendetta she has no part of.

"What do you mean 'they'? Was there more than just him?" I know the question is stupid, but I want to know how many people we will imprison or kill due to Asher's actions.

"At least two, there were two major spots that were set ablaze at the same time. The garden and a few houses in the village down the road. There's no way he could have done this all by himself."

I sigh in frustration. "Will you let me speak with him?"

"Just speak? Or are you still ready to fire that arrow?" He nods to the bow beside me and the quiver still strapped on my back. I give him a small smile before answering.

"Would you blame me if I did?"

"No, I'm not innocent either. I've taken a few down just to find you." His reply is hesitant. He is admitting a truth he never intended to say to me.

"I didn't know that. I thought you just bumped into me at the market."

Wren leans back on his arms, looking up at the herbs hanging to dry on the ceiling. I don't bother glancing at him. I keep my hands and eyes on Willow. "I killed one of Asher's guards. He was patrolling the border, and I taunted him to cross. Once I got the information, I killed him. I knew something wasn't right, I just had to know what."

"You're not a bad person, Wren. Just like if I take this one down, it doesn't make me a bad person either. He committed a crime. It's justice." After all the hurt and anger from the past few weeks, intentionally injuring Willow, trying to kill her... that's my breaking point. My heart has hardened towards the Air Kingdom. My attempts at finding a reason and finding the good in Asher are gone. There is no good in him, not even if he tries to be strong for his kingdom.

"There's a very fine line between justice and murder, Am.

Sometimes the difference is as simple as whose side you're standing on. I'm not saying you can't. I would never say you can't do something; I'm just saying don't cross the line out of hatred." I nod my head. But my mind nor my decision never waivers.

37

Amabie

I stand in the middle of the room, staring at the servant. He holds his head high, arms tied tightly behind his back. I can tell that Wren already had a moment with him because other than the arrow that I put in his knee, he has blood on the corner of his mouth and more blood still dripping from his nose.

A large man holds the top of his shoulders on either side of him so he can't move in either direction. I don't feel remorse for the man. I trusted him; Wren trusted him.

Still, he chose Asher.

The five of us stand in the center of a small and empty room in the basement of the chateau. All the walls are solid stone, like a cellar. The only light is a torch on the wall near the door behind us. The servant's face is lit up as Wren and I are silhouetted.

"Why?" It still doesn't matter his answer, but I want to know. Wren stands behind me, allowing me to take the lead. When the man doesn't say a word or even look at me, I grab an arrow from the quiver on my back and ready my bow. "Did you enjoy the hit to the knee? I see your other one is looking a bit lonely."

"You're not as fearsome as you think you are. Asher was right, you are weak," the man taunts, but I refuse to give in. I straighten my shoulders and take a step towards him.

"Oh, sweetheart, you haven't seen me when I'm pissed." I take the bowstrings and pull them tight before letting them go into his uninjured knee at close range. It travels right through, leaving a large, bloody hole. The man screams in agony, falling backwards on his ass while clutching his knee.

"You bitch!"

Wren tries to step forward at the insult, but I put my arm out to stop him, shaking my head no.

This one is mine.

I have an eerie veil of calm over me. The point of anger that surpasses rage, a calm without any feeling of remorse. He hurt my Willow. He tried to destroy my family all for Asher, and I need to know why.

I raise my eyebrow at him, readying another arrow. "Which body part is next, hmm?" I pause to let the man moan from the pain a bit longer. "Now, I want to know why. Why would you act against the Earth Kingdom?" Tears stream down his face now, mixing with the blood. I tip my chin up and take a deep breath, squaring my shoulders again. I'm shocked when I hear his choked and pained answering cry.

"He-he has my family. He has them being watched here." More cries escape the mouth of the man, but I don't react.

"You could have told us. We would have helped." A soft edge to my voice drifts in, but I harden myself against the emotion threatening to break my calm. Before I finish talking, the man is shaking his head so violently, that blood and tears are falling to the floor. "Where is your family?"

"North, ma'am. They are in Leifton." The man's sobs become louder and louder until I can't take the agony behind his screams.

With a tear threatening to spill over, I raise the bow again and pull back the string. My hands shake as white-hot tears finally escape, running down my face as I feel the salty taste on my lip.

"I will ensure your family is safe." My fingers loosen on the bowstring, and I fire.

The *thunk* of the arrow embedding in a wooden barrel behind the man vibrates through the otherwise empty room. This is my choice to save his life, and I must stand by it. I need to show that I will not back down to a threat or an attack, but will I indeed be any better than Asher if I take this man's life.

How can I command someone to death for taking the same actions I have taken? I made terrible decisions to save my family, frightened by threats from Asher.

Wren puts a hand on my shoulders for support, but I don't blink.

Shock is frozen on the servant's face, and he looks like he is about to vomit.

I feel the same.

Nausea churns in my stomach. For what I both did and didn't do. Even if it leaves a bitter taste in my mouth, I stand by my decision. Willow deserves justice, and I took that from her.

"Thank you. Thank you!"

Over and over, the man spews the words, crying his relief.

Without another word, I turn and walk away from this room. I need air to breathe. Wren follows me after nodding to a guard. When he reaches me outside in the open air, he grabs my arm and spins me around so I'm staring up into his concerned face.

"You alright?"

No. "Yes," I lie. I don't want to allow myself to think of his family. That man did the exact same thing I did, he sided with Asher to save someone he loves.

"Don't lie, Am. You're shit at it." I glare at him, but I still don't say anything. "I was thirteen when I killed my first man," Wren begins his story, but I cut him off, hand raised.

"I'm fine, I didn't go there."

"You're not fine, so shut up and let me talk." His words startle me enough to close my mouth. "I was thirteen, and I killed a human man because of a dare. A damned dare, Amalie. That man's eyes haunted me for years. It still does. And do you want to know how I killed him? With my magic. Did you ever wonder why I never used my magic when I was a half-fae boy?"

Wren waits for me to answer him, "I thought you couldn't." I shrug. I always thought not all half-fae have magic, and they only fully gain it once they come of age.

"I had magic, Am. But every time I used it or thought of using it, I would vomit. I know the reason you didn't do it. Still, you thought about taking your first life, which isn't a small decision. When the time comes, it doesn't mean that it won't haunt you, but eventually, you may become numb to it as I have."

I stare up at him, trying to read his forest green eyes. "Why didn't you ever tell me? Why lie?"

He takes my face in both his hands, smoothing his thumb over my bottom lip, "Because I didn't want you to think differently of me. If you believe all the bad things about me, then they become true." I turn my head to kiss his palm, silently promising to protect this man and his heart.

"Can you take me back to see her?" I change the subject, everything is all too heavy, and I need to focus on one important thing at a time. Wren nods, taking my hand and leading me around the corner of the chateau and into the kitchen again. "I want you here. Can you look after him later?"

Wren nods sternly, and I turn away, ready to see my girl.

Just as I am ready to reach out for the handle, Wren pulls my arm back.

"Leeha is inside." Those three words send my heart into palpitations. I can feel the burn of threatening tears once again.

I'm not sure if I'm relieved she's here or terrified that she cannot heal Willow. "Are you ready?" he questions, taking in my features. I don't know what he sees in my eyes, but he nods, leading me inside.

Willow is lying flat, belly on the floor, and her wings are still spread wide, almost reaching wall to wall.

"Hey, girl," I announce to her as I enter the room, giving Leeha a nod. I remove my quiver and bow, placing it to the side, and I kneel down in front of her head. Willow's large head lifts as her nostrils flare, and she begins sniffing my chest and neck. I look up at Wren but his mouth quirks to the side in a half-smile before sitting on the floor with me. I stroke her head, running my fingers through the crease between her eyes. Willow snorts before flopping her head in my lap, making me laugh aloud. She looks up at me through her beautiful vibrant green eyes that remind me of Wren's.

I can hear Leeha grinding up herbs behind me with her pestle and mortar. I glance back and ask her, "What did you give her? She seems more alert than she was about an hour ago." My fingers are still stroking Willow's face, tracing the lines around her eyes, nose, and mouth. The hard leaf-shaped scales beneath my fingers are soft like silk.

"Just a calming spell is all. I am mixing some pain relievers for her now." Leeha doesn't look at me as she replies, and her eyes are downcast in a sad look.

"Leeha, please be honest. How bad is it?" I'm afraid of the answer, but this baby dragon is *my* baby, so I have to know. She finally lifts her eyes to mine before answering.

"I cannot fully mend her right wing. There is too much damage to the patagium," She gives a small laugh at the confused scrunch on my face. "The thin webbing between the bones of her wings. I can heal the wounds, but I can't regrow her patagium." I stare down at Willow and her damaged wing to my left.

When I was a child, I used to take a leaf and rip out the soft blades between each vein; this is what I am reminded of every time I glance at her damaged wing. The edges are charred and black, carrying the stench of burnt flesh and pine.

"Will she still have full functions?" I know the answer before she says it, her lips purse, and her head drops again.

"She may have trouble flying, Am." I hear Wren's deep soothing voice beside me, but I don't look at him.

"Can't you give her something to mend it like you did when I was injured?" I ask her, my voice increasing in volume, which causes Willow to lift her head and grunt. My head snaps back to her immediately, and I realize that I have stopped petting her. She nudges my hand again, causing me to give a small, sad smile, and I run my fingers over her head again.

"Your ribs were broken, not gone. As I said, I can mend but not regrow. No healer can regain what has been lost. It's simply not possible. She does have tears in her wings, and we may be able to suture some of the smaller ones. It's the large ones that may pose an issue. Dragons can still fly with tattered wings if the rip or hole isn't too large. It's a waiting game at this point to see how her body heals."

"Will she be in pain? Will it hinder her in any way?" My voice cracks at the thought.

"She may have residual pain and tenderness. A wound with such severity could have continued side effects, it's hard to say. I heal humans and fae. I've never treated a dragon before." Leeha grabs the herbal paste she has made and walks over to Willow, who acknowledges her with a soft grunt but doesn't remove her head from my lap. "They may be able to restore their patagium over time, or she may be able to learn to fly with tattered edging."

Leeha leans down and gently applies the paste to the minor burns all along Willow's back, legs, and tail. Willow gives a low growl at each tender area but allows her to continue.

I look up at Wren, pleading for comfort or *something*. He takes in my face and says, "Either way, she will be fine. She will be back to her old self soon enough."

"But she's our baby, Wren. Doesn't your heart ache for her as mine does?"

Wren scoffs a laugh. "What a strange child we have made."

I crack a smile at him and snort, "Oh please, how can you be so nonchalant about this?" The smile leaves my face once again.

"I'm not being nonchalant. I am trying to hold it together and give you comfort. As much as I don't want to admit it, she has grown on me too. It pains me to see her injured, and it pains me more to see your heart breaking." Wren's voice is low, but he doesn't take his eyes off mine. I think Wren knows me more than I know myself sometimes.

I nod, then glance towards Leeha as she gathers the leftover herbal paste. She looks up at me as I take a deep breath.

"Thank you for helping her."

Leeha nods before standing to grab her supplies.

I don't look up when I feel Willow's body jerking and moving as Leeha and Wren try to hold her still and suture her wing. Even though Leeha promises that she has had enough pain relief, Willow still moans and fights to tuck her injured wing back tight against her body.

"Is there something we can give her that would knock her out?" Wren asks, frustration evident in his tone.

Leeha gives me a thick leaf to place under Willow's tongue, and she falls into a deep sleep moments later. Right now, I wish I had the same herb. My palms and forehead are sweating profusely, and I feel like I'm going to vomit from the smell of her charred flesh. But once they start removing the char to have an exposed area to clean and suture, I have to stand up and vomit into a bucket in the corner of the room.

My insides are empty, but my stomach continues to heave. I dry heave repeatedly until I feel a warm and large hand rubbing the center of my back, calming me. Wren leans down beside me, whispering in my ear.

"It's done; she's alright." He coos over and over, repeating the words like a mantra. Even though Wren sometimes pretends to not like Willow, his actions, words, and reassurances today truly show his feelings for her.

Hot tears run down my face like a tap someone forgot to turn off. I can't stop the sobs escaping as they become louder and louder, morphing into a wail. My mind runs in circles of hatred for Asher, anger at myself, sadness for Willow.

"Amalie, I have her stitched. She should be stirring in about an hour. Why don't you try to get a bit of sleep or have food and a bit of water? If you're going to be sick again, it's better to vomit something rather than nothing." I'm shaking my head as soon as she mentions food and water. I don't think I could stomach anything right now. "This is coming from a healer. At least have some water or perhaps ginger tea."

Wren stands and reaches out his hand to help me to my feet again. He stares at me, brushing my hair back from my face as he guides me back over to Willow.

Leeha, thankfully, has cleaned the wound and other areas where the embers burned her. She looks so peaceful sleeping, but when I glance at her whole body, she looks terrible. Seeing her like this isn't right .

I kneel beside her again, grabbing her large head and placing it in my lap as I did before. I stroke her face and neck over and over to calm her, but I think the action calms me more than her. She's breathing, small snorts escape her large nostrils, and I couldn't be more relieved. If she can make it through this, I can work with her every day to regain her balance and confidence.

I hear Wren's footsteps leaving the room, but I don't look up. My focus is on this girl in front of me. My eyes start to drift close as I curl myself over her sleeping figure. Ignoring the steaming tea Leeha placed beside me.

Wren enters the room with a crashing sound, banging into the door frame as he carries an arm full of supplies. My head snaps up at the sound, and I turn to stare at him, eyebrow cocked.

"Shit, sorry." He drops the blankets, pillows, and a canvas bag beside Willow. I still stare at him, expecting an explanation. "I thought I could at least bring you a blanket. I don't think she will be moving anytime soon."

I nod, giving him a small smile of thanks. I take Willow's large head and gently place it underneath the pillow Wren placed on the floor. I stand up to grab the blanket and drape it over her large and motionless body.

"The blanket was for you, not the beast," Wren says with a chuckle under his breath. I roll my eyes at him, ignoring his words. He grabs the canvas sack and pulls out a thick bedroll. "This is for you. I don't think you will be able to move her onto the roll." At that, I smile.

"Thank you," I mumble in my tired state. I didn't realize how late in the day it was or how exhausted I was from today's events. I move the bedroll beside Willow, lifting her left wing and tucking it carefully back into her side. The bedroll is so soft that I have no issue drifting to sleep once my body curls into Willow's left side.

38

Wren

I sit on the kitchen island, watching as Willow stretches her left wing and places it on Amalie like a blanket. The action seems instinctual because she doesn't even crack an eye or lift her head. Amalie told me a while ago that when dragons imprint on their mothers, they become instinctively protective. Like baby ducklings are drawn to the first person or thing they see; apparently, dragons aren't that much different from a duck. I have heard of the theory, but my anxiety eases slightly to see it.

Even when I leave for the capital to speak with my parents, she will be protected by the beast, and for that, I am forever grateful.

I jump off the counter and head through the door, searching for Finley. It doesn't take me long to find him. He is helping Seren and Cahira clean up the debris from Willow's garden.

"Fin!" I shout over their voices, chatting amongst themselves. His head snaps up at the sound of my voice. He drops the large piece of charred wood and approaches me. "How quickly do you think you could be ready to leave?"

"Really, leave now? It doesn't seem like the best time, does it?" Finley counters.

"I'm leaving the girls and Willow here. I already sent a leaf for Hadley to return. He will guard the chateau." Finley runs a hand through his hair. The top half is tied back in a bun while the bottom half is laying loosely over his shoulders. The black soot from the fire is smeared over his hands, clothing, and face, but he doesn't seem to mind.

"Alright...Where are we going?" By the crease on his forehead, I can tell that he's confused by my sudden change of plans, but it can't be helped. After what Asher did and how he is threatening my people to turn on me, I need to find a way to break this bond and stop a war before it begins. Because if Asher continues, there *will* be a war, and I will be the first to strike.

The best option I have is to go to my parents. They will have the answers I need.

"Capital. Gotta pay dear old mum and dad a visit." Finley gives me a wide full toothed grin, remembering the days when we would prank and dare each other ridiculous things. The King and Queen would always scold us for our wildness, but it didn't deter our adventures. Sometimes we brought Amalie with us, but it was just us boys for the most part. "When can you be ready?"

"An hour."

His statement is simple and exactly what I need. I clap him on the shoulder before turning away to pack a traveling bag.

I make my way through the halls of the chateau, not bothering to look in on Amalie and Willow. If I take the time to see her before I pack, I will change my mind about leaving her here.

I reach my bedroom door and turn the doorknob to enter. The room has been a lot cleaner since she came back. I suppose that's all I needed to get my ass in gear again.

The room is dark, as always. Wooden floors creak underneath my feet as I walk to the large oak armoire, pulling on the silver rings to open it. I pull out an emerald green jacket and spare outfit without really paying attention. When I'm finished, I shut the doors and head towards the bed to pull my traveling bag out from underneath it. I kneel down on the floor and feel under the bed blindly. My hand grazes across the hard wooden box I had prepared for Amalie. I seek to further torture myself, it seems, as I pull the box out and crack the lid to peek inside.

Inside is a letter I wrote to her, the bonding ring I planned to give her, and a handful of small trinkets I've collected over the years that remind me of her. The white gold bonding ring is in the shape of leaves and vines, followed by a large green emerald in the center, capturing the essence of the forest she loves so much. I hold the ring in my hands, closing my eyes for a moment just to make a promise to the world. A promise that I will break this cursed bond between her and Asher, at whatever cost. A promise that I will fight for this kingdom and no other members of Earth will suffer as the servant did. A promise that in the end, everything will be alright again.

I close the ring back in its box and slide it back under the bed. I reach for the fabric of my traveling bag again and pull it out. I shove the clothes in it roughly before turning to leave my room without a second glance. Who knows if I will ever be back here, but I am only moving forward from here on out.

A bottomless pit settles in my stomach. Whatever trial I need to go through to break this bond may break me as well. If it comes to that, I need to find a way that she will be okay, that the kingdom will be alright.

I make my way through the chateau to the kitchen again to find Amalie and Willow awake. I stop in the door frame, staring at the tears running down Am's face while Willow nuzzles her face into Amalie's chest. I purposely scuff my boot against the stone floor so I don't frighten either of them.

Willow raises her head and gives me a low growl of a greeting, at least I hope it's a greeting. We've had her for about three months now, and she still makes me nervous sometimes, not that I will ever admit that to anyone.

Amalie's head follows and turns in my direction, giving me a tear-filled smile. I'm trying to decide if it's happy tears or sad tears. Her features are giving me mixed emotions.

Amalie says simply, "She's awake." Then I know it's happy tears, thank the stars. I thought I was going to have to murder someone.

I nod and grin back at her, running my hand through my short hair. I move to hop on the counter island again. It's quickly becoming my new spot in the whole chateau. I drop my bag at my feet, which catches her attention. Her forehead wrinkles in confusion, causing her small nose to scrunch up.

"I'm going to see my parents for a few days. My guard, Hadley, will be back later today if you need him." I try to deliver the words as calmly and as a matter of factly as I can, but I knew she would question me.

"Why go now? You know I can't leave her here." Her hand travels to Willow's neck again.

"I know, that's why you're staying here with Seren. You two can watch over her recovery," I nod towards the dragon. "And for why I'm going now, I don't want to risk another chance for Ash-hole to get his claws in again. It will only be a couple of days."

I can see the thoughts turning in her head. She sits so still with only one hand moving in slow circles along Willow's neck.

"If you're gone more than a few days, I will come after you." She seems to give in to my plan easier than I thought she would, possibly because of Willow's current condition.

"If I'm going to be there more than a few days, I will send a leaf." I compromise.

She thinks over the counteroffer, nodding her head in agreement. "Fine." She huffs, clearly not happy about being left out of this adventure. We sit in silence before Finley appears in the doorway, bag slung over his shoulder.

"Are you two lovebirds finished? I'm getting nauseated listening to you two." His mocking grin makes me laugh as Amalie scowls at him.

"Oh, screw off, Finley." She rolls her eyes before turning back to me. "You be careful, don't be an idiot. I will kick your ass."

I hop off the counter and stride towards her. Leaning down, I give her a small kiss on the cheek. "Oh, I know you would. Look after our daughter, will ya?" I say as I give Willow a soft pat on the top of her head. She lifts her head and snorts in my face.

Amalie and I laugh at the dragon, but Finley interjects, "Congratulations, Kitten! I didn't know you were expecting!"

That makes me laugh even harder because the expression of shock and mortification on Amalie's face is the best thing I've seen in a while. Her cheeks immediately redden, and her eyes are so wide they may fall out of her skull.

"He means Willow, you dumbass!"

Both Finley and I laugh as we exit the kitchen and head to the stables to grab a horse for our journey north to the capital.

The stables are small compared to many others in the realm, but for the chateau, it's perfect. The small wooden barn houses three horses on one side, with hay and equipment on the other side. I walk over to the tan and white horse and prepare it for our trip while Finley does the same to the black horse beside me.

Once settled, we walk out of the stables and give each other a nod before mounting the beasts. We click our tongues, squeezing the horse with our legs and causing the steeds to take off in a run through the field and into the forest behind the chateau.

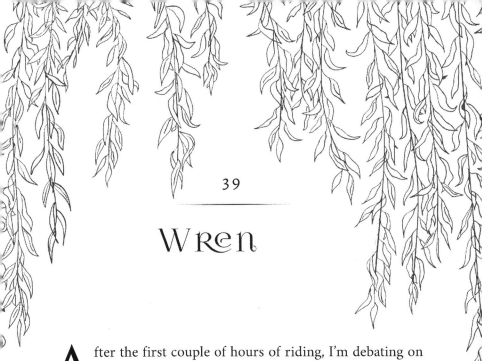

39

Wren

After the first couple of hours of riding, I'm debating on murdering my best friend. Finley had been reciting the same poem repeatedly, increasing in volume and adding his own flourish after each round. He is a couple of yards behind me, but at the volume he is belting out the words, it sounds like he is beside me. I spy the perfect opportunity to stop him in his tracks when we round a corner to see a low-hanging branch. I lift my hand and use my magic to extend the branch further as I pass underneath it.

"There was a fearless lady of earth
  Whose face was forever bright with mirth,
  She left her kingdom to join the Air
  Saving her love but falling in despair,

Five, four, three…

. . .

The lady never knew her lineage before
Now she will raise the throne to restore."

"Ah, ow!" I hear the branch snap on Finley's face, and I turn in my saddle, laughing loudly. "You, ass! I could have lost an eye."

"Oh, too bad. I was aiming for your voice box," I reply as soon as I catch my breath. Finley continues to glare at me but remains silent the rest of the way.

By the evening, we finally arrive in Willoughby, the Earth Kingdom capital and where Amalie and I grew up. Guards attempt to greet us, but I don't slow my horse. I head straight through the streets to the castle ahead.

Willoughby is a treehouse town instead of a typical city that one may encounter. The streets are trails and paths winding around different trees where homes and shops are hidden. Many newcomers don't know to look up to see the structures. They can walk right through the city and not even know they're there.

Finley and I guide our horses to the massive weeping willow in the middle of the city center. Above us, tiny lights illuminate the houses within and around the treetops, casting out the stars through the tight canopy of the trees.

The castle is inside the tree, connecting to other treetops like veins on a leaf. Once the guards reach us again, we slide off our horses and pass the reins to them. I take a deep breath before approaching the large door at the base of the tree, the door that leads to my parents.

Finley claps me on the shoulder before walking to the elegantly carved entrance. "Let's go. I need to get my face looked at."

I snort at his comment. "Oh, stars. You're fine. Maybe you should get your ego checked, in any case. I think it might be wounded," I retort, grinning widely at his glare.

"Excuse you, my face is my best feature. Besides these muscles," He cocks his arm and flexes to show off said muscles.

"Careful, you might need a new shirt too."

Finley laughs again, grinning so widely that his eyes scrunch and close. I roll my eyes at him, smirking as I reach for the door and turn the knob. Soft lights brighten the corridor and staircase leading up the tree to the main foyer of the castle.

The Earth kingdom has always been welcoming. We allow everyone with good intentions to enter our castle. Unfortunately, there is no way to know if their intentions are true, but that is one fault of the kingdom. Where we lack cautiousness, we excel in ruthlessness.

As we ascend the spiral staircase, small stained-glass windows spiral around us, following the path of the stairs. Fragrant flowering vines hang from the ceiling and lay on each windowsill, giving small animals and insects a home.

"Stars, why haven't they put in for a portal or something? I forgot how tiring these stairs were.," Finley complains behind me.

"Maybe you're just getting too soft." Finley's disagreement is evident as he picks up his pace, passing me on the staircase. He looks back and cocks an eyebrow at me.

"Who's the soft one now, huh? I could run circles around you, prince," Finley taunts as he takes off running up the stairs again.

If I'm being honest, I have gotten soft. I'm not telling him that, though. I've enjoyed my life at the chateau for far too long, almost forgetting the enchanted atmosphere of the Capital.

My parents must have been waiting for us because as we reach the top, my mother is standing with arms wide to embrace me. Instead, she gets a bear hug from Finley as he picks her up and spins her.

"Stars, I missed you, Haelyn! Did you bake anything for our arrival? I'm starved." Finley places my mother on her feet again as she reaches up and grabs his face with both hands. She is so short that she has to reach up on the tips of her toes.

"Finley, dear. When have I never had fresh cookies for you?" She leans back and places both her hands on her plump hips. "They're cooling in the kitchen." Finley takes off running again, down the corridor towards the kitchen. I roll my eyes at him and ascend the final stairs, taking in my mother's image and my father a few steps behind her.

My mother's chin-length rich brunette hair shimmers with hues of gold from the stained-glass windows around her. My father towers over her short stature, leaning his chin on her head. He has always kept a close shaved beard to rough up the top of my mother's hair as she moves her head under his chin.

"It's about time you found your way home." My father teases while my mother smacks his arm.

"Bryn, leave him alone. Welcome home, honey." She pulls me into a tight hug, surprisingly strong for such a small woman. Her pointed ears brush my chin as I pull her closer. "I got your message. It seems our girl got herself into some trouble?"

I nod my reply, still unsure of how to start this conversation. So, I ask a different question, "Hadley left, right?"

My mother nods. "Bright and early this morning." The tightness hiding in my chest subsides, and the nervousness I didn't know I felt leaves me knowing that he should be arriving at the chateau any minute, if he hasn't already. I make a mental note to send a leaf later.

I look up as birds begin to chirp, settling in the branches overhead for the night.

"Why don't you get settled in for the night, we can talk in the morning," my father offers, and I relent, giving in to the exhaustion of a day's ride. I clap him on the shoulder and kiss my mother on the cheek before heading for the wooden stairs to the living quarters.

I find Finley walking down the hall towards me with a

mouth full of cookies and one hand carrying another stack of them. I stop dead in my tracks, crooking my head to the side in wonder.

"What? It's pumpkin!" Finley shrugs in answer to my silent question and continues past me to his own room. I grin at myself and quickly recover, thinking about the tasks ahead and whom I left behind.

Tomorrow, I have to find a way to break the bond, stop Asher's antics, and get back to Amalie before he tries anything else. The task list is getting longer, and my head is starting to spin at the thought of it all.

Fireflies dance around the ceiling, casting a romantic and soft glow through the hallway, illuminating a path to my bed chambers. I can't help but wish Amalie was here again. The fireflies at night were her favorite; she would always compare them to the stars.

I reach my sizable wooden door. It's been so long since I've been here that I have to brush aside some vines that have grown over the handle. I grab the knob and turn, pushing open the door and breaking some vines as I do. The soft glow of the fireflies floats through the crack in the door, lighting my room ahead of me. I nod my thanks at them and open the door wider.

The tree has taken care of the dust, as the castle is essentially open and grown from the tree, so the light breeze doesn't allow dust to settle. I reach my bed, where wooden logs support the frame, and the blankets are soft spun silk.

Sitting down, I take off my boots and throw them to the side. I place my feet on the floor, feeling the grass and moss like a plush carpet between my toes. The grass floor never grows, but the vines do, and I've always thought of it as the tree taking care of us in its own way.

I reach into my jacket and find my quill, then I summon a leaf and write a short message to Amalie.

Miss me yet?

Smiling, I spell the leaf for a reply and send it off into the wind. I lean back on my bed and close my eyes.

A reply returns a couple of minutes later, the leaf landing on my face. I grab it and read the response.

Of course, I do.

I write back, *I meant the beast.*

A minute later, her reply floats through the canopy above me.

Ass.

That makes me laugh even louder. My favorite part of the day is bantering with her. I think she's more fun to tease than Finley.

I take another leaf and write again, not allowing a reply this time.

Goodnight, My Queen.

I fall asleep shortly after, thinking of the positives of the future.

When the morning birds chirp, I am already awake, and outside sword training with Finley as the sun begins to break through the canopy. I lay down my sword and Finley does the same.

"Tired already?" Finley taunts me.

"Nope, I just thought you would need the rest."

Finley laughs and claps me on the shoulder. We decide to meet my parents in the sitting room before breakfast, it's time to get this conversation over. I need to know how to break the bond and get rid of Asher and his power.

If I have to, I'm not opposed to killing him to stop this war from happening. If Asher continues on his path, my sword will gladly welcome him.

We reach the sitting room with my parents waiting,

speaking softly amongst themselves. When they see us enter, they stand to greet Finley and me. Before they have a chance to move towards us, I raise my hand and wave them off. I stride closer to the lounge and lean on the sofa beside my mother as she sits again.

"What's going on?" my father asks. I did send Hadley to inform them, but he either didn't give them the whole story, or they wanted to hear it from me.

"Long story short, I need to know how to break a bond." My mother's eyes bulge in shock at my words.

"Wren... you need to let it go." My mother's soft voice causes me more anxiety. My hands start to shake as she continues, "This is not something that is often done."

"So, it's possible. What do I have to do?" I don't want to listen to her advice and cautious tone. If there's a way, I'll do it.

"Wren, it's a trial of sacrifice. It would be a sacrifice you would not be able to make," my mother pleads, but Finley speaks up instead.

"How would that work?"

My eyes widen in surprise. That's a very valid question. I was anticipating some sarcastic comment or question, but I've never considered the possibility that I wouldn't be able to help her. I would be able to go through this trial to make the sacrifices so she doesn't have to.

My mother understands his question because she says, "If one were to break a bond for another, they would have to petition it to the council. Only the four elements combined can break the bond." I nod my understanding. The council is made of the four elders from each kingdom, and only the elders can use all four elemental magics in unison.

"Okay, so I'll go to the council. There's no reason I should be denied, even being the next heir." I stand up, straightening my shoulders.

"That's exactly why this is a bad idea, Wren." This time my

father chimes in. He's usually a quiet man, allowing my mother to speak for him, and is the type of fae who forces you to listen to each word simply because they are not often spoken.

"Please, it will be fine. I'll be fine. But if I'm not, can we put something in place?" I try to reassure them with my sense of confidence, but as I look around the room at the faces of my family and friends, I know their concerns. "Listen, I understand. But this is something you can't talk me out of. I will fix this and go home to her. If something doesn't go as planned, I want her to be okay. You would do the same," I tack on the jab at the end towards my father. If the roles were reversed, I know he would do anything for my mother.

My father exhales loudly. "What were you thinking?" My mother turns her head to him so quickly. Then, she glares at him, clearly unhappy with his acquiesce.

"Bryn! Yes, Amalie is our family, and she will be taken care of, but we are not discussing this option. Wren, please. She has less to lose than you do." She stands and grips my crossed arms. She looks into my eyes, pleading with her expression.

I can't look at her anymore. I'm torn between my stubbornness and my mother's will. I divert my attention and lean back to look at the canopy above us.

"You're not going to let this go, are you?" Her voice breaks at the end, knowing she can't change this. Her hands fall from my arms as she takes a step back. "Fine, let me go draft a letter of succession." I look down at her, but she turns on her heel and walks through the door without a glance back.

"Uh... yeah. What's a letter of succession?" The only second question Finley has asked in this whole conversation.

My father stands up and claps me on my shoulder before following my mother out of the room. I wait until he leaves to answer Finley.

"No matter what happens, good or bad. You're still getting your Queen."

40

Asher

The dagger slices through my mother's abdomen as my father watches, gasping for breath. My parents stare up at me, eyes wide with shock and confusion.

It had to be done; I'm just sad it needs to be this way. I would have been King if she stayed. In the end, it's all her fault. The only two ways to ascend the throne are by either marrying and being crowned or the death of the current royals.

Wren has his talons in her, I know that. She isn't coming back to me, but I don't need her here. I just need her alive.

"You did this!" I spit the words at my mother as she holds a bloody hand to her stomach. She drops to her bony knees, cracking against the stone floor as her mouth gapes open like a fish out of water.

"She doesn't deserve you. I wanted to save you from her."

My spies told me about her letter to Amalie, threatening her with Wren's life after her mother died.

That is why she agreed to marry me.

And here, I believed that she actually loved me. I believed that she felt the same way I did!

"You killed her mother and lured her to my side, for what? To kill her while she was in my arms?" my voice raises in anger. I can feel the beast inside me grinning at the malice.

"I-no, I wanted her gone before all that. The poison was meant for her. Please, darling, listen to me. She is no good for you. Please," my mother pleads for her life, yet her actions tell a different story.

I take the elegantly carved dagger and plunge it into her neck. Hot metallic blood sprays onto my face, coating my pristine garb as I turn to my father.

I feel the power flowing through my veins as the air is ripped from his lungs until the light in his eyes fades and his chest concaves from the pressure. I don't feel the remorse that I know I should. I can only feel the strength and the presence of air flowing through me. The element coaxes me into a delirium, edging on madness, and I embrace every moment of it.

"I'm sure you knew about her plan. You deserve the same fate," I say as the color drains from his skin, leaving him grey and ghoulish looking.

The silver crown still rests on my father's head, my crown. I walk over to him, stepping over my mother's fallen body, careful not to slip in the pool of blood on the cold stone floor. I reach my father, grab the bloody dagger I used on my mother's throat and stab it into his heart, exposing the hilt. His body takes the force without a jolt; no movement is left in his lifeless body.

I bend down and grab the crown from his head. Savoring the sound of his skull cracking on the floor.

I stand tall like a true king and place the crown on my head, securing my position in the court. I turn around again and walk to the grand throne at the far wall of the room, and I take my seat as I stare at their bodies.

My mind screams at me to feel something, but I only feel powerful, untouchable, and infinite.

I take another breath before standing to place the crown back on my father's head and shouting for the guards so I can initiate the next phase of my plan.

41

Amalie

Seren and I try to coax Willow to eat, but she isn't having any of it. I suppose I shouldn't say that. She's happy to have the significant portions of beef that Cahira was cutting up for the chateau. Seren waves a whole fish back and forth in front of Willow's nose, but Willow tucks her head under her one wing as I laugh at Seren's frown.

"Oh, for star's sake!" Cahira grabs a partial leg of a cow and tosses it at Willow, who perks up like a puppy. She uses her front claws to hold the meat in place as her sharp teeth saw and rip through the flesh and muscle. "Spoiled thing." Cahira huffs a laugh before continuing her butchering.

I look up at Seren. "Do you think we can get her up on her feet today?" My mouth purses in concern for Willow.

"Oh, absolutely! I believe dragons heal faster than humans do, so she will be fine in no time!"

I smile at her enthusiasm and nod to her in thanks. Willow continues to rip apart the leg, almost finishing it, bone and all.

When she finishes, she stretches out and yawns with a roar, causing us to giggle. Willow tucks her front legs in again and pushes herself up from the kitchen floor, swaying a bit to gain her balance. Seren and I jump up and grasp her large body to help her. Cahira runs to the door, opening it wide as we coax Willow outside into the fresh air.

Her leaf-shaped scales glisten in the afternoon sunlight like a thin coat of morning dew. Willow stretches her wings out wide, and I can see the muscles flexing underneath her scales.

I coax her to walk into the field in front of the chateau, but her body begins to lean further to the right as she takes a step. Seren tries to catch her and grunts under her weight. Willow corrects her balance by flicking her tail to the left, dispensing the weight. It only takes her a couple of minutes to start understanding how to keep her balance as her body adjusts to the pain that's being aided by herbs she is given. As her body leans in one direction, she flicks her tail in the opposite direction, throwing the weight and restoring her balance.

We spend hours with her outside, encouraging her to use her wings and wear off the herbs until she is leaping and running through the field. She did have a couple of falls, but overall, she did amazing.

I jump up and down, clapping my hands in excitement as Seren copies my actions. Willow turns and spies us cheering for her, and she runs over to me, head butting me in the chest. I reach out and hug her neck tightly, scratching the small horns that are just starting to poke through.

"Amalie! Willow!" I hear a familiar young male voice, and my head pops up, searching for where the voice came from.

It's Hadden, the guard Asher supposedly disposed of after the market. Fear and shock still my beating heart, and I take a few steps back. He notices my demeanor and pauses. Willow turns excited to see him, which confuses me even more.

"You're supposed to be dead." The words are stupid, but it's the only ones I can get out as I stare at him like I've seen a ghost. Hadden laughs at me. He seems so much younger than before. I realize why he felt so familiar when I met him in the Air Kingdom, Wren must have sent him.

When I was in the palace with Hadden-Hadley, for those brief moments, he seemed serious, older somehow. I narrow my eyes waiting for him to start explaining.

"Wren sent me to the Air Kingdom. I guess I messed up when we saw him at the market." He shrugs like it isn't a big deal, but I'm still trying to figure out how he's alive. Asher would have killed him for less.

When he doesn't explain further, I ask him, "How are you alive?"

"He let me go. *Dismissed* for not being able to uphold my duties."

I stare at him, more confused. There was a time when I believed that Asher was a good man, but he killed Semira, stole my magic, and tried to imprison Seren and me.

"I'm telling you the truth. Wren sent me to make sure you were safe. He wanted me to just be there in case you needed anything. When we saw him in the market, I shouldn't have let you talk to him, but I did. That was my infraction. Asher dismissed me, quite sternly too." Hadley's face is serious, no smile creases or cocked brows. I stare at him for a minute longer.

"Just like that?"

"Just like that. I didn't think Asher was all that bad until he did what he did to your friend. I'm sorry about that. Oh, and your magic. I heard about that one too." I'm still cautious, but I give him a curt nod before turning back to the chateau and calling Willow as I go.

Her stomping footsteps sound behind me, easing a bit of my anxiousness. I guide her back into the kitchen for more food before I try to set her up in my room.

Cahira is nowhere to be found, so I grab the large piece of beef she set aside and give it to Willow. Seren and Hadley follow in soon after, the setting sunlight pours through the open door, and I give them both a nod. "I'm heading to bed. It was a rough night last night."

"Good night," they both say, staring at Willow and me as we walk away.

I urge Willow to ascend the staircase. She's wary at first but doesn't have an issue after the first couple of steps. She is still small enough to move around in the chateau, but she won't even fit through the door in a couple of months. As we reach my room, she runs and jumps on my bed. Yelping a bit as she lands on her healing wound. I smile at her and move to the bed to curl my body around hers. She's the size of a giant wolf and takes up most of my large bed, but I fall asleep quickly, wrapped around my girl.

A leaf startles me awake as it falls onto Willow's nose, causing her to sneeze loudly. I pick it up and read Wren's elegant but scratchy scrawl, grinning as I grab my quill and form a reply.

Our banter is short but sweet. I want to ask him how he is, how his visit is going but I don't. I don't get a chance to. If he isn't back in two days, I am going to the capital. I need to solve my own problems. I can't let Wren do all the work every time.

I stretch my hand out and rub the webbing of Willow's wing before I drift back to sleep.

The early morning sunlight wakes me up, but I refuse to open my eyes until I hear my door open and shut. My eyes snap open so quickly, fearing it is Hadley, and he is betraying us as the servant did.

Instead, Seren slides through the door, tiptoeing to my bed as she does.

"I'm awake," I mumble into my pillow.

"Do you mind if we talk?" she whispers. Though, her unusual demeanor causes me to roll over and sit up in bed. Willow raises her head to look at Seren, then places it in my lap as Seren crawls on my bed. I lean against the headboard beside her once she's settled herself.

"What's on your mind so early this morning?" I sling an arm around her, drawing her closer to my chest to cradle her.

"I really like him," she mumbles into my body, making me chuckle at her admission.

"That's not new information. I can tell by the way you look at him. So, what's truly bothering you?" I press.

"I haven't told him any of my past." Her voice is small, and even though her head is on my chest, I still have to strain to hear her.

"If you believe he wouldn't want you because of your past, you don't know him very well." I've never known Finley to judge or condemn someone for what they did or what happened before. He's always been an action type of person. If someone made a mistake, it's the actions going forward that stand tallest with Finley. That is one of the main reasons why he's Wren's best friend.

Seren thinks over my words. She's silent for a couple of minutes before she takes a breath and continues.

"I have a child. *Had* a child." Her voice goes quiet for a moment after that. "She was two when she was killed. My mother was with her while I was at the Treaty Market, looking at fabrics. I came home to find our house ablaze. I couldn't save them." Her voice breaks, and so does my heart.

After the death of Semira, I've turned to Seren and relied on her heavily. I never realized that she might need to rely on me as well. I pull her tighter against me, cradling her head. I comfort her as I hear small sobs escaping from her. I want to ask her about her daughter, her mother. I want to know more, but I don't press her.

"That's why I couldn't use my magic when Willow was hurt. I haven't used it since that day. Every time I try, it brings up the memories of that day. I ran because I couldn't face looking at the charred remains of my life."

"Does your daughter have a father?" I dare ask the question. Partly to take the pressure off that day, I am also curious about my friend. She has lived a whole life without me knowing.

"Biologically, yes. It was a short relationship, and he decided he couldn't care for her not long after I met my girlfriend. She was so gorgeous, but after that night..." Seren's voice travels away in the wind as she collects herself again. "I left her. She probably thinks I'm dead, to be honest."

I only nod and hug her tighter, not forcing any more questions on her.

When her sobs start to subside and my night shift is wet from her tears, she sits up and releases a small giggle.

"I'm sorry I cried on you. It's a Water Kingdom thing."

I laugh at her. "Crying is a Water Kingdom trait?"

"No, just the amount of water with our tears. The more powerful fae can literally cry a pond of tears. Many of the legends speak of maidens crying an ocean of tears."

I smile at Seren. Her eyes are red, and her cheeks are blotchy, but she still looks like my beautiful blue-eyed friend.

"For the record, I don't think Finley will see you in a different light. He's too head over heels for you." She laughs and hugs me before thanking me.

I click my tongue at Willow to rise off my lap so I can slide off the bed.

"Hungry?" My question is directed at Seren, but Willow perks up and bounds off the bed. She spreads her wing attempting to fly, but she leaps and lands with a hard thud on the floor. "Stars!" I run over to her, but she springs back into action—all injuries and embarrassment forgotten at the mention of food.

Behind me, Seren laughs loudly.

Word came from the capital later that afternoon. I knew I should have gone with him. I should have known he would try something stupid to protect me, but I know for certain that I don't need protection this time. This time, this mistake will be mine to suffer and mine alone.

Haelyn sent the letter, not Wren. Of course, not him. I'm furious at this misguided hero mentality. Not every maiden needs to be saved, sometimes, the maiden needs to save herself.

I run out of the chateau, grabbing my bow and arrow on the way out. I sling them over my back before reaching the stables and grabbing the last set of reins hanging on the wall. I spy Seren as I place the bridle on the horse, raising my hand to wave her over as I tighten the buckles.

"Hey, going for a ride? It's going to be dark in a few hours." She looks up at the horse questioningly, nose scrunching and eyebrows raising.

"I'm going to the capital. Wren's going to break the bond."

"That's a good thing, right?" she queries.

I shake my head as I turn to grab the saddle and place it on the horse. "No, it's not. He said he would only find out *how* to break the bond. Haelyn, his mother, and the Queen of the Earth Kingdom, says he has to go through a trial to break it. I don't know what the trial entails, but it's not his responsibility to go through it." I glance at Seren to see her nodding, her face flat and severe.

"What do you need me to do?"

"You're not going to fight me on this?" I look at her questioningly, skeptical. I would expect her to try to talk me out of it, but I'm surprised by her words.

"I would do the same thing if I was in your position. I wouldn't want anyone to sacrifice something for me. As much as I don't like the idea, I won't stop you."

I exhale loudly, relief easing my taut muscles. "Thank you." I pull her tight into a hug, holding on longer than I usually do. I feel her thin arms encase me, returning the embrace. "Please look after Willow and deter Hadley. I will be back soon."

"You better." She pulls away and slaps me on my ass before I mount the horse. I yelp and giggle at her. "Now go yell at that man!"

"Oh, he's getting an earful." I laugh as I guide the horse out of the stables and across the field towards the capital.

42

Amalie

I ride the horse as hard as it will allow, but it still takes most of the night to reach the capital. I'm exhausted and aching from the windburn on my cheeks. Once I enter Willoughby, I dismount and greet the guards.

"I am Amalie, and I grew up here. I need to speak with Prince Wren." I strengthen my core, belting the words with authority as my mother taught me. The guards stare at me hesitantly before standing closer together, preparing to deny my request. "I know the rules of this kingdom. I have a pure heart and do not wish any ill will towards the kingdom or inhabitants." At that, the guard standing in the middle glances to his right, uncrossing his arms as he steps back and allows me to pass. I nod my thanks as I walk along with my horse through the forest paths.

Since most of my memories have returned, I remember enough of the place to know the journey between the Chateau and the Capital; I know the small shops in the treetops and the most enormous Willow tree in the center is where I will find the castle.

I find the large tree in the city center and open the beautiful door to enter the castle staircase. The fireflies on the ceiling are just beginning to dim as the sun appears through the canopy of trees. Exhaustion wraps me in a soothing blanket, and I am fighting the urge to sleep on the stairs.

Around and around, I climb the spiral until I reach the grand foyer of the castle. I have no idea if Wren is sleeping or training at this hour. He usually rises with the sun. I decide to run to his room first, and I am rewarded with the image of Wren's bare back as I barrel through the door.

Wren turns quickly, taking in my disheveled state.

"Stars! Amalie, what happened? What are you doing here?" His voice gets louder as he faces me. His shocked state stops him from advancing. His feet are frozen in place, his shirt still gripped in his hands. His eyes move frantically over my face, down my body and hands, checking for injuries but finding none.

"Don't," I whisper breathlessly from my run through the city and castle.

"Don't, what?" His nostrils flare, and lips curl. I can't tell if it's confusion or anger. Did he know I received his mother's letter?

"This is my mistake; this is my trial. I can't allow you to take my place."

He sighs heavily and begins to pace the room. Balling his shirt, he throws it to the corner of the room, destroying petals on a flowering vine.

"Damn it, Am! Just let me deal with it." I can see the anger brewing in each step, his footsteps muted on the grassy floor, but the thud of his feet is still audible.

"Why? Why do you want to do this so badly? Why do you think I am so weak that I cannot succeed?" I shout my questions at him as I stand taller and broader, holding my ground against him.

"You're not weak. We both know that." His voice is quieter, and he takes a loud, deep breath.

I move towards his bed and sit down. I try a gentler approach, softening my voice as I see his anger increasing. "Then what is it? Please, Wren."

"It's because I need control!" I can tell Wren is fighting with himself. He's fighting to keep himself calm by pacing throughout the room, his voice rising and lowering and fighting between shouting and whispering. He approaches me, kneeling before me, gripping my thighs tightly. "I can't lose you again. I won't, Amalie. I don't want to leave that chance to anyone, not even you. If I can't do this, then at least I can hate myself; I don't want to lose you and resent you."

I sit still, staring at his face until he drops his head into my lap, moving his arms around my waist. My mind is running through all the things to say, all the options and promises to ease his anxiety. I came here ready to argue instead I found myself with this broken man in front of me. I sigh and run my fingers through his thick dark hair. I fold over him and kiss his head.

"You're not going to lose me again," I whisper into his hair, unsure of what else to say.

The early morning birds begin to chirp through the canopy above us, signaling the rising sun. We sit in silence for a while, unmoving, unbreakable.

"Just let me fight for you, for us. I can't let another day go by where we have to lay down our future and safety for him." He spits the word, not wanting to say Asher's name.

As much as Wren wants control, I still cannot give it to him. I can't let him fight this battle for me. If things go wrong, at least it will be my choice. I just don't know how to make him realize that. Nothing that I say will force him to agree. That's when my own lie takes hold in my mouth, spewing deception after every word.

"Okay, I won't interfere." My lie is a whisper, and his loving kiss that follows my words breaks my heart further.

The deception of my actions may be the end of us, but that's the truth of lies, isn't it?

The truth is that when you love someone so thoroughly that you can't speak the truth to them. When the truth hurts the one you love, your only option is a lie. Not all lies are formed through malice but through protection.

I don't want to hurt Wren. I know he will be hurt when he discovers my plan, but he lied through omission, and I lied through my teeth. The line is a fragile tightrope swaying over a canyon.

"I love you." He kisses me over and over, breaking me as tears well in my eyes and spill over. "What's wrong?" he asks so softly as he brushes my tears away with his thumb.

I shake my head to wave off his concern. He gives me a small smile before he stands, extending his arm for me to take.

"Hungry, my dear?" I release a small giggle at his change in topic before linking my arm with his as he leads me to the main dining room.

"I'd actually like to see your mother, if I can. It's been so long." Wren grins wider, taking my hand into his and kissing my knuckles as we walk through the hallways.

He remains silent through our short walk, descending the staircase and turning to the east branch of the castle as we enter the dining room.

The room reminds me of the dining room in the chateau. It is all windows and looks more like a greenhouse. The only difference this time is that we are in a tree. Branches and vibrant green leaves intertwine through the ceiling of the room. Sitting in the center of the room is a long log-style table with an ivy centerpiece along the entire length. At the head of the table sits Wren's parents, Bryn and Haelyn.

Once Haelyn notices the smile on Wren's face, she moves

her eyes to see me standing slightly behind him. Her eyes go wide in shock before she stands up abruptly, smiling so big it causes the corners of her eyes to crinkle. The Queen rounds the corner of the table with arms stretched for an embrace. I move forward, leaving Wren in the doorway as I rush to his mother, hugging her tightly.

"Oh, my dear! I'm so happy to see you," she coos in my ear, squeezing me tighter.

"We need to talk," I whisper in her ear before saying louder for the room to hear, "I'm happy to see you as well. I've missed you both." I feel her nod her chin on my shoulder before we separate. She grasps my hands and looks at Wren, who is now making his way to the table.

He stands behind a chair, pulling it out for me to take, but his mother interjects.

"Actually, I would like to speak with Amalie. Just us girls." Her smile is so sweet and sincere that Wren doesn't question it. He simply sits down in the chair he was holding for me and begins to fill his plate.

I give Haelyn a smile of gratitude before she leads me out of the room.

We walk through the castle in silence until we reach her private study. I take a plush white chair in the center of the room as she sits beside me.

"You've received my letter," she says as a statement, not a question, though I nod anyway.

"Oh, Haelyn, I've made such a mess of things!" I can feel myself wanting to cry, but I don't want to cry in front of her. I want to show that I can be strong and can be a Queen.

"My son has told me little of your situation; I hope you are not offended." I believe she is referring to the words in her letter.

"I understand your fears and concerns, for I feel them too. I'm glad that you told me. Wren wouldn't have. That is why I had to lie to him." I hang my head, ashamed to admit I deceived her son.

"I'm glad you did." My head snaps up at her words, I knew she didn't want him in the trials, but I didn't think she would be pleased about it. I give her a confused look, and she laughs. "Amalie, I love my son, but he is an idiot sometimes. Given that his father was the same way. Earthen men are hopeless romantics; they need to save everyone. Still, he has much more to lose in this situation than you do, my dear."

"I told him that I won't interfere, but I need to."

"As you should," she replies curtly. "It truly would be a shame if he was at the wrong location for the trials to occur. A shame indeed." Her sly smile radiates through the room. I would laugh at her if the situation weren't so serious.

"What should I expect?" My question to her is asked with caution. I want to be prepared, but I don't want to know if it's bad.

"The trials to break a bond are a test of the inner self. Not of strength or skill. The bonds can only be broken with the utmost sacrifice. It is a test of intent."

Okay, that doesn't sound bad. At least I don't have to fight a great beast or engage in a battle of wits.

She continues, "Each kingdom will require a sacrifice. You must agree to each and act on one."

"So I agree to all, but I only act on one. Do I choose which one to act on?"

"No, of course not. My dear, that would be too easy. The council wishes to deter others from breaking their bonds, even if it was formed through deceit." She sighs, then takes a deep breath to continue, "The choice will be to the council and the council alone. I will not have any influence over the sacrifices."

My hands shake with anxiety and fear. Haelyn was right, Wren would have a lot more to lose than I do. He has a family, a kingdom, and his own magic. I do not.

I nod, standing to leave before Wren begins searching for us, but Haelyn stops me with her words, "This bond must be broken, sooner rather than later. More than just you and Wren are suffering."

I spin around, drawing my eyebrows together in confusion. "What do you mean?"

"Earth has claimed you, you may not have had physical magic, but your essence eases creatures of Earth. Asher's magic of air is not compatible. Earth and Water, Air and Fire. Only those elements may bond." My blood runs cold, and I hold my breath waiting for the rest of her words to fall on my ears. "He will go mad from the power, if he hasn't already. The longer he is bonded with Earth, the worse he may become."

I nod, still not understanding what this means of the past. Was it real before? Or was it an act from the beginning? I think to myself, trying to gather my memories. Asher never acted with malice until he gave me his ring.

"When the bond is broken, what will happen to him?" I ask the Queen.

"It's hard to say, if the bond was formed a while ago, he may recover slowly, or his mind may never fully recover." Haelyn stands and approaches me. She pulls me into a tight embrace, and I sink into her. "Your mother would be proud. She was no stranger to making the hard decisions."

My heart constricts at her words, securing my decision further.

43

Wren

They're taking too long—my mind whirls with anxiety. I sit beside Finley and across from my father, silent and wary. Just as I am about to stand up and search for them, the doors creak open, and my mother walks in, followed by my girl. I let out a sigh of relief at the sight of them both.

My mother sits down beside my father, placing her hand on his and giving him a soft smile. I rise from my seat and pull a chair out for Amalie, who thanks me as she sits. I try to catch her eyes, but she is focused on the plate placed in front of her, picking at her food mindlessly.

"Everything alright?" I whisper cautiously to her.

She nods with a small smile. "Just tired."

"Why don't you finish up your breakfast, then I'll take you back to my room." She sighs in agreement at my suggestion as she continues eating.

I watch as she eats, picking tiny pieces of her fruit apart before placing them into her mouth. The table is unexpectedly silent, raising the hair on the back of my neck.

"You sure you're alright?" I ask her again, whispering in her ear so I don't draw attention.

She leans over and places a soft kiss on my cheek. "Yes, Wren. Truly. I've ridden all night, and I only need a few hour's rest." Her bright amber eyes gaze up at me, a slight sparkle from the sunlight rising high above the canopy shimmers in her eye. She rests her chin on my shoulder and twines her arm around mine, placing her hand in the bend of my elbow. I cover her small hand with mine, giving her fingers a tight squeeze.

"Come, I'll walk you." I kiss her forehead before turning my head back to my parents. "I will be back." I remove her hand from my elbow and stand. Reaching out for her to take it again, I twine my fingers with her as we walk out of the dining room.

"I missed the smell of this place. It smells like fresh pine and spring rain. It smells like home."

Her soft words reverberate through my bones and squeeze my heart as her eyes flutter close. I lay with her in my arms until she falls asleep. I don't dare reply. I don't want to keep her from the sleep she needs. I watch her mouth part slightly, breaths becoming slow and even. I continue brushing her hair back from her face softly. I think about the future I will secure. Not just for us but for the entire Kingdom. I will ensure the best outcome for everyone. Establishing trading with the Fire Kingdom, their mastery in forging is the best of our realms. Create peace with the Air. Reason with the King and Queen about their son's behaviors and deceptions.

The sound of the door creaking open startles my reverie, and I look up to see Finley poking his head through the crack. When our eyes meet, he nods his head to the side in a *come here* motion.

I sigh, giving Amalie a soft kiss on her brow, and I roll over and slide off the bed. Grabbing my boots, I walk out the door, not wanting the thump of my heels to wake her, and drop them in the hall beside Finley.

"What is it?" I ask as I slide my feet in one at a time.

"Alizar is here," he says softly, clicking the door closed behind me. I purse my lips in bewilderment. "Semira's husband. He left the palace before she was killed. He wants an audience with your parents."

"Why?" I ask skeptically, but Finley raises his shoulders and drops them in a shrug. I stand tall after lacing my boots. "Where is he?"

"Library, he hasn't seen your parents yet. Thought you would want a word first." I clap him on the shoulder and nod my thanks before turning on my heel and heading towards the library with Finley in tow.

The man looks ghastly, and the stench of a man traveling on foot could be scented through the door. I have never met Semira's husband. He was always a shut-in, living in the village closest to the Treaty Market. Their marriage, to my knowledge at least, was fairly new. Perhaps a couple of months before Amalie was set to marry Asher. My blood boils at the thought, so I take a deep breath, banishing the image and greet the torn man in front of me.

"You're Alizar." Sure, it's not the most welcome greeting, but I'm not yet sure of his intentions for being here.

"Prince Wren." He bows. "I have come to join your battle against Air."

"Who says I'm fighting the Air?" I ignore his bow and bite back, none too kindly. It's words like his that start rumors.

"To be bold, the slaying of the monarchy said enough." His words confuse me further as I take a more severe glance at him.

His shoulder-length hair is matted and dirty. Under his eyes are thick, dark circles, and he looks twenty years older than he should. The poor man is pathetic, but I assume I wouldn't look much better in his situation. I decide to stride over to the dark ale on the table to my right and pour him a glass. Extending the glass to him, I nod as he takes it. I cross my arms before speaking again.

"Where did you hear this?"

"I never left the palace." His hands shake as he takes another sip, recalling his memories. "Semira...My wife. She never returned to me."

Suddenly I'm being ripped back into my own memories of the same situation not too long ago. When I waited hours for Amalie, and she never showed. I thought she had died. Only for this man, his love did die. I let him regain his composure again as he downs the glass of the liquid.

I give him a pointed glance at the glass, and he nods. Filling it again and passing the glass back, he nods again in thanks before continuing his story.

"I waited outside the palace grounds for her for hours, and she never came. I knew in my heart that something was not right. I knew it. That man-Asher." He spits his name like venom. "He killed her. I've seen him take a servant the same way my wife was killed. She was left on the floor without a breath of air in her lungs. The hollowness of her chest told me so. I wanted him dead; I still want him dead."

Alizar's words are dipped in malevolence and anger, promising revenge for his loss.

"And how do you plan to do that?" He looks like he wouldn't be able to swing a sword, let alone kill a bonded Fae.

"I don't know. I'm just a man. But you are a Fae Prince. You and your kingdom have the power to destroy him." He empties his glass again and places it on the table. "You've already defeated the King and Queen! I want to join you in defeating the prince as well. Please."

I shake my head, trying to recall how I defeated the royals. I haven't taken a step forward in this war. It is a game of chess, calculated and slow. The Earth doesn't start a war without a declaration. If people believe I murdered the monarchs, that is war declared.

"I did not." My words are sharp and straightforward, breaking through Alizar's shaking hands. He stills, eyes locking with mine in an unreadable expression. "I did nothing against the Air Kingdom. If someone has taken the life of the King and Queen, then good riddance, but it wasn't me."

"So, that's it. You're not going to do anything? You're not the great Prince Wren that everyone in the Earth Kingdom raves about?"

"I didn't say I wasn't going to do anything. I said I didn't kill them." I step forward, standing taller. "That bag of stale air deceived my future Queen, taking her bond through lies and deception alone. That will not go unpunished. If you want to join me, send word to the Elders. I'm breaking this bond. Then breaking his crown." I turn back and nod at Finley, who is leaning on the door frame, arms crossed. "Ready a horse, will you?" Finley smiles and nods before turning away.

"That's it?" Alizar asks again. I turn around and sigh.

"You keep saying that as if you're unimpressed."

"Not much to be impressed about," Alizar counters, making me laugh.

"I can say the same about you." I gesture to his disheveled state. "Why don't you clean yourself up? I'll show you to a room." I turn back towards the door. Just as I am about to walk out, he speaks again, stopping me in my tracks.

"Wren, you know this isn't over after breaking the bond. It's going to be a lot more than just taking his crown, too."

I don't bother to look back.

Each elder symbolizes the elements, working as one to unify the kingdoms.

They are the law—judge, jury, and executioner.

Two days later, I am standing on the dais beside my parent's thrones as the Elders walk into the vast room. They take their seats to the right of the thrones without a word or glance towards us.

"Thank you, Elders, for gathering." My father stands from his throne and bows, the crowd mirroring his actions. I notice Amalie standing near the back of the room with Finley, speaking softly between themselves.

I take a step forward to protest the bond, but I'm quickly interrupted. The throne room doors fly open with a heavy hand, and Asher walks in with the silver crown on his head.

"The King and Queen of Air are dead!" Asher yells, causing an uproar in the crowd.

"Prince Asher, stand down!" my father raises his voice into the crowd as the noise dies, hushed whispers breathe through the room. I stand unmoving, in shock at the outburst and interruption. All thoughts of bonds are gone from my mind and all I can see is red anger as Asher continues.

"King! King Asher," he corrects, lip curled like a snarling dog. "Elders, I am here to request the execution of their murderer, Prince Wren of Earth."

The Elders look towards me as the crowd begins to roar again.

44

Amalie

I watch as the council and spectators rise from their seats, shouting and pointing fingers at one another. I wonder how Asher could enter the Earth Kingdom since his intentions surely cannot be pure.

He has your Earth magic. A small voice in my head reminds me.

"He has a motive!"

"He's a liar! Our Prince wouldn't."

"Of course, he would!"

"Never trust the Air."

The shouts ring out through my ears, my eyes unfocused as I look around the room. Head snapping back and forth as more and more people join in. Human and Fae clash with words leading to chaos until Bryn uses his magic to shake the earth beneath the room, halting everyone's voices.

"I will not have this in my court!" Bryn's voice vibrates through the room, reaching the back walls of the court. "Prince Asher, please state clearly. What is your theory on the death of your parents?"

"King Asher," he corrects. "Prince Wren has threatened to

bring war to us all. He has threatened my life as well." Asher pauses for a moment.

"Is that all? This is the grounds you have to accuse my son and the future King of Earth." Bryn shakes his head, taking his seat on the throne again.

"This is not the only evidence I have!" Asher's face begins to turn red in anger. "He has sent numerous spies to my court to infiltrate our inner workings. He has plotted behind our backs, and he has plotted and succeeded to kidnap and corrupt our future Queen." At his words, I step forward to argue, but Finley grabs my arm and pulls me back. I look up at him in disbelief, but he shakes his head to not interfere. I lower my eyes to the floor again as Asher continues to speak, "He has killed my men. A guard of mine was found dead on Earth Kingdom territory."

An audible gasp sounds through the room. I knew this was not a lie. Wren did kill a guard, he admitted it to me. My heart pounds faster.

King Bryn's head snaps towards Wren, standing to his right as he stares daggers at Asher. Wren looks like the mirror of death, dark and dangerous and ready to strike. His fists clench in fury as he answers his father's question, never taking his eyes off Asher.

"I can't deny it." His words are incriminating and straightforward, and my stomach churns with the possibilities.

If Wren is found guilty with no motive, Asher would have the right to revenge. Impacting the same fate of his parents on the guilty. If the council can find motive, Wren would be stripped of his title and exiled.

I think of all the times I laughed with him and loved him. All the times we've fought and cried. That's when I realize in my heart that I remember it all.

I don't know when it happened. My life just became easier. Things made sense and felt like home. My memories came to me slowly, not all at once like I thought they would. The dreams, the thoughts, and the knowledge returning to me wasn't always overwhelming. It was like a soft drizzle before the rain. Now that I recognize the rain, it becomes a storm.

I gasp, tears streaming down my face as I watch my friend and my love leave my life again.

Asher pulls a dagger from his belt and tosses it on the floor, dried blood still on the blade and hilt. I stare at the dagger, eyes widening in recognition. It's Wrens' dagger. I would know that dagger because I was the one to carve the vines on the hilt.

"This was left in my father's chest," Asher spits, and the room goes silent. I glance up at Wren, not believing he would actually kill the King and Queen of the Air Kingdom, but he would do anything to save someone he loves, to save his kingdom. That is why I don't believe it was him. This act wouldn't save me, it wouldn't save his Kingdom.

It would destroy both.

I can see Wren's nostrils flare, but he doesn't move to argue. I notice his jaw tightening, fighting back the words I know he wants to say.

King Bryn closes his eyes while Haelyn turns to Wren with tears in her eyes. "Wren, please tell me this isn't your dagger."

Wren's only answer is to look down, almost ashamed.

"Do you see now? Do you see who your new King will be? He is willing to start a war and strike down anyone for a girl! A girl who isn't even his to claim!" Asher's voice grows louder as his words leave his mouth, growing more manic as he steps forward. "And he has the gall to protest my bond, our bond!" Asher gestures to me as if I agree with him.

I lose my calm, all the shock and fear leaving my body in a violent outburst as I stride towards Asher. I cock my fist back and punch him in the face. I shake my hand from the stinging pain as he falls to the ground.

"It is me who is protesting this bond. It is me who doesn't want you. It is me who killed your parents." The words leave my mouth before I even have a chance to stop the lie. Before I know it, I am grabbed roughly, my arms pulled behind me as flames are cast around my wrists in shackles. The flames don't begin to burn until I pull against the restraints. Blistering flames crawl up my arm, scorching my wrists and forearms. I refuse to scream from the pain. Instead, I hold still to stop the torment. The flames die down, but I can feel the burns up to my elbows on each arm.

Fire shackles.

As my mind comes back to the reality of the situation, I hear Wren screaming my name over and over while guards hold him back. I also refuse to look Wren in the eyes as Finley runs towards him. I can't face his torment.

I straighten my back, lift my chin, and glare at Asher. This is my fight, and I am not backing down. I know my actions were rash, but as Haelyn said, Wren has more to lose than I do. If this is the only option we are given, I will be the one to take it.

"Stop! Wait!" I hear Haelyn's voice ring through the room as her husband's did a few minutes prior. Heads turn in her direction as she speaks, but I don't take my eyes off Asher, and he doesn't take his eyes off me. "She still has the right to protest. According to the law, any bonded human or fae has the right to protest regardless of any current standings. Whether she is guilty or not, she has a right!"

She turns towards the four council members to the left of the room, waiting for their nod of approval. The few tense moments it takes for them to come to a final decision have my hands shaking so hard that I can feel the shackles growing warmer, threatening to burn me again.

"She isn't protesting anything!" Wren yells from beside the throne, trying to capture the elders' attention, but he goes unnoticed.

I speak over Wren, "I formally protest the bond of Air." I

speak clearly and with confidence, turning away from Asher. I only look towards the council. "Council, I invoke my right."

As if the four are communicating telepathically, they nod simultaneously. Sealing my fate once more. I let out a breath, daring to look at Wren now. His mother is speaking softly to him, and I cannot hear her words. Wren nods, and the guards release him. As soon as they step back, he bounds down the throne steps and runs to me. Before I can open my mouth to say a word, he pulls me tightly against him. His left hand rests on my upper back while his right curls around my head and laces through my hair.

My eyes fill with tears as I whisper to him, "I'm sorry. I'm so sorry."

"Why, why did you do that? Why admit to something you didn't do!" His voice begins to rise again, and he hugs me tighter. I can feel his hands shaking, but I can't hug him back with my hands bound behind me.

"This isn't your fight, Wren. I love you, but you must let me do this. Please." I can feel the tears spilling over now, landing on his tunic. He's shaking his head, but I continue, "It will be fine. You will be fine. If you want to do one thing for me, please just let me do this."

"Am, nothing good will come from this! You just confessed to killing the Air monarchy, not just the bond trials. I know you didn't. I saw your hands shake when you simply *considered* ending the life of the servant." He leans back and looks into my eyes. "I don't know how he got my dagger. It must have been from the servant or another spy. We will figure it out."

"Let me go through this. Then we will figure it out. Even if we aren't together at the end of all this, you will move on. You will find a queen," I assure him with a soft smile, hot tears running down my face.

"You are my Queen." His voice breaks, and so does my heart. I see a tear roll down his cheek, his sorrow mirroring mine.

He stares at me until Finley places a hand on his shoulder. "Time to go, man."

Wren pulls my face to his, kissing me urgently. His kiss is hurried and fierce but everything I need. "I can't let you go. You know, this isn't over," he whispers as he pulls away, touching his forehead to mine.

"Wren…" Finley urges again.

"We should have known this wasn't forever." He pulls back to kiss my forehead as I continue to say, "I love you. That is why I want you to move on."

A guard grips the top of my arm and pulls me away. I don't fight him as I move further away from Wren and Finley, not wanting to look back.

45

Amalie

I wait in an empty room, pacing back and forth, waiting for word on the trials. Waiting for word on my fate. The guards removed my shackles of flame, but I don't dare dwell on the blisters and scorched flesh on my wrists and up my arms. I kick myself for my rash mouth, but I can't entirely regret my decision. My punishment may be death in the end if they don't find my motives within reason. Striking Asher like that probably sealed my fate as well.

I stop pacing as the door cracks open and Finley slides into the room. I run to him, throwing my arms around his waist, happy to see a familiar face.

"Kitten, you've gotten yourself into quite the mess, haven't you?" Finley wraps his arms around me, squeezing me tightly.

"It was always my plan to protest. I just didn't anticipate Asher's accusations. I couldn't let that fall on Wren. We both know he didn't do it." I let go of Finley and peer up at him.

His face is dark with concern, eyes clouded, and his forehead creased. He looks almost as tormented as Wren did.

"I know, it will be alright. Wren is working on a plan, and

Haelyn is trying to get some insight into how to break the bond." I nod at Finley's words.

"Okay, just don't let Wren do anything stupid. Please watch over him, Finley. This is my choice."

"You got it, Kitten," Finley says with a smirk and a step back towards the door. "If Haelyn doesn't get information to you in time, just remember this." Finley takes a breath, counting each point on his fingers. "Each kingdom is known for something. Earth-grounded, practical, comforting. Air-intellectual, plotting, communication." He raises his third finger and continues, "Fire-passionate, confident, creation. Lastly, Water- compassionate, sensitive, and the realm of emotion."

I try to replay his information in my head. Carving the words into my memory.

"Thank you," I whisper as he slides out of the room, and I begin pacing again.

I lose track of time, it could have been hours or minutes, but I never stop pacing the empty solid wood room. Not all prisons have bars; some are mental while some are physical. I am in my own kind of prison.

A guard enters the room with fire shackles in hand. The cold iron clasps are placed on my wrists before the flames take over again, threatening my movements. I hold steady, only moving my legs as the guard guides me into a portal room. I gape at him in bewilderment but he does not say a word before shoving me towards a glowing portal.

The portal is a large, curved door on the wall. The glowing lights representing the four Kingdoms encompass the frame. Red, blue, green, and whites swirl and form in my vision as I am pushed through the door, the guard following closely behind me.

The room is small, about half the size of the throne room in the Earth Kingdom. Despite the smaller size, it feels less welcoming and more ominous. The walls are made of grey stone, carved with each symbol of the Elemental Kingdoms.

The Elders sit at the head of the room, staring straight ahead. All four thrones curved in a semi-circle around an altar.

Faces familiar and new stand on each side, leaving an aisle like a wedding ceremony. There is a short dais in the center of the room. The guard grabs my bicep, guides me down the aisle, and instructs me to stand on the dais. I take a breath but don't hesitate. I stand tall, widening my shoulders and lifting my chin to show confidence. Even if I do not feel confident right now.

I can feel my legs shaking under my dress, compensating for my hands that I can't move for fear of their flames. I don't look around the room, I stare straight at the elders.

The four fae appear almost identical. Each in similar robes of different colors corresponding with their kingdoms, a beautiful and sizeable glowing stone hangs from their necks in their Kingdom colors: three males and one female.

The female is wearing a red robe that drowns her figure but doesn't deter the intimidating aura she possesses. She is the first to speak in an echoing melodic tone, "Amalie of the Earth Kingdom. You are here to submit to the trial of bonds. In completing said trial, you will regain your inner self and extinguish the flame of bonds you share with King Asher of Air. Do you submit?"

At the mention of his name, Asher stands beside the dais but does not say a word.

I glance at him out of the corner of my eye. I see his heavy breathing, his hands shaking in anger, and I nod to the Fire Elder.

"I submit."

The Elders nod in unison as the Fire Elder sits back on her throne.

"King Asher," the Air Elder addresses him. "Please present the bonding token."

"Unfortunately, the token has been lost." Asher smiles at his attempt to stop the trial.

"Lost but not destroyed." The Elder says. In unison, all four Elders lift their hands into the air while the Elder of Air holds out his large palm. Smoke in a kaleidoscope of colors swirl and churn around his hand, presenting my wedding ring. The grin falls from Asher's face at its sight in the Elder's palm.

"We will not delay or play games, King Asher. If your bonded protests, she has the right to complete the trials." The Fire Elder snaps. I try not to cringe at her words. I don't like to be reminded of how close we were to actually being married.

Asher glares at her but doesn't reply. He nods and looks at the stone floor, submitting to the will of the Elders.

"Right, let's begin." The Elders turn their gaze to me as I stand straight-backed, still cuffed. I take a deep breath, wondering if Wren, his parents, or Finley are in the crowd watching. I close my eyes, shoving the thought of them out of my mind. I take a deep breath and calm myself.

The Elder of Earth stands, pulling the length of the long green robe behind him. "My daughter of Earth, Will you sacrifice the scepter of your lands, relinquish yourself of future sway, and live amongst the commonwealth?"

I take my time answering. I would sacrifice almost anything to break this bond as I work through his question—the Scepter of my lands. Relinquish future sway and live amongst the commonwealth. The Elder is speaking of my future as Queen of the Earth Kingdom. To lose my role as Queen would not be a difficult sacrifice. Finley's reminder of grounding and comfort makes me think that his question could mean that I truly lose the Earth Kingdom. *Does he mean I wouldn't live in the kingdom anymore?* If that is true. My answer still hasn't changed.

"Yes, I will." I breathe out my answer. My anxiety is growing, but I continue with the trials.

The Elder of Earth nods and bows before taking his seat while the Air Elder stands.

"Creation of Earth. Will you sacrifice the cognizance of mind, discard anamnesis once more, without hope of revival?" The Elder of Air Questions.

Finley said that the Air kingdom is the realm of intellectuals and plotting. Anamnesis. The word stuck out to me, meaning to look back on something or remember. I've already lost my memories once. I'm willing to do it again.

"Yes, I will," I repeat my answer, feeling more confident than the previous question.

Once again, the Elder nods and sits on his throne before the only female Elder rises.

"Devotion of Earth." Her voice is more fierce, fit for a Fire Elder. "Will you sacrifice the connotation of your heart, forfeiting the passions of the soul and extinguishing the fire within?"

My heart stops at her words. The question is double-edged. In my mind, it could mean either losing my love or losing my passion, my drive. If it is the first answer, I couldn't forfeit Wren's life. Not for the bond, not for anything. But if it's the second answer, would I be able to give up my passions? Would it be worth it, and what would I be in the end? I think back again; the Fire Kingdom is known for creation and intentions. I don't believe that the elders would ask me to destroy my love, so the answer would be to extinguish my passions. I close my eyes for a second before answering.

"Yes, I will."

The expressionless emotion on her face causes my hands to shake behind my back; hot flames begin to crawl up my arms and back.

"Lastly, the Ardency of Earth." The soft-spoken Elder of Water stands and speaks, "Will you sacrifice the fervor of heart? Forsaking your inner devotion and affection for affinity?"

I feel comforted by the Water Elder. His tone and demeanor remind me of an elderly man watching after his grandchild. I stand by my belief that I wouldn't have to sacrifice a love, perhaps just the idea of love. If Wren can survive a loss again but still live, I can agree.

"Yes, I will." I feel so heavy that I could fall to my knees, but I continue to stand tall. I glance to my right where Asher stands, still fuming but unmoving.

All four Elders stand and speak as one, "Your trial is to douse the ember of heart. Extinguish the flame of man and burn the adoration to cinders."

My eyes dart back and forth, unsure of their meaning. Douse the ember of heart. Extinguish the flame of man and burn the adoration. The terms are all of the Fire Kingdom. I try to recall her question.

"This is the sacrifice of the Fire, is it not?" I ask plainly. I want to know clearly what needs to be done. I need to know what the proper steps are to break the bond.

"It is." She speaks again, the Fire Elder moving forward to stand in front of the dais.

I am short on patience, and my anxiety increases after each moment of scrutiny. "Please speak plainly. What is your sacrifice request?"

"My dear. To obtain your inner magic once more, you must douse someone else's flame. Take the life of a loved one, and magic will restore the balance." There is a slight smile of malice on Asher's face that I see mirrored in the Fire Elder's.

I should have known.

Fire and Air are allies. I should have known they would work together to stop this bond, regardless of whether the Elder is meant to work for all the kingdoms in unison.

Silent tears run down my face. I've failed. I have agreed to douse a flame that I have no intention of doing so. I took a gamble on my ability, and I lost.

My hands shake, and my knees buckle. The only thing holding me up is the guard on my left, who grabs my bicep again, not allowing me to sink to the floor.

Minutes pass in silence. The crowd doesn't dare to make a sound until I hear a whisper through the room.

"Please, let me pass."

I crane my neck to look in the direction of the voice to see Alizar. A sob escapes my mouth as more tears slide down my cheeks. I can barely recognize him, his hair is a tad longer, but his face has sunken in. More sharp lines than before and dark circles line his eyes. When Alizar speaks again, my blood runs cold, and my ears ring.

"I would like to volunteer for your sacrifice."

46

Amalie

I sob.

There's nothing else I could do. With Alizar standing in front of me, offering his life so I can continue mine so that the kingdom can continue theirs without the wrath of Asher.

I stare at him with tears running down my face, but Asher interjects. "Unless she is in love with you, it won't work."

My pulse beats in erratic patterns, battling with my heart and my mind. I find myself equally relieved and devastated at his words. I exhale and look toward Asher, his smug smile sparking fury inside me. I once cared for Asher. I darkly wish that he would count towards the sacrifice bond.

The Water Elder stands, all heads snapping to his attention as he walks forward to stand beside the Fire Elder.

"King Asher, you must hold your tongue. You may be bonded, but you are not the one to protest. The words are up to the interpretation of the Elders and the protester." He turns towards Alizar now, addressing him in a quiet and soft voice. "We understand your selflessness. Please think wisely before offering yourself."

"I have thought about it. I've thought about it every day since this man murdered my wife. I have thought about it over and over. If I can free my wife's friend from the wrath of this monster, I will. For her. Then I will join her in the afterlife." Alizar speaks with a solid and unwavering confidence. Breaking my heart and validating my decision.

"If this is your wish." The Elder pauses a moment, seeming to be listening to someone speaking, "We will allow it."

A strong breeze blows through the room, wrapping my loose hair around my face and pushing the skirts of the Elders around their legs. I look over to Asher to see his fists clenched and jaw tight. His anger is growing more and more violent. The wind begins a violent assault, slamming people against the walls. I drop to my knees, trying to cover my face from the razorblades of wind cutting through my cheek. I tuck in as tightly as possible, hands still bound behind my back. I peek through my windblown hair to see Asher's feet moving closer to me. He kneels down and takes my chin in his hands, forcing my face up to his.

The wind stills in our small circle. I dart my eyes around the room, debris flying through the air like a tornado.

"I loved you, you know," he begins, but I don't pay any attention to him. I stare at the Elders, hoping they will intervene, but they simply stand there, speaking furiously amongst themselves. I can't hear what they're saying over the roar of the wind, but the three male Elders seem to be in an argument against the Elder of Fire. I am surprised that the Elder of Air hasn't sided with the Fire, but I wouldn't doubt if Asher bribed the Fire Elder with something. I wouldn't be surprised by Asher anymore. I know what he's capable of now.

"Asher. Stop!" I yell over the sound of the wind, but it falls on deaf ears. He doesn't seem to realize I've said anything. His thumb wipes the blood off my cheek from a small cut I've gotten from debris.

"I wanted this to work. I wasn't lying when I told you I

wanted you that first night. You're so perfect." His thumb continues to rub over my face as he speaks. His eyes were almost hazy in thought. "I wanted us to rule together, but you left me."

"I left because you killed my friend! You lied to me, Asher! Do you not know how insane you are?" I ask him. I want to smack his hand away, for him to stop touching me, but my hands are still bound.

"Your friend lied to you then tried to leave you! I wouldn't do that; I wouldn't leave you." His eyebrows turn down in what appears to be sincerity.

"Asher, if you truly love me, you will let me break this bond. If you believe in us, you will let us form it naturally. Not out of deception and false promises." My best bet might be to give into Asher, or at least, appear to give into him. If he hears what he wants, he might stop this. I can feel his hands shaking as they move from my face and down my neck, one hand lacing through my hair.

At his nod, I sigh.

"I'll let you break the bond but only if you promise to try again. Things will be better this time. You will be my Queen. We will have the bond we both deserve, even if I have to live without this much power for a little while. I'll do it. Just promise me." His words are louder, more frantic as he speaks, and I can see the madness behind his eyes.

Haelyn was right when she said that our magic does not merge well. I can see the destruction in his mind, how quickly he has deteriorated in the short time since the bond. That's when my assumption about his parents became a reality; he killed them. The dagger must have come from the servant that betrayed Wren.

I promise, Asher.

The moment the two words are out of my mouth, the wind dies, and the sound of the room comes back to life. The tornado dissipates as people begin to rise, assessing themselves. Asher doesn't move. He still holds me on the ground, and what a sight we must have been.

The enemy king and his lost bride, kneeling together, whispering promises that one never intends to keep.

"Let me go, Asher. Please." I use the calmest voice I can manage as I look into his eyes. Pleading for his cooperation. To my surprise, he does, and I see a flash of the man I was falling for.

The hope of Asher is still hidden underneath the magic tainting his mind.

The guard behind me, already standing, grabs my arm and pulls me to my feet as I look for Alizar. He's still kneeling off to the side of the dais, but I can't read his expression.

"Guards, please escort the King to a separate location for the duration of the trails." The Earth Elder says, glaring at Asher.

The man I knew is still on the surface as he gives me a small smile and brushes my cheek again before turning on his heel to leave. I could have cried a breath of relief. The malice leaves the room with Asher as two guards follow him out.

"Shall we continue?" The Fire Elder snarls, but I nod instead of verbally answering her.

"Sir, do you still wish to continue as well? Do you wish to join your heart in the afterlife?" The soft-spoken Water Elder asks, gesturing with his hands, palm up as if in invitation.

Alizar nods and stands before me. "Amalie, I have spoken to your Wren. Trust in him and allow me to fight this battle in my own way."

My breath comes out in a broken sob as my tears begin again. "Thank you." It's the only words I manage to get out before the guard releases the cuffs at my back. My arms feel equally weightless and heavy at the freedom.

"Let's proceed." One of the Elders says, but I don't take my eyes off Alizar. Memorizing his face at this moment. I imprint it into my memory.

The dark blue circles under his eyes, the sinking cheeks, and the grey complexion. I do not doubt that if Alizar did not volunteer to die now, he wouldn't be alive in a couple of months.

Some people believe that heartache isn't a valid form of death, but it is. Alizar is proof. The heart is unwilling to beat any longer after it has lost its purpose in life. Once the heart does not have a reason to beat, the body decides not to continue.

I convince myself I am doing the right thing. I convince myself that Alizar won't live anyway as I am handed a dagger engraved with the four symbols of the Kingdoms. Fire, Earth, Water, and Air merge together in one blade.

Alizar kneels before me, keeping eye contact as he smiles brightly, and I realize I've only seen this man smile when he was with Semira. My vision goes blurry with tears as I watch my best friend's husband give up on life to be with her.

I take a breath, step forward and grab his shoulder, hoping to give time for him to change his mind. But it never comes. He nods at me, still with a bright smile on his face.

I breathe in and plunge the knife into his chest.

His eyes go wide with pain, but the smile never leaves his face as blood escapes the corner of his lips. Blood spreads along his white shirt, creating a grotesque embroidery.

I feel like I'm going to be sick. My stomach heaves as I take a step back, leaving the dagger in his chest as he falls to the side.

Dead.

It takes a minute to feel the pain inside myself. I don't know if I'm screaming for what I just did or screaming because of the pain.

It is like fire and ice. Rocks and wind pelt my skin as the bond is ripped from Asher and placed back into my body. For a moment, I wonder if this is as painful for him as it is for me.

Forming the bond was effortless with a sense of ease while breaking it is torture. I fall to the ground again. This time, I don't get back up.

I'm still awake as the guards haul my body up, but I'm so broken from emotion and pain that I slump. Alizar's body is still lying on the floor. The crowd is still silent. Nothing has changed for anyone else, but for me, my world has been turned upside down in the vortex that Asher created. His own drive for his future ruined the lives of many.

"Amalie of Earth. We will name the punishment for the murder of the Air monarchs." The Elders speak in unison again, almost as if chanting.

I don't move or contradict their words. Nobody is here to fight for me, not even myself.

"We have heard the words of your sacrifice. We have heard your admission of guilt. Our decision is final."

My mind joins my body, and my knees lock in place as the pain begins to subside. I lift my head to stare at the four Elders, waiting for my punishment for my lie.

I nod slowly, realizing they are waiting for a reply or for me to acknowledge that they've spoken at all.

The Earth Elder steps forward from the line and speaks. "As you are a daughter of Earth, I will deliver judgment. Amalie, you will be sentenced to exile for your admission of guilt in murdering the King and Queen of the Air Kingdom." My ears begin to ring, and I force myself to listen to the rest of his words. "You will live amongst the outcasts in the Nightlands. You will not be welcome in the Elemental Kingdoms, and you will no longer feel the comfort of Earth."

The four stones hanging from the Elders' necks glow as their powers solidify my fate.

My mind runs in thoughts of Wren, Finley, Seren, Willow, my home, everything. Now that I've gained my life back, my family and friends, I lose them again. I look around now, looking for Wren. I need to feel the comfort of his arms, of his whispers that everything will be okay, but he isn't here. None of them are.

The tears pour from my eyes as I accept my fate.

To drive in the last nail, the Elder continues, "Your exile begins now." From the crowd, an older curvy fae woman in leather armor with long white hair stands forward and bows at the Elders. "This is Keitha. She will be your escort to the Nightlands. We wish you well, Amalie of exile."

And with that, the Elders leave the room, followed by the crowd and guards, leaving me alone with the woman.

I stand in an immobile trance as she places her arm around me in a motherly hug. I don't have time to say goodbye or grab anything before she leads me toward the portals.

"Come on, hon. It's time to go home."

Epilogue
Asher

The Nightlands are said to be the end of the world. No life grows, no sun will shine—eternal darkness with unimaginable beasts.

Guilt rips through me as I walk down the empty halls of the Castle. The Air Kingdom seems so quiet lately. The servants make themselves scarce, the guards are better not to be seen, and my family is gone—even my wife.

I didn't love her. But I know I could have. Amalie was one of those people with an infectious personality. She could make even the coldest of hearts warm and smile. I walk into my chamber, shrugging off my long charcoal-colored coat. I take my silver crown off my head and place it gently on my elegant, stone-carved display pedestal. It's dark in the room, and I turn to the hearth to add warmth and light to the melancholic room. I didn't realize I was speaking to myself until a voice interrupts me.

"You speak about your wife as if she is dead."

I whirl around to see a similarly dressed man. A man who could have been my twin if I didn't know any better. His hair is blonde and short like mine. Strong built and tall. He oddly resembles my parents, and my heart begins to beat. *Did I have a brother? Why are my parents keeping secrets from me?*

"Who are you? How did you get in here?" My voice vibrates through the empty room, bouncing off the stone walls and echoing through the mountains surrounding us.

"It's a shame that this place is so empty now, so devoid of

warmth and life." The man repeats my earlier thoughts before I went to the trials.

I walked through these halls for days on end, waiting for my time to see my wife again, if only to keep her safe. I suppose it didn't matter all that much, as I lost the bond anyways. She did promise me to try, but now she's gone. And so is the whole reason for having her in the first place. I made the mistake of trusting her, and look where that has gotten me. Alone in an empty castle, ruling alone with no bond. My magic was taken from me.

I run my fingers through my hair in frustration. I don't have any weapons on me, and I feel powerless without her magic running through my veins.

"I'll ask again, who are you?" My parents must have lied. This man must be a relative trying to take my crown. The crown I deserve. He looks too similar to be a coincidence.

"And who are you now, my dear friend?" The man whispers back into the dark room.

I stand there, staring at him as if he is an apparition. Eyes wide, palms sweating. A ghost from the hell beyond this land. I step forward, approaching the man in front of me. As I take a step, he mirrors my movements, causing my anger to ignite.

"Was it worth it, young king?" His haunting voice wraps around me as if he can reach into my own mind. I can hear his voice inside my head.

"Was *what* worth it?" I sneer back at him, growling at his pleased expression. He's wearing the same Air Kingdom grade uniform, which I believe is stolen. My mind churns like a vortex as I try to figure out how this man got into my castle, into my *bedchamber*. The intrusion is unsettling. I will need to increase the number of guards in the court and flush out the traitors that do not belong in these lands.

"When you used his dagger to take the life of your parents."

His tone is nonchalant. Like the question was simple or obvious, but instead, it plunges a dagger into my own heart.

"I didn't do that! You know I didn't," I deny. "Wren killed my parents; I saw him. He smiled at me as he did it too. If there is anyone to accuse, it would be the prince. Go haunt him."

The man smiles back at me, and I see red—the only color in this dull room. I move closer, standing face to face with the devil in front of me. Before he has a chance to speak again, I raise my fist and smash it into his face, shattering the mirror in front of me.

Blood drips through my fingers as his disembodied voice sounds through the room.

"Do you feel guilty yet?"

The story continues in book two of the Elemental Kingdoms series The Wrath of Deception

AUTHORS NOTES

I wanted to take the time to reflect on why I decided to write a book, this book to be specific. I have always wanted to write a book and hold it in my hands. Let it sit on my shelf just to know *I did that!* I have written many chapters and (almost) completed two books before this, only to delete them. I always had the mentality that I couldn't do it. And if I did, would it be good enough? It took many years (Eleven to be exact, if we are going by Facebook Memories- A post I wrote in 2010 "Almost finished writing the first chapter to a new story!") to finally build the confidence to just go for it. Highschool is a tough time for everyone, worse if you were bullied or didn't quite fit in. I didn't allow myself to express my interests out of fear of rejection. I showed my friends my book I wrote and was immediately told I should not be an author.

Words can change ambitions. Words can build or destroy. Now that I am older, I have regrets for not giving those words a chance.

I was laid-off from work due to covid. I had an enormous amount of free time, and a wandering mind. Amalie's story, in part, came from experiences-with a fantasy twist. The idea of trying to move forward from your past, good or bad, and build yourself a new future. The idea that not every hero starts off strong and wearing armor. Some heroes are knocked down and built back up only to find their strength in the toughest situations and stand up for what they feel is important in their life.

Fantasy is an escape for me. There are no rules to abide by, an author can write their fantasy story any way they like, and nobody can tell them that it's wrong. I think that's what I loved so much about this genre. I finally have the freedom to do what I love with no rules. I relate to Asher in looking for approval and acceptance but learning to overcome expectations and live life for yourself is something that Asher has not learned yet. It's a difficult lesson but necessary to truly enjoy what you do. Rejection is hard, and the fear of people not liking something you have put your whole soul into can be heartbreaking. But it's how you deal with it and how you move forward that matters.

Even if it isn't a bestseller. Even if I can't make a career writing books, it's okay. Because I accomplished my goals, and I loved every moment of it.

For anyone out there that loved this story or found that they could escape in this world for a few hours I just want to say: Firstly, I thank you! It is way more than I expected and I appreciate it with all my heart. Secondly, if you did read this book and connected with it or found your escape from reality. This book is for you. For anyone who needed to slip away for a short time to feel accepted, welcome, and embraced.

ACKNOWLEDGMENTS

I have to start by thanking my family for putting up with my crazy ideas.

To my mom, dad and sister. Thank you for all your love and support through this all. You all have given me strength to follow my dreams and to be who I really am. I'm sorry it took so long to listen to everyone, I suppose it was something that I had to learn on my own. But having your voices in the back of my head encouraging me, I realize that many others don't have the love and acceptance that you all give to me. I am so lucky to have you. Mom, You will never know how much it motivated me to keep writing to know that Grandma would have been proud. I wish she would have been able to read it, or at least know that I am writing.

I want to say a huge thank you to the *Bookstagram* community. I don't think I would have started writing again without it.

Elsie Quail (Lyndsay), I thank you for your motivation and friendship. You started as my alpha reader and became my "beast" friend. I am so happy for your writing journey, you are amazing and you will be successful! Your writing is beautiful, and I know Shadow Rose will be well loved by others, never doubt yourself.

I owe a thank you to Authors NJ Gray and Pru Schuyler. I wouldn't even have a book if you didn't push me to start writing. You two have planted the literary seed and allowed it to grow. Thank you! And for anyone reading this, check out their books. These ladies are amazing authors!

To Angie. I would be so lost without you. You have built me up and believed in this book. You have been a mentor, a therapist, an ear to listen to my ideas and rambles. Thank you for putting up with me. Thank you for taking on this project. And thank you for believing in me and my story. It means the world to me, you have no idea.

I want to thank my beta readers for giving me their love and excitement as well as their corrections and suggestions. You all have made this the best that it could be, I can't wait to work with each and every one of you in the future.

Thank you to my nephew Lucas. I promised you your own page and here it is!

Thank you for letting me brainstorm plot and character ideas with you. Our chats are responsible for quite a few fun ideas that made it so much easier to expand and grow into a full story. I hope one day you will have a dream or a goal and accomplish it. No matter how long it takes, I will be behind you every step of the way.

ABOUT THE AUTHOR

Lily Anne Rose is from a small town in central Ontario, Canada. Her two loves are books and animals. She is a proud cat lady with a dream to live in a tiny house with a nice view and write books. When she isn't dreaming up her next story, you can usually find her napping.

Follow her on Instagram @Lilyannerose.author

Manufactured by Amazon.ca
Bolton, ON